IC COMMUNICATIONS

Home of Irish Author Joe McCoubrey

PROUDLY PRESENTS

FORCE
OF
NATURE

By Joe McCoubrey

About the Author

Joe McCoubrey is a former journalist who reported first-hand the height of the Northern Ireland "Troubles" throughout the 1970's and 1980's, firstly as a local newspaper editor, and then as a partner in an agency supplying copy to national newspapers and broadcasters. He switched careers to help start a Local Enterprise Agency, providing advice and support to budding entrepreneurs in his native town, and became its full-time CEO. He retired to concentrate on his long-time ambition to be a full-time writer. His previous novels have all been published to critical acclaim. He lives in Downpatrick, County Down, and is proud of its historic connections to Saint Patrick, Ireland's Patron Saint.

BOOKS BY JOE McCOUBREY

THE MICK BOYLE SERIES
Force of Nature
Spent Force
THE QUINN SERIES
Thirst for justice
No place to hide
THE MIKE DEVON SERIES
Exposure to Truth
No Margin for Error
Absence of Mercy
Absence of Rules
Someone Has to Pay

FORCE OF NATURE

Copyright © Joe McCoubrey 2020
Ebook ISBN: 9780995468788
Publisher: Inishfree Communications

All characters in this book are fictitious and any resemblance to real persons, living or dead, is purely coincidental.

The right of Joe McCoubrey to be identified as the Author of the Work has been asserted by him in accordance with the Copyright, Designs and Patents Act 1988.

You may not copy, store, distribute, transmit, reproduce or otherwise make available this publication (or any part of it) in any form, or by any means (electronic, digital, optical, mechanical, photocopying, recording or otherwise), without the prior written permission of the publisher. Any person who does any unauthorised act in relation to this publication may be liable to criminal prosecution and civil claims for damages.

A CIP catalogue for this book is available from the British Library.

Dedication & Thanks

We have a new addition to the family and so this is especially for her – my granddaughter Anna Tate. Welcome to the world, princess. Not forgetting my wonderful grandsons Alfie, Rory, Ellis, and Michael. The family tree is growing!

Also, a big shout out to my partner Teresa, and my daughters Brenda, Lynda, and Lisa. Their support and encouragement keeps me wanting to do more.

Heartfelt appreciation goes to my editing team of Martin Graham, Mick Keane, Johnny McCoubrey, and Brian Willoughby for putting much-needed final polishes on the manuscript.

A special thanks goes to my crime and procedures consultant, who kept me right on all matters pertaining to technical and legal issues in respect of An Garda Síochána and without his input this manuscript would have contained flaws, which might otherwise have detracted from the story.

A quick word about a long-time friend and mentor, Brad Fleming, who has collaborated on all my books but, because of ill health, was unable to see this one through after the first few chapters. I missed his incisive and enquiring mind when it came to accuracy and conciseness, although I hope he finds that I followed his well-worn guidelines from our previous work. Get well soon, old friend. I look forward to us working together again soon.

ABOUT THE BOOK

Irish Garda detective Mick Boyle is back in the most challenging manhunt he has ever had to face.

Young girls are vanishing off the streets in a trail that leads from Downpatrick in Northern Ireland to Boyle's doorstep in Castlebar, County Mayo. The mystery killer has evaded capture in a spree that stretches back 10 years – and there is no sign that he intends to stop. He never leaves clues. He doesn't offer up bodies. He simply picks off his victims one by one before moving on to the next target.

But Boyle is determined to catch him – no matter what it takes.

The kidnapper is stepping up his activities and Boyle finds himself in a race against time to save at least one young girl from becoming another forgotten statistic.

ENDORSEMENT FOR PREVIOUS WORK
"Sometimes a book comes along that you instantly know......damn, I am now going to have to read this all over again for the sheer joy of the narrative. It means that I will have to swear off other books for a time as very few can provide the utter joy and delight of Joe McCoubrey's superb novel."
KEN BRUEN, international bestselling author of the Jack Taylor Irish crime series.

BOOK 1

EARLY DAYS
Downpatrick, Northern Ireland

Chapter 1
Downpatrick 2012

FIFTEEN-YEAR-OLD Jacinta Wilson closed the front door of the family home and skipped breezily down six steps that led to a pedestrian pathway beside a busy road junction. This was Church Street, the main thoroughfare for incoming traffic muscling its way at the end of a workday in Belfast, the capital city of Northern Ireland, twenty-two miles from the relative sedateness of the rural town of Downpatrick.

It was five o'clock on a warm July afternoon.

Jacinta had wolfed down the traditional Friday meal of fish and chips, anxious to escape the claustrophobia of the small, terraced house she shared with her mum and dad. Two weeks into the school holidays, this was a time for getting out, enjoying the sunshine, and chilling with her mates.

It was a time for dreaming big ideas about what to do with the rest of her life.

One thing was certain, as far as Jacinta was concerned. Whatever lay around the corner, it didn't include being cooped up in a provincial town where the only highlights on offer were lounging about at the local Dunleath Park, or dressing up for the monthly disco at the youth club, an antiseptic environment run by starched leaders who seemed intent on ensuring boys and girls kept their distance, particularly during the slow dances. What a pathetic bunch of losers!

Jacinta had always been a bit of a rebel. It hadn't helped that she was an only child, or that home life was constantly disrupted by an absent mother, who tried to hold down three separate cleaning jobs to compensate for an out-of-work husband, a shiftless forty-year-old whose days were spent in the pub, drinking away most of the pennies his wife earned. It was a toxic combination that led to endless arguments, which constantly chased Jacinta to the refuge of her bedroom.

There, at least, she could lose herself in oft-recurring fantasies, all of which centred on running away from home. There had to be something better than this, and Jacinta knew exactly what that something was. One way or another, she would find a new life in London. It would be a life of glamour and glitz, filled with modelling, or acting, or maybe meeting a rich man who'd give her all the things she deserved.

She knew she had the looks for whatever opportunities might come her way. Her long, flowing blonde hair and striking cobalt blue eyes accentuated an elfin face that was as beautiful as any she'd seen in glossy showbiz magazines. She wasn't a vain girl, although she often smiled inwardly at the tools God had given her, and how she intended to use them.

She told friends constantly about her plans. *Just watch! One day when you're looking for me, I won't be here. Just keep your eyes on the telly. Maybe I'll be a regular on EastEnders or stepping out with a movie star or footballer.*

In any other person, the words would have been dismissed as fanciful and attention-seeking gibberish. Not so in Jacinta's case. The matter-of-fact determination behind her assertions convinced her mates that she would actually do it. Sometimes, during school term, when she didn't appear for lessons, they'd thought this is it; Jacinta has hightailed it to London.

One thing Jacinta knew as she walked up Church Street that July afternoon, was that it was getting closer. She had made her plans as best she could. The time to act was near.

She smiled at passers-by, waved at a few neighbours seated behind draped windows, and continued to skip jauntily towards the main shopping precinct of Market Street.

Those fleeting glimpses were the last sightings of Jacinta Wilson.

When she failed to return home by midnight, two hours after her agreed curfew, a frantic mother started making telephone calls to friends and neighbours. It became a long night, punctuated by close relatives dropping into the terraced house to provide support and offer encouragement, although most were beginning to think the unthinkable.

The police were finally contacted at ten o'clock the following morning. The job fell to a newly minted Detective Sergeant, John Bonnaville, a taciturn and serious-looking individual, who appeared content to trot out the usual textbook drivel about statistics on teenage *Mispers*, ugly cop-speak shorthand for missing persons. He had barely stepped through the door before he covered all the trite bases. Probably gone off with a boyfriend and is too ashamed to come home. Maybe she got drunk and is sleeping it off somewhere. Was she depressed? Pregnant? Had she had a row with her parents? Was she being bullied?

A police constable who'd accompanied Bonnaville to the Wilson home, stepped in to cool the growing anger among those who'd listened to Bonnaville's bland and seemingly uncaring monotone. She'd promised the police would mount immediate enquiries and would fully support the family's desire to instigate a public appeal for searches to discover Jacinta's whereabouts. The PC also agreed to keep the parents informed with regular updates.

Once back at the station, Bonnaville appeared finally to latch onto the unease that surrounded Jacinta's disappearance. After discussing the case with the duty Inspector, it was agreed to mount a *treat-as-foul-play* investigation, until such times as the teenager was located.

Bonnaville was not a name to be found in Northern Irish genealogy. His family roots were in the heart of Cambridgeshire in England, from where his father upped stakes to become a senior law lecturer at Queen's University, Belfast. For a time, the young Bonnaville dallied in notions of forensics and criminal profiling as career choices but couldn't shake the vocation he felt to become a detective, preferably in homicide. Of course, he would need to start at the bottom, a prospect that didn't daunt him, even though it drew frequent criticism from his father, who'd hoped to see his son join the serried ranks of academia.

It was those memories of career decision-making that finally galvanised Bonnaville into positive action. This one would be done by the book. And then some. While uniforms and civilians mounted exhaustive searches for Jacinta, Bonnaville launched into a painstaking round of interviews, even going as far as to walk the streets of the town, showing Jacinta's photograph to the general public. The hours blurred into days, with still no trace of the girl.

If foul play were involved, the police adopted a default position – start with the family and work outwards from the centre. Check the mother, father, grandparents, aunts, uncles, and cousins. Move on to friends, casual acquaintances, and then people with influence in the victim's life, such as schoolteachers and employers. Look at anyone with whom she might have come into contact recently – a new boyfriend, workmen in a housing redevelopment near her home, or the regulars at a new dance class she recently attended at a small church hall.

No-one particularly liked Bonnaville's line of questioning, though for the most part they accepted his urgency for directness. Some of his subjects struck Bonnaville as being either eccentric, shifty, or downright weird. Enough to want to harm the girl? It was just too early to say, but he made notes against several names, with the intention of doing some follow-ups at a later stage.

What did emerge from his countless interviews was a picture of a girl who'd wanted to leave home, something common enough among teenagers, but seemed to resonate particularly in Jacinta's case. There was no denying the lure she'd felt for London, a fact even admitted to by her mother who'd initially hoped it was a passing fad but had conceded it had been deep-rooted for many years.

A search of Jacinta's bedroom yielded scrapbooks full of places of interest in London, including many references to acting and modelling agencies. Several diaries were crammed with heartfelt notations about living in the West End, going to theatres, and dining at the best restaurants. There was something stirring, yet plaintive, about the scribbles of a lonely child who appeared to crave nothing more than a little attention and a bit of limelight.

That made Bonnaville switch tack. He looked at the ways in which a teenager might get to London, including ferry and air routes, the latter unlikely because of the higher degree of security at airports. It would be much easier to hop onto a ferry from Belfast to Heysham in Lancashire, or one from Larne to Cairnryan in Scotland. She could even have hitched a ride to Dublin to grab a seat on one of the crossings to Holyhead in Wales. She could have saved money for a ticket or persuaded some misguided friend to take her as part of a vehicle berth. Nothing could be discounted.

Her photograph was issued to all terminals, although the chances of anyone having seen her were remote. A better prospect was circulating her details to London modelling and acting schools and agencies, since those were her professed destinations. If she were making good on her promise, she'd turn up at one of them sooner or later.

Lastly, as a matter of standard procedure, Bonnaville sent Jacinta's file to the Metropolitan Police and the UK Missing Persons Bureau. But with more than a quarter of a million such cases each year, he did not hold much hope of a result from either resource.

Four weeks after the disappearance, the police investigation reached a standstill. Bonnaville had to concede defeat in his attempts to find her, and reluctantly sat at his desk to write a final report, a case summary that could have only one conclusion. She was officially classified as a *Misper*, unlikely to be found unless she wanted to.

It did not rest easy with Bonnaville, but there was nothing more that could be done. It was not unusual for youngsters to get swallowed up by a big city, yet something about Jacinta's single-mindedness seemed to suggest that was not what happened here. Maybe one day he would discover the true nature of her disappearance.

Bonnaville took his first day off since the investigation had started. He made his way to the Quoile River, less than two miles from Downpatrick town centre. It had been quite a while since he'd found time for Pike fishing, but he needed the solitude and serenity to wind down and recharge badly worn batteries.

As he relaxed on a canvas seat on the east bank of the river, he was not to know that barely two hundred yards from his position, and thirty feet below the murky surface of the fast-flowing waters, the badly-abused body of Jacinta Wilson was lying on the riverbed. It was wrapped in a hessian bag and weighted down with a breezeblock.

Chapter 2
Downpatrick - two years later

Patti-Ann Weston loved Friday evenings.

That's when she got to be a normal teenager. No schoolbooks, no homework, and no worrying about a planned career as a doctor. On Fridays, she stopped thinking about A-star grades, what university she would attend, or what branch of medicine she would specialise in.

This was a time for make-up and boys and letting down the long-flowing golden locks she'd inherited from her mother's side of the family. She got to wear jeans and sneakers and sequinned tops. And then there was the jewellery, a dazzling array of bling that included pierced-ear diamond studs and a sparkling Michael Kors watch that granny had bought her for doing so well in the end-of-term exams.

Best of all, she got to stay out late with her friends. Eleven o'clock was hardly staying out late, but it was better than being cooped up at home, dreaming of the dishy Eamon and wondering if some of the other sixth formers were muscling in on her territory. She knew he liked her a lot, even if she wasn't always available for the half-price Tuesday blockbusters at the local cinema. Things would change soon. They had to.

Patti-Ann's problem was that she was an only child. Her mum and dad doted on her, wrapped her up in cotton wool, and were too protective by far. She loved being spoiled; loved the attention, and the clothes, and the latest gadgets that were bought for her at every opportunity. They were quite simply the best parents in the world, even if they hadn't moved past the stage of realising she was a teenager, practically a young woman who craved a bit of independence.

Her dad worked six days a week on a local building site. Mum held down two jobs, one as a school dinner lady, the other as a home-help for an elderly man who lived on the other side of town. Patti-Ann knew the sacrifices were mostly for her, and she adored them for it, although she wished they would spend more on enjoying their own lives. They deserved to be pampered, just like she was, and she was determined to make it up to them when she qualified and set up practice as a GP in her own town.

She had always been good at mapping out goals. She liked the idea of setting targets and seeing how quickly she could achieve them. For now, though, she just wanted to chill out.

It was a beautiful summer evening in late May. School holidays were just around the corner, and Patti-Ann was determined to make it the best break ever. She had a part-time job in a local supermarket and would see her friends - and Eamon - every evening and weekend for eight glorious weeks.

This was her time to blossom. The thought made her tingle with excitement as she walked down Saul Street, a hilly area of Downpatrick, one of many towns carved out among the rolling drumlins terrain of County Down.

It was a half-mile walk to the town centre. Normally it would take about five minutes for Patti-Ann to reach the junction with Scotch Street, a pedestrian-only link to Market Street where her friends would be waiting. She took a little longer this evening, mainly because she stopped often to talk to neighbours who were lounging in their front gardens, making the most of the strong sunshine. Despite an eagerness to get to her rendezvous, she couldn't simply walk past them, not when they were being so friendly.

In truth, she loved the chance to listen to her mum's pals. They were always so kind and considerate, and Patti-Ann enjoyed the way they made time for each other. The whole street was like one big extended family.

At Scotch Street, she descended four steps to a cobbled open-air area thronged by people going to local takeaways and bars. She smiled and nodded and pushed her way through the crowd, hoping her friends were still waiting – and praying that Eamon would be among them.

It was a cramped spot, barely eighty yards in length but it seemed to take ages to negotiate a clear path. Finally, she passed the entrance to the Arts Centre, walked around the Town Hall corner, and emerged into Lower Irish Street, a busy traffic route that was thankfully free of pedestrians. Just a hundred yards to go before she crossed into Market Street.

But somewhere along those one hundred yards, Patti-Ann Weston dropped off the face of the earth.

Detective Sergeant John Bonnaville was counting down the days to a three-week holiday when he got the news of Patti-Ann's disappearance. He had planned a road trip across America's western states, after which he'd return to a new posting as a Detective Inspector at one of the Police Service of Northern Ireland's stations in Belfast. The promotion had come through just a week ago, and he couldn't wait to get started.

But now everything had changed.

Thoughts of Montana, Colorado, and Arizona evaporated in an instant. They were replaced by images from two years ago, all to do with the smiling face of Jacinta Wilson, the one that got away. The one who still haunted him with feelings of inadequacy.

Even from the early reports coming into the PSNI station house at the top of Irish Street, the similarities in the cases of the two girls were too strong for Bonnaville to ignore. Two fifteen-year-olds gone missing in broad daylight in the centre of town. Both were blonde, both had no siblings, and the timings of their disappearances – in the first real days of summer – couldn't be explained away as mere coincidences. Was there a Solstice beast out there, unable to suppress his urge to kill after waiting two years from the date of his first victim?

Bonnaville knew the idea was fanciful in the extreme. When he tried to articulate it to the area's Chief Inspector, it sounded even more ludicrous, a nebulous link that was being woven without any real regard for the facts. After all, Jacinta Wilson was still officially a *Misper*, and Patti-Ann Wilson had only been reported overdue at a friend's house by several hours. Hardly conclusive proof of a serial killer at large.

And yet, there *could* be something tying together two seemingly unconnected incidents. The Chief Inspector finally decided on a full-scale search operation, with more than five-hundred civilian volunteers joining in, to comb waste ground and pick their way through scores of derelict buildings. A team of ten detectives interviewed friends, relatives, schoolmates, neighbours, ex-offenders with any history of violence, and everyone who'd seen or talked to Patti-Ann on her last walk from home.

Bonnaville, against the urgings of his superiors, cancelled his leave and took charge of a specific element of the investigations. He spent days sifting through the names and interviews from Jacinta Wilson's cold case, looking for links or intersections with the current investigation. A handful of teenagers had shared friendships with both girls, but those were only tentative at best, mostly to do with attending the same school, or youth club, or drama group. Something to be expected in a small town.

There were no connecting lines with adults, although it did strike Bonnaville as interesting that a building contractor, whose squad of men had been carrying out redevelopment work on houses close to Jacinta's home, was still engaged on other jobs, one of which was in a small cul-de-sac on the same street where Patti-Ann lived. It was probably to be expected that a builder would need to keep his business afloat by constantly bidding for small local jobs, but it was at least worth another look.

Twenty interviews later, Bonnaville could find nothing untoward among the squad of workers. They were the usual mixed bunch of trades – plumbers, electricians, brickies, decorators, and chippies, the insider appellation for joiners – but none of the individuals stood out as having something to hide, and none displayed any signs of guilt or unease when answering Bonnaville's often bullish questions.

As the days progressed, rumour and suspicion were rife within the tight-knit community. Everyone, it seemed, had a theory, and with each wild allegation the list of potential suspects grew. The disappearance of the vivacious teenager touched the lives of many, none more so than Patti-Ann's sixteen-year-old boyfriend Eamon Vickery, whose family later had to leave the area because of the innuendo and harassment that trailed in the wake of whatever happened on that May evening.

Despite poster campaigns and media appeals, nothing broke loose. Eventually the manhunt scaled down, and people went about their own lives. Friends did their best to keep Patti-Ann in the public eye. They set up a Facebook page and posted regular pleas for help. They held candlelight vigils, organised special events to raise funds for newspaper adverts, and printed two thousand leaflets, which were posted through doors and stuffed behind car wipers in local parks. As the months passed, their enthusiasm waned. There were no sightings. No fresh leads for police to pursue.

Once again John Bonnaville came up empty-handed.

Chapter 3
Downpatrick – a year after Patti-Ann Weston

The elderly couple always took a late evening stroll along a gravelled path that followed the twisting turns of the Quoile River. No matter the weather, they never missed their daily routine. It helped give them an appetite for supper and made it easier for them to sleep away the tiredness of their exertions.

It came as no surprise to them to find a man stooped over a bundle close to a fishing platform, one of many that made the area so popular among locals. What did surprise them was that the figure was wearing a large, hooded jacket, despite the mildness of the summer evening. The man's face was screened from view as he jumped at the sound of the couple's arrival. He sprang to his feet and bolted off, never once looking back, or giving a clue to his identity.

The elderly couple moved forward tentatively to look at the abandoned bundle. It was a long hessian sack, rolled into a crude circle, and secured with coils of black electrical wiring. Something about it made the old man recoil.

PSNI officers were on the scene ten minutes after the couple had punched through a frantic call on their mobile phone. The restraints on the bundle were cut away and the hessian cover sliced open. Inside, they found the body of a seventeen-year-old girl.

John Bonnaville, now a Detective Inspector based in Belfast, got a courtesy call from one of his former Downpatrick detectives. It was about a possible homicide involving a teenager at a local river. Bonnaville dropped everything and raced to the area.

Forty minutes after leaving Belfast, Bonnaville stepped inside a crime-scene tent erected around the gruesome riverside discovery and immediately took in one glaring feature of the dead girl. The victim had long blonde hair.

She was later identified as Martina Quigley, born and raised in Belfast, and in Downpatrick that day to make a surprise visit to her grandmother. It was the first time her parents had allowed her to make the bus trip on her own, but it was not something they were worried about. By all accounts, Martina was a mature, level-headed girl who was used to acting independently and responsibly, often running errands into Belfast city centre for family members and neighbours. She had four younger siblings, three brothers and a sister, who all looked up to Martina as a second mother.

Bonnaville was able to track Martina's last movements through the simple expediency of the bus route into Downpatrick and the grandmother's address, which was a single-storey house on the Strangford Road, close to the town's cricket club. Martina would have alighted from the bus near a large roundabout and walked the rest of the way, a distance of two-thirds of a mile, to her destination. She would have had to cross the road, go past a row of terraced houses, and swing into a more secluded area that stretched for about five-hundred yards.

It was confirmed that she had arrived at her grandmother's shortly after eleven o'clock in the morning and left that evening in time to walk back for the seven o'clock express to Belfast. The bus driver was able to tell police that he picked up no passengers at the roundabout, meaning that Martina had somehow met her killer during that short, fateful walk along the Strangford Road.

How was that possible? The idea that Martina's killing was opportunistic was barely credible. People weren't just snatched off the street for no reason. The perpetrator had to be someone the girl knew, perhaps even someone who had followed her from Belfast to Downpatrick. Nothing else made any sense.

Bonnaville had to concede there were no interconnecting lines for an enquiry to take in Downpatrick. Martina had no friends in the town. The only times she had been the area was with her family or, as in her final journey, by herself, to visit her grandmother. She had never gone anywhere else whilst she was in Downpatrick, so there was no prospect of casual acquaintances she could have made.

The enquiry was taken out of Bonnaville's hands and transferred to Belfast where detectives would chase down everyone with whom Martina had contact during her short life. If her killer were to be found, he would be among those who knew her.

Bonnaville argued strongly that Martina's death mirrored the disappearances of two previous teenagers in Downpatrick. The physical appearances of all three girls showed a pattern that could not be ignored, but try as he might, he could not come up with anything other than that slim thread. None of the people interviewed in the previous cases could have had any links with Martina, a girl who had lived her life outside Downpatrick. There was just nothing to work on.

In one last desperate attempt to keep control of the investigation, Bonnaville requested that a detailed search be carried out at the Quoile River. He wanted a complete drag of the riverbed, hoping it might reveal clues to the other missing girls. By then, Patti-Ann Weston had been gone for more than a year; Jacinta Wilson for three years

The request was denied.

One senior officer described Bonnaville's interest as "obsessional" while another said it was "fanciful in the extreme." The bottom line was that no-one wanted to commit resources on a line of enquiry that could have only one inescapable conclusion. The idea that a serial killer might be at loose was not a concept the public should be exposed to.

Bonnaville was told to stay away from the case. Over the next five years he never forgot the three girls.

BOOK 2

PRESENT DAY
Castlebar, Republic of Ireland

Chapter 4

THEY ALWAYS DID these things at six o'clock in the morning. It was as good a time as any, although someone in the bean-counting department of An Garda Síochána had probably sweated needlessly over a spreadsheet to determine the maximum impact of a raid designed to sweep up suspects and evidence before the culprits had a chance to get wind of what was going on.

It worked most of the time. But not always.

The complication on this June Friday morning was that there were four raids, planned simultaneously across the county after months of laborious stake-outs, endless tails on vehicles coming and going from the premises, and behind-the-scenes grafting by forensic accountants attempting to link a myriad of companies and business activities.

The one common denominator was Padraig Flynn. Better known to the criminal underworld as Big Paud, he had his fingers in every grubby money-making pie west of Dublin. Drugs, money-laundering, protection racketeering, red diesel fraud, and the import of counterfeit goods – from cigarettes and whiskey to Gucci shoes and knock-off denims. Whenever something was being traded under the counter, Big Paud made sure he got his cut of the action.

The Guards reckoned his little business empire netted him somewhere in the region of ten million Euros a year, all in cash, and all hidden away in probably more than a dozen secure locations. Just enough was brought to the surface to fund several legitimate businesses, the most convenient, from Flynn's point of view, being a chain of betting shops that helped to wash some of the proceeds of his other nefarious activities.

This allowed him to live in open grandeur on a sprawling fifty-acre estate near Castlebar. A pillar of the community, a noted benefactor to numerous charities, and an all-round sleazeball to those who could see past the veneer.

Detective Inspector Mick Boyle was most definitely at the top of the can't-fool-me column. Five minutes after restoring his reputation following a bleak period in a colourful career, Boyle pinned a photo of Flynn to the top of a noticeboard in his new Castlebar offices and decided this particular fox had run its course. Boyle's recently formed county-wide taskforce had its first priority assignment.

Shut down Big Paud Flynn, once and for all.

Not surprisingly, Boyle grabbed the front passenger seat of the lead vehicle of the two-car convoy that drew to a halt just outside the open-gateway entrance to Flynn's estate. A large metal arch spanned the entrance, bearing the gold-plated title of *The Ponderosa*.

The car engine ticked over as Boyle waited for the appointed time, less than two minutes away. He fidgeted with three small folders, each containing a search warrant. It was the pedantry nature of police paperwork that demanded separate warrants for the house, for the large, detached garage building, and for any vehicles belonging to the home occupants. Many a case had been thrown out of court because of illegal searches of areas not specifically mentioned in the authorised documentation.

Boyle looked up at the imposing facade of the large, three-storey house. There were ten distinct structural sub-divisions across the frontage, each no doubt denoting the demarcation of individual rooms. Jeez, he'd seen smaller hotels! Each sub-division contained ornate window paneling, with twelve panes of glass in each panel, making a total of a hundred and twenty per floor, minus the space needed for the massive porch area jutting out at ground level like a miniature castle. Boyle started counting the sheets of glass, making his way from the top floor in a precise clockwise sweep across and down the building.

"I know what you're doing. It's that numerology thing again, isn't it?"

Boyle smiled and looked across at his driver, Detective Sergeant Paul Brogan, one of the force's new breed of fast-tracked university recruits who one day would turn policing into a minefield of computer-generated crime scenarios and databases capable of cross-referencing perps who shopped at Sainsburys or those who liked raspberry jam with their doughnuts. The world was going mad! To be fair, Brogan was not like that. He had a copper's nous for the old-fashioned, down-and-dirty detection methodologies, and Doyle liked him immensely. The pair had developed a strong bond since the younger man's posting as a greenhorn Guard, fresh from his studies in Criminology, and ready to conquer the world until he butted heads with the realism of Boyle's earthy world.

"Did you really just say numerology?" Boyle harrumphed. "What the feck did they teach you in Trinity College? The word you're looking for is

Arithmomania, which any self-respecting analyst will tell you is the best possible way to relax and find your equilibrium." Boyle knew it was in fact a form of OCD, a compulsion to count numerous objects, but he was not about to admit that to his young colleague.

Brogan threw back his head and roared with laughter. "Yeah, whatever! Why don't you just admit you were counting the blades of grass in the front lawn, or the number of clouds in the sky. I'll bet you know by now how many doors and windows there are in that big house yonder."

"As a matter of fact, I do," Boyle retaliated. "You can learn a lot from knowing such things."

"Such as?"

"Well, for starters, I now know how many rooms we have to search, and whether there are any escape routes we might have to cover. A good policeman has to get the basics right before rashly running through front doors only to find that all the bad guys have bolted out through some side entrance he knew nothing about."

Brogan was unimpressed. "Bullshit! You can't see the sides of the house from here. Why don't you just admit to having an annoying little habit that serves no useful function?

Boyle was about to respond when his wristwatch pulsed against its alarm setting. "Time to go. Let's roll!"

Brogan floored the accelerator, sending the silver Rav4 hurtling up the driveway, closely followed by a squad car belonging to an Armed Response Unit, in this case four men who had been comprehensively briefed by Boyle prior to the searches getting the go-ahead.

The convoy slid to a halt beside the porch, and six pairs of shoes crunched across the gravel. One officer carried an Enforcer, a tubular battering ram that delivered three tonnes of impact force, more than enough to shatter the sturdy, deadbolt locking mechanism on the front door.

The officer stepped forward, holding the battering ram in a two-handed grip. Just as he was about to swing it towards his target, a set of lights bathed the porch in a blinding flash, and the door swung open to reveal three figures standing with their arms folded across their chests.

There was no mistaking the huge bulk of Big Paud Flynn. He was a bear of a man, easily six-five and carrying somewhere north of twenty stone, most of which was covered by a white Aran sweater that looked capable of framing a family-sized tepee. An out-of-proportion gut stretched the garment as far as it would go, no doubt the result of too many whiskies and beer chasers, if the burst blood vessels on his bulbous nose were anything to go by.

He had thinning brown hair and a forehead full of creases that underlined his seventy years. Bushy eyebrows and thin, turned-down lips added menace to a face that many an unfortunate had probably cowered away from over the years. All in all, Big Paud was not a man to be trifled with.

Standing beside Flynn was his son, Jerome, a slovenly-looking chip of the old block, who wore a cutaway, sleeveless t-shirt and jeans that seemed to defy gravity below a chunky waistline. As an attempt at debonair casualness, it was a wardrobe malfunction of the worst kind.

But it was the third figure that grabbed most attention. One look at the designer three-piece suit

and smug grin was enough to send something heavy to the bottom of Boyle's stomach.
Oh fuck! What's he doing here?

Chapter 5

"ISN'T THAT TYPICAL of our beloved Guards! Why use a perfectly good doorbell when you have a battering ram to satisfy an urge for the theatrical? Never mind the mess, or the cost, or the inconvenience, just so long as the guardians of the law get to play their little control games."

It was a voice that grated with Boyle. Too much rounded vowelling, an over-the-top concentration on enunciation, and too heavy on the plummy tones that underscored his roots in South East England. A privileged jerk who'd become one of the youngest QCs in the London circuit courts and had the distinction of being *called to the bar* in more countries than any of his silken-robed peers. This was Myles Winstanley, a heavyweight in the legal profession, and a friend to anyone from the dark side who could afford his impressive fee structure.

Rumoured to be on annual retainers of two-hundred thousand Euros, plus a daily rate of five thousand, Winstanley had no shortage of takers. He'd arrived in Dublin five years ago to lead the defence team for the head of a local crime family charged with a succession of feud murders. It was an open-and-shut case until Winstanley chiseled away at the prosecution's paper trail and exposed a succession of chain-of-evidence errors that ultimately resulted in the case being thrown out of Dublin Central Criminal Court in a blaze of headlines, all of which featured the remarkable prowess of the lead defence barrister.

The offers rolled in. Winstanley had gone back to London for three weeks to wrap up his affairs and returned to Ireland to begin the most lucrative chapter in his life. All told, it was estimated he was now banking more than two million euros a year, after taxes, the kind of money that could provide a luxury estate of his own, plus a yacht and membership of some of the most exclusive golf clubs in the country.

Boyle had suffered under Winstanley's cross-examination techniques in a drugs case listed at Galway Circuit Court several years before. The thirty-five minutes he'd spent on the stand was taken up with overt references to Boyle's alcoholism, his failed marriage, and the fact that he'd been demoted after hitting a colleague so hard the man had spent several months in hospital. It hardly mattered that Boyle had never been classified as a heavy drinker, or that the reason he'd broken the man's jaw was that he'd had found him in bed with his then wife, it was enough for Winstanley to attack the credibility of the witness rather than stick to the facts of the case. Boyle tried to convince himself that the exchange was merely par for the course, something all lawyers engaged in, but somehow Winstanley had made it too personal, and had taken way too much delight in Boyle's discomfiture. The two men had left court that day as implacable enemies.

And now, here they were face to face again.

Winstanley grinned and shifted his eyes towards the paperwork held in Boyle's hand. "I take it those are warrants? Kindly hand them over and remain where you are until I've had a chance to read through them."

Despite his growing anger, Boyle almost burst out laughing. "In your dreams, counsellor. As I'm sure you know, you'll find nothing there about me waiting around for your approval. What you will see is that I can effect whatever immediate entry I deem reasonable and take any steps necessary to secure evidence pertaining to our investigations into your client. Any attempt by you, your client, or others, to frustrate the execution of these warrants will amount to obstruction of justice, for which I will be obliged to make arrests."

Winstanley began a slow handclap. "Bravo, Inspector, I see you've been reading up on your law. Nice to know the Guards are paying some attention to the legal niceties."

Boyle shoved the warrants hard into Winstanley's chest, shouldered his way between Big Paud Flynn and his son, and stepped into a massive foyer that resembled a museum chamber. The floor was covered in marble tiles and surrounded by plinthed statues, paintings mounted on easels, and an array of tasteful furnishings, including two large chaise longues which added a much-needed splash of colour to the antiseptic look of the place. Big Paud had shelled out a lot of money to an interior decorator with minimalist design ideas.

Boyle waited for his officers to join him in the centre of the area before he turned back to Winstanley. "Make sure you keep out of our way. Wouldn't want to lock any of you up now, would we?"

"You're plainly enjoying yourself, Boyle," Winstanley snorted. "Just make sure you don't cause any damage, such as putting holes into partition walls, or needlessly ripping up floorboards. I warn you, there's a thin line between doing your job and causing unwarranted vandalism."

"Now, there's a thought," Boyle scoffed. "I suppose if I wanted to hide a stackful of euros, the best places would be under the floorboards, or sealed into walls. Thanks for the tip, counsellor."

Winstanley walked forward, his face a mask of determination. "You'll find nothing. My client is a highly respected businessman who is well known in the community for providing employment and supporting charitable causes. His many commercial dealings are beyond reproach, so much so in fact that were it not for his enterprises, this little western corner of Ireland would be a much poorer and disadvantaged area. You should be thankful we have men like Padraig Flynn in our midst."

Boyle felt a familiar creep of anger rise in his chest. "Let's get one thing straight. Your client is a criminal of the worst kind. He milks the very people you purport he serves. He takes everything they've got, and when he bleeds them dry, he moves on to his next victims, never caring whether whole families go without food or clothing because they're in hock to him and his henchmen. Those who try to fight back usually end up in hospital, or much worse, depending on whether this sleazeball gets out of bed on the right side every morning."

Big Paud balled his fists and made a rush towards Boyle. He was held back by Winstanley. "Be patient, Padraig. Let the Inspector have his little bit of fun."

Flynn stepped back, glaring daggers at Boyle.

"That was impressive," Boyle told him. "Has he taught you to roll over to have your tummy tickled?"

Flynn exploded. "I'm warning you, copper. You

might feel safe now when you're surrounded by all your flunky officers, but you won't always be like this. Take a care, especially when you're on your own, or with that pretty new wife of yours."

Boyle looked as if he were about to go into an apoplectic rage. The colour rushed to his cheeks and his breathing became laboured, his chest rising and falling at too many beats than was natural. He was about to throw a right cross into Flynn's face when he felt his arm restrained by Sergeant Brogan. "Don't rise to the bait, boss," he whispered.

The seconds ticked by while Boyle brought his breathing under control. He counted off from one thousand to one thousand and ten in his usual OCD way of coping with stress. Finally, he was confident enough to speak. "I could interpret what you just said as threatening a police officer in the commission of his duties, or I could just assume you meant it as a personal hands-off warning. Either way, let's be clear about one thing. If you ever mention my wife again, then all your money, and all your henchmen, and whatever protection you think this smarmy lawyer of yours can provide, won't make a blind bit of difference to the fact that I'll come for you. And when I do, you'll know what it's like to be on the receiving end of a lot of hurt."

The tension in the foyer was palpable. Heads bowed and feet shifted as everyone waited for the next act to play out. The merest spark could explode the confrontation into a full-scale free-for-all. It was Winstanley who took it upon himself to diffuse the situation. "Alright, we've all had our little bit of fun. What say we act as professionals and bring this rather unseemly episode to a conclusion. I must tell you, Chief Inspector, you're wasting your time.

There's nothing here of interest to you."

"I'll be the judge of that," Boyle responded.

"Just trying to be helpful. I mean, surely An Garda Síochána can't afford the resources needed for a fishing trip of this nature, not to mention the other raids that are being carried out as we speak across the county. A lot of people are going to be left with red faces when you come up empty-handed."

Winstanley's words struck a nerve with Boyle. A look of indecision crossed his face, as he stared across the room at a large painting, depicting some sort of historic meeting around the time of the Easter Rising, judging by the old-fashioned paramilitary gear. Boyle counted fifteen faces in the frame, at the centre of which was the unmistakable figure of Michael Collins, then a lowly recruit in the ranks of the Irish Republican Brotherhood, the group responsible for the failed attempt at independence in 1916. Five years later, Collins led his country – or at least twenty-six of its thirty-two counties – into a total breakaway from English rule.

Somehow, the message of resolve and patience resonated with Boyle at that moment. "You know what, Counsellor? You're right. This is a waste of time. There's nothing to be gained by us being here. It's obvious we'll find nothing; your client is an innocent man; and an Irish astronaut landed on the moon ten years before Neil Armstrong."

Boyle nodded at his team and marched out through the door, leaving Winstanley and the Flynns staring open-mouthed at their departure.

Chapter 6

BROGAN WAITED until the convoy was back on the main road leading away from the Flynn estate before he spoke. "Mind telling me what that was all about?"

Boyle slumped in the passenger seat and knuckle-rubbed his eyes. "We've been blindsided. That bastard Winstanley wasn't there by accident at this time of the morning. They knew we were coming, which means someone tipped them off, which means we have a serious leak somewhere in our set-up, or in the Office of the Director of Public Prosecutions, or in the District Court offices where the warrants were approved."

"Jeez, Mick, that's a bit of a stretch. It could be that Flynn just happens to start work early in the morning, or his lawyer could have stayed over from a party the night before. You need to be careful before you start flinging around accusations."

Boyle understood Brogan well enough to know he was trying to be cautious. Their relationship was such that they could speak plainly to each other, confident that friendship came a long way before rank.

"You heard him," Boyle said. "He knew about the other raids. He wouldn't have got that unless somebody told him in advance. No, we've got a leak the size of the River Shannon, and we were left up the creek without a paddle."

"That's a pretty impressive analogy, even for you,

Boss. Seriously though, you're obviously right, but let's go easy until we know a lot more. I think we should look at who had access to the information and then see if we can find any links to Flynn or his lawyer."

"Aye, and therein lies the rub," Boyle said. "We had to jump through a lot of hoops to get the warrants. This went on for months, with a lot of higher-ups extremely fidgety about mounting such an operation in the first place. We both know Flynn has a lot of clout and has greased enough palms to ensure there's always someone looking after his interests. Christ, there must have been more than a hundred people involved in processing the requests for these warrants. Where the feck do we start?"

"Well, if you'd wanted easy, you'd have taken early retirement and helped Belle run that pub of yours. It's not fair to leave the wife to earn the real corn while you're out gallivanting across the county on wild goose chases."

Boyle smiled at Brogan's attempt to lift the mood. Belle Mooney, now Mrs Boyle, had been his childhood sweetheart, but it had taken some wrong choices for Boyle to finally see the wood for the trees. Belle had inherited her father's pub and was in the middle of a major refurbishment, thanks to an injection of cash from the sale of the Boyle family home shortly after their marriage. The couple lived in an apartment above the pub, which had spacious grounds to accommodate an extension and a new beer garden.

"Don't let Belle hear you call it a pub. It's a fine-dining restaurant and conference centre, or at least it will be by the time she gets through with it. Thankfully, she's keeping her famous steak pie and chips on the menu. And just for the record, she's glad I'm not there, getting in the way. I mean, have you ever seen me try to pull a proper pint of Guinness?"

"Point taken. Now, what are we going to do about the mole?"

Boyle fished in the pockets of his suit and brought out a small A7-sized spiral notebook. "First things first. The other teams need to be notified that we're busted. Might as well call off the searches and return everyone to base."

He flicked through the pages looking for the names of the team leaders, grabbed his mobile phone, and began making calls. Five minutes later he settled back into his seat, his mind already racing ahead to where things would go from here. One thing was for sure: there would be a lot of shit flying around, most of which would end up painted across his own face. Par for the course.

Welcome to Mick Boyle's world!

Belle Boyle, née Mooney, was at her happiest. She was in the kitchen preparing early breakfasts and a select lunchtime menu, which didn't include steak pie and chips, although she did make a large deep-plated one earlier and clingfilmed it on a shelf at the back of the refrigerator. At least tonight's dinner was taken care of.

Workmen were already on site, dismantling the scaffolding at the rear of the property, and moving in earth-clearing equipment to prepare the garden for the next phase of development. The upstairs was finished, providing a new master bedroom; a second room that was needed for a nursery; a new guest room; and a new bathroom, complete with walk-in shower, something that suited Mick because of his usual rush to work. The downstairs bar and lounge areas were also wrapped up, with attention now turned to creating a new dining area and small conference room to the side of the building. Another three weeks should see everything in full working order.

As usual, Belle dished out coffee and croissants to the workers before they launched into their day. There was a dozen constantly on site, and none passed up the opportunity to visit the kitchen. She had just placed a mug in front of the foreman when she heard a loud banging noise coming from the front bar.

"Service! Where the feck is everybody?"

Belle glanced up at the kitchen clock. It had just gone past seven-thirty. She shouted over her shoulder. "We're not open for another three hours. Come back later."

The response left her dumbfounded. "Yeah, well the door was open. Time was when Mooneys had a reputation for looking after its regulars. Suppose that's what married life does to you."

There was something about the voice that was vaguely familiar. As she walked through to the bar area, it suddenly hit her, even before she spotted the large figure leaning against the counter."

"Jacko McStravick! What takes you back here?"

Her visitor threw back the counter hatch and grabbed Belle in a bear hug. "Sure, darlin' I missed my favourite barmaid. I just couldn't stay away any longer. Where's that ingrate of a husband of yours?"

Belle thumped against McStravick's chest. "Put me down, you big ape. If Mick walks in, he'll do you for common assault and lock you away, just for the hell of it."

"Aye, that he probably would." McStravick set her on her feet and walked back around the counter. He looked around the lounge, his eyes settling on a cubicle to the left side of an ornate open fireplace. "Many's a grand time I had there. God, it's great to see the old place again."

"Stop being so mushy, Jacko. It's only been a year or so. What happened to the new life in Salthill? Weren't you living in a caravan beside the sea?"

McStravick wiped an arm across his mouth. "It's been fourteen months and two weeks, but who's counting? I traded in the caravan, as you called it, for one of those new-fangled motorhomes. It's luxury on wheels and lets me go wherever the feck I please. Should have done it years ago. Now, my mouth's as parched as a…… better not to go there. What about a drink?"

"Are you mad in the head at this time of the morning?"

"Ah, come on Belle, I was down in Killarney this past week and I've been driving through the night. I've a fair druth on me, I can tell ya. What about helping a weary traveler with a pint of the black stuff?"

"Jacko McStravick, if you think I'd risk my licence for your old blarney, you've got another think coming." Her eyes softened. "Have you had breakfast? What about a fry-up and a big mug of coffee?"

He winked at her. "Now, why didn't I think about that?"

Belle shook her head and wandered off towards the kitchen, realising she'd just been railroaded by a master conman. McStravick was once the big wheel in Castlebar, running a string of criminal activities, most of which were petty larcenies and dealing in stolen goods. He always drew the line at the hard stuff, like drugs, though he was notorious for using his fists more often than his brains. At almost seventy years of age, he still looked like he could handle himself, something that befitted a former bare-knuckle champion of Ireland. For all his faults, he was an incorrigible rogue, the kind of larger-than-life character who always created a breath of fresh air mixed in with an acceptable level of devilment.

Belle knew McStravick had a lot of history with her husband, but when push came to shove, Mick had stood in the big man's corner and helped him stay out of jail for the murder of a notorious serial killer, who'd numbered McStravick's sister among his victims. There was a certain bond between the pair, even if both would never admit to it.

"I like what you're doing to the place," McStravick told her thirty minutes later as he washed down the last forkful of an enormous breakfast. The helping of four sausages, four rashers of bacon, two black puddings, a pile of beans, and a stack of potato bread hadn't stood a chance against a hungry bear's onslaught.

"What are you going to do with yourself, Jacko?"

"Thought I'd park up the motorhome down at the tourist site in Meadow Lane. The owner owes me a few favours, so I reckon I can stay as long as I like. Thinking of grabbing me a small retail unit in High Street, and opening an antiques den, all legit with no dodgy goods."

Belle shook her head. "You'd better go straight. Mick will be watching you, and I kind of think you owe it to him not to put him in an embarrassing situation."

"Don't worry, darling, old Jacko knows what side his bread is buttered on. I don't forget people who did me a good turn, and your old man is right at the top of the list. I'll keep my nose clean, but I can't guarantee I won't have a few laughs at his expense along the way. Sure, wouldn't life be dull without it."

Belle rose from the seat, kissed McStravick on the cheek, and walked towards the kitchen, muttering to herself. *Somehow, I think we'll be glad to see a bit of dull by the time Jacko's finished.*

Chapter 7

THE POTHOLED LANE was barely two hundred yards in length. It stretched from an old, secluded thatched cottage to an ungated entrance by the side of the busiest road leading into Castlebar. It took less than a few minutes' walk to be magically transported from the rural Ireland of the eighteenth century to its more clamourous modern day reincarnation. The sight of a rotted pony-and-trap rig abandoned against one wall of the cottage couldn't have been more incongruous when compared to the helter-skelter of HGV leviathans and family saloons that rushed in a blur in both directions of the N5 link to Westport.

It was a walk that fifteen-year-old Megan McGrath knew well. She'd been doing it on an almost daily basis since primary school days. She knew the characteristics of every tree, and thornbush, and cracked pavement slab between her home and the centre of Castlebar, which was about a mile from the laneway entrance. It was a journey for her of usually no more than fifteen minutes, less so today because she was in a hurry to meet with best friend, Siobhan Cunningham, who she knew was secretly planning Megan's surprise sixteenth birthday party. Hardly a surprise, since Megan already knew most of the details, though she pretended not to overhear the numerous conversations that were supposed to have been out of earshot every time her inner circle had met during the past week.

She'd heard that Siobhan was in charge of getting a venue. No better person! She was an expert at forged IDs. If Siobhan couldn't get the group into the new upstairs nightclub at Foley's, then nobody could. It was as good as done.

As Megan skipped happily along the pavement, she failed to notice a van pull over into another lane entrance just ahead of her. It was only when she got within twenty yards that she spotted the driver struggling with a large map covering the steering wheel and half the windscreen. He looked up as she approached, activated the side window, and spoke directly to her. "Excuse me, Miss, I'm lost and need to get to a job interview in Castlebar within the next ten minutes. Can you help me? Am I near the town yet?"

Megan didn't think it strange that the man could have failed to see the plethora of kilometre markings that dotted the N5. She stood back warily and pointed ahead. "You're nearly there. When you go around the corner at the top of this straight, you'll see traffic lights. You should keep to the inside lane and that'll take you into the town centre."

"Thank you," the man said. "Do you know Mooney's pub? That's where the interviews are."

"Yes, go down the main street and take a right at the second set of traffic lights. It's only a few yards from the junction."

"Do you know if there's parking nearby? I really can't miss this interview. My wife is depending on me, what with a new baby and all."

Megan looked at the well-dressed man and felt sorry for him. "They're doing work at Mooneys, so the only parking is at the end of the street in a church park on the right-hand side."

The man shot her a puzzled look. "So, I take the inside lane and go through two traffic lights before turning right? Then I go up the street and turn left for the church park?"

"No," Megan responded with a touch of exasperation. "Don't go through two traffic lights. Turn right at the second set of lights. If you miss the turn, it'll take you another ten minutes to get back because of the new one-way system."

"I'm sorry for the mix-up. It's just that this job means everything to us. I don't suppose there's any chance of you showing me. If you're going that way, it really would help a lot."

The driver watched as Megan's face displayed a series of conflicting emotions. He waited patiently while she filtered through the options. Finally, she spoke. "It can't do any harm: besides, I'm meeting my friend close to Mooney's, so it looks like I'll get there a lot sooner than I thought."

The driver smiled and reached across to open the passenger door. Megan slid into the seat and fastened the seatbelt. She waited for the van to reverse back onto the road but was startled when it suddenly lurched forward. Before she had time to say something, a large hand clamped across her mouth, releasing a sickening sweet smell that almost made her vomit. Panic rose to the surface and she kicked out at the dashboard, breaking the heel of one of her sandals. She felt herself go weak. Her eyes glazed over. And then there was nothing but blackness.

Siobhan Cunningham was becoming frantic. It was now almost an hour since Megan was supposed to meet for a planned lunch and shopping trip to the new boutique in Market Lane. She'd sent more than a dozen texts, each one becoming more urgent, but still no reply.

Where are you, babe?
What's keeping you?
Have you found something better to do?
This isn't funny. Get back to me now!

Siobhan had gone online through her iPhone to check Facebook, Snapchat, and Messenger, but no activity was registering against Megan. Finally, she put a call through to Megan's mobile, frowning at the robotic voice message that announced the service was unavailable.

She waited another ten minutes before reluctantly calling Megan's home. She didn't want to bother her parents, but she needed to know if everything was okay. What if Megan was meeting a mysterious boyfriend? No, she couldn't keep that a secret!

"Hello, Mrs McGrath, it's Siobhan Cunningham. Is Megan at home?"

"No dearie, she left a long time ago to meet with you. She said you two had planned to go to the shops, though Lord knows that girl has enough clothes to last her for the next five years. Are you saying you haven't seen her yet?"

Siobhan bit her lip, wondering how best to proceed. "She hasn't turned up, Mrs McGrath. It's not like her to be late. I'm really worried."

"Oh dear, now you've got me worried. What should we do? Should we call the police? Are you sure she's not with some of her other friends?"

Siobhan could hear crying on the other end of the line. Then there was a scream. "Malcolm, Malcolm, our Megan has gone missing." Malcolm was Megan's dad. He'd know what to do.

The seconds stretched into a minute before a second voice came on the line. "This is Malcolm McGrath, am I speaking to Siobhan?"

"Yes, sir."

"Contact all your friends and see if anyone has spotted Megan. We'll get in touch with her granny and aunts to see if she's gone visiting. Let us know as soon as you hear anything."

"Shouldn't we contact the Guards and............"

The line had gone dead.

Castlebar police station sits in an island junction between the Mall and Pavilion roads. The distinctive triple-peaked structure is one of An Garda Síochána's most tasteful properties, its outward appearance more suited to a town manor estate than a place of work. A circular driveway, carved between a well-clipped lawn and flower beds that had the look of many hours of devotion, swept around the front of the building. The only blemish – and a clue to its real function – is an ugly radio, satellite and cellphone mast sweeping skywards from the rear to provide a jarring barrier to the rows of private houses situated beyond.

The front lobby was an unusually serene place,

filled with the starched smell of police stations the world over, but without the hustle and bustle normally associated with a busy cop shop. Pop-up information stands positioned between upholstered fabric seating provided points of interest for the visiting public, not that the station encouraged contact from the people it served. All calls and incident-logging were routed through the Garda Information Services Centre at the mainly civilian-run Michael Davitt House on the other side of town, leaving the local station free from the distractions of mind-numbing paperwork.

The man in charge of day-to-day operations was Superintendent John Delaney, who managed to keep a tight rein on the various detective squads, uniformed beat and mobile units, and the support staff of clerks, IT operators, and scenes of crime specialists. At any given time, Delaney knew where everyone was, what they should be doing, and whether their casework was up to date. He was a stickler for detail, though he presided over his domain with a caring and affable demeanour that made him immensely popular among the ranks.

Delaney would have been the first to admit that the real organiser was desk sergeant, Colm Moriarty, a twenty-five-year veteran who had the ability to bawl out a Superintendent with the same gusto as he would a first-year Guard. The deep-rooted, universal respect for Moriarty was as much due to his even-handedness as it was to the fact that he was a champion of back-covering, always ready to ensure the men and women at the station were not treated unfairly by those looking for an easy target in their climb up the career ladder. In short, nobody messed with Moriarty unless they were doubly sure of any grounds they thought they had for bringing complaints or disciplinary cases against a fellow officer.

Most of Moriarty's morning had been spent getting the lowdown on the failed searches at Big Paud Flynn's various properties. It hadn't surprised him that they'd come up empty-handed, but what stuck in his craw was that it appeared there had been a tip-off. Mick Boyle believed that was what had happened, and that was good enough for Moriarty. It was certainly enough for him to start mounting his own fishing expedition to uncover a possible source of the leak. All the paperwork had come across his desk, and if anyone was responsible for the cock-up, it was down to Colm Moriarty to get to the bottom of it.

He was sorting through the files in a steel cabinet when the main entrance door flew open, banging against a corner unit with such force that it shook Moriarty's beloved reception counter. A young girl ran across the open space and sagged against the laminated top, her shoulders splayed across the surface, and tears running freely down her cheeks.

"Steady on there, Miss, what seems to be the trouble?"

Siobhan Cunningham gasped for air. "It's....it's Megan! You've got to find her."

Chapter 8

THERE ARE LOTS OF ways of pushing the wrong buttons on Mick Boyle. Not noted for patience, or for turning the other cheek, Boyle would be the first to admit he had anger management issues, especially when it came to some of the lowlifes he encountered on the job, and particularly so those for whom violence was second nature. It was all very well playing by the book, respecting the rights of suspects, and tucking them into their cells at night, but every so often the only thing these bozos understood was delivered with a stronger degree of force than a slap on the wrist. Yeah, he'd crossed the line a time or two, but who was counting?

It was not to say that Boyle was overly aggressive. Always careful not to leave a mark on his victims, he preferred a well-delivered punch to the solar plexus than one that altered facial features, no matter how ugly the visage in question was to start with. At just under six feet, and heading into his mid-forties, Boyle was no Conor McGregor poster boy, but there was scarcely an ounce of fat on his lean frame, and his regular visits with Brogan to the local gym helped keep things in trim, particularly a recent introduction to various forms of martial arts, which had honed his reflexes still further. He didn't go looking for trouble, but it was enough for Mayo's criminal fraternity to know he wouldn't shy away when the occasion arose.

He'd mellowed over the past year, a subtle transformation that could be put down to only one reason. When Belle Mooney had re-entered his life and helped him out of the car-crash of a failed marriage and a career heading for the rocks, everyone around Boyle could see the emergence of a new man. Belle was a feisty woman with a deep-rooted sense of caring for the world around her. From an early age, she'd found an equilibrium that brought contentment into her life and allowed her to worry more about the plight of others, so much so that she threw herself wholeheartedly into church and charitable work, while trying to balance the hectic demands of running a business. There were no airs or graces about the latest Mrs Mick Boyle. What you saw is what you got. For most people, that was plenty more than they'd a right to expect.

The idea that someone would want to do harm to Belle was making her husband's blood boil. Big Paud Flynn's barely veiled threat had shifted the stakes to another level. What had started out for Boyle as a determined operation against a criminal enterprise, had now been ratcheted up to a full-blown personal vendetta. One way or another, Flynn was going down.

And he was going down hard.

Boyle had been locked in his office for the better part of an hour. It rankled him that someone had blown the whistle on the dawn raids of Flynn properties, but how much time and effort could he spend on finding the culprit, and what good would it do at the end of the day? Flynn would still be in business, laughing all the way to the bank, or wherever he stashed the bulk of his ill-gotten gains. Nothing would change, life would go on, and Boyle's team would have to start again to try to build another case.

Feck that! There had to be another way.

The answer was staring him in the face. Six months of mind-numbing stake outs had been washed out with one phone call by a dirty mole. Shipments tracked, employees followed, photographs taken, reports filed, databases updated – and yet not one arrest made, nor any illegal goods seized, simply because Boyle and his men had stood off, trying to build the big picture in the hope of collapsing the whole deck of cards in one foul swoop. It was time for a change of tack. Time to hit Big Paud where it hurt the most.

If nothing else, the surveillance operation had amassed a wealth of intel. Names, dates, places, people, vehicle registrations, routes frequently taken – all of which could now be used to throw a spanner into Flynn's apparently well-oiled machine.

Boyle stirred from his reverie, rose from behind the desk and headed to the squad room at the end of the corridor on the first floor of the stationhouse. He was greeted with a scene of pandemonium as detectives mingled with uniforms around a noticeboard that displayed a large map of the Castlebar area.

"What's the flap about?"

Paul Brogan moved away from the melee. "A teenage girl's gone missing from the town. Superintendent Delaney is looking to use all the resources we have."

"When did this happen?"

"It's been a few hours now since she was last sighted."

Boyle threw Brogan a puzzled look. "It's a bit

early for a panic? Don't we wait at least twelve hours before the cavalry is called out?"

"It's my call, Mick." Boyle turned towards the sound of the new voice and saw the worried look on Delaney's face. "I may be overreacting, but I don't like the circumstances of this disappearance. The missing girl is Megan McGrath and the family say she always keeps in touch when she goes out. None of her friends have seen her in almost three hours, and her mobile phone appears to have been disconnected. I've got a bad feeling about this, Mick."

"Fair enough, John. Is there anything you need from us?" Although he had offices at Castlebar, Boyle headed an independent task force that was kept apart from the normal business of the station. Doing Delaney a favour was the least Boyle could offer to help repay some of the support he'd got from his counterpart in recent times.

"Can you let me have two of your detectives for interviews with the family and friends? I want to get that paperwork out of the way as soon as possible."

Boyle turned to Brogan. "Reassign Black and Byrne to Superintendent Delaney for the next few days." He was referring to detectives Mark Black and Noel Byrne, who'd been seconded to the task force from their previous posts in Galway.

Delaney was already disappearing back into the crowd when he called over his shoulder. "Thanks, Mick."

Detective Gardai Colin McCartney and George "Custer" Armstrong were waiting in a small general activities office when Boyle and Brogan extricated themselves from the downstairs conference room. They were the remaining two members of the task force, and both had worked tirelessly over the past six months to build a case against the Flynn empire.

"How do we hunt down this fuckin' mole?" McCartney asked in his usual direct manner.

"We don't," Boyle told him emphatically. "I've wasted enough time on paperwork. We'll let Sergeant Moriarty ferret for the rat while we turn our attention to more affirmative action."

"I'm all for that, Boss. What have you got in mind?"

Boyle pulled a plastic chair from a stacked pile and straddled it, propping his chin on an arm draped across the backrest. "We're going to use the information gathered over the course of this investigation to start shaking Big Paud's tree. I want his vehicles stopped and searched on a constant basis; I want his hoods brought in on any pretence for questioning; we'll get the Customs boys to carry out random red-diesel checks on all identified trucks; we're going to show our faces at every location where we know shady deals are happening. In short, I want Big Paud to realise that wherever he or his cronies go we'll be there watching them."

"That's going to be a lot of legwork," Custer Armstrong chirped in. "Will it do any good? I can't see us getting much from it, other than a severe case of fallen arches. Come to think of it, aren't we supposed to have flat feet anyway?"

Boyle smiled at the humour attempt. "Yeah, I don't expect to get lucky by seizing container-loads of contraband goods. Big Paud's too smart to be caught out in the open, but how will he fare if he's completely boxed in?"

Brogan pivoted in his chair, a wide grin pasted across his face. "I see where you're going with this. It doesn't matter how's he's moving his stuff: it's enough for him to worry that we're around every corner, watching everything, and making it almost impossible for him to operate. It could work, but we'll need a lot of extra feet on the ground."

Boyle shook his head. "That's not going to happen. News of our failed search operations has already reached the NBCI. I'm expecting a call any minute now from the Commissioner himself, so we can kiss goodbye to additional support, or even overtime as far as taking action against Flynn is concerned." Boyle was referring to the National Bureau of Criminal Investigation, headquartered in Harcourt Street in Dublin, which had oversight responsibility for the task force, ultimately signing off on the request for multiple search warrants.

"You're saying we'll have to do this on our own?" Armstrong asked with incredulity.

"Fraid so, Custer. When we get the team back up to full strength, after the search for the missing teenager, we should be able to make enough inroads to cause Flynn to sit up and take notice. I want his people lifted on a regular basis and brought in for questioning on everything from drunk and disorderly to jaywalking to running a red light. Who knows, apart from taking them out of circulation for a few hours, we might actually get one of them to say the wrong thing? Anything's better that sitting on our thumbs feeling sorry for ourselves while that mob gives us the run around."

"I'm with you one hundred per cent," Brogan said with feeling, "but we need to be careful around that barrister of Flynn's. That's one guy who will take great delight in lodging complaints of harassment."

"Oh, you can be sure we'll certainly be harassing

his client," Boyle responded. "I don't doubt for a minute that Myles Winstanley will be on our case, but you let me worry about how we deal with his representation when the time comes. We'll do things by the book, and hope that Big Paud, or one of his band of merry men, make a mistake sooner rather than later."

Chapter 9

MOONEY'S BAR, soon to be a fine dining restaurant and conference centre, was in full swing with early evening revellers when Boyle pushed his way through the throng shortly after seven o'clock. They were a noisy, but good-natured bunch, none more so that the group of men enjoying the end of the working week, and no doubt looking forward to a lazy Saturday filled with nothing more than betting shops, horseracing, and football. Boyle recognised some of the men who'd been working on the renovations and threw a quick nod in their direction as he ducked under the counter and headed for the kitchen.

As usual, Belle was scurrying around, putting the final touches to more than a dozen plates of food, most of which contained the Friday night special of cod and chips. Her assistant, Andrea, scooped up half the plates and settled them across her arms in a well-rehearsed balancing act before she backed out of the kitchen through a swing door that led directly into the main lounge.

Belle wiped the back of a hand across her forehead, blew out her lips in a sigh, and mumbled: "Finally, I'm glad that's over."

"I'll bet you are," Boyle said playfully, knowing she hadn't realised he was standing behind her.

She turned quickly and flung her arms around his neck, planting a lingering kiss full on his mouth. "You're home early. I didn't expect you for another hour. You're just in time to help me clear up."

"I thought we hired full-time people for that?"

"Don't be such a grump. Andrea and her husband Johnny are looking after the bar tonight while we relax upstairs over dinner. You can give me ten minutes here, and then head up for a shower. We have a special guest tonight."

Boyle frowned. "What, a guest on Friday evening? Must be someone special. Don't tell me your cousin Marjorie and her kids are coming around?" Boyle always pretended the three boys, aged ten, eight and six, were too much of a handful, though in truth he loved spending time with them.

"No, it's not Marjorie, but you'll just have to wait to see who it is. I'm looking forward to your surprise."

Boyle spent fifteen minutes going through the motions of stacking the dishwasher and wiping down surfaces before he was chased from the kitchen. Upstairs, he walked into the bedroom, immediately spotting an opened flat cardboard box lying on top of the bed and shaking his head at his wife's latest online shopping purchase. She was the queen of *Amazon*, with one package or another arriving with regularity every two or three days. This time the label read *Marks and Spencer*, and he smiled at the knowledge of what was inside the box.

It was another off-the-peg two-piece suit, the latest in Belle's attempt to increase his wardrobe beyond the jeans and pullovers he normally wore. "You're an Inspector now and have to dress accordingly," she'd chided him when the first suit had arrived less than a week ago. "You have to be smart, and you need to have at least two suits so that the men can see you take your job seriously. A suit sends out the right message about how you view your responsibilities."

To be fair, she was right about his dress sense. His new job meant a lot of meetings with the top brass, many of which were held in formal settings in either divisional headquarters at Galway, or in the NBCI offices in Dublin. He couldn't fault Belle's choice of apparel, most noticeably the selection of shirts and ties she'd bought to complement the suits, but he'd drawn the line at letting her loose on his footwear. Boyle favoured heavy-duty safety shoes, the kind that came with reinforced uppers, and made life more practical when chasing down criminals across wasteland. They were also pretty useful for kicking out when things got a bit hairy during the course of making arrests.

He pulled the suit from the box and held it up, nodding his head in approval. It was a conservative, mid-blue textured design that felt as though it could withstand the rigours of the job. It contrasted with the dark-grey outfit he was currently wearing, either one providing him with a look of respectability, even if he longed for denims and sneakers.

The door to the upstairs dining room rapped at precisely eight o'clock.

"That'll be our guest," Belle said as she rushed across the room.

Boyle, now dressed casually after his shower, swivelled in his chair and watched in amazement as the visitor was ushered into the room. "You! What the feck are you doing here?"

Jacko McStravick clutched a bunch of flowers, which he handed off to Belle, and ignored Boyle's outburst. "God bless everyone in this fine house. May yous be in heaven a half-hour before the devil knows you're dead."

Boyle rose to face the big man. "Still the same old blarney. Thought you'd left us for good. Wait a minute, something happened in Salthill, didn't it? Don't tell me you're on the run? I knew you couldn't keep out of trouble."

"Mick! Stop that." Belle shot him a look of annoyance, as she guided McStravick to the table. "Sit down and welcome, Jacko. Dinner is coming right up."

The two men glowered at each other for several seconds before McStravick offered a handshake. Boyle – aware that his wife had stopped on her way to the kitchen – took the huge paw and shook it several times in a less than enthusiastic manner. "I have to say you're the last person I expected to see. Please tell me I don't have to worry about anything you got up to in Salthill."

"You feckin' Guards are all the same. Run a man down, why don't you, even though he's as innocent as the driven snow."

"Innocent! Jacko, I wish I had a Euro for every time you've broken the law. I could have retired years ago."

"Yeah, that might well have been so, but I'm a changed man. That incident with me sister made me sit back and take stock. I don't mind admitting I was a feckless idiot, and I'm still not sure why you helped me out. But I'm grateful to ya, and I wouldn't dream of causing any embarrassment to you or Belle. I owe you, Boyle, even if you don't want to hear such nonsense from the likes of me."

Boyle was taken aback by McStravick's statement. He'd seen the big man vulnerable on only one other occasion when he'd confessed to killing his sister's murderer, by the simple expedient of tossing the man off cliffs at Shore Point, close to Westport. McStravick had spent months cruising the county in the hope of coming across the hitchhiker killer, his patience finally rewarded when the man thumbed a lift in the early hours of a dull September morning. After Jacko had delivered a severe beating, the man admitted to his guilt, and earned a one-way trip down a hundred-yard plunge to the Atlantic Ocean. It was Boyle who'd persuaded McStravick to slightly alter his story to one that placed him in the area by chance – thereby eliminating the possibility of premeditation – with the hitchhiker's death coming only after McStravick acted in self-defence. It was enough for the Director of Public Prosecutions to decide on no further action.

As far as Boyle had been concerned, McStravick had done the world a favour, and deserved a second chance. The incident hadn't made the two men bosom buddies, particularly given their previous history when McStravick had led Boyle's team on a few merry dances caused by his tendency to fracture the law. However, he liked the big man and hoped that was all behind them.

"You owe me nothing, Jacko. Just keep out of my hair, and we'll both get along just fine."

"Don't you worry about that, my stuffy Garda friend. I'm opening an antique and gifts shop in the town and settling down to the quiet life."

Boyle almost exploded. "I swear to God, Jacko, if you start dealing in dodgy goods, I'll have you. I want to see proper paperwork for everything, and I'll make sure there are regular inspections of every item, including those stashed under the counter."

"For feck's sake, give a man a break. Who made you the guardian of morals in Castlebar?"

Belle stepped into the room and immediately sensed the tension. "That's enough from you two. There are bigger things to worry about than the pair of you flexing your macho muscles. What about that poor lass who's gone missing? Is there any news yet?"

The wind went out of Boyle's sails. "It's not looking good, darling. There are search teams out all over the town and surrounding areas, but it's been more than ten hours since she disappeared. Unless something breaks soon, we have to assume the worst."

"Oh my God," Belle sniffed. "The poor parents must be frantic. I know Mrs McGrath and I know that girl was her whole world. How is she ever going to cope?"

Megan McGrath's eyes fluttered open as she gasped for air and felt shivers run through her body. It took a few moments for her to focus on a single bulb which cast shadows across dirty concrete-block walls and rows of shelves that were filled with rusty tins, oily rags, and an assortment of dust-covered tools.

She tried to sit up, but something was preventing her. She was lying on top of a bed with her hands and feet tied to the four corners by crude strips of plastic wiring that bit into her skin. She tried to shake away the fogginess trapped behind her eyes, but every movement brought on a fresh wave of nausea, causing the room to spin, and sending pinpricks of pain up and down her spine.

What bothered her most was the cold. It was like being trapped inside a large freezer store, the same as the one they had at Wilson's butcher shop when she had visited there with her mum. How long could someone stay in a freezer before they stopped breathing?

She looked down again and realised she wasn't in a freezer. Her clothes had gone. She was naked!

Before panic had a chance to take hold, she heard the dull slap of footsteps and the creaking of a door. She turned towards the sounds, watching in wide-eyed hysteria as a man stepped into the room. She recognised the face immediately as the man in the suit who had asked her for directions.

Now she understood. She'd been kidnapped and this man was going to rape her! She tried to wriggle free as the man approached the bed carrying a bundle of clothing under one arm and holding a large, serrated knife in his free hand. He just stood there with a look of disgust, his eyes moving up and down her body as he waved the knife, slicing it through the air in a series of chopping motions, as if he were practicing a frenzied attack. He walked towards the bed, bending down to grab her head when she attempted to turn away. He pulled her face close to the blade of the knife.

"Don't ever turn away from me again, little princess." His voice was laced with menace. "I will let you live for now. Your sole purpose is to do exactly what I tell you, but the moment you stop pleasing me, or refuse to carry out my orders, I will start chopping you up in little bits and stuff you in one of those."

His eyes drifted across the room to a small stack of brown hessian bags.

Chapter 10

THE LORRY DRIVER almost leapt from his seat as he rounded a bend in a minor road that bled onto the N5 just outside Castlebar. At six o'clock in the morning, the last thing he expected to see was a cluster of commercial vans and people in uniform straddled across a potholed carriageway that hardly deserved to be called anything other than a rural lane. You had to live in the area to use this sorry excuse for a byway, a fact reinforced by an unbroken string of weeds that meandered up the centre of the surface where a white line would be on a normal road.

And yet, here they were. A bloody convention of do-gooders and stuff-shirted assholes, out and about and sticking their noses into matters that shouldn't concern them. Stopping hard-working citizens going about their business. Who did these feckers think they were?

The driver worked these thoughts into an anger that would be ripe for explosion as soon as he drew in front of the makeshift barricade, which comprised of three foldable wooden struts, each no more than a yard wide. Set side by side, there was no space left at either end.

Not that the driver had any intention of crashing through this particular roadstop.

As he drew closer, he realised the uniforms were not those of patrolling Guards. These were Revenue snoops, the kind of feckers who'd crawl up your ass if they thought you were hiding something. The driver's anger abated almost immediately, to be replaced with a pasted-on smile that he hoped would see him on his merry way without any hassle.

His journey plan was to link up with the N5 and shoot straight eastwards to Dublin. From there, he would sling south to Wexford and an appointment at a builders' yard on the edge of town. He carried with him a load of scrap windows and doors, which were a by-product of one of Big Paud Flynn's legitimate businesses. He would tell this to the Revenue men, they'd take a good look, and wave him through.

The cover story and the contents were all true. What the driver would neglect to say was that he would pick up a consignment from a container unloaded late last night at the nearby Rosslare Harbour. Now, that was a load he would not want Revenue poking through!

The driver wound down his window, stuck out his head, and flashed a set of nicotine-stained teeth at the men below him. "Morning officers. What takes you out so early on this fine Irish day?"

As greetings go, it wasn't a bad icebreaker. But it didn't cut with the bulky official who strode forward from the main group. "Sir, cut your engine and get down from the cab. We will be carrying out a full inspection of this vehicle, so please stand back and let us do our jobs. Make sure the rear compartment is unlocked."

There was not much the driver could do but obey. For the next forty minutes he watched as four men and two women from the unit swarmed all over the truck. They then walked behind the barricade and held a conference in front of one of their vans.

Eventually, the man in charge approached the driver waving a clipboard.

His tone was sombre and officious. "This vehicle is being impounded for breaches of the Road Traffic Acts of 1961 to 2006....."

"Here, you can't do that," the driver interrupted.

The Customs man continued as if he hadn't heard. "Such breaches include the illegal use of red diesel, driving a vehicle without a current valid road licence, permitting a vehicle to be on the road with sub-standard tyres, and carrying goods which are estimated to be in excess of the permitted weight limit. Do you understand everything I have just told you?"

"Yes, yes," the driver mumbled, "but I have to be in Wexford before noon. Can't you take this up with our office and let me be on the way?"

"I'm afraid you're going nowhere. We will be putting a call into the Guards, asking them to arrest and process you for these offences. In the meantime, this lorry will be towed to our centre in Galway for further examination."

The driver shook his head in bewilderment. All he could think of was Big Paud Flynn and how he would react to the loss of one of his trucks and the delay in picking up the consignment in Wexford. He suddenly thought about the illegal diesel plant where he'd filled up this morning before embarking on his journey. He needed to warn Big Paud in case these feckers knew where it was.

Unknown to the driver, he was already too late in raising an alert.

At about the same time he'd been stopped at

the roadblock, a second Revenue team had swept into an apparently disused farmyard at Knockranny, to the east of Westport town centre. They found a hive of activity, including four commercial vehicles lined up at pumps under the dilapidated shell of an old barn. The searchers uncovered four twenty-thousand-gallon tanks standing on makeshift brick platforms, and a stash of cash crammed into several boxes on a shelf below the counter of a portacabin office.

Early morning, it seemed, was the best time to transact illegal business.

All vehicles on site were impounded, eight men were put under arrest, and a pile of invoices and receipts were bagged for evidence.

"Don't fucking tell me to calm down," Big Paud Flynn exploded as he digested news of the morning events. "This is all Mick Boyle's doing and you need to stop him."

Myles Winstanley was seated across the room, a briefcase resting on his lap as he watched his client's rage grow with every passing minute. "All I'm saying, Paud, is that you need to stop over-reacting. I agree that Boyle is probably behind this little series of inconveniences, but don't fall into his trap. He's trying to throw you off guard. He's hoping you'll do something that will leave you vulnerable."

"Inconveniences? Is that what you call what's been happening?" Flynn threw a glass ashtray across the room and watched it smash into pieces against the brick wall. "I've lost a bunch of vehicles and a lucrative diesel operation and you think that's nothing more than an inconvenience?"

Winstanley maintained his unflappable

demeanour. "There's nothing to tie you into anything. The trucks belong to a company registered offshore, the diesel plant is under the name of the farmer who holds the title deeds to the property, and none of the men who were arrested are on your books as employees. You're free and clear unless you start making waves. My advice is to take the punches and pick your fight on another day. Boyle's got nothing, so just keep him that way."

"That's all fine and dandy, but if I continue to sit back, that fucker will strip me bare. Over the past week I've had three men arrested for getting into a fight, one done up like a kipper for drink-driving, and four banged up as illegal immigrants. There's only so much of this I can take."

Winstanley stood up and brushed a hand down his expensive overcoat. "As your legal advisor, I must warn you against doing anything precipitous. Boyle is undoubtedly trying to gum up your works, but he's doing it through third parties, such as the Revenue service, which means there is no clear trail back to him. I'll file a general harassment notice, and I suggest you ignore Boyle for at least the next few weeks. If I know Boyle, he'll keep pushing, but let's wait for him to make a mistake."

"And then what?"

"Then he's mine. To hell with harassment, I'll file suit about abuse of office, operating personal vendettas, and squandering valuable public resources. I'll throw enough civil actions against Boyle to tie him up for the next year or so. But you've got to give me time to put these things into motion."

"Okay," Flynn said with an air of resignation, "I'll wait to see what you come up with, but I warn you, I won't wait forever. Sooner or later, something will have to be done about Boyle."

Big Paud Flynn watched through the office window as Winstanley crossed the yard and climbed into an expensive Mercedes. As soon as the car roared through the open gates of the compound, Flynn lifted the desk phone and pressed an intercom button. "Get in here now!"

Ten seconds later the door burst open to reveal Big Paud's son, Jerome, this time with his younger brother, Seamus, a twenty-stone freak with a pockmarked face and bulges in all the wrong places as a result of dangerous daily intakes of steroids and pints of Guinness.

"Is Winstanley going to sort out Boyle?"

Flynn senior looked at his offspring with a tinge of regret. "Why is it that you always open your big mouth before you're spoken to? Haven't I told you a hundred times to take the time to weigh up a situation before planting your size twelves into places where they're not welcome?"

"Uh?"

"Never mind. You let me worry about Boyle. Right now, I need to move the shipment of drugs from Wexford to here."

"Me and Seamus can take care of that."

"There you go again, spouting off when you should be listening. You can't be involved in the transfer, not least because if you're stopped, they will have a direct line of evidence back to me. Get Mikey and Paul to pick up the load. Tell them to use their own cars and to travel separately, at least an hour apart. The goods should fit in the car boots and if any one of them run into trouble then at least we've halved the odds of part of the shipment getting through. I have suppliers waiting anxiously for us to fill their orders."

Jerome Flynn shifted uneasily on his feet. "Why not just use one of the trucks or vans?"

"Haven't you been listening to a word I said? We're under scrutiny, particularly with our commercial vehicles. This way is safer. Mikey and Paul are expendable. You're not."

The unexpected praise lifted Flynn junior's spirits. "That's smart, Pa. Maybe while the boys are off to Wexford, me and Seamus could take care of Boyle?

"No, leave Boyle alone for now. I must admit, however, I'd love to somehow ruffle the bastard's feathers."

Chapter 11

THE ODD THING about the mid-morning briefing at the Castlebar station of An Garda Síochána was that Boyle looked like a man who already had his feathers ruffled.

Despite effusive updates from his team about the success of the Revenue raid on Big Paud's diesel depot, Boyle paced the head of the room wearing a scowl that didn't match the general atmosphere. He was like a man who'd just been told he won the Lotto, only to discover that all he was getting was six Euros for matching three numbers.

"Come on, Boss, cheer up. We've hit Flynn where it hurts most – in the pocket," Sergeant Paul Brogan said in an effort to lighten the mood.

Boyle stopped pacing and pulled up a chair. "Look, I know this was good work and I'm not knocking anyone's effort. It just seems like a pyrrhic victory, nothing more than an irritation that Flynn will probably shrug aside and continue on as if nothing happened."

Brogan smiled. "Pyrrhic is it? You keep using these words and we'll have to add *sesquipedalianist* to your list of accomplishments.

"Sesqui-what?"

"It means someone who likes to use big words, although usually it only refers to words that are very long and multisyllabic. I guess in your case we'll settle for calling you a *logophile* or a *grandiloquent*, both of which simply mean a person who loves words."

It was Boyle's turn to smile. His number two always had a knack for pulling him out of a dark mood. "Okay, Professor Brogan, as ever we're grateful for the benefit of your university education. How about instead of saying a pyrrhic victory, I state simply that it all seems so feckin hollow and empty?"

"Still not buying your description of what's gone on over the past week or so," Brogan said in a more serious tone. "Big Paud is minus a couple of trucks, at least six men, and twelve-thousand Euros taken from his diesel farm. We keep this up and he'll be out of business in six months."

Boyle nodded in acknowledgement. "Guess I am looking for too much too soon. Those were good tip-offs which I reckon we can add to over the next few weeks. What have we left in the pipeline?"

Colin McCartney raised his hand. "We've still got the matter of Big Paud's night club in Galway. We know he's operating high-stakes poker outside hours and a well-planned raid might just see him lose his licence."

"The big nights are usually Fridays and Saturdays," piped up George 'Custer' Armstrong. "If we case the place on one of those days and make sure all the players are still on the premises, we should be able to call in a successful bust. These poker sessions don't usually break up until four or five in the morning, so keeping an eye out shouldn't be a problem."

"Alright, Custer, you've just talked yourself into a stake-out this weekend," Boyle told him. "You're going to need some back-up so I'll see what's happening with Byrne and Black." He was referring to the two detectives who had been seconded to the search for the missing teenager.

Just then, the briefing room door opened, and station sergeant Colm Moriarty walked in carrying a small folder. "We've got Joe Dennehy down in the cell. He was the driver of the lorry stopped this morning by the Revenue boys. His solicitor is here and demanding we set up a formal interview. Anyone care to take a crack at it?"

It was Brogan who responded. "Yeah, I'll go through the motions. Unlikely we'll get anything out of him, but we need a statement prior to releasing him. Have you got a charge sheet?"

"Yes," said Moriarty with a gleam in his eye. "We've thrown as much as possible at him. It's not enough for detention, so I'll guess we'll release him after you're done. I'll see to it he gets an early date in front of a district court judge."

Moriarty placed the folder on the table in front of Brogan and turned to leave.

"Just a moment, Sarge," Boyle said. "Any word on the missing girl?"

The shoulders drooped on the normally unflappable Moriarty. "Nothing, not even a whisper. It's been four days now and the search has all but been called off. I'm afraid there's not much hope of finding that wee lassie alive."

Megan McGrath *was* alive. She could move freely around the kitchen, or at least as freely as the fifteen-foot chain manacled to her ankle would allow her to move. This was where she spent most of her time, making food and keeping the floors and walls gleaming with constant washing and polishing. One speck of dirt was rewarded with a back-handed slap across her face, something her jailer seemed to relish, judging by the number of times he dished out the punishment.

Her eyes were swollen, as much from bouts of crying as from the assaults, but at least she was still living. She kept telling herself to hang on. Every day was a victory. Every day brought hope that someone would find her. Those were the high points. They were precious to her. She had to keep positive. She couldn't let the darkness and despair eat away at her soul.

Megan couldn't figure out her captive. He hadn't touched her sexually. Apart from stripping her naked and forcing her to wear a dreary maid's outfit, he hadn't looked at her with lust or longing. His glances showed contempt and hatred. It always seemed that at any moment he would lose his cool and plunge a knife into her frail body.

She did her best to avoid raising his temper. She learned how to be totally subservient, to call him *sir*, and to make sure his food was exactly the way he liked it. She washed his clothes, cleaned his boots, and sat meekly on her little wooden stool whenever he was in the room. Which thankfully was not too often.

He spent most of the days – and some nights – away from the cottage. Those were her best times. For the first few days she had tried unsuccessfully to cut through the heavy chain that was bolted to the concrete floor. After breaking two kitchen knives she gave up and spent the solitude gazing forlornly through cracks in the shuttered windows.

All she saw was trees. There was a small clearing in front of the cottage, but everywhere else was trees. She was in the middle of nowhere with no hope of someone stumbling across her prison. She never saw wildlife, or heard the sounds of engines, or was able even to relish the sunlight, which was blocked out by those damn trees.

What she could see was a van parked to the side of the house. It was the same one in which she had so foolishly accepted a lift. *God, if only I hadn't been so naïve!* Her captive also used another vehicle which she had never seen but judging by its throaty roar she guessed it was a big saloon, which was kept at the other side of the house, away from view to the rear of the compound. She had heard its menacing comings and goings, preferring the sounds of its departures to the nightmares of its arrivals.

Her captive was a workman. He had two sets of all-purpose dungarees, one of which always had to be kept cleaned and ironed ready to wear. He changed sets every two or three days and she had noticed little things that made her think he was an electrician. His toolbox must have been kept permanently in the van, but Megan had seen bits of plastic wires snagged in the pockets. It wasn't much of a clue; probably not even a clue at all. But thinking about things like this helped to keep her sane by working her brain instead of accepting tacitly what was going on around her.

She never knew why he stayed out some nights. There was no pattern to his disappearances, and he never told her in advance. When he did show up, he acted as if his absences hadn't happened. He seemed to relish keeping her off guard.

The usual daily pattern was that he brought her out of the basement room every morning at exactly 7 o'clock, locked her into the chain in the kitchen, and pottered about in the other rooms until she had made breakfast. He usually returned to the cottage at six in the evening, waited for her to clean up after dinner, and then led her back to the basement. During the day, the chain stretched only as far as the confines of the kitchen, although this included a small toilet cubicle which was situated near a reinforced rear door.

On the nights when he didn't return, she was expected to curl up in a ball on the kitchen floor and use towels for a pillow.

Megan wasn't sure how long she had been there. The days and nights seemed to merge into one large nightmare. What she did know was that one of those missing days had been her birthday! She was sixteen now but didn't get to celebrate with Siobhan or the rest of her friends. She wondered if they missed her. The thought made her even more depressed. She flopped onto the stool, buried her face into her hands, and cried.

The raucous sound of an engine brought her sharply out of the melancholy. She glanced at the kitchen clock and realised she'd lost track of time. She'd forgotten to boil the pot of potatoes to go with the braised steak which was in a ceramic dish on a low heat in the oven. She jumped from her stool and raced to the cooker, switching on one of the hob rings just as he walked through the door.

"What the fuck is this? Why isn't my dinner on the table?"

Megan kept her eyes averted. "I'm sorry, sir, I don't know what came over me."

The man flung one of the chairs across the room and advanced menacingly behind Megan. He bent over and shouted into her ear. "This isn't working out. It's time to replace you."

Chapter 12

BOYLE STEPPED OUT of the shower shortly after 7.30am on a bright Monday morning. The warm glow of a yellowing sky matched his mood as he towel-dried and walked whistling into the new spacious bedroom, a welcome by-product of his wife's extensive renovations.

"Someone's in a great mood," Belle said from her propped-up position in the bed." She was holding a teacup, her eyes fixed on an iPad, no doubt browsing through the Amazon site for more shopping bargains, thought Boyle.

"And why wouldn't I be happy," Boyle said over his shoulder as he disappeared into the walk-in wardrobe. "The raid on Big Paud's nightclub on Saturday couldn't have gone better. I'm looking forward to seeing how he reacts to the potential loss of his licence."

The club raid in the early hours of Sunday morning had netted more than a twenty high-rollers, all with drinks at their poker tables and enough cash lying around to keep a small country going for a few years. The money couldn't be confiscated, nor could much be done against the players for participating in the illegal gathering. Most likely they'd get a slap on the wrist, but for Big Paud the ramifications were more serious. His staff had made the mistake of ringing up drinks on the bar tills, thus leaving evidence that alcohol was being sold and served outside permitted hours.

"But surely if Big Paud wasn't on the premises

there's nothing you can do against him," Belle offered as a way to let her husband keep talking up his success.

"Ah, but he's the owner and ultimately responsible for ensuring the proper running of the place," said Boyle. "Not being there doesn't help him avoid the consequences. He'll get a hefty fine and hopefully face an order to shut the place for at least six months until he can convince a judge that this kind of thing will not happen again. To a man like Big Paud, that's a huge loss of face. He's used to people thinking he can do just about anything he wants, but we're hitting him where it hurts and sooner or later, he'll snap."

Boyle sorted through the rails on his side of the wardrobe and selected one of the Marks and Spencer suits Belle had bought for him. He matched this with a white shirt and crimson tie and added his trusty work boots to complete the ensemble. Why not look good as well as feel good, he thought. He pulled on the suit coat and emerged into the bedroom to rummage in a locker for his shield wallet and belt holster which he clipped onto his waistband before sliding in a Sig Sauer. He bent to kiss Belle. "You take it easy today," he told her.

"For goodness sake, stop fussing, Mick. I've still four weeks to go. There'll be plenty of time for rest when I get closer to my time."

"I know, darling, but you do tend to overdo it. Let Andrea and Johnny take the strain at the bar and the kitchen, at least a bit more than you're letting them do now."

"I will, I promise. Me and Baby are doing fine."

The mention of his soon-to-be first-born lifted Boyle's spirits and he started up again with his whistling drone as he marched out of the room and down the stairs. He walked through the rear of the bar premises and out into the street where he'd parked the Toyota Rav4. Instead of turning right, he spun the wheel in the opposite direction and glided through the early-morning traffic making its way into the centre of the town.

It was a whim, something he couldn't pass up. Two miles outside town, he rolled to a stop beside a walled-in complex that housed a half-dozen industrial sheds and a large office block, which took up one side of the compound. Boyle eased forward until he was blocking the main entrance, a twin-gate mechanism that was already swung open below an arch with curved lettering. A name was garishly carved out in red metal lettering – *P Flynn & Sons, Door & Window Manufacturers.*

The yard inside was buzzing with activity. Boyle counted six commercial vans in the firm's familiar livery of red and black painted squares behind various photos of their main products. He counted more than twenty workmen, moving back and forth between the vans and the sheds, carrying wood-encased panels destined for installation at the many sites serviced in the county by what was one of Big Paud's so-called legitimate businesses.

Boyle knew it was a front. But knowing and proving were two different things. All he could hope for was to keep chiselling away at the edifice in the hope that something would break loose. Put enough minor irritations in Big Paud's way and maybe, just maybe, a crack would appear, which would lead to a mistake, which might just be enough to bring everything crumbling down. It would be a long, patient game, but Boyle's head was already in it. The big question was how long would it take to tip Big Paud over the edge?

The raids on the diesel depot and the nightclub, combined with the arrests of key workers, ought to be nothing more than irritants to a professional felon, used to sparring with police whilst hiding behind a façade of respectability. But by getting into Big Paud's face and showing him that this was a personal crusade, Boyle was banking on blindsiding his quarry into making some rash moves.

And that's why Boyle was here. Out front and visible. Taunting.

Boyle wasn't sure what he expected to find but was rewarded with the sight of the big man pacing across a window in the upper floor of the office block, one of his sons hot in pursuit. There was a row going on, which was obvious from the finger-pointing and gesticulating and Big Paud's florid cheeks as he held court. Suddenly, he stopped and gazed out the window, his eyes coming to rest on Boyle.

Boyle sat motionless, allowing a smirk to wash across his face as he stared at the big man. Flynn's son, Jerome, appeared at his father's side and raised a middle finger, his lips flapping in what Boyle guessed was a foul-mouthed rant.

The outburst made Boyle's smile grow wider. He slipped the engine into gear and eased away from the entrance, once again feeling the urge to whistle.

Boyle was still smiling when he drove through the gates at the Castlebar Garda Station and headed to the car park at the rear of the building.

As he climbed from the vehicle, he spotted Sergeant Moriarty appear at the top of the steps, his hands fumbling for the cigarette packet he always kept in the breast pocket of his tunic. Boyle decided he would join him, despite promising Belle he would give up "those damned weeds."

The look on Moriarty's face, however, told Boyle the mood of the morning was about to get darker.

"Something tells me that you appearing here just as I arrive is not a coincidence," Boyle said.

Moriarty lit a cigarette and held the packet out for Boyle. "Just wanted to give you a heads-up before you go in there," Moriarty responded as he nodded back towards the door. "Some things you should know, and a cool head is what I'm hoping will result from a little advance chinwag."

Boyle waved away the offer of a cigarette. "Just spit it out, Sarge."

The two men had an easy rapport. It had been that way since Boyle's initial transfer back to Castlebar after a less than spectacular stint in Dublin. Moriarty was the glue that held the station together, but he'd recognised in Boyle an incredibly talented and down-to-earth investigator who'd reinvigorated the fortunes and wellbeing of this neck of the woods. More than colleagues, the two had become firm friends.

"Jeez, Mick, it's been quite a morning, and it's not yet eight-thirty. Quite a few developments overnight, and two interesting visitors as soon as we opened the doors."

Boyle's eyes clouded over. "Who's in there?"

"One has already left. None other than our favourite legal-eagle, Myles Winstanley, here to complain about the persecution of his client, the downtrodden Paud Flynn who apparently just wants to earn an honest crust but is being prevented about going about his lawful business by us terrible Guards." Sarcasm dripped from every word.

Boyd couldn't help but smile. "So, Big Paud is hurting and he sent his highly-paid stooge to put the squeeze on? What exactly did Winstanley want?

"Wants us to stop trying to tie Big Paud into illegal activities, of which he has no knowledge or interest – Winstanley's words not mine – and he threatened to take out an injunction against one particular Guard if he doesn't stop a personal and slanderous campaign – again Winstanley's words – against the said saint, known as Padraig Flynn."

"I take it that was me he was referring to? I hope someone gave him short shrift."

"The Super dealt with him and you can be sure Delaney didn't cower in front of the great man."

"So, what's the big deal here?"

Moriarty dragged on his cigarette and threw the stub into a sandbox. "Those developments I was telling you about. The big one is that....."

"Wait a minute," Boyle interrupted, "you said there were two visitors. Who was the other one?"

"Chief Superintendent William McCluskey."

Chapter 13

WILLAM "BILL" McCLUSKEY was not just one of An Garda Síochána's most influential higher ranking officers, he was also the father of a Guard who was beaten to a pulp by Boyle in a famous incident that marked the end of Boyle's once meteoric rise in the National Bureau of Criminal Investigation in Dublin.

The fact that McCluskey junior was caught sleeping with Boyle's first wife was hardly grounds for mitigation, particularly so when the father had stepped in to engineer a demotion for Boyle and a reassignment to County Mayo. At the time, Boyle was too distraught by his wife's infidelity to care much about what was happening to his career. But then he teamed up again with Belle Mooney, a former hometown sweetheart, reinvented his professional standing, and earned back his missing stripes.

Using his new status, Boyle went after McCluskey senior. He threatened the Chief Superintendent with union-led legal action for harassment and the cover-up of his son's serious breaches of professional standards.

Boyle had been out of order in delivering the beating, but as far as standards in public office went, the actions of both McCluskey Senior and McCluskey Junior were a lot higher up the scale of no-nos. Had Boyle pursued his action, there could only have been one winner – and two losers. McCluskey had wilted under Boyle's attack.

"Thought that bastard had agreed to resign?" Boyle said to Moriarty.

"Yeah, but it seems like it hasn't gone through yet."

"So, what the feck is he doing here?" Boyle made to brush past Moriarty, but the big Sergeant grabbed him firmly by the arm."

"There's something you should know, Mick, before you go blundering in there."

"Are you trying to tell me he's somehow involved with Big Paud? Was it him who give the tip-off about our search warrants?"

"You're getting ahead of yourself, Mick."

"Is he here to shut down my investigation?"

"In a way, yes, but there's....."

"No fecking way. I'll finish with him what I started with his son."

Moriarty stepped closer to Boyle. "Will you just hold on a moment? It's not about Big Paud."

"What then?"

"Another wee lassie went missing last night."

Boyle rapped twice on the door and stepped quickly into Superintendent John Delaney's office. A larger-than-life figure was sitting facing Delaney, his back to Boyle, his attention focussed on a file lying on top of the desk in front of him.

Chief Superintendent William McCluskey turned at the sound of Boyle's entrance and immediately stood to offer his hand. "It's good to see you again, Detective, although I wish it was under better circumstances."

Boyle ignored the handshake and walked to the side of the desk to fix the station visitor with a withering glare. "I think we're past all that, don't you? I thought you were due to retire before now."

"Inspector Boyle, remember your place, please," John Delaney barked with less enthusiasm than he would have used if he had meant his words to be a reprimand.

"It's quite alright, John," McCluskey interjected with equanimity. "Yes, the paperwork has been slow, but I'll be out of everyone's hair in a few months."

"I'm sure that's not what Boyle meant, sir."

"Oh, I'm sure it's exactly what he meant." McCluskey turned to Boyle. "But let's put that to one side for now. I'm here to reassign you to a case that is catching fire all around the country."

"You mean the missing girls?" Boyle said.

"I see word travels fast in a rural station. Yes – and this comes from the top – you are to head up a manhunt for the bastard behind these disappearances. You have your own local resources and can call on uniforms and detectives from Galway. Plus, we'll send you whatever manpower you need from Dublin. Nothing will be denied this investigation. Your supervisor will be Detective Superintendent Shane Horgan, who will expect you to contact his Galway office for daily briefings and will pass on any relevant information directly to me. As Senior Investigating Officer, you can pick and choose who you want, bring in any outsiders, such as psychiatrists or anyone you might think appropriate, tear this county apart, if that's what it takes, but most of all put an end to this madness. The public is up in arms and the Commissioner has promised that we'll leave no stone unturned."

"Why me?" Boyle asked, already certain he knew the answer. McCluskey's appearance here could only mean it was McCluskey who had put Boyle's name forward, which meant that McCluskey was hoping Boyle would fall flat on his face.

"Don't be modest, Boyle. You know this county like the back of your hand, and everyone remembers you as quite the star from your successes last year when you recovered those priceless paintings and brought an end to the country-wide investigation into the hitchhiker killer. Should be right up your street."

And there it was! Damned by faint praise. Boyle saw through the sham but decided to stay quiet. On one level, he begrudgingly admired McCluskey for sacrificing his own career to save that of his worthless son. You didn't get to rise up the ranks without being a formidable character, someone who would have relished Boyle's complaint in his early days but was not prepared to risk the spotlight falling on his offspring. And so, McCluskey had backed down, although it must have rankled.

Boyle reluctantly dropped onto a spare chair and pulled the desk file closer. "This everything we have on him?"

"Mostly family statements and investigation notes from a number of prior disappearances around the country, including in Northern Ireland where a detective was convinced this bastard had struck a few years back. There were two, or possibly three, unsolveds there plus one in Cork and one in Kilkenny. And now we have two in Castlebar. Might not be the same guy involved in all cases, but they've got to be worth a look as a starting point."

Boyle nodded in agreement. "I'll clear my decks immediately, but I want one thing understood. This will be not be a public relations exercise. If you say there are resources being made available, then I want them the moment I ask for them. If I have to tread on a few toes, I want to know that Dublin has my back, and most of all I want everyone to understand there's going to be a big overtime bill for all this. I'll hold my nerve and stay the distance. Just want to be sure that the same goes for everyone else."

McCluskey rose and moved to the centre of the room. "You're the flavour of the moment, Boyle, so you'll get what you ask for. If I were you I would remember, however, that this is all about results. You've got exactly six days to make an arrest."

The girl squirmed on the bed and tried to make sense of her surroundings. All she could see were bare brick walls and rows of dilapidated shelves which were cluttered with rusty tins and soiled rags. Overhead, a single bulb swung on a small chain fixed into wooden floorboards that told her she was in a basement. It was cold and damp and dreary.

That's when she noticed she was naked and that her hands and legs were tied to the four corners of the bed. A rush of panic forced the air from her lungs. She had been kidnapped and she was going to die!

Suddenly, a man appeared at the end of the bed. Panic give way to shame. She had never let a boy or a man see her naked. She was mortified. She tried to roll and turn to hide her body from the glare of the stranger. And then she remembered. This was the man who had stopped to ask for directions. The next thing she knew was waking up here.

The tears started flowing down Siobhan

Cunningham's face. This must have been what had happened to her friend Megan McGrath. Was this the same man who had kidnapped and killed Megan? Had he raped and tortured her before disposing of her body in some shallow grave or deep well?

She screamed.

The man moved quickly forward until he stood over her. He was carrying a bundle of clothes in one hand and a large knife in the other. "If you ever scream again, I will kill you." His voice was low and menacing. "You are here to tend to my needs. If you do exactly as I say, I will let you live, but I don't care either way. Girls like you are sluts. The world will be a better place without you. Sooner or later, that's how it's going to be."

Chapter 14

BOYLE NEEDED TIME to think. They'd just dumped a poisoned chalice in his lap. Nothing irked a cop more than a case of missing children. Throw in possible sexual abuse and murder and the stakes soared from high to almost impossible. One mistake, one overlooked clue, could mean a child's life. It was the kind of investigation that could leave permanent scars.

Ten minutes locked away in his office brought Boyle to one inescapable conclusion: the odds were already stacked against finding the two Castlebar teenagers alive, but he would make damned sure the girls would be the kidnapper's last victims. He would cast a net over Mayo and surrounding counties so tight that the bastard would pop to the surface before he had a chance to continue his spree.

Right now, however, he couldn't give up on the missing girls. He *had* to believe he could track them down. He *had* to make everyone believe Megan and Siobhan were still alive, holed up somewhere waiting for rescue, praying the Guards would do their jobs and find them.

Boyle scratched away on a notepad, segmenting the blank pages into squares, each representing components of a large grid which summarised how he wanted to proceed. The resources needed would be vast but that was the least of his worries. Satisfied he'd covered all the bases, he rose and walked quickly out of the office and down the hallway to where Delaney was patiently waiting.

He spoke as soon as he stepped into Delaney's den. "I know this is going to sound strange, John, but I need you as my number two on this. I'll put Colin McCartney in as the Incident Room Co-ordinator to handle the flow of work from the detectives, but I'll need more than an IRC on this because of the heavy input that will be required from the uniforms. The logistics are frightening, and I'll feel a lot safer knowing you're in charge of monitoring what's going on."

"I'd have been insulted if you hadn't asked," Delaney responded with typical bluntness. "What way do you want to play this?"

Boyle drew up a seat and placed his notepad on the desk. "I want two hundred uniforms out and about searching every house, outbuilding, warehouse, abandoned vehicle, and disused property within the town limits. Our men have to be told they need access to all areas to check bedrooms, basements, attics, and garden sheds. The majority of residents will readily agree, but if there are any problems the uniforms are to sit tight until we get a search warrant. I was hoping you'd speak directly to District Judge Callaghan to have him stand ready to sign these off like sheets of confetti."

Delaney nodded his agreement. "These are exigent circumstances, so normal rules won't apply. I'd bet on the public understanding and co-operating with our aim of clearing potential hiding places as soon as possible, but it makes sense to have a legal fallback if we run into difficulties."

"That's what I was thinking," said Boyle. "Where are we on putting together the search teams?"

"I've already got eighty Guards crammed into the downstairs conference room waiting for instructions and more will be arriving from Galway later this morning. I'm guessing that by lunchtime you'll have your compliment of two hundred. Sergeant Moriarty will handle the logistics in his usual efficient manner."

"Good," Boyle said, knowing Delaney would have been on the ball immediately. "Next, we need mobile units to operate outside the town, starting with a five-mile radius and extending as we go through the operation. I need you to commandeer everything on two or four wheels and get them out into the country areas, again checking all types of properties. The mindset of our searchers has to be to assume that each place they visit is where the girls are being kept. This is not about speed; it's about doing it right first time, every time."

"Don't worry on that score, Mick. Our boys and girls are fired up about what's happening. You won't hear them talking about lunch breaks or overtime. They'll keep at this until something shakes loose. What else do you need?"

"That's a pretty heaped plate as it is, John. I'll take the lead with the detectives. We'll scour the file of missing girls, re-interview families, and take a fresh look at some of the previous scenes where abductions took place. It's a long shot, but you never know where you're going to find patterns and clues unless you start at the basics. I'll bring in a psychiatrist to see if we can develop a profile of the kidnapper and learn what makes a bastard like this tick, and I want Garda Detective Roisin Munn transferred here from Galway. She's earning quite a reputation for herself these days and I'm going to need a woman's perspective at the heart of the investigation."

Boyle paused and looked down at his notes. "I also think it would be useful to chat to the detective from Northern Ireland who was convinced about a serial killer operating on his doorstep almost ten years ago. There are definite patterns between his missing girls and what I've seen from the reports from other regions. Might be worth having him join the team, but I'll know better when I travel to Downpatrick to take a look for myself."

Paul Brogan, Custer Armstrong, and Colin McCartney were waiting patiently in Boyle's office when he returned from his briefing with Delaney.

"I hear we've landed the big one," Brogan said.

"Yes," Boyle responded as he walked behind his desk and sat down. "You'll be the IRC on this. That makes you the most important cog in the machine so if you need support, don't be afraid to shout out. All decks are to be cleared until we nail this feckin bastard."

"Does that mean we drop what we're doing with Big Paud?" The question came from Armstrong.

"To hell with Big Paud." Boyle almost spat out words. "The fate of two little girls is more important than that useless piece of garbage. Forget about Flynn and let's talk about how we're going to proceed."

Boyle filled them in on his discussions with Delaney. "The uniforms will take care of the searches. Our job is to look at what little facts we have and try to make some sense of them. We start from scratch and we go through everything as if it's a first go at understanding what happened to at least seven girls we know about. There might have been others, so the first job is to review all cases of missing teenagers going back at least fifteen years anywhere in the country. Some of them, particularly in the early days, probably didn't raise flags about a serial abductor, but might make more sense now with the benefit of hindsight."

"How do you want things divided up?" asked McCartney.

"As IRC, I want you to start dealing out the files among the team. Get them to scour for any points of intersection. These definitely appear to be random snatches but the one thing we can be sure of is that our culprit is the common denominator. He's been at all locations and has developed a cover for being there. What is he? A travelling sales rep or a workman or a retired weirdo spending his days acting like a glorified tourist? I had a quick read at the cases in Downpatrick where the detective seemed to take a special interest in a crew hired by a housing contractor. That's maybe a starting point."

"It would be useful to talk to that detective," Brogan chipped in.

"Way ahead of you. I intend to travel to the North to speak with him and maybe invite him back. In the meantime, can you use your university sources to get us a psychiatrist? I want someone who's young and eager and is barely one step removed from being a criminal profiler."

"I'll see what I can do," Brogan replied, "but why not use some of the experts they have in Dublin? The NBCI taps into a full professional network and has even some of its own people working full-time on preparing all kinds of reports on the criminal mind and what makes it tick."

"No," Boyle said emphatically. "If they were proactive in the way they should have been, these kidnapping incidents would have been flagged up before now. I know that's probably a bit unfair, given the separation of timescales between each incident, but I'd still prefer having someone take a look with a clean slate."

"What about us?" asked Armstrong.

"You'll be in charge of re-interviews. I'll get you another six detectives from Galway, and if you need any more just let me know. I want you to revisit the older scenes and feedback any fresh data to the IRC. Concentrate on trying to discover whether there were strangers in the area around the dates of the disappearances, and in particular check out if there were any builders or contractors operating in those areas."

Boyle paused for a moment, his eyes clouding over. "I'm heading out shortly to interview the parents of the latest victim. I'll stick as close as possible to this case, but I want a full briefing on all the other cases every morning and evening until we put this thing to bed."

Chapter 15

BOYLE SAT IN his car staring out through the window at a gleaming black PVC door under the small porch of a detached three-bed house. The door colour matched his mood – and no doubt that of the two people who lived there. It was a well-kept house, with a clean red-brick façade and a sloped grey-tiled roof that bore the signs of regular power-washing. The small driveway was swept clear of leaves and the front garden was awash with the rainbow colours of flowers of countless varieties. The whole picture spoke of pride and commitment.

The house was part of a forty-unit estate just off the main road at the edge of Castlebar. One of a number of developments around the town in a blitz of housebuilding twenty years ago, it was likely where Siobhan Cunningham first came into the world and where her parents now waited in dread for news that she was still alive.

Boyle sucked in a few lungfuls of air and climbed out of the car. It had been a long time since he'd done anything like this. He desperately wanted to turn around, get back in the car, and drive away. But, of course, he couldn't. Two anxious people were waiting to hear from him, hoping he would bring comfort, no matter how small, but most of all looking for reassurance that he would find their daughter.

It was not something Boyle could promise. He knew he'd done as much as he could in putting together a framework for the search, but that's all it was. A framework. Nothing would go according to plan. The investigation would twist in all directions, pushing Garda resources into areas which could not be foretold. Rumours and possible sightings would spin their heads, meaning that every new scrap of evidence needed to be checked out before getting back on track. What they craved, more than anything, was a large slice of luck, the kind that would lead them directly to the missing girls and the man responsible for their abduction. But you couldn't rely on luck, which was why they were operating within a tried and tested framework.

And praying for the best.

The front door of the house opened as Boyle approached. A Garda family liaison officer, a young man in his early twenties, stepped onto the porch and nodded a respectable salute. Boyle admired these officers greatly. There would be two of them, working continuous 12-hour shifts, to relay vital information and keep loved ones abreast of what was going on. It was the shit-end of the stick, but you wouldn't think it to watch these officers go calmly about their duty.

The Guard spoke softly to Boyle. "The parents are Bob and Mary and they're in a pretty bad way, as you can guess, sir."

The officer had mentioned the parents' names in case Boyle had forgotten them. He hadn't, but it was nice to see the young man was ready to keep him on his toes. Boyle glanced at the officer's badge number and his name. Willoughby.

"Are there many other people inside?" Boyle asked.

"About a dozen, sir, mostly all family members,

although several of the neighbours have been helping out making tea and bringing in food."

"Okay," Boyle responded. "I need you to clear everyone out into one of the other rooms while I talk alone to the Cunninghams."

Willoughby went ahead of Boyle into the house and down a short hallway to a door on the right. A drone of voices stopped immediately as Boyle was announced.

"This is Garda Detective Inspector Boyle who is the Senior Investigating Officer in the search for Siobhan," the young man said. "He would like to speak alone with Bob and Mary, so I would ask you all to please make your way to the kitchen."

The sea of faces quickly parted to provide Boyle with a view of Mary Cunningham, hunched over in an armchair, dabbing a white handkerchief against bright red eyes, and looking twenty years older than the forty-one that was shown on the single print-out of data which Boyle had taken with him from the station. Her husband was sitting protectively on the cushioned arm of the chair.

Boyle waited until the last person had cleared the room before making his way over to the couple. Bob Cunningham stood and shook Boyle's hand and stood back to allow him access to his wife.

"I'm sorry to meet you in such circumstances," Boyle said as he took a seat opposite. "I came here to assure you that we are doing everything we can to find Siobhan. We have just begun the biggest ever search in the history of the county and none of us will ease up until we find out what happened to her."

Mary Cunningham sat up straight and stared at Boyle. "I know you, Mr Boyle, and I know your wife, Belle. I've seen you around quite a lot and I know you are good people. One of ours, which is a comfort, because I know you will make sure Siobhan is brought safely back to us."

Boyle spent a few minutes updating the couple on how the search was proceeding and then turned his attention back to the real reason why he had visited in person. "I have to ask you some questions about Siobhan and her friends, in particular boyfriends, and whether there have been any strange happenings over the past few weeks."

"What do you mean by strange happenings?" Bob asked.

"Anything unusual," Boyle said. "Did Siobhan mention seeing any strangers around, or was she worried about being followed? Did either of you notice anyone paying particular attention to her or maybe you saw some vehicles in the area that were out of place. It's not something you would have thought much of at the time but looking back it might be important."

The couple exchanged glances, and both shook their heads. "Our Siobhan is a smart girl," Mary said with pride. "She knew not to talk to strangers, especially after what happened to her best friend Megan....oh, my God, is the same man involved? Did he take our Siobhan the way he took Megan?"

It was a question that had tormented Boyle over the past few hours. It seemed likely the same abductor was responsible for the girls' disappearance, yet everything about that flew in the face of the other abductions around the country. These had all seemed random, opportunistic even, with a considerable gap – in terms of both times and locations – between each one. So why had the pattern suddenly shifted? Two abductions within a matter of weeks and two victims who knew each other intimately. Why had they been targeted? Had the perpetrator moved into an escalating phase, which would mean he would strike again – and soon?

"It really is too early to speculate," Boyle replied weakly. "Rest assured, we will follow very possible lead, and yes, that includes consideration that the same man is involved with both Megan's and Siobhan's disappearances."

Mary Cunningham burst out crying. "But that means she could be dead, the same as poor Megan."

"No," Boyle said as forcefully as possible. "We haven't given up on Megan still being alive. Our investigation is focussed on finding them both. You have to hold on to that hope."

"I know, Mr Boyle, I know. But it's so hard."

Boyle quickly changed direction. "Tell me. Have you had any work done about the house lately? Any workmen been about in any other parts of the estate?"

Mary shook her head. "No workmen. Bob does all our work. He does everything around here, including our new garage which he built last year and has come in very handy as a spare area for our washing machine and freezer." She smiled at her husband. "Poor Bob, I think he wanted that garage for his van and tools until I took over much of the space."

"Never thought it would be any other way," Bob said graciously.

"What about the rest of the estate?" Boyle persisted. "Notice any workmen or contractors around lately?"

"Do you think it was a workman involved?"

Bob asked.

"No, just covering all the bases like I said."

"Come to think of it, the Murphys down at the corner of the estate built a new extension last year. I think they added a bedroom and sun lounge."

"What's their house number?" Boyle asked.

"It's number 22, the one with the big hedge."

A *big hedge* was an understatement for the 20-foot barrier that surrounded the house at the corner of the estate's cul-de-sac. It was a well-maintained yet forbidding green wall that hid the house completely from the view of neighbours and passers-by and spoke of a siege mentality that some people liked. Not Boyle. He preferred openness and clear views of what was around him. Goodness knows, he thought, Ireland doesn't get enough days of sunlight for someone to go blocking it out when it does decide to come around for a visit.

The front door opened before Boyle had walked half of the short driveway. A frail, elderly gent, probably somewhere in his eighties, stepped out and eyed his visitor suspiciously. He was dressed in a tartan shirt, brown cardigan, and brown corduroy trousers that looked like they had enough material to make a second pair. He stood in a pair of threadbare slippers and waited patiently for Boyle to explain his trespass.

As Boyle walked forward, he opened his wallet to show his credentials. "I'm sorry to bother you, Mr Murphy, but I'm investigating the disappearance of one of your neighbour's children and wanted to ask you about the workmen who were here several months ago."

The old man's demeanour changed immediately. "Bad business that. Hope you catch the bastard. Come on in and tell me how we can help. My wife Dora's at the back of the house in our new sun lounge."

Boyle followed the man slowly down a long passageway into a bright room that had more glass than concrete.

"What do you think of our new lounge?"

"Very nice, Mr Murphy. I wanted to ask you about the contractor who carried out the work." Boyle felt like telling his host he could have saved himself a lot of money by trimming at least fifteen feet off the rear hedge but thought better of it.

"Please call me John or Spud. The nickname is obvious, but I stopped growing my own vegetables years ago. The old back just wouldn't let me continue which is why we decided to use the space for an extra room. But tell me, why is it important that you know about the contractor?"

Boyle trotted out the usual following-all-leads explanation and waited for John Murphy to supply the information.

"Let me think for a moment. It was a small firm over in Westport. Think they went by the name of Anderson or Sanderson."

Mrs Murphy spoke for the first time. "It was Anderson. Their business card is in the top drawer," she said, nodding towards a small cabinet in the corner of the lounge.

Chapter 16

ANDERSON & MADINE announced themselves as builders of high distinction. They promised quality and affordable renovations for the private and commercial sectors and underlined a guarantee of commitment and expertise from their large and expanding workforce. That's what it said on the business card and on a faded nameplate across the front of the entrance to a small yard at the end of an alley close to Westport town centre.

Boyle admired the firm's attempts at positive marketing as he stepped out of his car and surveyed a dreary enclosure with just enough room to swing the proverbial cat. He walked over to a portacabin and was greeted by a mild-mannered girl who sat behind a computer desk and nodded towards a large man who stood in front of a filing cabinet. "You've got a visitor, Mr Anderson."

"I heard him, Sheila. What can I do for you, Inspector?"

Boyle liked the man instantly. He was an imposing figure, just short of six feet, with a smile as wide as the room, and a handshake that could crush a good-sized stone. There was warmth to the voice and a sincerity that was obvious. "I'm checking up on work you carried out for Mr John Murphy over at Castlebar a few months ago. It was a sun lounge..."

"Jesus, don't tell me there's been an accident. That was a solid job, so couldn't have been anything we did. Mind you, I'll not shirk my responsibility if something went wrong."

Boyle realised why he had taken a liking to the man and why his firm probably kept busy despite the appearance of its surroundings. Here was an honest soul who no doubt delivered an honest job. "My apologies, Mr Anderson. I should have explained right off the reason for my visit. It's got nothing to do with your workmanship."

The big man wiped his brow and sat down behind a desk while Boyle outlined the disappearance of Siobhan Cunningham from the same estate where the work had been carried out at the Murphys. "We need to check everything, Mr Anderson, which is why I'll need a full list of all the men who were in that job. It's important, for the purposes of elimination, that no-one is missed out."

"Good people, the Cunninghams. Don't deserve what's happened to them. I guess no parent deserves it. The work we did for the Murphys was a straightforward job, just a few days to get it sorted. Mind you, the old man knew what he wanted. He had all the plans already drawn up by an architect and had the building permission in place together with full details of the materials to be used. He was hawking around for suitable quotes and I guess we undercut the competition."

"I'm more interested in the people involved rather than the process," Boyle said.

"I understand entirely, Inspector, but I can assure you none of my men would have got tied up in anything so ghastly. There's just me and my partner, Jim Madine, and two other full-time staff. We're a small ship but we get the jobs done."

"Have you ever carried out work in Cork or Kilkenny or in Downpatrick in the North of Ireland?"

Boyle asked.

"Did a few new homes in Kilkenny a number of years ago but we've never been to Cork and wouldn't undertake jobs in the North. Too much travel and too much hassle with VAT and currency conversions."

Boyle thought for a moment about the answer. "You mentioned there are only four of you, but surely you'd need bigger squads for new-build projects?"

"Yep, but we have access to plenty of self-employed individuals and groups. That's how ninety per cent of the building trade works these days. You want something done, you hire one of these squads for a set fee based on outputs. Saves us having people on our books and processing payrolls and it suits the men who can claim their own expenses against earnings. Ask me, that's the way it'll all end up. No more firms with big overheads, which explains why we're in this shithole instead of paying fancy rents for yards and offices we don't really need."

Boyle smiled. "Fair enough, but I'll still need a complete list of all the men, including the self-employed squads, who worked on the Murphy job and the one in Kilkenny. Come to think of it, Mr Anderson, it might just be better if you provide me with a full database of all the people you have access to for any job."

It was Anderson's turn to smile. "We don't do databases or spreadsheets or any fancy graphs, but Sheila there will be able to get the information you need."

"Already working on it," the girl said over her shoulder. Several minutes later, a desktop printer stared spooling out sheets of paper. "We might not have a database, but we do have a full contacts list, sub-divided into the various trades," she said proudly.

"Do you have addresses or contact numbers?" Boyle asked.

"Both," Sheila replied.

Boyle's iPhone trilled as soon as he'd left Anderson's office. He hit the green accept button and climbed back into his car.

Paul Brogan's voice boomed out. "Where are you at?"

"Had to take a few small detours after visiting the Cunninghams. I've got another builder's list to add to the ones we already have. Anything come up?"

"Nothing special," Brogan told him. "I tracked down a psychiatrist. She completed her doctorate at Trinity last year and is currently working on secondment at University College Hospital in Galway. Says she's willing to meet with us this evening, if that suits."

"Notice you mentioned *she* – is there anything I should know?" Boyle responded playfully.

"Just a friend. I met her in Trinity when she was doing her Masters and think see might give us a solid perspective on what we should be looking for."

"Okay, set her up for about seven o'clock. I want to swing home and grab a bite to eat. Maybe shower and change before heading back."

Boyle's "bite" was a full three-course meal which Belle insisted he finish. "Knowing you, it will be another late-nighter and I don't want you collapsing for the lack of food," she told him.

"Are you kidding," Boyle laughed as he looked

down at the heaped plate of roast beef, potatoes, and vegetables. "It's not me who will be collapsing. Have you been taking it easy today?"

"I told you this morning to stop fussing. I feel great and Andrea and Johnny helped really well to process the lunchtime orders. They are also going to take over full bar duties from six o'clock, which will leave me time to visit the Cunninghams. I know Mary from the library reading group."

"She told me that when I saw her this afternoon," Boyle said.

"You've already met her? How is she? Poor thing must be going out of her mind with worry."

"Not an easy thing to deal with," Boyle agreed. "They have a full house over there, what with family and neighbours. If I were you, I'd give it a pass for a day or so. It's beginning to take on the feeling of a Wake and that's something they could do without. They need to hold onto some semblance of hope that their daughter will be found alive."

"Do you think she will be, Mick?"

He glanced across at the television screen. The main RTE news bulletin was running a constant loop of videos showing the massive Garda search operation under way. Announcers relayed information about more than two hundred officers being involved, helped by the same number of civilian searchers. The scenes brought a lump to Boyle's throat. It was something that had to be done, no matter how forlorn the hope of finding the teenagers. At the very least, the clampdown would restrict the movements of the kidnapper, leaving Boyle and his detectives free to pour through the endless background work of revisiting past cases looking for that needle in the haystack that might provide a vital link.

It was going to be patient, monotonous, and gruelling work. It was not that previous case investigations had been slipshod, far from it. Each additional case, including the current ones, simply added new layers of information and potential intersecting lines. It was his job to find them. The problem was that he didn't know if he was up to it.

He turned to Belle and spoke softly. "I wish I knew, darling."

Chapter 17

THE FADED DENIMS and *Snow Patrol* t-shirt were not what Boyle was expecting when he was introduced to Brogan's psychiatrist friend.

The biggest surprise, however, was that Dr Connie Dunne looked impossibly young for someone to be at the head of a profession that Boyle associated with old grey-haired men in pin-striped suits and briefcases as big as their egos. Not for the first time, Boyle had to remind himself to stop generalising people. He tried to mask his initial stunned look and held out his hand, hoping his visitor hadn't noticed his disappointment.

She had.

"Many of my colleagues would frown at your appraisal," she said through a warm smile and a mouth full of pearly teeth. "I'll take it as a compliment that you probably think I'm too young to be here, or that I don't fit the mould. It's something I hope is to my advantage."

Boyle reddened slightly but relaxed quickly in the face of the charm offensive. "Forgive me for staring. You're certainly not what I expected but that's because I'm an old dyed-in-the-wool fuddy-duddy who needs to get out more. Can we start again? It's good to meet you, Doctor Dunne. I appreciate you coming in to help us."

"Nice save, Inspector, but no apologies needed. Please call me Connie. I don't know if I *can* help, but I'm willing to give it a go. Paul has filled me in on what's been happening, and I've taken a scan through your files on the abductions around the country. It's an intriguing case."

Boyle shot a mischievous glance at Brogan. "Paul tells me you're just what we need, a fresh perspective on our usual theories about psychopaths and what makes them tick. We'll take any help we can get," he added, gesturing to Brogan and Dr Dunne to take their seats.

"Let me begin," Dunne said, "by offering an overview of psychopathy. I promise to keep it short, although goodness knows it's a complex and ever-expanding field. No two psychopaths are the same and it's equally certain that what triggers them differs greatly from one subject to another. What I can tell you is that their characteristics are usually broadly similar, in that they are cunning and manipulative people with a grandiose sense of their own self-importance. They almost always have a glib and superficial charm and display a complete lack of remorse or guilt.

"In broad terms, psychopaths need stimulation, which leads them to act impulsively, often with no long-term goals, other than an insatiable desire to quench whatever sparks their latent urges. For the most part, they see themselves as being on a crusade, something that only they understand as an issue to be corrected. The rest of us are out of step, in their minds, and as such they are fearless in pursuit of their objectives. The combination of all these factors is a reason why many psychopaths have longevity, often becoming what are known as serial killers. They simply don't care, and as a result evade detection because they don't conform to natural patterns, which means they are not usually the type of people to come under the purview of police, even during the most high-profile investigations."

Boyle leaned back in his chair and puffed out his cheeks. "Not what I wanted to hear, Doctor. I've been given less than six days to find this bastard. Isn't there anything you can say that will help me narrow down the search?

"I'm afraid not," Dunne said with an air of resignation. "There's no magic formula here. The best I can do is suggest you're looking for someone between the ages of mid-twenties to late thirties."

"That's quite a leap. How can you be so precise?"

"From what I've read in the files, the first reported abduction was twelve years ago. Our knowledge of psychopaths is that they are mostly not late developers. These urges that I spoke of usually start manifesting themselves from late teens to early twenties, so it's not that big of a stretch to suggest that the first abduction was in fact the first manifestation of your man acting out his impulses."

"You're sure it's a man?"

"Most definitely. His targets are young females, which suggest that the perpetrator has a fixation against the opposite sex."

Sergeant Brogan swivelled in his chair to face Dunne. "What kind of fixation are you talking about?"

"If only I knew," Dunne said with honesty. "In truth it could be anything. A young boy humiliated by a sister or a mother or a teacher or his first girlfriend or someone who rejected his advances. Somewhere within his past will be a female who belittled him in some way; held him up to scorn and caused him to be rejected. For the true psychopath, such treatment is unforgiveable, not something that can be overlooked. Remember what I said about self-importance? This breeds a need to be accepted, almost revered by those around him. The slightest disconnect from this notion can lead to a trigger for revenge."

Boyle suddenly became interested in where this was going. "Is it possible then that the first victim was the one who caused the trigger. Could she have been the sister or girlfriend or whatever of this fiend?"

"I would say definitely not. It usually takes a while for the psychopath's dangerous emotions to bubble to the surface. It's not the actual person who caused harm that becomes the subject of his crusade, but rather it's the *type* of person which will feature in his desire to put things right. All of the victims I've read about are teenage girls, all of whom were blonde-haired. That's his *type* of victim. That's who he's gone after and will continue to target."

Boyle was momentarily deflated, and it showed. "So, there's nothing to be learned from the first victim and her acquaintances? She was not the cause of his trigger, but rather a random target who simply looked like the cause of his wrath?"

"Yes, I would say that's the case."

Boyle rose from his seat and paced the room. "Okay, Doc...Connie, let me see if I can tie you down to some specifics. At the moment, our working theory is that the abductor could be an electrician or someone labouring on building sites. How does such a man fit your profile?"

"Not terribly well, I'm afraid," she said with a shake of the head. "Your typical psychopath is a leader, not a follower. He'll be someone in authority, usually in a good job, used to giving orders and having other people jump through hoops for him. He's the most important person in the room and he believes that other people accept that as a fact. If you think he's connected to the construction sector, he'll be in a position of authority, probably either as the owner of the company, or at the very least a site foreman."

"So not an electrician, or a member of a roving squad of self-employed workers?"

"He could very well be an electrician, but he will most likely be the head of the squad, the one who finds the jobs and hires the others to be part of his team. Such a leadership role will assuage his need to be top man, so to speak."

"Excellent," Boyle said. "That gives us something to work on. Do you have anything else to add"?

Connie Dunne looked at the files in front of her. "If you don't mind, I would like to take these away and study them some more. There's still a lot I want to know and understand about the victims and the circumstances of their disappearances. Also, I would ask that you keep me abreast of any developments over the next few days, especially allowing me to look at interview notes from any suspects you question."

"I'll go one better," Boyle responded. "I'll let you sit in on any interviews that we think are significant. It might be useful for you to take a close-up look at anyone we think might be our perpetrator."

"I'd be happy to do that."

"One moment," Brogan interjected. "I'm

puzzled about the timing of these abductions. The gaps between the incidents in Cork, Kilkenny, and Downpatrick were fairly big, usually at least a year, yet here in Castlebar we've had two abductions in just over a week. Are we dealing with the same man, or is it a case that what's happened to the two missing girls here has nothing to do with what happened to the others?"

Once again Dr Dunne shook her head. "The description of the girls in all cases leads me to believe they are all connected. They are, or were, all blonde-haired teenagers, a link that can't be overlooked. Of course, it's possible you have some sort of copycat in Castlebar, but I don't think so. There are just too many inter-connecting lines about the *type* which the victims represent, and anyhow there has been no real public information which ties them all together, hence not much for a copycat to go on."

"How then do you explain this sudden escalation in activity? Why so little time between the Castlebar abductions?"

"That's the thing that worries me the most," admitted Dunne. "It could be that his appetite is beginning to get out of control, or that he is entering a final phase, which would be the worst possible thing."

"How so?" asked Boyle.

"Well, either way, you could be looking at someone who has reached the end of the road. Maybe he doesn't want to do this anymore, or maybe he thinks he hasn't achieved as much as he wanted to by spacing out these events. Could be he craves more evidence that his crusade is working."

Boyle was almost afraid to ask his next

question. "What exactly does that mean?"

"It means he'll keep kidnapping girls, and probably killing them, until he's caught. He'll relish it as a challenge to see how many he can notch up before you can stop him."

Chapter 18

BOYLE FACED an enlarged detective team an hour later and brought them up to speed on the discussion with Dr Dunne. Six additional officers had been drafted in from other parts of the County and most had already hit the ground running by spending the day going through the PULSE database, the Garda's much heralded computer system for real-time recording of all police investigations. It was an acronym for Police Using Leading Systems Effectively and was capable of storing names, addresses, personal data, interview notes, and crime scene photos. Basically, any Garda interactions with the public were stored there, ready for quick retrieval and cross-referencing.

The only detectives missing from the briefing were Custer Armstrong and the newly recruited Roisin Munn. They had been sent to Cork to re-interview the central figures in the first recorded abduction and had been forced to stay overnight to follow up on at least one man who had so far proved difficult to track down.

Might be something. Might not.

Boyle got straight down to business. "Updates, please."

Sergeant Brogan was the first to speak. "One of the chief IT guys over at Michael Davitt House has spent the day extracting all names from the PULSE system with any connections to the previous investigations. He's downloaded it onto a Microsoft

Access file which has been passed to two of our secondees from Galway." He nodded towards a man and woman sitting at the rear of the room.

"Have you added the names from the list I got this afternoon from Anderson Madine Builders?"

"Just completed it an hour ago, sir," the female detective answered.

"What about names from the Northern Ireland investigation? Are we sure everything from Downpatrick was included in the file we were sent?"

"Yes, all names have been added, but I'm not sure how complete it is. I put a call through to the Police Service of Northern Ireland and I'm waiting for them to get back to me with the contact details for the detective who was in charge of the investigations there back in 2012 and 2014."

Boyle's anger flared, and it showed. "How long ago was this? What was the name of the investigator?"

The detective shifted uneasily in her seat. "I made the call about five hours ago. Apparently he's on leave and they're trying to track him down. His name is Inspector John Bonnaville, currently stationed in Belfast."

"Five hours!" Boyle's rage was now fully blown. "Don't they know how important this is? The lives of two young girls are at stake and the PSNI don't seem to be capable of even tracking down one of their own."

"I'll put another call through immediately, sir."

"Don't bother. I'll do it myself and there'll be hell to pay if this Bonnaville is not available at the end of a phone within the next hour."

A rap on the door of the briefing room stopped Boyle in his track. All heads swivelled towards the interruption as Sergeant Moriarty stepped inside.

"What is it, Sarge?"

"You've got a visitor."

"I'm kinda busy. Take the details for me."

"Think you'll want to meet this particular visitor. It's a PSNI Inspector by the name of John Bonnaville."

"**I** was on a fishing trip in Donegal and dropped everything as soon as the station reached me. Thought it best to come directly here. To tell the truth, I was going to reach out to you as soon as I heard about the disappearance of your girls but thought maybe I'd wait to go through proper channels in case you would resent any interference."

Bonnaville had a pronounced English accent which grated slightly with Boyle. Within minutes, however, he warmed to his guest who was still dressed in his fishing gear, complete with a floppy green-coloured sunhat which was resting on his knee. Boyle had left the briefing room along with Brogan to meet the Northern Irish detective in one of the nearby interview offices and was immediately struck by the man's enthusiasm and desire to help.

"What we need to be sure of," Boyle told him, "is that all the names of those interviewed in Downpatrick are included in the file we were sent. There's no doubt your cases and ours are linked, so it's important we start from a solid base."

"I'll review what you were sent and see if anything's missing. I was not a party to what was passed on to your people, but I'll be able to spot any gaps."

Boyle nodded his thanks. "Tell me, Inspector,

what made you positive that the three incidents in Downpatrick were linked? As I understand it, only one body was recovered and there was speculation that the other missing girls had actually run away to England."

"I never believed that" Bonnaville said. "The physical similarities between the girls was just too striking to ignore, as you're finding out now with your cases. My only regret was that at the time we were not aware of the earlier disappearances of the two girls from Cork and Kilkenny. It might have strengthened my hand if I'd known about them."

"How so?"

"Let's just say I met with some opposition in trying to tie all three together. The idea of a child serial killer was not something anyone wanted to admit to, particularly with strong circumstantial evidence that one of the girls had been planning to run away to pursue a modelling or acting career in London. I was not involved directly in the third investigation, but I tried to get them to drag a local river. Unfortunately, the resources were just not there."

"You're saying the river was never dragged?"

"It wasn't considered a priority. I've always wondered if it holds some dark secrets."

Boyle glanced across at Brogan who understood the silent message. He pushed back his seat and left the room without a word.

Bonnaville caught the subtlety of the moment. "Are you intending to make a formal request to dredge the Quoile River?"

"Seems the obvious thing to do, given the new developments that have taken place here. I take it you agree?"

"Absolutely," Bonnaville beamed. "This case has haunted me for over eight years. I guess every detective has a touch of the one that got away, but this has really bored into my soul for such a long time. I need to know one way or another where those other two girls ended up. I guess a formal request from you guys in the middle of what is becoming a high-profile case across the whole country will leave it impossible for the authorities in the North to say no."

"It probably won't move us along very much," Boyle admitted, "but you never know what forensics might come up with if we do recover another body. Right now, I'll take any straw I can clutch at. No two crime scenes are the same, even if the perpetrator is a common denominator. Your riverside body was the only ever one recovered, but who's to say that our killer didn't leave evidence at the other locations? They all make mistakes which makes our job simple – find the mistake and you find the killer. The greater the number of bodies we find, the better the chances of getting our man."

Boyle paused to weigh up the man seated opposite. "I need you to stick around for a bit. In particular, it's important that you review our Downpatrick-based file as soon as possible to check for completeness. I can arrange to bring you in some sandwiches and put you up for the night in one of our local hotels."

Bonnaville stood up immediately. "Point me in the right direction. My leave is not due to expire for another week and I'd like to help in any way. I promise not to get under your feet, but it would mean a lot if I could be around when you nail this bastard."

Boyle shook his guest's hand. "Be glad to have you on board."

Bonnaville leaned back in his chair and clasped his hands behind his head. "I've waited a long time for this killer to emerge again. Don't get me wrong, nobody wants to see other young girls put at risk, but it always seemed obvious to me that this guy wouldn't go dormant forever. This double kidnapping is out of sync with what we understand about his previous modus operandi, and it could be that these two incidents are going to be what traps him."

"You think we have a shot at nailing him?"

A smile crossed Bonnaville's face. "Ever see that Tom Selleck TV series called *Jesse Stone*? He had a great recurring line that referred to 'copy intuition.' Everything tells me that this kidnapper-cum-murderer has gone one step too far. It's got to end sometime, so why not here in Castlebar?"

"That's the kind of positivity we're going to need around this place. I think you and I are going to get along just fine."

Bonnaville nodded and headed for the door.

"Just a moment," Boyle stopped him with a raised hand. "Is there anyone who stood out as a possible suspect among those you interviewed? Any name who we can use to start our cross-referencing?"

"I ran into a lot of dead ends," said Bonnaville. "I liked a few guys from a building site, but their alibis were cast-iron."

Boyle's interest peaked immediately. "A building site? Tell me about them."

"One was a kid with an acne-scarred face. He was a general dogsbody on the site and a bit of a weirdo, if I'm being honest. Didn't have much formal education and was a bit slow on the uptake. His social skills were somewhere south of zero."

"What about the other person?"

"He was top of my list. Guy by the name of Michael Kelly who seemed very sure of himself and practically smiled all the way through a number of interviews. But I couldn't trip him up, and, like I said, he had a cast-iron alibi."

"What did he do on the building site?"

"He was an electrician, which was why we took such an interest. The body that was found on the riverbank had been tied up with electrical wiring."

Chapter 19

"**M**ICHAEL KELLY. Is he on your database?"

Boyle and Bonnaville had rushed out of the office into the briefing room and were standing over the table glaring at the detective in charge of cross-referencing from the PULSE system.

The Guard danced her fingers across the keyboard and stared at the computer screen. "Yes, there's a Michael Kelly showing up in the original Cork investigation. Says here, he was an electrician on a building site. Interviewed twice but marked as *not likely* in the system. Seems he's a Dubliner with an address on the southside."

Boyle's pulse was racing. "Not bloody likely! I need to speak with Custer Armstrong to find out the name of the guy he's trying to track down in Cork." He was already hitting the speed dial on his iPhone as he walked across to the side of the room. He glanced at his watch. It was still only 11.00pm. Custer and Munn were probably having a nightcap in one of the local bars.

"This better be good, boss. I'm trying to get some beauty sleep here ahead of an early start."

Boyle had to force himself not to smile. "Listen Custer, this is important. What's the name of the man you've stayed behind to locate?"

"Michael Kelly. Apparently he's not a native of here. Originally from Dublin but travels around the country to get work wherever he finds it."

"Bingo," Boyle shouted. "He could be our man, Custer. Sit tight and I'll send a full team down to you and another team to the Dublin address we have on the database."

"Hardly likely he'll still be around here after so many years. Wouldn't we be better joining up with the team in Dublin?"

"No, your first instinct to look for him there was sound enough. Maybe he met someone and took up with her or maybe he's found a new base and is no longer at the Dublin address. I want to track down everyone with whom he came into contact in Cork, including workmates, barmen, landladies, or betting shop owners. You know the drill. Find something that will help us locate him if we draw a blank in Dublin."

Boyle ended the call abruptly and started pointing at the detectives. "You heard what's going on. I need two of you to join up with Custer in Cork and four to head to Dublin. Sorry about the lateness, but you need to hit the road immediately. As far as the Dublin address goes, I want some urgent action, even if that means getting people up in the middle of the night. It should take you less than three hours to get there, so don't be afraid to ruffle feathers. I want this man in custody and brought back here as soon as possible. Arrest him on suspicion of kidnapping and murder. Feedback anything you get to the IRC the second you get it. I'm afraid none of us are going to get much sleep tonight."

Boyle tried to reel in his emotions. Was this a breakthrough, or was he getting too far ahead of himself? If experience had taught him anything, it was to avoid falling into the trap of assuming a case had reached the end zone. Maybe this Michael Kelly was the man they were looking for – and at the moment everything pointed in that direction – but there was always a price to be paid for not keeping a wary eye on other aspects of the investigation. Certainly, Kelly had to be their prime concern at the moment, although something nagged at the back of Boyle's mind. It couldn't be that easy, could it?

He knew the hard part would not be about linking Kelly to the abductions and deaths. If he were the guilty party, the mountain to be climbed would be proving a case against him. Much more important, could they squeeze the man into revealing the whereabouts of Megan McGrath and Siobhan Cunningham? Were the girls still alive? Would Kelly give up the information?

Boyle's thoughts were interrupted by Brogan who walked into the room and pulled him away from rest of the group.

Brogan whispered. "I eventually got through to the Chief Constable of the PSNI who seemed a bit miffed about us not following correct procedures. Seemed to think the request was based on a tenuous supposition and that it should have come direct from our own Commissioner."

Boyle threw his hands in the air. "Jesus, save us from the by-the-book brigade! If he wants to speak to our Commissioner, then that's what he'll get. I think it's time for our esteemed Chief Superintendent to earn his corn and deliver on his promise to pull out all the stops to help this investigation. I'll call McCluskey now and impress on him the importance of getting the Commissioner to tell the PSNI to get off their arses."

"Tread carefully, Mick."

"You know me, Paul, the very essence of tact and discretion."

Boyle was pleasantly surprised by McCluskey's reaction. "If you think we can learn anything from dredging this river in Downpatrick then so be it. I agree it should have been done back in 2015 and I'm sure the Commissioner will take the same view. I'll get onto it straight away."

Part of Boyle wanted an argument, but on reflection, after McCluskey disconnected, he could understand why the Chief Superintendent was being so compliant. He wouldn't want to be seen as having hampered or impaired the investigation should it come to a review at a later date, at which point, Boyle surmised, his own actions would be called into account if he failed to apprehend the killer. McCluskey was looking at a win-win situation.

It was for that reason that Boyle had not mentioned the news about a suspect. He knew McCluskey would be all over a possible lead and would seek to insert himself into the middle of things if he thought the investigation was reaching a critical point. When asked by McCluskey how the case was progressing, Boyle had issued the standard non-committal response of "actively pursuing some leads."

Boyle dismissed the conversation with McCluskey and called Belle. "Hope I didn't wake you."

"No, just lying in bed reading a new book. Are you going to be home anytime soon?"

"Not for a while yet. We've had a bit of important information and I need to chase it down. I'll stick around here for a while before heading back and grabbing a few hours in the spare room."

Belle became noticeably animated. "Do you mean information about finding those poor girls?"

Boyle cursed himself for talking so freely. "No darling, nothing so spectacular yet. We're trying to track down someone who might help us to move things considerably forward, but there's no reason to believe we're going to find the girls just yet. Please don't mention this to anyone."

"Mick Boyle, you know better than to say that to me! I know the rules. I don't talk out of school and I'm angry at you for suggesting otherwise."

Now he was in trouble. "I'm sorry, darling, I didn't mean that the way it came out. I've always been able to talk freely and openly with you about my work. There's nobody I trust more. Forgive me?"

"On one condition," she teased, trying to mask the fact that she wasn't really angry. "Make sure you come home as soon as possible and don't leave in the morning before I get the chance to make breakfast."

"Perish the thought. Nothing would keep me away from your bacon, eggs, and all the trimmings."

"Now I know you've got a guilty conscience. Talk about trying flattery to cover your back. Love you."

"Love you, too."

Chapter 20

THE DREADED FOOTSTEPS sounded on the stairs, making Siobhan Cunningham go stiff with fear. She was curled up in a corner of the dank room, a position she hadn't moved from since her kidnapper had forced her to put on the drab uniform and left her with nightmare thoughts about what might be ahead.

Suddenly, he was standing over her. "It's time for you to start earning your keep. You'd better do things right or you won't like what's going to happen."

He walked to the bottom of the stairs and motioned for her to follow. She rose with difficulty, her legs cramped from a long sit, and inched her way behind the menacing figure. She used her feet and arms to mount the concrete stairs, emerging into a kitchen where she was blinded by the harsh rays of a fluorescent tube. Despite the glare, she could make out another figure standing beside a sink, wearing the same uniform she was. The figure turned.

It was Megan!

Siobhan forgot about her kidnapper and her predicament and rushed forward, wrapping her friend in a hug. "Oh Megan, you're alive."

The two girls held tight to each other, tears streaming down their faces, and incoherent words spilling from their mouths.

The man moved quickly, prying them apart with difficulty. "That's enough of that. If I ever see you doing this again, I will kill you both. The last thing I need is two sluts pretending you actually care about someone other than yourselves. Well, you don't fool me. Your type is all the same – vain, arrogant brats who think the world revolves around you, and to hell with anyone else. It's a lot different here and the sooner you understand that, then the better your chances of survival."

He slapped both girls hard across the top of their heads and walked angrily from the kitchen, shouting over his shoulder. "Get that place cleaned from top to bottom."

The man walked down a short hall to a lounge at the front of the house, slamming the door behind him as he shuffled across threadbare carpet to flop onto a old armchair. It was a drab room, filled with furniture from decades back, and reeked of alcohol and stale cigarettes, the by-product of which had yellowed the walls and a thick curtain that was always drawn shut. It was badly in need of a thorough clean, but he'd be damned if he'd let the sluts into the privacy of his inner sanctum.

He fought to get his rackety breathing under control and reached out subconsciously to open the middle drawer of a dresser. The photograph was sitting on top of a pile of junk items. He pulled it out and looked at the face staring back at him.

Bitch!

The image was faded and creased by regular handling, but the face was as clear and stark as he remembered it when she walked out him. He was just thirteen years' old back then, abandoned by a slut mother who thought more of herself than her family. He recalled the intervening years, being made to look after his younger brothers, and always at the end of a beating by a brute of a father who didn't know how to cope.

The six-year-old had to grow up quickly. He was better than the hand he was dealt. He stuck to his studies, took the abuse, and plotted a future without snotty brothers and a slob parent. When he turned seventeen, he headed for school as usual, dropped his brothers at the front gate, and strode to the *Bus Éireann* depot at the other side of the small village just outside Kilkenny where they lived. He'd arrived in Dublin three hours later and disappeared into the city's underbelly, changing his name, and finding work on a building site. He had brought with him forty Euros he'd stolen from his father's bedside locker the night before.

He was never sure when the urges had started. All that he knew was that one day he woke up and realised he needed the taste of payback against all the blonde-haired sluts who were corrupting the world, just like his mother had. It was a feeling that simmered and festered until he reached his twenty-second birthday.

He had driven his work van south to Kilkenny, anxious to put distance between his home and the place where he would act out his fantasy. He couldn't believe how easy it had been.

The girl was wearing a short skirt, high heels, and a top that hardly covered her ample cleavage. She was walking alone, shortly before dusk, on a poorly lit street with little traffic and no other pedestrians. Without thinking, he braked alongside her, jumped out, and hit her hard with his clenched fist. He hoisted her unconscious body into the back of the van and raced away, not stopping until he reached a secluded wood at the edge of town.

What happened next was still a pleasant memory for him, one that he'd replayed over and over in his mind. He'd opened the rear doors, leaned in, and put his hands around her neck, squeezing hard until she bucked and kicked and went still. There was no sexual gratification in it. He couldn't think of these young whores that way. He'd simply wanted to end her life; to stop her inflicting pain and hurt on others, the way his mother had.

He'd scooped out a shallow grave deep in the woods and tossed the body inside. Over the years, he'd always wondered why it hadn't been found. Perhaps that's the way it was meant to be, although part of him wanted people to know what he'd done. It was the same for the other bodies. No-one had ever found them. And that made him increasingly angry.

The man placed the photograph carefully back into the drawer and used a remote control to turn on a portable television. A news bulletin showing lines of policemen searching a wooded area near Castlebar, brought him quickly to attention. He slapped his knee and smiled. *Fools! You haven't a clue what you're doing. Not even close. Not even close.*

Suddenly, he became serious, replacing his grin with a creased face of anger. *I'm doing this all wrong. They have to know why this is happening.*

And then he relaxed, realising for the first time why he had changed his pattern. When he'd snatched that Megan girl, he never intended to kill her immediately, just like all the others. He had planned it in his head for some time. He wanted to see what it would be like to humiliate her, maybe even teach her the errors of her slut ways. It would only take a day or two for her to realise that people like her had no place in the world. Then he would kill her.

Why then had he decided to let her live for longer? And why had he decided to go out and pick up another girl, Megan's best friend, to do the same thing with her? It had seemed a good idea at the time. Two for the price of one. But it had been a stupid and senseless break from his normal routine. It had brought a lot of attention to his actions. The police wouldn't rest this time until they caught him.

That's it! That's why!

He wanted the attention. After years of going unnoticed, he'd earned the right for people to know what was happening. He didn't crave notoriety, but he did want recognition for what he'd done. His deeds were carried out on behalf of society, and at the very least they should be brought out into the open where people could judge the contribution he had made.

After all, he had this home away from home in the middle of nowhere. It was his by right and they'd never find him here. It was the perfect base from which to carry on doing whatever he wanted.

The idea that he should stop suddenly vanished from his thoughts. He would instead ramp up his efforts, make the public aware of the need for people like him, and get the whole country talking about the saviour in their midst. And there was an easy way to achieve this.

He'd kill the two girls and dump their bodies where they could easily be found. Then he'd pick up another girl, and another, and another. He'd taunt the police and he wouldn't stop until they found him.

But they never would. He was smarter than them.

Chapter 21

BOYLE DIDN'T GET the sleep he'd hoped for. Nor did he get Belle's start-the-day fry. He settled for three hours on the couch, a quick shower, change of clothes, and a mug of black coffee. It was six in the morning when he gently nudged Belle awake and told her he needed to get back to the office.

She bolted upright. "Look at the time. Let me get you something to eat."

"No need, darling, we'll be having a working breakfast at the station," he lied, his head spinning with the possibilities presented by the day ahead. He didn't want to lose a second in the hunt for Michael Kelly, knowing the lives of two young girls depended on tracking down their only real lead.

"Things are happening, aren't they?" she asked tentatively.

"Too early to say. I promise, I'm not being coy because at the moment it's just an important angle that we need to look closely at. The sooner we can tie it off, one way or another, the better it will be for the investigation to move into other areas, if we need to." Boyle could have said they were working on multiple fronts, as was normally the case. No matter how strong the Kelly lead was, it would be a rash detective who put all his eggs in one basket. And Boyle was determined to be anything but rash.

"I understand, darling," Belle responded in a voice that confirmed she knew exactly where he was coming from.

He leaned over, kissed his wife tenderly, and headed for the door. He was parked at the kerbside in front of the restaurant and found himself heading left, a detour that was becoming commonplace these days. He hadn't forgotten about Paud Flynn, nor had he given up hope of catching the big man unawares in one of his greasy ventures, not that he expected anything so simple, particularly this early in the morning. The murder case was getting his full attention and Big Paud could wait his turn. Nonetheless, a drive past the crime boss's base of operations somehow kept him connected to something he didn't want to lose sight of.

Traffic was virtually non-existent, except for a few Garda patrol cars which were continuing the search for the two girls. The murky dawn of a September day provided sufficient light for Boyle to glance across gardens and laneways, peak into parked cars, and watch for any pedestrians acting suspiciously. Nothing appeared out of the ordinary.

Not until he rounded a corner in front of Big Paud's office and warehouse compound.

It was only a fleeting glimpse but there was no mistake in Boyle's mind that he saw a stooped figure, dressed fully in black, drop down from a side wall into the Flynn complex. Not a normal entrance for an employee, even for one who had forgotten their key to the main gate. Besides, there was no vehicle parked near the perimeter.

Boyle slowed to a stop, reacting to an instinct to investigate what was happening. But then he smiled. Big Paud was about to be the victim of a break-in.

Not wanting to interfere in the commission of a

crime which could only be beneficial to the community, Boyle chuckled, switched off the engine, and lowered the car windows. He sat for a few minutes until he heard the sounds of banging and tinkling glass. Not exactly a silent intruder. *Fill your pockets, son,* he mused and restarted the car.

Sergeant Brogan had beaten Boyle into the station. So too had just about everyone else, judging by the hubbub of activity which greeted him on the first-floor suite of offices. It looked like nobody had gone home, which made Boyle slightly guilty for stealing away.

"We got access to Kelly's Dublin address a few hours ago," Brogan told him. Unfortunately, no-one was there, and judging by a small mountain of junk mail in the hallway, it doesn't look like anyone's been there for a few weeks. Nothing incriminating found so far at the scene, but I've told the team to pull the place apart."

"Has he done a runner, or he is simply on one of his building-site jobs elsewhere in the country?"

"Take your pick."

Boyle tried not to let his disappointment show. "Okay, we take it from the top and chase all angles. Do we know what sort of vehicle he drives? Can we track if he has a mobile phone registered in his name? What about bank accounts and using credit or debit cards? It's impossible these days not to leave a digital print somewhere."

"Already on it," Brogan stated matter-of-factly. "I'm waiting for the banks to open to check for accounts in Kelly's name, but we've pulled the online records from the RSA which has him as the registered owner of a 2008 Ford Transit Courier. It's one of those ubiquitous white jobs, bought from a dealer in Howth three years ago. Currently fully taxed and insured."

"Has the Road Safety Authority got information on previous vehicles owned by Kelly?"

Brogan lifted a folder. "We have his complete history here. He's owned various vehicles over the last ten years, almost always small commercial vans of one model or another. We're checking to see if any of these were reported in witness statements or police notes at the times of the other kidnappings."

"What about mobile phones?"

"No luck so far. I emailed requests to the main service providers, but to be fair, that was in the middle of the night. We'll chase them down again when offices start opening in a few hours."

"That could be the key," Boyle said. "The easy thing will be able to ping his location once we get the phone details."

"Assuming of course that Kelly's got a phone with GPS features. It would be just our luck that he's one of those people who use disposable pay-as-you-go phones."

"And there's me thinking you were always a glass-half-full guy."

"I guess you're rubbing off on me," Brogan countered.

Boyle slipped his serious face back on. "Let's recap on what else we need to be doing. I've got a list that appears to keep getting bigger and I'm afraid something will fall through the cracks."

"I know where you coming from. Because we've despatched teams to Dublin and Cork, we're beginning to get stretched. We have to keep those teams in place for now, but that means drafting in more resources. I have two uniforms trawling through CCTV around the Castlebar area over the past week or so. It's not nearly enough. Another three or four bodies would be helpful.

"I'll ask Superintendent Delaney and Sergeant Moriarty if they can redirect some men. Anything else?"

Brogan picked up another file. "The Downpatrick angle worries me, if only because it is the one we know least about. The request for the river dredging has gone through, but we've no indication when this might start, and on top of that we must make sure we allocate enough detectives to continue the follow-up interviews from all the previous investigations."

Boyle nodded. "I can still call in more detectives from Dublin. In fact, it might be better if we let them take over the search of the Kelly house there, as well as any addresses that Armstrong and Munn have come up with in Cork. Yeah, let's bring our own teams back to base. We should also make full use of Inspector Bonnaville who strikes me as an efficient officer. Give him free rein to double-check our Downpatrick file and to liaise with the database cross-referencing guys. I trust him not to miss anything."

"Every little will help," Brogan agreed. "I just wish we could push things quicker on finding Kelly."

"The thing is that we don't know his current whereabouts, but we do know where he's been."

"What are you getting at?" asked Brogan.

"It's simple," Boyle stated. "What's certain is that if Kelly is our man, then he has been in the Castlebar area on at least two occasions over the past seven days when the girls were snatched. Could be he's found a base around here, which means we start looking more extensively for this Ford van on our own doorstep. Now that we know the vehicle details, and we have Kelly's driving licence photo, we start visiting every building site in the county. That means covering new housing sites or renovations of any kind, in fact anywhere we spot a skip or a wheelbarrow."

"That's going to add to manpower pressures."

"I'll get Delaney to pull as many uniforms as necessary away from the searches. This has now become our number one priority, meaning we concentrate on being proactive rather than reactive. I want as many mobile units as possible to be out there scouring for this van. Something tells me that we'll get Kelly sooner rather than later."

Chapter 22

THE GARDA MOBILE patrol driver parked at the kerb opposite a new-build housing site shortly after nine o'clock in the morning. It was one of those upscale sites, marked out for ten three-storey detached houses, each featuring different shades of grey slate roofs and walls in the latest architectural fad for the modern living look. Two units were almost finished, complete with driveways and generous front and rear garden plots. Prospective owners would have to shell out at least a half-million Euros if they wanted keys to these particular homes.

The Guard was not thinking about designs or prices. His focus was on a white Ford Transit Courier which was parked alongside several works' vehicles in a cul-de-sac area at one end of the development. It was close enough for the policeman to read the number plate which tallied with the one shown on the day's alert sheet pinned to the dashboard of his patrol car.

He'd found Michael Kelly's vehicle.

His first thought was to drive onto the site and look around for the suspect. It was a notion that lasted only a few seconds. This one had to be done by the book. If Kelly saw the approach and was spooked into doing a runner, there'd be hell for the cop to pay for his rashness.

His pulse was racing as he lifted the base intercom handset and pressed the open channel button. He waited patiently for a response from the switchboard at Castlebar.

"CB105, go ahead."

"CB105, this is Mobile Foxtrot India 7789. Urgent, I repeat, urgent. Have sight of vehicle at the top of today's briefing notes. Alert appropriate investigating officer. Over." The guard was careful about divulging too much information on air.

Less than three seconds elapsed before a different voice responded from base. "Foxtrot India 7789, are you certain you have the right vehicle? Have you still got it in sight? Over."

The patrol officer recognised Sergeant Moriarty's voice. "Affirmative, CB105. The vehicle is parked. Refer to grid reference A101 to B366. Over." Once again, the need to keep vital information away from nosy eavesdroppers was paramount in the messages swinging back and forth. It was for that reason that An Garda Síochána used their own large-scale map references of areas within individual station jurisdictions. The last thing anyone needed was a gaggle of press photographers and television crews arriving at the scene of a reported incident.

"Be advised, Foxtrot India 7789, to sit tight and let us know if anything changes. Support is on the way. What is the topography? Over."

"It's a main road, CB105. A large building site surrounded by open fields. No other secondary exits apparent from my viewpoint. Over."

Colm Moriarty was in Boyle's office a minute after ending his call with the patrolman. "We've located Kelly's van. It's at a housing development site on the N9 between Westport and Newport, approximately three miles from Newport."

Boyle jumped from his seat. "Brilliant stuff, Sarge. Are we sitting on it?"

"The mobile unit that called it in has eyes on the vehicle and is awaiting back-up. What do you need from us?"

Boyle shouted at the top of his voice for Brogan who was in the next room. While he waited for his number two to react, he told Moriarty. "I'll take whatever you've got. The road is to be sealed off at both ends and we need to check for any escape points. What do we know of the area?"

"Apparently a big site surrounded by fields. Might need to get some uniforms into the fields in case Kelly legs it in those directions."

"Agreed, get them moving. And remember, Sarge, Kelly must be taken alive at all costs. If he's our man, then only he knows where those girls are."

Moriarty bumped into Brogan on his way out of the office. "What's the flap?"

Boyle rushed towards him. "We think we've got Kelly. Get whoever of our team is left in the building and meet me in the rear car park. Believe it or not, he's only about twenty minutes from here."

It was a good forty-five minutes before Boyle was satisfied everything was in place for an orderly takedown. There was no such thing, he knew, but the planning had to be done. After that, you just had to react to whatever presented itself.

As soon as he received confirmation that a squad of thirty uniforms had thrown a semi-circle cordon around the rear and sides of the site, about two hundred yards away in the fields, he issued last-minute instructions to his detectives and climbed into his RAV4 with Brogan in the passenger seat. Six other detectives boarded two vehicles and waited while Boyle nosed sedately towards the site entrance. There would be no high-speed antics, with screeching tyres and sirens. It didn't make any sense to announce their arrival in advance.

Boyle's car crunched over the site's unfinished road surface and stopped beside a man loading debris onto a large builders' skip. Boyle got out and showed the worker a picture of Kelly. "I'm looking to talk to this man. Is he here?" No name given. No point in confusing the situation if Kelly was operating under an alias.

The labourer studied the picture, although his attention was more focussed on Boyle than the image held in front of him. "Who wants to know?"

There was always a know-it-all, self-important twat everywhere. Boyle was in no mood for the man's posturing, so he flashed his badge and held it beside Kelly's photo. "Don't look at me, look at the damn picture. I need an answer now or you'll find yourself on an obstruction charge. Is this man on site?"

The labourer quickly lost his bravado. "I think so. I think he's one of the sparks crew working on final fixes at those two houses down at the end," he said, pointing to the left of the site.

"Put your damn hands down and stay here beside the skip until we're done."

The man dropped his arm just as two other vehicles carrying the rest of Boyle's team rolled to a stop behind the RAV4. Other men working on the exterior of houses at this part of the site, seemed to sense something was happening. Eyes turned in the direction of the policemen, and several power tools suddenly faded off. The tom-tom drums were beating up and down the development.

Boyle reacted quickly and turned to his team. "Sergeant Brogan and I will take the front entrance at the end house. I want four of you to check the adjoining house, two each front and rear. The other two will remain here."

He took off on a run, reaching his target house in less than ten seconds. He stepped through the open doorway, signalled Brogan to the right, and headed into a room on his left. He met two workmen on a traverse through the ground floor, but none were Kelly. He showed the second man Kelly's picture and got a raised arm. "That's the boss. He's upstairs to the front, but he'll insist you wear a hard hat before you go up there."

Boyle ignored him and raced back to the front of the building where the staircase was located. He met Brogan in the hall and pointed upwards. He counted fourteen steps on his way to the next floor, taking them two at a time, not caring about the noise of his boots on bare wood.

A figure appeared on the landing as Boyle reached the top. The photo in Boyle's jacket pocket didn't show dust marks on the face, or a three-day beard stubble, or a wool cap perched jauntily on top of a square head, but there was no doubt in his mind that the man facing him was Michael Kelly. He was wearing a threadbare blue jumper over the top of a wrinkled checked shirt and had bulky multi-pocket trousers that were home to a variety of screwdrivers and pliers.

But it was a large claw hammer in Kelly's right hand that caught most of Boyle's attention. It hung loosely by Kelly's side as he studied Boyle with a puzzled look, his eyebrows raised in a silent query.

It was the only reaction Kelly had time to think

about.

Boyle sprang forward, wrapping his arms around Kelly's midriff and pinning the hammer to his side. Brogan stepped neatly behind Kelly and grabbed hold of his right wrist, twisting it backwards and upwards. Boyle let go when he knew Kelly was immobilised.

"What the fuck's going on," Kelly shouted.

This was the part Boyle had been waiting for. "Michael Kelly, I am a Garda Síochána Detective Inspector. I have reasonable cause to arrest you on suspicion of kidnapping, false imprisonment, and murder. You will be brought immediately to a Garda station where you will have the right to consult a solicitor in respect of the charges which might be brought to bear against you. Do you understand what I've just said?"

"Understand? Are you out of your fucking mind? I know nothing about kidnapping and murder. You've got this all wrong."

Brogan flashed a smile at Boyle. "Wish I had a Euro for every time I heard that."

Chapter 23

THE PRESS CORPS was waiting in their usual animated cluster at the front of the Castlebar station. Two TV crews were already set up on the front lawn, their tripod-mounted cameras swivelling back and forth from the roadway entrance to the large copper and steel Garda emblem fixed to the wall above the main door, no doubt checking their focus in anticipation of the arrival of a convoy. Boyle counted ten photographers with outrageously-sized lens designed to pick up nasal hairs from a half-mile away, and there was a similar group of reporters, each holding pocket notebooks and pens, ready to scribble anything to add colour to what would otherwise be bland copy about a suspect being taken into custody.

"How did they hear about this so fast?" Brogan muttered from the back seat where he kept watch on a handcuffed and subdued Michael Kelly.

"Mobile phones and social media are the curse of our times," Boyle responded. "Probably one of the site workers couldn't wait to put himself in the limelight, or maybe it was a motorist pissed off at being held behind one of the roadblocks on the N9. Too easy these days to reach out to the world in the blink of an eye. Wouldn't be surprised to see a video from the site arrest appearing on Facebook or whatever. Glad I decided to change into a nice suit."

Boyle eased the RAV4 across the intersection close to the station, flicking the indicator light only at the last moment to signal his intention to enter the curved driveway. There was no convoy, just Boyle's car. He'd left his full team back at the building site to interview the workers and supervise the removal of Kelly's van, which would be taken to a warehouse for full forensic dissection.

The arrival of a single vehicle got the attention of the press huddle, but not enough to put them on full alert. Boyd swept up the driveway and disappeared behind the building before a camera was raised or a notebook opened. He braked in front of the rear door and waited while Brogan bundled Kelly into a service hallway. Then he parked in his usual spot and walked casually towards the steps where Sergeant Moriarty suddenly emerged.

"Thought you could use one of these," Moriarty said as he held a cigarette packet in front of him.

"I don't care what anybody else says, Sarge, but when you get right down to it, you're not such a bad guy." Boyle took the offered cigarette and light and sucked hungrily. "Boy, that hit the right spot."

"Nice job out there, Mick. Do you think it's him?"

"Baby steps, Sarge, baby steps. By the way, your boys did great this morning."

"How many times have I told you that the suits would be lost without the uniforms?"

"No argument here, Sarge."

Moriarty glanced briefly behind. "How do you want to play this, Mick?"

"Got to be by the book, but I want a first crack with him before the presence of a solicitor. Wait twenty minutes before your log him in and then wait another twenty before you track down his brief, assuming he has one, which I doubt. That'll give us a bit more leeway with one of the standby court-appointed solicitors."

"Don't suppose you need me to tell you to tread carefully. I'll buy you a bit of time, but sooner rather than later everything will have to go on the record. I'll process him as a person of interest before any formal charges and I'll enquire about his legal representation. I'll even fetch him a cup of tea and a biscuit, though I hope the bastard chokes on it."

"Now that you mention it, I'll have a cup along with one of your stashed chocolate digestives."

Brogan was waiting outside an interview room. "He's safely tucked away, but we didn't fool the press. There's already TV and radio bulletins announcing that a man has been arrested in connection the disappearance of the girls. They're gonna need a statement before too long."

"Gonna? Don't tell me my university-educated Sergeant is slipping into Americanisms before he reaches the rank of Commissioner. We're *going* to give out a statement, but only after we test the waters with Kelly. Can you call your friend, Dr Dunne, and see if she can join us as soon as possible? I want to hear her impressions of Kelly."

"I'll get right on. Just gimme a moment to mosey on down to my office," Brogan replied with a phoney American accent.

Boyle shook his head and pushed open the door to the interview room. Kelly was sitting in front of a bolted-down grey table, his wrists handcuffed to a small bar that protruded from one side. He lifted his head and glowered at Boyle. "This is fucking ridiculous. Why am I here? I want to see a solicitor."

Boyle pasted on his best smile and took a seat

opposite Kelly. "The station Sergeant will be along shortly to take some details. Do you have a solicitor, or do you need us to get one for you?"

"No, I don't have a solicitor. Who the fuck goes around with a solicitor on retainer? You'd better get me one, and I'm not saying anything until they get here."

"That's your prerogative. Just thought I'd get some basic details to help save time."

Kelly rattled the handcuffs against the holding bar. "Are you fucking deaf? I'm not talking to anyone until I have legal support. Just what is it that you think I've done? What evidence do you have?"

Boyle threw him a best-friend look. "I'd feel the same way as you, but I'm sure you understand that I also can't say anything about our case until a solicitor is present. Wouldn't be fair on you. I want to make sure you have all the help you can get." The last sentence was said with a foreboding drop in tone. Boyle was making it clear that Kelly – if he didn't already appreciate it – was in serious trouble.

"Look," Kelly said in a pleading voice, "this has got to be a case of mistaken identity. Tell me what I'm supposed to have done."

"You're an electrician, aren't you? I gather you move around a lot."

"I'm an electrical sub-contractor. I go where I can find the work. Not easy these days, but I look after my crew and make sure they've always got a job to go to."

"Where do you stay when you're on the move?"

"Depends on the job and the location. If it's too far outside Dublin and it's for more than a week, I usually find a B&B or small hotel."

"Must be hard on your family. What about your

wife or girlfriend?"

"I'm single and unattached. I go where I want, when I want."

Boyle raised an eyebrow. "No attachments at all? Do you have problems with women? What about little girls? Are they more to your taste?"

Kelly rose from his seat and rattled the handcuffs again. "What the fuck are you suggesting? Is this about those girls that went missing from around here? Do you honestly think I had something to do with that?"

"You tell me. Did you know any of the girls?"

"No, I fucking didn't."

"What about the girl who went missing in Cork when you were there on a job ten years ago, or what about the girl who went missing when you were on a job up North, in Downpatrick, five years ago?"

Kelly slumped back in the seat as if he'd being hit with a sledgehammer. A shadow passed across his eyes and he stared in shock at Boyle. "Sweet Jesus, this is bad, isn't it?"

"As bad as it gets," Boyle told him.

"You've got to help me. I didn't do these things. There has to be another explanation."

"That's what we're here to find out," said Boyle.

Chapter 24

THE FORMAL INTERVIEW with Kelly started in mid-afternoon. The paperwork had been processed by Sergeant Moriarty, and a local solicitor by the name of Pierce Hamilton had been rounded up. Dr Connie Dunne arrived in time for the proceedings to start. In truth, things had been delayed until she could get away from her desk at University College Hospital in Galway.

Before they entered the holding room, Boyle brought Dr Dunne up to speed with his informal chat with Kelly. "To tell you the truth, Doc, he seemed sincere. His shock at being attached to these crimes looked genuine. I'm getting a bad feeling about him."

Dunne nodded in acknowledgement. "The thing to remember about the true psychopath is that he is always in control, always capable of turning on emotions to suit the circumstances, and always convincing. He prides himself on manipulating people. It's second nature, like a defence mechanism that's difficult to break down."

"It will be interesting to see what you think of him. I can't let you sit in on the interview, but I've set you up in a small anteroom with sound and a two-way mirror."

"I must admit I'm looking forward to it," Dunne nodded. "The thing that struck me most about your conversation is when you said he corrected your description of him as an electrician."

"Made it clear he was an electrical sub-contractor who looked after his boys and kept them in work."

Dunne smiled. "Remember that I told you yesterday that the psychopath has a grandiose sense of their own self-importance. They have to be leaders, not followers, and they have to make people understand the difference. That's what I think your Mr Kelly was doing when he rebuffed your electrician tag."

"So, you're saying that man in there is a psychopath and could well be the kidnapper and murderer?"

"Not at all. A good old down-to-earth egotist is probably more self-centred and fuller of their own importance than a psychopath. There is, however, a big difference between the two species. Let's find out which one Kelly is."

Boyle shook his head in bewilderment. "Why do I feel more and more that I'm out of my depth here?"

Interview with Michael Gerard Kelly commencing at 14.05 on September 23rd, 2020. Present are Detectives Michael Boyle, Paul Brogan, and Roisin Munn, who is taking notes for a full transcript to be available immediately after the conclusion of the interview. Also present is Mr Pierce Hamilton, of the legal firm of Hamilton, Hamilton, and Morris, which is representing Mr Kelly. I am now addressing Mr Kelly directly: You are not obliged to say anything unless you wish to do so. Anything you do say will be taken down in writing and may be given in evidence. Do you understand what I have just said?

Boyle's opening statement was greeted with impatience by Hamilton. "Yes, yes, can we move things along? My client is fully aware of the circumstances of this odd gathering and is willing to cooperate fully to clear up what is obviously a misapprehension on behalf of An Garda Síochána."

Notetaker Munn scribbled feverishly. She had arrived back from Cork with George Armstrong less than ten minutes before being roped into the proceedings. She glided a biro awkwardly across the paper, cursing herself for not taking the trouble to learn shorthand. But then why should she? She was a detective, not a bloody secretary.

A frustrating aspect of Garda interviews is that everything said during questioning has to be written down. It does little to help the free flow of conversation, but until legislation keeps pace with the demands of officers on the ground, the use of exclusively digital recordings is still a pipedream. The notes can be later typed for convenience, but the original hand-written pages are the official record, which must be kept on file.

Hamilton was noted as an old-school lawyer, one who espoused substance over style. He was the senior member of his firm and a frequent visitor to Garda stations where he got on well with policemen and recognised the difficulties often imposed by their jobs and the legal restrictions which governed how they went about things. He was known for always trying to chivvy out a deal but was a straitlaced professional when it came to formal interviews.

Boyle adopted a similar stance and threw Hamilton's words back at him. "I'm delighted to hear that your client has agreed to cooperate freely. Perhaps, if he is open and honest with us, we can all learn whether we have misapprehended some disturbing discoveries which place Mr Kelly at the scenes of at least five abductions over the past decade."

"My client has naturally informed me of the coincidental nature of his presence in Cork and Downpatrick when several abductions took place. I'm not sure how you're getting to five with your count."

"Your confusion is understandable, Mr. Hamilton," Boyle said affably. "We can start in Kilkenny in 2008 when a young girl by the name of Jennifer Ross went missing and was never found. She was just fifteen. We have no way of knowing if your client was in the Kilkenny area around that time, but we would like him to clear that up for us."

Hamilton leaned across to whisper in Kelly's ear, and then listened to a long reply, which Kelly also whispered. "My client points out that he was just seventeen at the time and was completing his electrician studies at the Dublin Institute of Technology. You should easily find his records."

"Doesn't mean he didn't slip away to Kilkenny for a weekend," Boyle countered.

"Please tell me you've got more than supposition and fairy stories, Inspector."

"Let's move forward two years to Cork in 2010 when sixteen-year-old Sally Gardiner disappeared. During police investigations at the time, Mr Kelly was interviewed because he was working in the vicinity of where Sally lived."

"Interviewed and released," Hamilton pointed out.

Boyle continued as if he hadn't heard the solicitor's interruption. "Two years later, and for a period which lasted three years, another three girls went missing, this time in Downpatrick in Northern Ireland. Once again, we find that Mr Kelly was in the area at the time of at least one of those disappearances."

Boyle held up his hand to cut off another interruption. "I want to fast forward to the present and the two missing teenagers from Castlebar during the past fortnight. Lo and behold, once again we find Michael Gerard Kelly at the scene."

"Hardly at the scene, Inspector. Be fair," Hamilton said. "The man's work takes him all over the country. These are merely coincidences."

Boyle could sense that Hamilton didn't really believe his own argument. "Twice maybe could be construed as a coincidence, but it's stretching it a bit to suggest that three times is anything except a pattern, which puts your client in a tricky spot as far as alibis go. And we only have his word that he was not in Kilkenny in 2008. That would be a full house, which even your considerable powers of persuasion would find difficult to explain. How about we start coming clean at your side of the table?"

To his credit, Hamilton remained unruffled. "What you have is little more than circumstantial. You're tilting at windmills without a shred of proof that my client had anything to do with the sad disappearance of these poor girls."

"What we have," Boyle snorted, "is nothing from your client to refute a damning case being built against him. Isn't it time we heard directly from him? Why doesn't he take the opportunity to tell us all about his times in Cork and Downpatrick and Castlebar and maybe even in Kilkenny. Tell us what he did at those locations, who he worked with, who he met, who he socialised with, and whether he knew or heard of any of the girls. I mean, he had to be living on a different planet not to realise what had happened in Cork and Downpatrick and now here in Castlebar while he was working on building sites. Why has he not come forward before now? Did he not think it odd that tragedy seemed to be following him around?"

"Nice speech, Inspector, but I'm not sure what it is that you want."

"What I want is to hear directly from your client. I want to see some openness and transparency, not to mention a desire to help us find the real killer. If he wants us to believe he's innocent, this is his big chance. If he's guilty, tell us where he's stashed Megan McGrath and Siobhan Cunningham. He can't have it both ways."

"That's not how this works, and you know it," Hamilton said. "Put your cards on the table and ask anything you want. Otherwise I suggest you stop this fishing expedition."

Boyle leaned back in his seat and fixed Hamilton with a glacial stare. "All we're doing here is looking for the truth, Pierce." It was the first time he'd used the solicitor's first name, a deliberate change of course in an attempt to bring the formality of the interview down by a few notches. The little speech he'd given Hamilton was designed to test the waters. Boyle had to admit there were things about the suspect that just didn't add up and he had a feeling that Hamilton himself was beginning to see some wriggle room for his client. Did this always have to be adversarial? Was there a way for both sides to get what they wanted?

Boyle decided to stick with the carrot approach. He leaned across the table towards Hamilton in what he hoped was a conciliatory gesture. "Look, Pierce, we both know how this works. Despite your understandable protestations, I know that you know there's a lot of dangerous ground underfoot for your client. We have enough compelling evidence to hold him for a week, after which we both know I'll get an extension to pursue enquiries, then we'll hold him for another week, and I'll get another extension, and on and on we'll go until after Christmas. At some point months from now, we might just have put the finishing touches to our case, which means he'll be locked up for the rest of his life. Don't you think you should talk that over with him?"

Hamilton thought he caught a glimmer of compromise in Boyle's words. "Seems to me, Inspector, that you're looking for the best of both worlds. You don't honestly expect my client to enter into a friendly tête-à-tête with a shark such as yourself waiting to pounce on the most innocent of remarks? No, I'll think we'll keep this within the normal rules of engagement, so to speak, unless of course you have a firm offer for my client."

"You're in no position to ask for anything," Boyle responded. "I'll repeat what I said about finding two missing girls. That's what's important, not your client's sensitivities. Convince us of his innocence and let my team get on with finding them. Every minute we waste here is stealing a precious minute from their lives."

"What exactly are you asking?"

"Help us out by getting your client to move out from under your protective umbrella. We have his van and we want access to his current digs for a full forensic sweep. You know we can get search warrants, but why delay things by even a few hours."

Hamilton went back to his lean-and-whisper mode. After a few minutes, he turned to Boyle. "How about a short recess to allow me to converse fully with my client?"

"Agreed," Boyle said and glanced at his watch. "Interview suspended at 14.46."

Chapter 25

BOYLE BLEW THE cigarette smoke into the crisp afternoon air and cursed his weakness. He was taking more and more of these damn things, particularly to help ease the stresses of his caseload, something he'd promised Belle he wouldn't do. Somehow, he'd gone from one or two a day to a full packet. When the hell had that happened?

He pushed the thought aside and took another deep drag. If he was hoping for inspiration from the nicotine, he was sorely disappointed. He couldn't get a read on Kelly, who'd sat almost expressionless during the interview, and was showing no signs of pointing the searchers in the direction of Megan Campbell and Siobhan Cunningham.

Boyle's biggest fear was that they'd do the usual dance-don't-touch routine with Kelly and get absolutely nowhere over the next few days. The guy simply didn't look like someone who would admit to anything. Boyle knew that the solicitor was right to describe the case as circumstantial, and unless forensics could come up with something to tie Kelly to the two missing girls, there was not enough to charge him with any prospect of a conviction.

"Mind telling me what that was all about in there?"

Boyle hadn't heard Brogan open the rear door and step onto the railed porch overlooking the car park. He turned to face his deputy. "What part are you talking about?"

"For starters, what was all that nonsense about asking Kelly to agree to searches of his van and digs? We both know that Superintendent Delaney was drawing up the papers before we started the interview and that warrants will be signed off by the District Judge within the next hour. We found where Kelly is staying, so there's nothing for him to give us that we don't already know."

"Yes," Boyle nodded, "but I need to prise open that prick's silence. Agreeing to the warrants is a simple gesture, but one that might indicate willingness to give us more. The trick is to get him talking, to get him to believe he's in control and that we have nothing unless he tells us what he knows. I'm betting he wants to talk, but his solicitor is holding him back. If Kelly's our man, he'll want to watch us squirm. He'll want to taunt us, to show he's superior to us, and to prove there's nothing we can do to stop him."

"Spoken like a true psychologist."

Boyle spun towards the door and stared in surprise at Dr Dunne's appearance. "Jeez, it looks like we've got a convention going on here."

"You know what they say about Mohammed and the Mountain." She flashed a smile and glanced at the cigarette in Boyle's hand. "If you've got one of those to spare, I'll think I'll join you."

Boyle opened the packet and offered one. "Life's full of surprises," he said. "There's me thinking you were one of those health freaks who pounded the treadmill and gorged on gluten-free."

"Oh, it would shock you to know that I have all the vices," she said teasingly, her eyes turned towards Brogan.

Boyle caught the inflection but said nothing as he lit Dunne's cigarette.

She inhaled a lungful, blew the entrails sideways, and turned back to Boyle. "That was quite a speech you were giving about getting Kelly to talk. Mind telling me where you got your degree in psychology?"

"I got it on the street. Every time we pick someone up, even for a minor offence, it's all mind games. There're all barrack-room lawyers who like to think we're nothing but plodders who don't know our asses from our elbows. Sometimes it's better to let them think we're clueless, so that they can fill in the gaps for us."

"And you think Kelly is like that?"

"No, I don't," Boyle said with emphasis. "He's cut from a different cloth. There's an air of superiority and cockiness about him that I can't get a read on. As far as we've been able to ascertain, he's never been in trouble before, not even a speeding ticket, but he's sitting in there like someone who's seen it all before. I can't figure it out."

"I have to admit," Dunne said, "he's a cool customer."

"You're the expert, Doc, so what are your first impressions?"

"I haven't seen enough to form an opinion yet. I like your tactic of getting Kelly to start talking. That's where he'll show his character. Get him to tell you about his childhood, his parents, his siblings, his girlfriends, the more trivia the better. Was he good at sports? Did he like school? What did he think of his teachers?"

Brogan interrupted. "Isn't that all a bit of diversion? We need to hear what he has to say about the kidnaps and murders. Won't his responses to those questions not tell you more about him than what he did when he was a kid?"

"The two elements are not mutually exclusive," said Dunne. "If this man's actions were triggered by something in his past, we have to see if he'll lead us there without knowing that he has. People always speak freely about their childhood memories, good or bad, and that's where we'll start to understand the type of person he is and, more importantly, the type of person he has become. I'm particularly interested in what he says about girlfriends, but I would suggest you get Garda Munn to probe in this area. His reaction to being questioned by a woman might tell us a lot."

"Okay," Boyle said with a flourish, throwing his cigarette butt into a sand bucket. "I don't want to get too bogged down on this out here. We'll do as Dr Dunne suggests, but time is pressing, and we need to move things forward. I want to keep the focus on the bigger picture."

"What have you in mind?" asked Brogan.

"I need you to sit out the next part, Paul. Stick with Superintendent Delaney and Sergeant Moriarty and get those warrants executed. This thing is going to hinge on forensics, so make sure we get fast-track access to the labs at Galway. Also, switch the team to tracking down everything they can find about Kelly, particularly about his time at the Dublin Institute of Technology. Speak to his tutors, check his exam grades, and see if he's the bright spark that he likes to think he is. And, by the way, there was no pun intended there."

Pierce Hamilton was waiting in the hallway for Boyle as he stepped back into the building.

"Right, Mick, my client has decided to play ball with you. He's agreed to talk about himself and what he's being accused of. I warn you, however, that I won't tolerate you going into places you shouldn't."

"I just want to move this forward, Pierce. We both know it's in Kelly's interest to start talking. Who knows, he might even persuade us that he's as innocent as driven snow?"

"What about that bullshit with warrants? I'm well aware that you've got enough circumstantial evidence to convince a Judge to issue warrants, so why ask for Kelly's permission, which by the way, he has freely given?

"Just wanted to establish a baseline of cooperation," Boyle replied. "How about we get on with this?"

"My warning still stands. I'll cut you off at the knees if you get too far ahead of yourself."

"Perish the thought."

Boyle's sparring with the solicitor was interrupted by Superintendent Delaney who approached the group with a frown that Boyle knew didn't bode well. There was always something about Delaney's demeanour that presaged the message he was about to deliver.

Boyle broke away from Hamilton and Dr Dunne to meet the station commander at the entrance to an empty office. "What's happened, John? Don't tell me there's a problem with the warrants."

"I wish that's all it was, Mick. I'm afraid this is a bit more serious."

"For heaven's sake, spit it out."

"Big Paud Flynn's barrister has gone ahead with a formal filing of an harassment complaint against you."

"Jeez, has Myles Winstanley got nothing better to do with his time? I can't be bothered with this nonsense. Tell him I'll see him in court."

Delaney shook his head vigorously. "It's gone beyond general harassment, Mick. The papers he's filed are claiming that you were at Big Paud's office complex early this morning and trashed the place. They have five vehicles out of commission, an office which has been ransacked, and a store which has suffered untold damage in terms of customer orders. They're claiming the costs will run into six figures."

Boyle sucked in air, remembering how he watched a black-clad figure scale Big Paud's perimeter wall shortly after six a.m. He shook away the image and turned to Delaney. "That's a load of bull. Any Judge worth his salt will throw it out the window in a heartbeat."

"The thing is, Mick, they claim they have CCTV footage of you outside the premises at the time of the attack."

Chapter 26

CHAIRS SCREECHED across the tiled floor as the small group took their seats at the table in Interview Room 4. By agreement, Kelly's handcuffs had been removed and he'd been given a comfort break before the start of proceedings. Boyle shook aside the harassment bombshell and launched straight in.

Interview with Michael Gerard Kelly recommencing at 15.40 on September 23rd, 2020. Present are Garda Detectives Michael Boyle and Roisin Munn. Also present is Mr Pierce Hamilton, of the legal firm of Hamilton, Hamilton, and Morris, which is representing Mr Kelly. Sergeant Paul Brogan is no longer present but may join the interview at some stage.

Once again, Hamilton, kicked off proceedings. "For the record, my client is willing to cooperate fully with this investigation in order to establish his innocence. For that reason, he has given his wholehearted permission for police to search his vehicle and premises and is happy is answer any questions about his whereabouts at the dates and times of the incidents which were referenced at the first interview."

Nice one, Boyle thought. Take credit and show a spirit of helpfulness which would jump out from the printed page once the interview was transcribed. "I'd like to begin by asking Mr Kelly to tell us about himself. Just a little potted history of his life and career will suffice to help us get to know him."

"What do you want to know?" Kelly said.

Garda Munn leaned forward, a wide smile running across her face. "Oh, just the usual, Mr Kelly. Tell us about your family and schooldays and how you carved out a career as a successful businessman."

"Not much to tell, Typical childhood. My mother died young and I had to help raise a younger brother. My father was not always around, so I learned from an early age how to stand on my own two feet. That's why I went to college and made something of myself."

"Ever bullied at school?" Munn probed.

"No chance. I knew how to take care of myself."

"Did you find studies easy?"

"They were alright. Wanted to be an electrician but there was nothing in the secondary school to help with this, so I got a place in the technology institute. Finished top of my class and started out as an apprentice in a local company. Did my time and quickly started my own business."

"That was quite a big step," Munn said. "Weren't you afraid of failure, particularly with so many businesses going bust at the time you started up?"

"Naw, I was better than most of the cowboys around at the time. I offered quality jobs and earned a reputation for professionalism and fair prices."

"What about girlfriends?"

The change in direction took Kelly by surprise. "What...what about them?"

"Did you have any?"

"Course I had. What sort of question is that?"

"Just wondering. You're not married are you?

What about a regular girlfriend or fiancée?"

"Don't have any. Women tend to be too demanding and distracting. Casual is good enough for me. That way, I can move on with no questions asked."

"Do you mean casual as in casual sex?"

Kelly's nostrils flared and he stared at Munn with a look of hatred in his eyes. "Are you offering, darling?"

Boyle quickly interrupted. "That's enough of that nonsense. Keep a civil tongue and answer the questions with a degree of respect."

The solicitor held up his hand to stop Kelly from responding. "Quite right, Inspector, although I think we've fully explored your colleague's little trip down memory lane."

"Almost," Boyle said. "Tell us about your brother and father. Do you still keep in touch with them?"

"Not much to tell. We all went our separate ways. As far as I know, my brother is working in Dublin City Council as a dustbin man, and my father is still probably propped up against a bar counter in one of his many locals. Haven't clapped eyes on either one in more than five years."

"Is that their choice or yours?"

"Fairly mutual, I'd say. We've nothing in common. If they want to live their lives like bums, that's their decision. Me, I've got higher ambitions."

"Such as?" Boyle asked.

"I'm a successful businessman. Got my own squad of sparks with plenty of work around the country. The next step is to set up a city office offering electrical engineering expertise to the big multi-nationals. That's where the real money is at and I intend to grab a share of it."

"How come you get so much work around the country?"

"You've got to cultivate your contacts. They're known in the business world as key referrals, influential people who can refer potential customers in your direction with a recommendation that they use your services. Big builders, small builders, architects, surveyors, developers, and housing associations. That's a full-time job on its own. Sometimes you've got to grease a few palms, which is worth it if you want to be included in most sites these days. Then there's Government tendering procedures, which follow the European guidelines, which are a bloody nightmare of endless paperwork and form-filling. I persevered with these and taught myself how to respond quickly to tendering opportunities. That's where the big jobs and big profits are to be found."

Boyle nodded as if he agreed. "Tell me about the job in Downpatrick in 2015. How did you get it? Not many firms from the South travel to the North."

"Got it through one of my contacts. You take what you can get, particularly when the money's good."

"And did you meet Martina Quigley while you were in Downpatrick?"

"Who?"

"She was a very attractive sixteen-year-old whose body was discovered being dumped by a man near a local river."

"Never heard of her," Kelly said morosely.

Boyle ploughed on. "What about what happened in Downpatrick a year earlier when Patti-Ann Weston went missing?"

"Same thing. I know nothing about that."

"Let's go back another two years to 2012. Were you in Downpatrick at that time, and did you know Jacinta Wilson?"

Kelly's solicitor almost leapt from his seat. "That's quite enough, Inspector. We've already covered this ground. My client did not know these girls. Can I remind you that he was interviewed, as were several hundred others, in connection with one of the disappearances? The police at the time found Mr Kelly to be highly cooperative and had no reason to continue having an interest in him."

"Doesn't mean they didn't have their suspicions," Boyle said.

"Inspector, I thought we'd agreed to move on."

"Different times, different girls, simple questions," Boyle said affably. "How many times did you visit Downpatrick?"

"You've got this all wrong," Kelly shouted. It was the first time he'd raised his voice. "I was only in Downpatrick once, in 2015. Stayed there for about three weeks on a housing contract. I never met any of the girls you mentioned."

"And you can prove that?"

Hamilton interrupted. "Do you mean can he prove he was only in Downpatrick once or that he can somehow prove he had never met the girls? The latter has already been asked and answered and frankly I don't see how he can add anymore."

"Where were you in 2012? What jobs were you working on at that time?"

"I was still in my apprenticeship then," Kelly replied with a more confident air. "It was the same thing as in Kilkenny. The firm moved us around a lot, so I'll guess you'll have to check their records to find out about the sites we worked on."

"What was the name of the firm?"

"Sporran Electrics, based in Dublin. Don't know if they're still around. Wouldn't surprise me if they've gone out of business. Didn't recognise talent when they had it."

Boyle looked across at his prisoner and decided to call it a day. "We'll take a break."

"Come on, Inspector," Hamilton pleaded. "I can't go through another one of these today. I have a ton of work waiting back at the office. Why not bail my client and arrange for a fresh session when you have something concrete? After all, he's got a job to complete and isn't going anywhere."

The solicitor's comment made Boyle smile. "Nice try, Pierce, but I think we'll keep Mr Kelly overnight until we get results from forensics on his van and digs. He'll get some fresh clothes and a hot meal and a nice bed downstairs in the cells. Your office will be contacted know when we're ready to resume tomorrow."

Chapter 27

DAYLIGHT FADED by late afternoon. The gloom in the enclosed rear yard of Mooney's Bar made everything invisible, which was why Belle had installed sensor lights as part of her recent extensive makeover. They should have kicked in the moment she stepped outside to dispose of a black plastic bag of rubbish. But they didn't. All that faced her was darkness.

Her immediate reaction was one of annoyance, not because she would have to go back inside to fetch a torch the way she did prior to the renovations, but because it was one more example of irritating faults she was finding about the workmanship of the crew who had now packed up and left the site. Cracks in the ceiling in the bar, interior doors that didn't close properly, and temperamental plumbing all added to her growing list of complaints. The site foreman had referred to them as a 'snag list' which would be attended to after three months. It was normal, he said, a case of the building settling into its new persona.

Easy for him to say, Belle thought. He wasn't the one to have to get a torch to move about the yard. He'd be getting a piece of her mind first thing in the morning.

She turned to go back inside and glanced at one of the sensor lights mounted on the wall above the door. The glass was shattered. The whole unit must have blown out. Did that mean all the new electrics were faulty? That foreman would be getting a call much sooner than first thing in the morning.

And then she heard it. A faint, muffled sound coming from the keg store on the right side of the yard. She peered through the gloom, shocked to see a flickering light dance across a small gap at the bottom of the store door. Someone was in there!

Belle was too angry to be afraid. She stomped back into the bar kitchen, retrieved a torch from a cupboard under the sink, and marched out into the yard, tracking the path provided by the powerful beam of her DeWalt square-faced LED lamp. Just as she reached the store, the door swung open and two large men emerged, each shielding his eyes from the glare which greeted them.

The first man angrily swiped the torch from Belle's grasp and pushed her roughly to the ground. A pain shot through her hips and she gasped at the thought of her baby.

"Lookee here, it's the copper's bitch," the man said as he stood menacingly over Belle's prostrate figure. "What say we rough her up some?"

"Please, no," Belle pleaded. "I'm pregnant."

The second man moved forward, a look of pure evil on a face she recognised. "That's all we need," he screamed, "another fuckface copper coming into the world. I'd be doing everyone a favour if I kicked that bastard out of you. If you want to blame somebody, then tell that good-for-nothing husband of yours to keep his nose out of other people's business."

"No, no, please don't....." She saw the thug draw back his right leg, knowing she was powerless to stop what was about to happen. She curled into a ball, her arms protectively covering her stomach.

But the assault never came. A third figure, little

more than a blurred silhouette, suddenly caught Belle's attention. She stared in disbelief as a huge fist swung through the air, catching the second man flush on the side of the head, and sending him sprawling across the yard. His legs gave way, crashing him headfirst into two large gas cylinders propped against the wall. He crumpled to the ground and remained still.

Belle recognised the unmistakeable shape of Jacko McStravick. "Oh, thank goodness," she whispered.

Jacko turned away from her to confront the other intruder. He was a half-second too slow, the realisation obvious in Jacko's face as he tried to dodge a thick rubber torch heading straight for the bridge of his nose. The slight movement diverted the torch onto Jacko's right cheek, the impact splitting his skin and sending stars across his eyes. It was a knock-out blow, at least for most men, certainly those who didn't possess Jacko's old ringcraft as a bareknuckle fighter. He'd learned how to take a punch, to stay in the fight, to not go down.

But that was a long time ago.

Jacko staggered, feeling the strength race from his body. He could barely lift his arm to ward off the next blow, which caught him on the side of the neck, and a third, which glanced off the back of his head, finally bowling him over. He fell beside Belle, knowing he was out of the fight, and cursing his weakness for not being able to defend her. The grey fuzz in his head slowly darkened and he passed out.

"Jacko, Jacko, please wake up!"

Belle's voice brought him to the surface, his eyes slowly adjusting to his surroundings. He was still in Mooney's yard, lying on the damp concrete, his head cradled in Belle's lap. He felt as if his skull was on fire, with waves of pain queuing up to wash ashore every few seconds. He had trouble seeing out of one eye, but he shook his predicament aside to stare at Belle, not quite believing she was the one offering comfort.

"What the hell, Belle, are you alright? Where are those two bastards?"

"I'm okay, Jacko, thanks to you. They've gone."

McStravick sat up gingerly, wiping blood from his cheek, and checking the yard in case Belle had only imagined the flight of the assailants. "Did they touch you after I passed out? Are you sure you're alright?"

"Stop fussing over me, Jacko. We need to get you to hospital. I think you're going to need a few stitches and get checked over for concussion."

The big man brushed aside her words and rose to his feet, offering his hand to ease Belle from her seated position. "No hospitals or doctors. A drop of your finest brandy and a pint of stout will have me dancing a jig in no time."

Belle tried to force down a smile, but it was a losing battle. "I swear, Jacko, you are the most incorrigible man I've ever known. I'll make a deal with you. Doubles all round, provided you don't tell Mick about this."

"Don't you know who those cowards were?"

"Yes," Belle admitted. "I recognised Jerome Flynn, and I'm guessing the other one was his brother Seamus."

"Yeah, Big Paud's excuses for sons. Why don't you want Mick to know? Those two need locking up, although I wouldn't mind five minutes alone with them before that happens."

Belle linked her arm through McStravick's and guided him towards the keg store. She wanted to see what her intruders had been up to but, more importantly, she didn't want anyone to overhear what she had to say. It was an enclosed yard, but you never knew who was walking by on the footpath outside the rear wall.

Damage to the store was minimal. Belle reckoned she must have interrupted the men before they'd got started on trashing the place. Their intentions had been obvious, judging by a sledgehammer lying on the floor beside two smashed pumps and three upended kegs, still with their feeds to the bar attached to the neck fittings. She knew the hammer did not belong to the pub. They must have brought it with them.

Belle breathed a sigh of relief and turned towards McStravick. "We got off lightly. God, they could have caused us a lot of grief, certainly enough to put us out of commission for a good while. Whatever's happening between the Flynns and Mick is getting out of control, if this is what they're resorting to."

"Is that why you don't want Mick to know? Don't you think it would be best if you told him what's happened here and let him nip this thing in the bud?"

"C'mon, Jacko, you know Mick. The first thing he'll want to do is go round there and knock a few heads together, particularly if he knows that they assaulted me."

"And why is that so bad? Those fellas have got a beating coming."

Belle shook her head vigorously. "And just

where would that leave Mick? He's a policeman and he's supposed to act accordingly. He's had a bee in his bonnet about Big Paud Flynn for the past year and I'm worried he'd let this cloud his judgement. It could be the end of his career if he turns up on the Flynn doorstep and starts throwing punches."

"Yeah, I can see that" McStravick said. "Any man would do the same. I still think you're wrong to keep Mick in the dark."

"It has to be this way. You've got to promise me, Jacko, that you'll keep quiet about this."

"Since when have you ever known me to go blabbering to the police? Goes against the grain to be a tout. Seriously though, I'll keep your secret."

She reached up and pecked McStravick on the cheek. "Thank you, Jacko, you can have free breakfasts every morning."

"Oh, you'll certainly be seeing a lot more of me, I guarantee it. Someone will have to keep an eye on you in case those bastards try something else."

"I don't need protection, but I love you for offering it."

The big man blushed and turned away, his face suddenly a mask of anger. If Mick Boyle couldn't exact revenge on the Flynns, it was down to Jacko McStravick to see they got their comeuppance.

Chapter 28

THE QUOILE RIVER in Downpatrick is a largely benign waterway which offers little evidence of its former glory as a busy shipping channel. It was from here that a paddle steamer service to Liverpool once operated from Steamboat Quay, which also served the nearby town with supplies of coal, timber, and slate. All that remains of the river's commercial heyday is the burnt out timbers of an old sailing ship, which found a final resting place on the riverbank, coincidentally a distance of only a few hundred yards from where a killer had been interrupted while trying to dispose of the body of Martina Quigley in 2015.

Five years after that tragic event, eight frogmen finally entered the river in search of its secrets. They were members of the PSNI Underwater Search Team, who spread out in fifty-yard gaps following the Quoile's natural flow towards a tidal barrier at Strangford Lough, the largest inlet in the British Isles and a gateway to the Irish Sea. In parts, the river was shallow enough to wade through, although most of its seven-mile length required diving to depths of more than thirty feet. The initial quadrant chosen for the search was less than two miles, a stretch that would take the searchers more than two days to complete. After that, they would try downstream, an unlikely alternative, given the nature of tidal flows, but one that had to be followed. The orders from above had been clear. Leave no riverbed stone unturned.

The activity drew interest from passers-by on a tourist footpath that followed the Quoile's meandering path. The police could have sealed off three car parks which serviced the area at various points, but in the end it was decided it simply wasn't worth the hassle or the resources needed. News of the activity would leak out, whether the public was close up or cordoned off at a distance.

The Underwater Search Team's briefing had been less than enthusiastic. This was little more than a PR exercise, a cross-border cooperation thing that was more to do with politics than with policing. No prospect of finding anything. Still, the men needed to keep up with their training and test new equipment. Always look for an upside.

The man in charge of the divers was having none of the negativity. His men were professionals, used to dealing with high-stress situations, and methodical in their approach. This would be no different. The search would be as slow and as painstaking as any they had carried out. Each diver was given a grid, bank-to-bank and for thirty yards in breadth. Stop and surface for a five-minute break every fifteen minutes, tea and biscuits at 11.00, sandwiches at 14.00.

They entered the water at exactly 0800. Each man carried probe sticks and side-scan sonar equipment capable of detecting buried human remains. Two dinghies were used for the deeper stretches and an onshore magnetometer was on hand to analyse materials which were considered by the divers to be worth a second look. Experience had taught them that a piece of debris, perhaps broken off from a larger item, could give a clue to a much bigger discovery.

The morning tea came and went, so too the afternoon sandwiches. The search quadrant had shrunk considerably, although more than a mile still remained untouched within the target area. Another two hours would lead to a halt being called to proceedings. Then they would come back the next morning and start all over again.

Except they didn't need to.

Twenty minutes after resuming from the sandwich break, one of the divers surfaced and signalled frantically to the onshore supervisor. He could have taken off his scuba breathing apparatus and shouted his message across the thirty-yard expanse. Instead, he used hand gestures, the meaning clear from the constant pull-down of his right arm. It was like someone playing a one-arm-bandit coin machine. *Jackpot!*

Boyle was at home, his mind in a turmoil from the events of the day. The business with the break-in at the Flynn complex was a distraction he could do without. It didn't look good that he was captured on CCTV outside the premises, even more so because of the clever stacking of harassment incidents which had been compiled by Big Paud's lawyer. Best case scenario was that that the complaint would be left on the back burner for a few weeks. Worst case? He could be pulled off active duties while the matter was being investigated.

Boyle knew the paperwork had already made its way to the Assistant Commissioner's office for Governance and Accountability. The good news, if it could be called that, was that the AC's office would have to refer the matter directly to the GSOC, an independent statutory body whose sole function was to deal with complaints against the police by members of the public. The wheels were known to grind slowly within the Garda Síochána Ombudsman Commission, a fact Boyle was hoping would work in his favour.

The Commission could demand that Boyle be placed on administrative leave, which was highly unlikely because of the average nine-month period they took to conclude investigations of complaints, or that he be reassigned to desk duties, also unlikely, given that Boyle had already consulted with his own acronym, the AGSI, the association of Garda Sergeants and Inspectors, which was not a union, because it was unlawful for a member of the force to join a union, but which to all intents and purposes was exactly that. The AGSI rep had assured Boyle that his back would be covered.

It didn't mean he was in the clear. For starters, he would have to attend an initial complaint briefing in Dublin sometime over the next two days. It was a monumental pain the neck, a date Boyle had no intention of keeping. He had more important things to deal with.

Which brought his attention back to the aftermath of the second interview with Michael Kelly.

Boyle hadn't liked the way things had gone. The longer he had sat with Kelly, the more convinced he'd been that he was not the man they were looking for. There was just something in the way Kelly had deported himself during the two sessions, giving none of the usual 'tells' that guilty people tended to transmit through body language, such as pupil dilations, throat-swallowing movements, or nervous tics. Boyle kept his views to himself when he'd asked Dr Dunne and Paul Brogan to join him in his office.

"Let's get straight down to it, Doc, do you think we've just been sitting across the table from a kidnapper and murderer?"

"Usually I'd need at least three or four interviews before forming a definitive opinion," Dunne said, "but I sense you want a knee-jerk reaction which I'm happy to give you, with the proviso that my opinion might change if I had further access to Mr Kelly."

"Knee-jerk will do for now."

"Okay, here it is, and you're not going to like it. No, I don't think Kelly is a kidnapper and murderer. He's certainly capable of it, and he's got a lot of personality traits that fit the profile, but there were just too many significant markers that makes me think he would fall short of actually committing these crimes."

Boyle decided to play Devil's Advocate. "What about all that psycho-babble about the man we want being full of his own importance and having issues with women. You heard him in there, spouting off about how good a businessman he is and how his previous employers didn't know talent when they saw it. And what about all that love-em-and-leave-em demeaning attitude about girlfriends?"

Dunne smiled. "The latter statement could be attributed to a dozen men I know. As for the rest of it, there's no doubt that Kelly sees himself superior to those around him. There are narcissistic elements to what he says and believes but, in my opinion, they are defence mechanisms, barriers, if you like, that he's put up to protect himself from certain vulnerabilities."

"I didn't see any vulnerabilities."

"These come from his background," said Dunne. "He had a pretty miserable childhood, what with the early death of his mother, the presence of an alcoholic father, and the pressure on him to help raise a younger brother. Despite all this, he stuck to his studies and had the will to take himself off to college to learn a trade. Not just that, he started his own business, one that he seems to have made quite a success of. Everything has been a challenge and continues to be so. That's why he's probably a bit of a loner, defending himself against returning to his former status as a general dogsbody who was supposed to do everything that a missing father should have done."

Brogan chirped in. "Why couldn't he be all that and still a killer?"

"Good question," Dunne said. "He could be all these things, an independent soul, a successful businessman, and a hands-off individual, while still being a killer. However, I get the impression that Kelly is driven by a different type of obsession. He needs to be successful which means being better than anyone around him. There's no room for anything else, much less a time-consuming crusade that could eventually result in him being locked up for life. In his own mind, I think Michael Kelly considers he's already been locked up for too long because of his childhood and that he enjoys the freedom of making his way under his own terms. That's why it doesn't surprise me that he's cut ties with his former life, for example his father and brother. They simply don't fit in with this new confident, upwardly mobile entrepreneur. He has goals yet to be attained and which require his full focus."

"So, on balance, you would rule him out?" Boyle asked.

Dunne was non-committal. "I'd still like to hear some more from Kelly. People have a habit for surprising you with their ability to mask true emotions, in much the same way that lie-detector tests can be rendered useless by certain individuals. The human psyche is capable of multi-levels of deception. The trick is to find out what level Kelly is on."

Chapter 29

BOYLE WAS IN the spare room again. He wanted time to figure things out, which meant a few hours of heavy reading under a bedside lamp, not something that would have been fair on Belle. She had looked tired and drained when he'd arrived home and was unusually quiet. He reckoned the pregnancy was taking a toll on her, even if she was doing her best to hide it from him. He'd kissed her goodnight and promised to slip out quietly in the morning.

Propped up on three pillows, he started turning the pages of the typed interview manuscripts, hoping to find something that he'd missed, something that changed his mind about Kelly being the killer. In the hours that followed the interviews, he had become more and more convinced that they were heading down a blind alley with Kelly, a view that seemed to be shared by the psychiatrist, Dr Dunne, notwithstanding her reticence about fully committing to the man's innocence.

Before he had left the station, Boyle had presided over a full briefing with his team. There was no positive news. The searches of Kelly's home in Dublin, his digs in Castlebar, and his work vehicle had yielded no evidence, damning or otherwise, that Kelly had had any connections to the missing teenagers. Various items of clothing and carpets from the van had been sent for forensic analysis to the laboratory in Galway. It would be at least another twenty-four hours before any results were back.

The massive Garda search for the two local girls had so far drawn a blank, despite covering hundreds of miles of land around Castlebar and Westport, stopping more than two thousand vehicles at random checkpoints, and being given access to hundreds of homes and outbuildings in housing estates and remote farmhouses. For the moment, the girls had simply vanished into thin air.

Boyle knew the uniform officers would keep going. They took this kind of thing personally, partly because it was on their own patch, but mostly because there were a lot of married men and women within their ranks. What if it was my daughter? It was a question that would push them through the exhaustion barrier. They would grab little sleep until Megan and Siobhan were found.

Boyle glanced at his watch. It had just gone past midnight, meaning that Megan's disappearance was entering the eighth day and Siobhan's was now in its third day. Hope of finding them alive was dwindling exponentially with each passing hour. Somehow, Boyle needed to bring fresh impetus to the enquiry, either by proving Kelly was responsible or by cutting him loose and changing direction.

Which was why he was pouring through the notes from Kelly's interview. *Find something, dammit!*

His first read-through of more than twenty typed pages was a quick go-around, intended to focus his thoughts before a more detailed line-by-line dissection. The transcriber had done a brilliant job, arranging the text in short, manageable paragraphs, and printing it out in a double-space format that was easy on the eyes. Here and there,

Boyle underlined a sentence, or drew an asterisk on the generous side margins to remind him to take a closer look at a section during the second reading.

There was nothing much in Kelly's first interview. All the talking at the suspect's side of the table was done by his solicitor, Pierce Hamilton. Boyle re-read only a few parts of the notes.

Inspector Boyle: *I want to fast forward to the present and the two missing teenagers from Castlebar during the past fortnight. Lo and behold, once again we find Michael Gerard Kelly at the scene.*

Mr Hamilton: *Hardly at the scene, Inspector. Be fair. The man's work takes him all over the country. These are merely coincidences.*

Inspector Boyle: *Twice maybe could be construed as a coincidence, but it's stretching it a bit to suggest that three times is anything except a pattern which puts your client in a tricky spot as far as alibis go.*

Mr Hamilton: *What you have is little more than circumstantial. You're tilting at windmills without a shred of proof that my client had anything to do with the sad disappearance of these poor girls.*

Boyle threw the manuscript down in disgust and lifted the second bundle of stapled notes. There was much more meat here for him to get his teeth into. This was the session that Kelly got the chance to speak, and somewhere in here, Boyle reckoned, was a clue to his uneasiness about Kelly's guilt. He scanned a number of sections but stopped at one particular piece of dialogue.

Inspector Boyle: *How come you get so much work around the country?*

Mr Kelly: *You've got to cultivate your contacts. They're known in the business world as key referrals, influential people who can refer potential customers in your direction with a recommendation that they use* *your services. Big builders, small builders, architects, surveyors, developers, and housing associations.*

And there it was! That's what had been nagging at Boyle. So far, the investigation of the various building sites around the country had centred on building companies and their sub-contractors and site workmen. There was a whole raft of other people who would have regular access and a reason to be present at such sites. Kelly had laid it all out for him – architects, surveyors, developers, and housing associations. Professionals who came and went and were so far overlooked in the attempts to trace potential suspects. And Boyle had missed it!

The next piece of text made him cringe even more.

Inspector Boyle: *Tell me about the job in Downpatrick in 2015. How did you get it? Not many firms from the South travel to the North.*
Mr Kelly: *Got it through one of my contacts. You take what you can get, particularly when the money's good.*

Boyle thumped the crumpled pages in disgust. He hadn't asked the obvious follow-up questions. Who was the contact? How many other jobs had Kelly got through this particular person or company? Rookie mistake. How the hell had he let this slip past him? The potential in this was enormous, particularly if Kelly was proven to be innocent. Boyle was still convinced that building sites were a strong lead, so if Kelly were not the link, could there be someone else among the list of professionals who had been on sites in Kilkenny, Cork, Downpatrick, and Castlebar?

He reached for his iPhone and punched in Brogan's number. His wristwatch told him it was just after two in the morning.

"Do you realise what time it is?" Brogan answered good-naturedly.

"Sorry about this, Paul, are you at home?"

"Yes, I left Custer Armstrong and two others to hold the fort. What's up?"

Boyle talked Brogan through his theory. "We need to get on this, pronto."

"Agreed," Brogan replied. "I'll get Custer to start checking all the site information again. There could be something in the files or online that will help us fill in some blanks, but failing that, I'll get him to start making phone calls. Don't see why I should be the only one who gets woken up in the dead of night."

"In the meantime, I'll contact Hamilton, the solicitor, to see how early he can meet us at the station. I think Kelly is best placed to help us kickstart this new line of enquiry. I'd love to wake him up now, but if we talk to him without Hamilton's presence there could be hell to play."

"Yeah, not worth the hassle, Mick. Oh, there's one more thing. The police up North reckon they've found a body in that river in Downpatrick. News just came through a few hours ago, but things are a bit sketchy. They're keeping their cards close to their chests until they can make a positive identification."

"It's got to be one of those other missing teenagers, Jacinta Wilson or Patti-Ann Weston." The names of all the potential victims over the past twelve years were ingrained in Boyle's memory.

"Sure looks that way. Our PSNI friend, Inspector Bonnaville, legged it as soon as he heard. Says he wants to be there for the confirmation and to be the first to tell the family. He has certainly taken this whole thing to heart and has promised to keep in touch with us as soon as he is sure of anything."

"He's a good man, Paul. We can be confident of hearing from him." Deep down, Boyle was delighted that his hunch about the river had been confirmed. He'd risked a lot by demanding the Garda bigwigs brought pressure to bear on the PSNI for a full-scale dredge. Sometimes it worked, oftentimes it didn't. This time, Boyle had just banked a lot of credit. He might need it in the days ahead, particularly with the Flynn complaint hanging around his neck.

Chapter 30

MEGAN AND SIOBHAN hugged each other tightly. They were sitting on a blanket of towels on the hard tiles of the kitchen floor, wondering what had happened to their abductor. He hadn't been home in more than thirty hours, the first time he had been away from the place for so long. Maybe he had an accident or, better still, maybe the police had caught him! They had allowed their hopes to soar over many hours, but now they were back to brooding about the hopelessness of their situation. No-one was going to come crashing through the door to their rescue. If they were going to get out of this place alive, they would have to do it by themselves.

Before they could do anything, they needed to get out of their chains. Megan had previously used a kitchen knife to force the lock around her ankle, but it wouldn't budge. The kidnapper had noticed the scrapes on the metal and had beaten her mercilessly, with a warning that if she tried it again he would kill her. She had believed him.

"It's useless," she told Siobhan, as she rattled the chain. "It's one of those mortice-type locks that's virtually impenetrable."

Siobhan didn't reply. She stood up and grabbed the chain, moving across the floor to trace its path to the point where it was fixed to the wall. It was a low-down anchor point, a square metal plate that was fixed to the wall with a large bolt, the sort that must have been drilled deep to secure the macabre fitting.

"We'll never get that off," Megan snorted.

"I know, but what if we were able to dig around it? These are old walls and the cement might give away easily."

Megan stared at the fixture. "We haven't got any tools. We'd need a hammer and chisel to make even a dent in the wall."

Siobhan smiled and hobbled over to the cutlery drawer. "We'll use whatever we can find," she said, fishing out two dinner knives and a pair of scissors.

"What if we get nowhere and just make a lot of mess? He's bound to see that we were up to."

"Fuck him," Siobhan said angrily. "What's the worst he can do, kill us? He's going to do that anyway. What have we got lose?"

Megan sniffled back a tear. "Let's do it."

Three hours later, with cuts on their fingers and blisters on the palms of their hands, the girls sat back exhausted and surveyed their work. They had started with a frantic attack on the brickwork, their efforts slowly running out of energy, as the blades of a dozen knives snapped and littered the floor. But they kept at it, going through the cutlery drawer with determination. They were down to the last few forks and spoons when Siobhan called a halt and brushed loose gravel from the small hole they'd made around the plate which held the screw.

The opening was about two inches in depth. It revealed the twisting spiral of the bolt disappearing into the brickwork. They had no way of knowing how far in it went. There could be another six inches, in which case there was no hope of completing the task before their kidnapper returned. The girls helped themselves to a drink from the kitchen tap and sat down on the floor, despair evident on both their faces.

Siobhan's gaze travelled across the room, eventually stopping on a brush propped against the rear door. An idea formed in her head. They could stick the brush into the gap they'd made between the plate and the wall and use it as a lever to prise the bolt away from its stubborn recess. She jumped up and rushed over to pick up the brush, explaining her thoughts to Megan as she jammed the brush into the hole.

Both girls strained hard, pulling the brush towards them, the veins in their necks swelling with the effort. Despite the pain of the blisters in their hands, they kept going until a strange wrenching sound emitted from the wall. The bolt was moving! Then the brush snapped, and they fell backwards, a tumble that seemed to drain away the last of their enthusiasm. They both started crying simultaneously, each lying on their back, staring at the ceiling.

Megan was first to stir from the melancholy. She raised herself on an elbow and stared at the broken brush, one half still wedged behind wall plate, the other half lying on the floor. "Hey, we now have two levers! Double the effort, double the chances."

The girls quickly moved back to their original positions, readjusting the pieces of brush shaft to the sides of the bolt. They each pulled back on their new levers, moaning and screaming with the effort. The bolt emitted another cringing sound – it was definitely moving.

A wash of bright light suddenly lit up the

corners of the kitchen. It filtered in through the windows in a glare that could only have come from outside the house. It must be car headlights. Which meant only one thing – the kidnapper had returned! Megan and Siobhan stared at each other, fright evident on their pale faces. They looked at the mess on the floor, knowing there was no way to cover up what they'd been doing before he entered the room through the hallway leading from the front of the building.

Their fear and trepidation were replaced a minute later by the sound of a thunder rattle which seemed to bounce off the surrounding trees with a welcome series of echoes. The light they had seen was not from a car, but from a lightning strike which had preceded one of nature's noisiest roars.

The realisation sent a burst of renewed hope through their bodies. They got back on their knees and restarted the attack on the metal plate and its captive bolt. Adrenaline coursed through their bodies and added strength to their assault. Suddenly, the bolt gave up its stubborn resistance and eased away from its housing. The metal plate and the bolt fell to the floor between the girls' knees.

They were free.

They stood rigid for several moments, not quite sure what to do. The back door to the cottage was bolted shut and was never used. Their kidnapper always used the front door at a part of the house they had never seen before. That was their obvious means of escape, though they had no way of knowing what lay beyond. Where were they? Where could they run to for help?

As if by telepathy, they gathered up their chains and walked gingerly towards the door leading to the hallway. It was dark outside, and the only ambient light came from the kitchen fluorescent, which didn't show them all the way forward.

"Fuck it," Siobhan said, reaching for a switch on the wall. The sparkle of light made them blink and turn away, but it was only a momentary delay. They rushed down the space, bumping against each other as they tried to synchronise the restriction caused by being linked together at the ankles with the same chain. Before they reached the front door, Megan peered into a room, guessing it was their kidnapper's private place.

"Wait", she said, we need to find some coats. "It will be cold out."

Siobhan nodded her agreement. The girls stepped into the room, found a light switch, and began rummaging in a standalone wardrobe. They each selected an overcoat, threw them over their shoulders, and walked back to the front door. Mercifully, there was a thumb-turn handle which rotated easily, allowing a gust of cold air to rush by them. They walked outside and looked around.

They were surrounded by tall trees and could just make out a lane which ran in both directions at the front of the house. A white van was parked against a small garage. Siobhan, who was just a few months short of her seventeenth birthday, had started driving lessons with her father in a disused quarry compound, and knew she could handle the vehicle enough to make a quick getaway. But when they tried the doors on the van, they were locked. There was no time to go searching for a key, especially if it meant going back into a house they had no intentions of ever stepping foot in again.

They turned towards the lane and agreed to go

right, knowing that was the direction they had heard the kidnapper come and go. There was thick foliage on either side of the lane, so they agreed to stay on the track until they heard the sounds of any approaching car. They set off, their eyes refusing to help cut through the gloom of the night. They were in the middle of nowhere, with trees cutting out any prospect of help from the night sky, which itself had turned to inky blackness ahead of a thunderstorm.

They linked arms and stumbled forwards, trying to keep to the centre of the potholed lane, but discovering every few yards that they were wandering unknowingly against the tall-grass fringes, beyond which stood large menacing trees, silent and foreboding sentries ready to block any attempts at escape. They quickly became totally disorientated. To make matters worse, the rain started, drizzly at first, then heavy straight-down spikes that added to their cold and misery. They tripped over their chains several times, and with each fall they knew they couldn't continue.

Reluctantly, they left the lane and felt their way into the fringes of the forest, stopping at the first big tree trunk and sinking to the ground in total despair. They both realised they should have searched the cottage for a torch and brought food and water. But it was too late to turn back.

They wrapped their coats tightly against their bodies, huddled together, and fell asleep,

They were less than two-hundred yards from the cottage.

Chapter 31

BOYLE WALKED INTO a flurry of activity, not to mention a thoroughly disgruntled senior solicitor, who was pacing across the front counter in the Castlebar station. It was 7.00am on Saturday morning, day four of Siobhan Cunningham's disappearance and day nine for Megan McGrath.

Pierce Hamilton greeted Boyle with a snarl. "You'd better have a damn good reason for this request at such at an ungodly hour on my day off."

"Relax, Pierce, I promised you a few hours ago that it would be worth your client's while to talk to me as soon as possible. I genuinely believe he can help us move the spotlight away from himself and down another avenue."

"Are you saying you are prepared to release him if he cooperates?"

Boyle knew he had to come clean. "Look, I can't let him go until the forensics are in, but what I will say is that I'm leaning towards Kelly being innocent. Work with me and I promise to move things forward as quickly as possible. I just need a few names from him."

"I'll need more than that, Mick."

Boyle ushered Hamilton into a side room and explained his theory about the range of professionals engaged on building sites. "Our initial thoughts were that the kidnapper was hiding among the workers, and for a time we were even convinced it had to be an electrician, which was why we concentrated on Kelly. I admit it was a bit of the cart-before-the-horse reaction after discovering Kelly's presence at the sites in Cork, Downpatrick, and Castlebar during the times of the disappearance of the girls. That might have blinded us to the fact that maybe there were other people on those sites on the same dates. We're obviously chasing down that angle, but your client can help to speed that along."

Hamilton came to a quick decision. "Give me five minutes with my client and then you can see him."

The subsequent interview with Kelly lasted just fifteen minutes. By agreement, it was not formally recorded, which helped to put Kelly at ease, and he showed a new willingness to cooperate. He could offer little information about those who were on site with him in Cork, explaining, not unreasonably, that he was still an apprentice and took little notice of those around him, particularly men in suits. He was more knowledgeable and forthcoming about the sites in Downpatrick and Castlebar, where he was a sub-contractor, having started his own business by then.

He supplied the names of key professionals, including those who have helped him get the electrical contracting work through the 'referral' arrangements he had explained at the second of his formal interviews. At the end of the session, Boyle was left with five names.

Ernest Magorrian, main building contractor.
Basil Tweedy, Quantity Surveyor.
Colm McIvor, Mechanical Engineer.
Owen Patterson, Architect.
Michael Holding, Housing Contract Manager.

The sheet of scribbled names was in Boyle's hand when he raced into the upstairs Incident Room within minutes of ending his chat with Kelly. All the desks were manned, a fact that didn't escape Boyle's notice as he threaded his way to the front of the room. Garda detectives were known to put their shoulder to the wheel when circumstances demanded.

Paul Brogan was writing on a whiteboard as Boyle moved up to his shoulder. The surface of the board was roughly boxed out into four squares headed by the names of the locations where girls had gone missing –

Kilkenny
Cork
Downpatrick
Castlebar.

Inside each square were lists of names that Boyle knew were persons already identified as being present on building sites near these cities and towns on the dates of the disappearances of the teenagers. The detective team had certainly been working hard during the night, red-eyed with file cross-referencing, punching numbers, and waking people from their sleep. They had coaxed and cajoled a directory of names of anyone with any reason to be near the sites, including skip-hire companies, roofing specialists, heavy machinery drivers, bricklayers, plasterers, landscapers, and interior designers. They were adding to the list almost every hour and were still waiting to track down some more people who could help them expand the search.

Boyle held up the list supplied by Kelly, quickly shifting his gaze back and forth to the whiteboard, but realising there were just too many names to read.

Brogan came to the rescue. "Call out your names and I'll check what we have so far from each location."

The buzz in the room tailed off as Boyle called out his names and the locations associated with them. One by one, Brogan responded with two standard replies:

Check, already here.
Not listed, I'll add the name.

Several minutes later the process was completed. Boyle and Brogan stepped back to look at the results, aware that they were joined by the other detectives, now gathered in a semi-circle around the whiteboard.

"There!" The shout was from Custer Armstrong, who stepped forward to jab a finger into each one of the squares. "This guy is here, here, and here. Three out of four can't be a coincidence, can it?"

"Hang on a moment," shouted IRC Colin McCartney, "here's another one who's in three of the four locations." He pointed at one of the names."

Boyle's spirits began to soar. "We need at least one hit that fills all four squares."

Brogan nodded. "Our big problem is the Kilkenny site. Too long ago and not enough detail about what went on there and who were the key players. It was a big commercial job, a combination of shops and offices in an out-of-town site. The contractor has since gone bust, which means all we've had to go on for the moment is standard information held online by the Department of Housing, Planning and Local Government. We should know more in about an hour or so when the Department's offices open up for the day."

"Don't put all our eggs in one basket," Boyle

replied. "Contact our Kilkenny station and task a few detectives with chasing down some names on the ground. Get them to speak to the contractor to see if he has any old records, and what about interviewing the owners of the development. They'll know who they paid money to for their new shops and office complex."

Brogan flicked his head towards Armstrong, who immediately dived for his desk and lifted the telephone.

Boyle stood silent for a moment, looking at the scroll of names, willing one of them to jump out at him. It wasn't going to happen, he knew, but at least they had a starting point, or rather two. "Listen up, everyone, I know you've had a long night and are going to have to face an even longer day. Keep adding to these names and pay attention to anyone else who starts to fill the boxes. Flag up the three-timers immediately and, needless to say, punch an alarm button if we get a hit in all four squares. For the moment we concentrate on the two names we know were at least three of the sites."

All eyes drilled back to two circled names on the whiteboard.

Owen Patterson, Architect.
Basil Tweedy, Quantity Surveyor.

Chapter 32

SEVENTY MILES from the Incident Room, Owen Patterson turned off the main road and steered his silver Audi A8 into the narrow opening at the front of the lane. The turn-off wasn't signed, nor was it visible to passing motorists unless they knew where to look. Vegetation had all but screened the gap from view, although the remainder of the three-mile lane was slightly wider.

Patterson, not his real name, regretted the small entranceway scratches on the bodywork of his seventy-grand motor. But, hey, he changed regularly every two years and always got the best trade-in offers, so what was the big deal? Besides, he was a self-made man with an ample reserve of cash. He could afford to take a hit on general wear and tear and depreciation of asset value.

The Audi's suspension was not built for the potholed surface. The low wheelbase meant reducing his speed to barely twenty miles per hour, particularly if he wanted to avoid scraping the bottom of the chassis or causing more serious damage to the hydraulics or driveshaft.

Daylight filtered down through the tree covering, although he needed sidelights to cut the natural gloom of the track. He'd been away since first light yesterday morning, scoping out potential sites to dump the bodies of the two girls. He wanted to do it close to Castlebar, but police activity in the area was just too great. He had taken the Audi and wore his best suit to avoid suspicion as he cruised approach roads to the town, quickly fanning out his search on a wider circumference, that took in nearby towns. He spent part of the night in a hotel in Westport and checked out two hours ago to finish his surveillance. Finally, he had found what he was looking for.

It was an old office-block building at the entrance to an industrial estate, which was still used by several businesses located in warehouses at sites dotted behind the dilapidated offices. That meant there would be vehicles coming and going past the site entrance. Which meant that if he propped the bodies of the girls against the wire-meshed front gates of the entrance block, they would be noticed fairly quickly. Around three or four o'clock in the morning would be the best time for the disposal.

His mind was made up.

He bumped over the last of the potholes as the cottage came into view. He had taken a gamble on using the building, but he knew how the owner operated. It was one of a number of such places the man owned in remote places, which were used as little more than dumping grounds for the storage of valuables he liked to keep away from the attention of the authorities. The sites were rarely visited. It would defeat the purpose of their existence to do otherwise.

Patterson knew there would be a stash of cash. There always was with this guy. And he knew where to look for it. It was always the same. A mock pig pen constructed somewhere in the grounds, shaped and cemented and hinged with a steel door. Lock in the stash and cover the surface with pig shit and manure. No-one would think of looking too closely, much less start scrambling around in the filth.

But Patterson had no such qualms. He found the foul compound almost immediately. It was butted against the left side of the cottage and give up its treasures after a frenzied attack with a shovel, which Patterson had grabbed from the garage. He hit the jackpot with a box of vacuum-packed Euros, a bigger haul than he'd expected, but the bastard could afford it. Besides, he owed Patterson a lot more than that! There were also bundles of drugs, five or six different varieties, each distinctively coloured, and showing through their wrappers as a mixture of pills and powder. He had ripped open the packages and scattered the contents into the soil and manure. It was an exquisite memory.

Patterson parked the Audi and stood for a moment to stretch out the stiffness in his back. He glanced towards the side of the building, his eyes falling on a window to the kitchen where he knew the girls would be. He would get this over quickly. No sense in having to look at them and listen to their pathetic moans for any longer than necessary. He would strangle them, put their bodies in the back of the old work van, and rest up for the remainder of the day.

He walked to the front of the cottage and froze. The door was swinging on its hinges. He raced inside, throwing open the door to the kitchen, and taking in the destruction of the wall where the chain had been bolted. His heart skipped a beat, wondering if the police had somehow found his captives. But that would mean the place would be crawling with people, unless of course they were hiding out there, waiting to spring a trap.

The idea was pushed away as soon as he saw the broken knives and brush shaft. They girls had obviously freed themselves, something which in other circumstances he might have praised them for. But their actions had now placed him in jeopardy. He needed to find them, or failing that, he needed to get as far away from this place as possible.

He pulled over a stool, slumped down, and let what he called his 'methodical reasoning' take stock of the situation. They couldn't have made it too far, certainly not to the end of the laneway. If they had, the sight of them in chains would have meant someone picking them up immediately, which would have led the police directly here, assuming the pick-up was longer than twenty or thirty minutes ago. If it had happened in less time than that, then he still had some wriggle room, but not much.

Stay or go? He weighed the pros and cons as dispassionately as if he were drawing lines on a scaled map of a new building project. After a few minutes, he found the scales evenly tipped. But they were always going to come down on only one side of the equation. *They can't be allowed to live.*

Patterson stormed back up the hall and into his private den. In the bottom drawer of an old cupboard he rummaged around until he found a torch and one more important item. It was wrapped in greaseproof paper, the smell of gun oil obvious as soon as he lifted it free. A Colt Python double-action revolver chambered for .357 Magnum cartridges, enough to blow a fist-sized hole through the little bitches. Or any cop who got in his way.

Before he could do anything, he needed to get ready for a flight to safety. He scrambled to the side of the bed and retrieved a large cardboard box, which contained the cash he'd found in the garage. He carried it outside and paused to look at the Audi, reluctantly deciding to abandon it. If the police learned about him from the girls, they would tie him to the vehicle in no time. Better to take the van. He would get another Audi when he settled in a new location with a new name.

He had already decided to torch the cottage, so now the Audi would have to go up in flames with it. He lifted a bunch of keys from his pocket, opened the rear door of the van, and tossed in the cardboard box, covering it with an old painter's sheet, which lay among a jumbled mess of tools. Next, he walked to the garage, emerging with a five-gallon drum of kerosene that he placed behind the van. He would set his fires as soon as he disposed of the girls.

He patted down his clothes, checked the revolver in his right-hand coat pocket, and started a slow walk back up the lane.

Megan had heard the sound of the car engine first. She prodded Siobhan and both listened to it drive past to the left of their location. To their horror, they heard it stop within a few minutes, the sound of the door opening and closing confirming that they were closer to the cottage that they'd thought. He would find them if they didn't do something quickly.

They were cold and tired and stiff all over. At least there was a bit of light that showed the forest in all its majesty, the rows of trees stretching hundreds of yards away until they were swallowed up in the distant gloom. That's where they needed to head to.

The going was tough on them. The forest floor was uneven, littered by debris from the trees and pitted with indents caused by burrowing animals. There were clumps of bushes, most with prickly points, and clusters of nettles that grabbed at their already swollen ankles, adding another layer of pain that made it impossible to make much progress. But they stumbled stoically onwards, cutting a zig-zag path that made them reach out gratefully for the comfort of each tree they passed.

Fear drove them forward, despite the noise they were making and the dread of being discovered. The farther they made it into the comfort of the forest, the better their chances of getting away. At least that's what they tried to convince each other about.

Until they heard the sounds of footsteps and saw the sweep of a torchlight bounce of a tall tree immediately ahead of them.

Chapter 33

BIG PAUD FLYNN was feeling pleased with himself. Things couldn't have gone better over the last twenty-four hours, thanks to a break-in at his depot that would have caused him to go apoplectic with rage in any other circumstances. No, this one had a silver lining in the shape of his nemesis, Garda Detective Inspector Mick Bloody Boyle, being caught where he shouldn't have been. It was pure poetry!

Seeing Boyle on the CCTV system at the time of the incident was a gift from heaven, a chance to finally nail the bastard by ensuring he would be kept permanently away from Big Paud's business interests. Things could pick up again, all wheels turning just as fully as they were before Boyle had started throwing spanners in the works.

Of course, Big Paud admitted with a grin, the image of the intruder inside the compound was not really Boyle. At the same time as one camera picked up the intruder smashing vehicles and windows, another camera showed Boyle driving away from the front of the site. However, that particular piece of information was not one that Big Paud was willing to share with anyone, including his barrister, the honourable Myles Winstanley, who himself was too eager to make a case against Boyle.

The feed from the interior camera had already been wiped. No sense risking a subpoena for evidence discovery, not when there was a sufficient compelling pointer placing Boyle in a tricky situation. Circumstantial it might be, but highly prejudicial and embarrassing for Boyle nonetheless, particularly when set beside a lot of other stuff that Winstanley had carefully crafted to show blatant harassment by Boyle against *P Flynn & Sons, Door & Window Manufacturers.* You couldn't make it up, Flynn whimsically thought.

His mood was shifted suddenly by crashing sounds coming from outside his office. Suddenly his door sprung open, crashing violently against a stud wall. The shape of a large man framed the gap, his lips curled in fury and his fists balled ready for a fight.

"I know you," Flynn shouted. "What the fuck do you think you're playing at?"

"I know you too," Jacko McStravick yelled through a torrent of spittle, "and I'm here to tell you to lay of Belle Boyle, or you'll answer directly to me."

Flynn was genuinely puzzled. "What the fuck are you talking about? Who the hell is this Belle Boyle?" The connection only dawned on him as soon as the words had left his mouth. "Do you mean the copper's wife? What's she got to do with you?"

Jacko walked menacingly forward towards Flynn's desk. "I'll tell you what she has to do with me. She's a good friend, probably the only one I've got in these parts, and I don't take kindly to you ordering your sons to rough her up. The woman's pregnant, for God's sake, but even if she weren't I'd still be here to tell you it ends now."

A look of shock crossed Flynn's face. "You're talking bollocks. Jerome and Seamus wouldn't do something like that. I've no grudge against the woman. We both come from the old school,

McStravick, you know the one where there's honour among thieves, and everything is kept at a certain strict level. I know all about your own twopence-halfpenny villainy down the years, but from what I heard you always kept things within boundaries. That's what I do, albeit on a much higher level than you ever managed to operate on. As far as I'm concerned, wives, girlfriends, and children are untouchable. What sort of men would we be if we couldn't deal with business affairs on a man-to-man basis?"

"Words mean nothing, Flynn. I was there. Saw the assault on Belle with my own eyes. How do you think I got these marks on my face?"

Flynn stared daggers for a moment before pressing the intercom on his desk. Jacko could hear a ring tone in the outer office where the secretary station was located.

"Mary, get Jerome and Seamus out of the workshop and tell them to come up here, right now, and I mean, NOW!"

Jacko wasn't impressed. "Cuts no ice with me, Flynn. It's obvious you can't keep those boys in check, which means someone's going to have to do it for you."

"Meaning you? Don't make me laugh. By the look of your face, the boys gave as good as they got."

"Yeah, well backstabbers and cowards get lucky once in a while, but there won't be a second chance for them. Next time, I'll face them head-on and there's only one way that will end. They'll be intensive care for months, but that's only likely if I decide to go easy on them."

Flynn rose angrily from his seat and walked to the side of his desk. "Is that a threat that's supposed to worry me? You're an old man with delusions of grandeur. I could have you snuffed out as quick as snapping my fingers."

"Not a threat, more of a promise," Jacko responded calmly. "If anyone goes near Belle again, I'm going to get really mad, the sort of madness that doesn't give a damn about the Guards, or repercussions, or spending time in jail. I'm going to hurt your sons very badly, and then I'm going to make you wish you'd never heard the name of Jacko McStravick."

Flynn was about to step fully around the desk to confront Jacko, when the office door swung open again and Jerome and Seamus strode confidently in. Jerome was in the lead, his eyes widening when he saw Jacko. "What's that bastard doing here? Guess he needs another lesson about keeping his nose out of other people's business."

Jerome's words were still tailing off when he lunged across the room, his right arm already swinging as he prepared to land a haymaker on Jacko's head.

McStravick stood his ground, his arms hanging loosely at his sides, and his weight solidly wedged on his heels, waiting for an explosive transfer of power into one of his trademark short, but vicious, jabs.

But he never got to give the boys a demonstration.

Big Paud quickly stepped into the gap and threw a solid punch into his son's midriff. Jerome buckled immediately, a rush of air exploding from his lungs and signalling that the fight had suddenly left him. He buckled at the knees and sank to the floor, not quite understanding what had just happened.

His brother Seamus didn't fare any better. A massive sideswipe of Big Paud's arm caught him across the cheek, sending him reeling across the room.

Jerome spoke from his position on the floor. "What was that for?"

"That's for roughing up the Mooney woman."

"I swear, we didn't. We just wanted to throw a scare into her, after what her old man did in thrashing our yard."

Jacko stepped forward and looked down. "That's a barefaced lie, typical of a bully and a coward. I saw you throw her roughly to the ground and threaten to kick her baby out of her stomach. You would have done it too, if I hadn't come along."

"Jesus wept," Big Paud said. "Is this true?"

"It was only a threat. I wouldn't have really done it."

The anguish on Big Paud's face was obvious. "Somehow, I don't believe you, boy. Listen carefully to what I have to say. That woman is to be left alone and in fact you are to keep your nose out of everything that doesn't concern you. Don't go near the Boyles again and don't do anything about anything unless I tell you to."

The two youths gathered themselves and walked sheepishly out the door, their eyes refusing to make contact with either their father or Jacko.

When the room was clear, Big Paud turned to Jacko. "Satisfied?"

"For now, but my promise remains."

"Yeah, well here's a promise for you, McStravick. Don't come back here. My orders only apply to the Boyles. If I were you, I'd start looking over my shoulder. You'll be sorry that your Garda friend asked you to do his dirty business."

Jacko shrugged. "Mick Boyle knows nothing about this. His wife hasn't told him and neither have I. You'd better hope it stays that way."

Big Paud watched Jacko's back all the way out of the office. He settled into his chair, opened a drawer, and pulled out a bottle of Tullamore Dew Irish Whiskey. He poured three fingers into a tumbler and swallowed the contents. As an attempt at pushing back a growing sense of frustration and regret, the liquor failed miserably to hit the right spots. He despaired for his two sons. Oh, he loved them well enough, but that didn't blind him to their shortcomings. He knew they had always been a bit slow on the uptake, lacking basic commonsense or a moral compass that might have helped to correct their innate stupidity. As the years wore on, he knew their character flaws would never be repaired. They got all the worst parts from their mother. *The Bitch!*

His eyes misted over, suddenly hit by the memory of a third son, the eldest and smartest of his three boys. If only he were here now. Things would be different. He would have someone to lean on, someone to take over the reins when the time came. But it was not to be. He had been taken from Big Paud much too soon. The loss had never really gone away.

Chapter 34

"YOU HAVE REACHED the offices of Basil Tweedy & Company, Quantity Surveyors. How may I help you?" Clipped, professional, assured. As telephone introductions go, it wasn't a bad first line of defence.

"I need to speak with Mr Tweedy as a matter of urgency," Boyle said. "Is he in his office?"

"May I ask what you are calling about?"

"No, you may not. It's a matter that's strictly between myself and Mr Tweedy. Can you please get him for me?"

Silence while the woman gathered her thoughts. She sounded like a secretary or a private assistant. Could be an office manager, or a senior partner, or the outright owner of the business. Boyle was trying his best to stop pigeonholing people on a first impression. Some days, he actually made it work. Other times, like now, he didn't have time for niceties.

The voice came back on the line. "Mr Tweedy is a very busy man and can't just take any call without knowing the reason for it."

"This is Garda Detective Mick Boyle. I need to speak with Mr Tweedy. Please transfer this call immediately."

The response lost the frost of the earlier exchanges. "I'm sorry...truly, it's just that we get...so many calls about marketing, or sponsorship or...oh, I should have said that Mr Tweedy is not in the office at the moment. He's out at one of our sites."

"And where would that be?"

"He's at one of our contracts, a major new housing development on the N9 near Newport. He should be there for another hour and then he is scheduled to visit a prospective new client in Galway. He won't be back in the office until late afternoon. I can give you his mobile number."

"Yes, that would be helpful," Boyle said.

She read out the number. "Do you want me to contact Mr Tweedy and tell him to expect you?"

"That won't be necessary."

Basil Tweedy stood beside a Range Rover close to the site entrance on the N9. Boyle guessed at the man's identity from the fidgety way he eyeballed all vehicles approaching the area, no doubt careful to keep private whatever business the Guards had with him. He wore a hard hat, a high viz yellow vest, and a pair of black wellies – an ensemble that was strikingly at odds with the expensive three-piece suit that fitted snugly over a lean frame. Boyle guessed his age at around forty.

Boyle buzzed down his driver side window as he drew alongside the man. Before he had a chance to speak, the face leaned forward into the opening. "Are you Detective Boyle?"

So much for asking the secretary or the personal assistant or the senior partner or whatever, not to make contact.

"Mr Tweedy, I presume," Boyle said as he opened the door and forced the man to step backwards. "I don't have time for niceties. I'm here to talk to you about the disappearance of a number of teenage girls."

The passenger door of Boyle's Rav4 opened and Paul Brogan stepped out, quickly making his way around the car to stand menacingly beside Tweedy. The surveyor's eyes switched from Brogan to Boyle and then inwards to the building site. He licked dry lips and tried to hide his discomfort.

"I know, of course, that you have already been to this site and arrested a man in connection with those disappearances. It's been all over the news. Are you here to follow up enquiries, though I don't see how I can help? I never met the man. No reason to. Can't tell you anything about him."

Boyle knew that people tended to babble when addressing the police. Particularly if they had never dealt with them before, and especially when they didn't want to be part of a formal investigation. Sometimes the reaction signalled guilt or a sense of hiding something. Oftentimes, it was just a case of Joe Public not understanding how these things went and wanted to demonstrate their willingness to talk.

A professional businessman such as Basil Tweedy should be more composed, Boyle thought. But then it took all sorts.

Boyle moved a step closer. "This is about you, Mr Tweedy. On at least three occasions when girls went missing in Kilkenny, Cork, and here in Castlebar, you were at building sites close to the location of the disappearances. That strikes us as very strange. Care to comment?"

The colour drained from Tweedy's face. "You can't be seriously suggesting I had anything to do with those?"

It was not an unexpected response. Talk about déjà vu. Boyle had been down the same road with Michael Kelly and was not about to jump to conclusions a second time around. But Tweedy represented another tangible lead that needed to be diligently hunted down.

Boyle fixed the man with a forced smile. "You're probably right, sir, but surely you must see it from our point of view? We need you to tell us about those locations and what you were up to. It's in both our interests that we clear you from our decks, so to speak, and move on to other matters. I think it best if you come with us for a chat at the station. Voluntarily would be best, but we can do it another way."

"No, no, of course I'll help. Would you mind if I drove my own vehicle? Where are we going?"

"Castlebar Garda Station. I'm happy for you to take your own car. Sergeant Brogan here will sit with you."

"Will this take long? I have an important appointment in Galway."

"Probably best if you cancel it. By the way, do you know if the development architect, Owen Patterson, is on site?"

Tweedy raised his brow. "Do you also need to speak to Owen?"

"Please, just answer the question."

"No, he's not here. Not due back for another site conference for at least a week.

The interview with Basil Tweedy couldn't have gone better. Despite showing considerable apprehension, the man turned down the need for legal representation and was happy to speak freely and to have Dr Connie Dunne present during the session. Boyle had explained who Dunne was, an introduction that seemed to amuse Tweedy as he looked at the young woman dressed in jeans and sneakers with a rock band motif spread across the front of her t-shirt.

The questions covered much of the same grounds as those from the Michael Kelly interview. Family background, schooldays, friendships, and girls. Tweedy was a married man with three young daughters, ranging in ages from sixteen to ten, and rarely liked to be away from home, even on jobs that took him hundreds of miles away. He always travelled back to his base in Westport, even if it meant driving through the night. A solid, unspectacular, conventional human being. Boyle believed everything the man said and judging by an almost imperceptible nod from Dr Dunne, so did she.

The conversation moved quickly to the professional side of Tweedy's life. The jobs he had worked on, the interactions on building sites, his rapport with other professionals.

Boyle wanted to move directly to a discussion about some of the other names on Brogan's whiteboard squares. "I mentioned Owen Patterson to you before. Have you had much contact with him at other sites?"

"In our business, you tend to bump into the same people at various locations, although all this European tendering nonsense is making it harder to win local contracts. I once had to deal with a German architect who didn't speak a word of English, which I can tell you is not much fun when you're having to constantly go through an interpreter. I'm sorry, I'm digressing, yes I've worked with Patterson on several occasions. Can't say I like the man."

"Why is that?"

"Too full of himself, Inspector. Thinks he's better than anyone else, and I don't care much for his business practices."

"How do you mean?"

"Well, he offered to get me some work under the table. Said he could arrange it if I was prepared to pay him a cut. I gave him short shrift, I can tell you."

"How did he take the rejection?"

"Water of a duck's back. Didn't faze him at all. Said there were plenty more fish in the sea."

Brogan interrupted at that point. "Mr Tweedy, but can you tell me if Patterson was on the Kilkenny development site with you in 2008?"

"Yes, he was lead architect. Even cockier in those days, if that's possible."

Boyle flashed a questioning look at Brogan.

The huge grin said it all even before Brogan spoke. "That gives us our first four-out-of-four on the squares of names."

Chapter 35

WEARINESS VANISHED from the detective room in a heartbeat. It was as if someone had opened a window and used an industrial-scale blower to disperse a fog of lethargy that until now had held everyone in its all-pervasive grip. Lack of sleep and general exhaustion offered scant defences. News of the four-timer was a different matter altogether.

It had a galvanising effect. The mood changed dramatically, buoyed by the realisation that they were facing a major breakthrough, an honest-to-goodness, diamond-studded shift in direction that they hoped would lead to a positive conclusion. Of course, no-one wanted to actually give voice to what they were thinking. There were a lot of seasoned pros behind the cluster of desks, most of whom had learned the hard way how not to get too far ahead of themselves. Still, this was big. It had all the makings of a game-changer.

Boyle didn't need to tell them what they needed to do. Nonetheless, he stated the obvious. "Owen Patterson. Who is he? Where is he? Where's he been? I want his life story from the cradle to now, and I want it in less than an hour. Hit the phones, scour every database we've got, take to the streets, talk to people, do whatever is needed to find this guy. Divide up into pairs and don't be afraid to tell me if I've overlooked anything."

Speech over, Boyle turned and headed out the door, leaving behind a scene reminiscent of a stock exchange trading floor on a day of heavy buying and selling. Shirt-sleeved men and women were now on their feet, cupping phones under their chins, waving pieces of paper in the air, and shouting orders at each other. In the midst of the melee, Brogan tried, and failed miserably, to bring order.

Back in his office, Boyle allowed himself a moment to share in the euphoria before switching on his desktop computer and scanning his email folder. It was crammed with bold-type message headings demanding attention. The first four on the list made him cringe. They were from the Assistant Commissioner's office for Governance and Accountability, confirming that Boyle's attendance was required at an initial complaints briefing in Dublin at 2 p.m. this afternoon. *Damn Big Paud Flynn to hell!*

Things were no better when Boyle opened his iPhone and saw a list of missed calls. He'd forgotten to reset the mute button and was now faced with another list, this one dominated by his AGSI representative, also no doubt trying to plan for the Dublin appointment. He ignored them and turned his attention to his message folder, which had more than twenty unopened texts. Only one grabbed his attention. It was from Belle.

Hi babe, just checking how you are. Sorry I missed you again this morning. We need to catch up. How about a nice sit-down dinner tonight? xxx

He wanted badly to call her. Tell her how things were going. But what exactly would he say? We're chasing another promising lead? It sounded banal. Instead, he tapped the keypad and sent a reply message.

I'm good. R U resting up? Dinner sounds great but what say you put your feet up and let me get us a

Chinese carry-out?

His phone pinged immediately, as if Belle was sitting waiting for him to make contact.

Sounds good to me. See you later. Love you xxx

Boyle was still smiling when station commander John Delaney put his head around the door. "Quite a flap going on. Do you think this Patterson will end up being the right guy?"

"Everything's screaming towards his direction, John, but we've already got our fingers burned once with Michael Kelly, and I'm not about to pop the champagne corks just yet."

"Speaking of Kelly, what to we do with him?"

"Keep him on ice until forensics come through. Should be later this morning. If there's nothing showing, we'll release him. Can you look after that if I have to suddenly rush out of here?"

"Are you going to the complaints hearing in Dublin?"

"Not a chance. Too much happening here."

"Jesus, Mick, have you at least let them know?"

"Haven't got round to it yet."

Delaney shook his head. "Want me to smooth the ground? They'll understand that you're needed here, but I doubt they'll agree to more than a twenty-four-hour postponement."

"Thanks, John, I owe you one. And not for the first time."

An hour later, Brogan was the next visitor into Boyle's office. "We've made a lot of progress in tying down Patterson."

"Give me the potted version."

"Appears he's got an office in Roscommon. We tracked it down via a website, one of those cheap build-your-own jobbies that only runs to a standard page with a bland stock photo of an architect's cluttered desk. No picture of Patterson and just a mobile number, which appears to be out of use. Strange way to run a business. Want me to rustle up one of our local boys to go check it out?"

"Hell, yes," Boyle responded, "and get them to send at least two cars. I doubt they'll find anyone in situ, but no sense taking chances. Anything else?"

"Quite a lot. We can't find any record of an architect by the name of Owen Patterson before he surfaced at the Kilkenny job in 2008. Bit of a coincidence in the date, don't you think?"

"You know what I think of coincidences."

"Yeah," Brogan parroted, "no such thing. Anyway, motor vehicle and taxation histories on Patterson also didn't start until that time and we can't find any of the usual professional memberships or social media links that you would expect a businessman to use. It's as if he was conjured out of thin air twelve years ago and has done his best to keep anonymous ever since. As far as we can tell, he's never owned or rented a property, although we do have a full sleeve on the cars he's been driving during that period."

"What does that tell us," Boyle said impatiently.

"My guess is that property ownership has been hidden behind business firewalls. Easy to construct a company and put its name on title deeds, but buying a car is a bit more personal, particularly because he seems to have had a habit of changing them on a regular basis. Likes his expensive toys, does our Mr Patterson."

"What does that mean?"

"He's currently driving around in an Audi A8, which is good news for us because it has all the bells and whistles, including current-generation satnav and manufacturer locator software...."

"...Please tell me we've got a location for him."

"Not yet," Brogan said, but shouldn't be long. We're in touch with Audi and expect some results within the next thirty minutes."

"I want a full team ready to roll as soon as that information comes in."

Brogan turned to go, but suddenly remembered something. He held out a sheet of paper. "Here's Patterson's photo from the RSA database."

Boyle stared at the two-inch head-and-shoulders picture, unaware that Brogan had already left the office. The face that looked back at him was a grainy black and white photocopy of a standard driving licence mugshot, which failed to pick up telltale lines and creases or to give clues about eye-colouring or facial bone density or nasal contours. What he did get was a round-cheeked, emotionless, fair-haired man whose gaze penetrated the lens, yet betrayed no hint of character or soul. Beneath the picture was the usual database details, which revealed that the holder of the licence was aged thirty-six and had an M1 classification entitling him to drive vehicles designed and constructed for the carriage of up to eight persons.

There was something about the face that troubled Boyle. It was familiar in an abstruse way, somehow a total stranger, but one who rang a memory bell. Had Boyle met him before? Had he run into him at the N9 building site? Was he a face in the background when they'd taken Michael Kelly in for questioning? Hard as he tried, Boyle couldn't bring it to the surface. But something was there. Or was it just his imagination?

The intercom on his desk shrilled angrily. Boyle lifted the handset. "We need you next door," Paul Brogan said without preamble.

Boyle rushed to the detective room. "What have you got?"

Brogan nodded at Custer Armstrong. "Show him."

Armstrong swivelled his desk monitor towards Boyle. "This is a GPS eXchange Format file detailing all the routes taken by Patterson's Audi over the past few months."

Boyle bent forward for a close-up look at a screen full of wavy-lined text. "Looks like a plate of spaghetti. How the hell are we supposed to make sense of that?"

Armstrong smiled. "Just wanted to give you a glimpse of the raw data, which has now been transferred to a mapping application." He pressed a few keys and the screen changed to a coloured topographical background, complete with the place names of counties throughout Ireland. "This tells us the routes taken by the vehicle. I've washed out everything except recurring trips, to see if we can define a pattern of travel."

"Please tell me you've got something, Custer."

"Your wish is my command. How about a single location where the vehicle has visited almost daily over the past month and is currently still there?"

"Where?"

Armstrong tapped a finger on the screen. Right here, a place called Glencool Forest, near Longford."

Chapter 36

A THREE-CAR CONVOY carrying twelve heavily armed detectives screamed out of the entrance to Castlebar Garda Station, lights flashing and sirens wailing as they barrelled through traffic. They had seventy miles between them and Glencool Forest and were not intending to waste a minute.

Boyle's trusty Rav4 led the way. As usual, he was accompanied by Brogan in the passenger seat with Armstrong and Munn hanging on for dear life in the rear. Brogan was on his mobile phone, relaying messages back to base where John Delaney had taken charge of co-ordinating the operation.

Delaney, per instructions from Boyle, had already mobilised armed units from Longford to dash to the scene as quickly as possible and to hold the fort in readiness for the Castlebar convoy, which had an estimated arrival time of ninety minutes. A last-minute plea had also gone out to the Irish Army's RDF base at Boyle, County Roscommon, asking if they had a military drone, which could be tasked immediately to the sky over Glencool. Despite being just a Reserve Defence Force base, they were fully equipped with all manner of drones, including those fitted with thermal imaging. The base commander assured Delaney that one would be on site within a matter of minutes and that the operator would open a direct line to Brogan's mobile number.

It hadn't been wasted on Boyle that the base

carried his name. Perhaps it was a good omen. He hoped so.

Fifteen minutes into their journey, Brogan's phone activated. It was not a number he recognised and he switched immediately to loudspeaker. "Brogan here."

This is Sergeant McLoughlin in charge of drone project 1257. We are over Glencool and have a visual of a major fire deep in the forest, approximately five miles from the main road.

Boyle's heart sank. "Ask him if he's picking up any heat signatures other than the fire? Tell him to start a pattern outwards from the seat of the blaze."

I heard that, sir. Visibility is virtually zero at the fire location. Too much smoke. I'll take Clive down for a closer inspection with the thermal. Could take a while to get into a full search pattern.

"Who the hell is Clive?" asked Brogan.

Sorry, sir, Clive is the name of the drone. We give them all names to help keep tabs on them.

Despite his foreboding, Boyle smiled.

Brogan thanked the operator and cut the connection. Barely a minute elapsed before it rang again. This time Brogan recognised the Castlebar station number.

"This is Delaney. Just got reports from the Longford mobile units that they are on site at Glencool and have encountered a large fire. There's a cottage, an outbuilding, and a car ablaze. Nothing much they can do. Fire services have been alerted and are on their way."

"Any signs of people in the area?" Boyle tentatively shouted across to Brogan's handset.

"Nothing so far, Mick."

"Any idea of the make of the car?"

"Yes, it's an Audi, but from what I gather, it has already been reduced to a shell."

Boyle thanked Delaney and retreated into a succession of dark thoughts. Was the blaze a funeral pyre for the two teenagers? What were their last days like? What had Patterson done to them? But the one question that kept leaping to the front of his mind was one that had haunted him for the past few hours. *I should have got on the bastard's trail earlier. I allowed myself to be sidetracked by Michael Kelly and now two girls are dead because of my stupidity. Fucking idiot!*

The sense of guilt wouldn't go away. Despite a growing dread about what he would find at Glencool, Boyle's foot pressed heavier on the accelerator, the big SUV swaying across the small N5 carriageway, forcing oncoming drivers to take evasive action.

The next fifty minutes dragged on. Boyle cursed every vehicle that hampered his progress, none more so than a large tractor and trailer combo, which refused to move to the side of the road, despite the incessant sirens and horn blaring in its wake. The farmer eventually found a pull-in space at a gated entrance to a field and raised a two-finger salute at the convoy as it rocketed by.

Finally, they reached the Glencool entrance lane, which was easy to spot because of a Garda patrol car parked sideways across the opening. The uniformed driver, alerted to the incoming sounds from his position in front of the vehicle, raced around the bodywork and jumped behind the wheel to manoeuvre a gap for Boyle and the others.

Boyle was forced to slow his progress, as much due to cloying smoke, which hung from the trees to the surface of the lane, but mostly because his beloved RAV hit a pothole, which sent a jarring crunch into the vehicle's interior. Boyle thought he heard something metallic snap, but he pushed on regardless.

The familiar voice of the drone operator peeled out from Brogan's phone. *Project 1257 reporting. I have a small heat signature approximately five-hundred yards from the main building. It's a faint thermal, but definitely indicates either a person or a large animal.*

"Is it just the one signature?" Boyle asked.

Affirmative.

Not what Boyle wanted to hear. It could only mean that Patterson was loose in the grounds. Which meant he had already disposed of the girls. He swallowed hard and forced himself to respond with an air of authority. "Okay, we're on site. Can you hold position until we take stock?"

Affirmative. Clive has at least two hours still left in the tank.

The scene that greeted Boyle and the team was one of pandemonium. The two-hundred-yard stretch before the cottage was crammed with police vehicles and at least thirty high viz jackets could be seen through the gloom. Ahead of the police cars were two large fire tenders surrounded by the familiar figures of black-suited and yellow-helmeted personnel, many of whom were training hoses on the dying embers of separate blazes. The hoses fed directly back to the tenders, exhausting the onboard supply of water. Boyle knew that some of the fire crew would be scouring the perimeter looking for access to hydrants, if indeed a place this remote were linked to a mains supply.

Breathing apparatus seemed to be the order of the day. The thick swirling smoke carried with it a toxic mixture of pollutants, forcing the Guards to resort to holding handkerchiefs up to their faces. In an old building such as this was, there was an added fear of the presence of asbestos, but none of the uniforms were ducking out of their duties. Boyle motioned them to come forward to his position.

He waited for them to gather around. "Listen up. We believe we have a dangerous man somewhere out here. We have a thermal imaging drone above us and will shortly be entering the woods in search of him. As soon as we get an updated fix, we'll move in on a line. Assume our subject to be armed and take all possible precautions."

He swivelled back to Brogan. "How do we play this?"

"Not going to be easy, boss. We have no way of downloading the drone's imaging so we're in the operator's hands as far as directing us to the location. At the moment we are presenting too big a cluster, which makes it difficult to give him a starting reference for our actual location in relation to the heat signature he's picking up."

Boyle scanned the area. "How about we send a single officer back up the lane and get the pilot to take a bead from him?"

"That'll work."

Boyle turned and issued instructions to a nearby Guard. "Walk out at least two hundred yards and wait for our signal."

As soon as the officer disengaged himself from the group, Boyle signalled Brogan to contact the drone pilot.

"Project 1257, we are standing south-east of the

main fire site. We have a man walking away from us. Can you pick him up and let us know where we are in relation to the thermal site in the woods?"

I see your man. Walk towards him for about a hundred yards and then turn to your right. Your subject is approximately four-hundred yards north west in the trees from that point.

"Understood 1257. I'm going to plug earphones into my mobile to cut down on chatter noise. We'll start the search with two lead persons, the remainder of the group fanning out from us on either side. Keep us advised if we stray off track."

Will do. I'll monitor you all the way. Good luck.

Boyle pulled his Sig from a rear paddle holster and turned to face his men. "You all heard that. Check your weapons, line up at ten-yard intervals, and follow me and Sergeant Brogan after we've covered the first fifty yards. Slow and easy, please. Keep safe."

Chapter 37

THEY MADE painstakingly slow progress. Had to be that way. Too many factors working against them. The natural darkness of the forest, the barrier of smoke – even this far from the burnt-out cottage – and a pitted, dangerous ground that magnified the sound of their feet crunching against broken twigs and dry leaves.

Every so often, Brogan's arm shot out to signal a slight change in direction, courtesy of information fed through his earphones from the drone pilot. When Brogan and Boyle altered course, the men and women on their flanks followed suit. Everyone was on edge, expecting an armed assailant to spring out at any moment from behind the trunks of one of the large sycamores.

But so far they encountered nothing. Except for a few rabbits scurrying across their path and causing sharp intakes of breaths until the searchers figured out what had caused the commotion. Onwards they tramped, torches aimed with one hand at the forest floor to help pick their way, guns held in front with their other hand to sweep the terrain. If any figure suddenly appeared, it was likely they'd be cut in two by a spontaneous volley from nervous trigger fingers. The training manuals or exercises didn't cover this kind of situation.

Boyle was aware of the dangers. There wasn't much he could do to mitigate them. He trusted his men, but self-preservation held away. If Patterson was intent on a confrontation, then he'd have to face the consequences. Better to take him alive, but infinitely better to put him down than to let him roam free.

Brogan leaned into Boyle's shoulder and whispered. "Drone pilot says the signature hasn't moved. He's now about three hundred yards directly ahead of us."

"Think he's injured, or dead?"

"Can't be dead, otherwise we wouldn't be getting body heat. Maybe it *is* just an animal taking refuge from the smoke."

Boyle shook his head. "Assume nothing. Far as I'm concerned, it's Patterson. We don't relax until we know for sure, one way or another."

They plodded on, their progress helped by an unexpected clearing, which stretched for about a hundred yards ahead. It was devoid of the heavy smoke, which had characterised the trail so far, leaving them with enough natural light to sprint ahead. Back under the embrace of the trees, they settled into their earlier rhythm and tiptoed forward, keenly aware they were getting close enough to their quarry to alert him to their approach.

Five minutes later Brogan signalled another switch in direction and two minutes after that, he called a halt with a raised fist. Not daring to whisper, he mouthed at Boyle. *Twenty feet dead ahead.*

They both eyed a tree directly in the path of Brogan's pointed arm. They were about to enter the last, potentially lethal, part of their search.

Boyle swung his torch behind and to either side to alert the rest of the team. Everyone stopped and followed Boyle's arm-waving orders to remain in position. His gesticulations made it clear that he and

Brogan were going ahead alone.

Torches were switched off and placed on the ground. Boyle held his pistol in a two-handed grip as he walked to the left and watched Brogan step out in the opposite direction. They closed in on the trunk, paused for a silent countdown, and leapt to the front.

Boyle gasped at the sight that confronted him.

He could make out the shape of a man's overcoat, as he tracked his eyes over the prostrate figure, from bottom to top, and came to rest on a mop of hair peeping over the wide shoulder lapels.

Wait a moment – there were two heads!

Not daring to hope, Boyle knelt down and gently folded back the top of the coat. The eyes were closed, the face dirty, and the hair matted, but there was no doubting that he was staring at Siobhan Cunningham. He watched a slight heaving motion in her chest and heard the faint sounds of ragged breathing. She was alive.

Suddenly, a second face emerged from the bundle of clothing and stared directly at him, her face a tortured canvas of fear. It was Megan McGrath.

She screamed. The best sound Boyle had ever heard in his life. The second girl bolted upright and joined in the screams. It was a chorus Boyle could listen to all day.

He moved back holding his hands out in a placatory gesture. "It's okay, you're safe. We're from the Garda Síochána and we're here to take you home."

The girls stopped their screams and exchanged glances. Boyle give them time to understand their situation, watching carefully as their moods changed, transitioning through various stages from initial horror to final realisation.

Siobhan sprang from the covers of the coat and wrapped her arms tightly around Boyle's neck. "Is it really true? Are we safe? Thank you, thank you."

"You certainly are," Boyle said, failing miserably to blink away tears that were starting to stream down his face.

Emergency rescue blankets were brought forward by the fire crews who also snapped oxygen masks over the girls. In between gulps from the cylinders, Megan and Siobhan drank greedily from water bottles and munched on power bars, which appeared magically from the coat of one of the officers. A crew paramedic declared the girls to be in a poor physical condition, at which point an ambulance was ordered up from Longford.

Stretchers were brought in from one of the fire tenders and the girls were eased gently onto them. Throughout the fuss and ministrations, they held hands tightly, refusing to be separated and chattering incessantly into each other's faces.

Boyle walked away from the scene to gather his thoughts. They had been fooled into thinking Patterson was the one giving off the thermal image signal, not the two girls, who had been so tightly wrapped against each other that they must have appeared as a single bleep on the drone pilot's screen. Thank goodness for technological flaws.

The presence of Patterson's burnt-out Audi at the cottage site was proof of his involvement, but Boyle needed to be sure. The girls were in no condition to be questioned in any detail, something he was happy to leave for a few days, Still, he needed confirmation. He pulled out his mobile phone and brought up Patterson's driving licence photo.

He walked back to the stretchers and bent down. "I know you girls have been through a lot, and I promise not to bother you too much. Will you take a look at this photo and tell me if this is the man who abducted you?"

Megan and Siobhan recoiled in unison when Boyle held up the phone. "Yes, yes, that's him. Take it away, please."

Boyle nodded and walked off. He clicked out of the pictures gallery and opened his favourites' folder. John Delaney voice came online within a second.

"What's the news, Mick?" The urgency in his voice was palpable.

"All good, John. We've got Megan McGrath and Siobhan Cunningham and they're alive. A bit the worst for wear, but they'll make it."

A crescendo of noise burst across Boyle's handset. Delaney had just shouted a 'whoopee' and was sharing the good news with anyone within earshot.

Boyle waited for the background commotion to die down. "John, can you let the parents know?"

"I think that should come from you, Mick."

"Nonsense, we're too far away and this has to be done immediately and in person. Mind if I suggest you take Sergeant Moriarty with you. He's put a lot into this investigation, and I think he should be there to represent the rank and filers."

"Excellent idea, though mind you I'll have to work hard to stop him blubbering."

"Cops don't cry," Boyle responded, somehow forgetting his own earlier little outburst.

"Just one more thing, Mick. A huge congratulations to you and the team. Those girls are alive because of you. You've given them a future and you've given this community a real reason to trust and respect the force. We are all in your debt."

"Knock it off, John. It was an all-round team effort, even if we did need a bit of luck."

"Luck be damned. Oh, what about Patterson? Any sign of him?"

"Nothing. He seems to have flown the coop before we arrived."

Silence for a moment before Delaney responded. "We need to get the bastard. Anything you want me to do at this end?"

"Patterson will keep. Don't worry, we'll get him, but right now you have two very important house calls to make."

Chapter 38

OWEN PATTERSON was no more. He'd swapped his identity and had no intention of being caught by the Guards. Driving sedately on the outskirts of Dublin, he banged the steering wheel of the battered work van and cursed the turn of events that had robbed him of the pleasure of killing the girls and parading their bodies for the world to see.

He'd searched those damn woods for almost an hour, finally abandoning the pursuit in favour of self-preservation. Not knowing where the girls had gone, he couldn't risk staying around in case they had somehow made it to the main road. He was not ready for capture just yet, not when there was still so much to be done.

He'd marched back to the cottage and prepared for a fast getaway. The car would have to be left behind. Too much there to tie him into the abductions. The girls would probably help the police to put together one of those stupid identikit pictures, but without his name and background they'd really have nothing. Just in case, he would switch to another one of his aliases and put as much distance as possible between himself and Castlebar.

The cash and a holdall of clothes were thrown in the rear compartment of the van, a vehicle that was registered in a different name and would be an anonymous way of crossing the country. Finally, he sloshed the kerosene into the house, the garage, and the Audi, the resultant whoosh of flames bringing a wry smile before he set off on the next stage of his adventure.

He figured Dublin was the best place to lose himself for a while. A pair of spectacles, a false moustache, and maybe even a wig, would be transformational. They'd never find him. Yes, he'd hole up in a two-bit motel for a few days and then head to Connolly Station. The railway offered the best option to go anywhere in the country.

But he didn't intend to go just anywhere. He'd already made up his mind.

He was heading back north. To Downpatrick, the scene of his greatest triumphs.

Sunday morning meant only one thing in the Boyle household. Mass at the Church of the Holy Rosary in Castlebar. Belle never missed a weekly visit, a routine that was pursued with less vigour by her husband, though to be fair, he went whenever the demands of work allowed him to.

Boyle was in a buoyant mood when he threw back the bedroom curtains and savoured the day ahead. His entire team had been stood down for a well-earned rest and he himself relished the chance to recharge the batteries before going full tilt again in the search for Owen Patterson. That could keep. Belle's appointment with God could not.

"How about we go to the noon Mass and then grab a nice roast over at Mulgrew's Restaurant? Maybe even take in a coastal drive over near Westport?"

Belle rose from behind the quilt covers. "Someone's in a good mood."

"Yeah," Boyle agreed. "It's days like this that

make you realise all the shit in the world can be pushed to one side, if only for a little while. Let's make use of it while we can."

"Oh, Mick, it'll be great to have you all to myself for one whole day. How about we have an early breakfast and go for a drive before Mass?"

"Your wish is my command."

"And by the way, why would we go to Mulgrew's when our own restaurant has started serving Sunday dinners? I'm not about to give trade to the opposition while we're still trying to build up our own clientele."

"What an uncharitable thought for a good Catholic lassie, and her about to go kissing the altar rails," he chided. "Talk about double standards!"

Belle flung one of her pillows playfully across the room at Boyle. "How is it double standards to want the best for your husband and child? Our cuisine is much better than Mulgrew's, and it's a lot cheaper."

Boyle grinned. "I just think you need time away from the place. Andrea and Johnny can look after the restaurant and bar, and they will have plenty of support from the weekend bar staff."

"No, I'd rather come back here. We can take our meal in our own upstairs dining room and enjoy each other's company for the rest of the day."

"Okay, you've convinced me. Now, get up and get dressed."

Boyle had barely walked halfway up the path leading to the front entrance of the church when he regretted his decision. People stopped and stared, some moved forward to shake his hand, others patted his back. Most Massgoers simply wanted to hear details of how he'd discovered the missing girls.

News travelled fast in a relatively small community. Television and the jungle drums of social media saw to that. Boyle's face was plastered across the Sunday tabloids, one of them even declaring him to be *The Hero of Castlebar*.

He put his head down and arrowed his way as fast as he could under the gothic portico, mindful that Belle could only amble slowly, and aware that she was less reticent about talking than he was. He dipped his hand in the Holy Water font and whispered in her ear. "This was a bad idea. Let's go home."

She didn't respond. Simply hooked her arm around his elbow and almost physically dragged him forwards. People swivelled on their bench seats to nod politely in his direction, his discomfiture rising by the second as he fumbled his way into a pew.

Thankfully, the start of Mass drew all heads towards the front of the church. The Parish Priest, a youthful incumbent in the post by the name of Fr Martin Graham, was in control and eager to share in his parishioners' general feeling of wellbeing.

"My brothers and sisters, we are gathered here on the feast day of The Nativity of the Blessed Virgin Mary, which celebrates the birth of Mary, the mother of Jesus. How fitting it is that we might reflect that it was perhaps the intercession of Mary which has led to a rebirth in our own community. Two of our daughters have been returned to us and we give thanks for Mary's guiding hand and for the peacekeepers who reunited our children with us."

A spontaneous round of applause echoed across the chapel. People stood and turned their heads towards one spot. Boyle felt their gaze, his face reddening with embarrassment, his head bowed in a silent prayer for the ground to open up. He felt Belle's hand squeeze tightly against his wrist. It was the only thing that stopped him from getting up and fleeing out the door.

He knew people meant well. He could even understand their unfettered joy over Megan's and Siobhan's rescue. But he didn't deserve their praise. That belonged to the hundreds of officers who'd put their heads down and done the donkey work, never caring about recognition or bouquets. Perhaps, in the end, that's who these people were really acknowledging. He just happened to be the Johnny-on-the-spot, and maybe he should be happy to accept the limelight on behalf of everyone.

He tried to push the notion aside as little more than sentimental claptrap, but decided to hold onto it, at least for the next fifty minutes. Fr Graham was not noted for short sermons when it came to the Liturgy of the Word part of the service.

The lunchtime trade in Mooney's was in full swing when Boyle escorted Belle to a seat in front of a roaring fire and walked to the bar. The events at the church had left him with a thirst and the need for a cigarette. He could do something about the first craving, but little about the second. Not while Belle was around.

He carried a pint of Guinness and a freshly squeezed orange juice back to the table. "I've just asked Andrea to carry two full roast dinners up to the apartment in about thirty minutes. Gives is time to get a few in."

"Don't rush it, Mick. I think you've earned a bit of downtime. I'll tell Andrea to make that an hour from now."

Boyle nodded his agreement and swallowed half the contents of the glass in two gulps. He wiped the foam from his mouth and let his eyes wander across the other patrons, his sweep stopping abruptly at a familiar face. Jacko McStravick was showing a right-side profile, one that was full of cuts and bruises.

Boyle rose angrily and crossed the room, tapping Jacko on the shoulder. "What happened to you? Thought I told you to stay out of trouble?"

Jacko looked up and smiled. "Walked into a lamppost, didn't I?"

"Don't give me that old flannel, Jacko. You were in a fight. I'll be damned if I let you start up again with all your old ways. I warned you I would run you out of town if I got even a hint that you were messing around."

Belle arrived at Boyle's shoulder. "Please, Mick, everyone's listening. Leave Jacko alone."

Boyle dropped his volume. "I told you McStravick was a good-for-nothing bully. Judging by the state of him, it must have been some fight. I'll bet if I get our boys to nose around, they'll find some poor bastard taking up a valuable hospital bed."

"It wasn't like that," Belle whispered.

"What do you mean? How do you know about it?"

"Because...because Jacko was injured trying to protect me."

Chapter 39

BOYLE COULDN'T DECIDE if anger was more dominant than shock. He was in the couple's private upstairs living room, staring in disbelief, first at Belle, then at Jacko. He could tell that their versions of events were stilted. They were failing miserably at trying to brush aside the confrontation with the Flynn brothers as little more than a verbal spat.

"You were thrown to the ground?" he asked Belle incredulously. "Were you hurt? Did you go the doctor? Why the hell did you two try to hide this from me?"

"It was nothing, Mick. I sort of stumbled, but I'm perfectly alright."

"Don't lie to me, Belle. I can tell there's more to it than that."

"I admit I was scared, but Jacko stepped in before anything bad could happen."

"Anything bad!" Boyle exploded. "They fucking broke into our yard, vandalised the place, and assaulted you. How much worse do you think it could have been?"

Belle buried her face in her hands. "Please, Mick, I don't want to talk about it anymore. The images in my head makes me jumpy just thinking about it. I need to stay calm and concentrate on not stressing the baby."

Boyle instantly mellowed. "I understand, darling. Just relax and stop thinking about the

Flynns. You leave them to me."

"No, Mick, don't do anything. The reason why I didn't want to tell you was precisely because I knew you would fly off the handle. You can't afford to get tangled up with these people."

"Besides," Jacko cut in, "I went round to see Big Paud yesterday to straighten a few things out..."

"So, now I need you to do my talking as well as my fighting?"

"Wasn't like that," Jacko said. "I was just thinking of Belle and wanted the Flynns to get the message to stay away. For what it's worth, I don't think Big Paud had anything to do with this. He looked genuinely shocked when he heard what'd happened, and he give those two boys a right belting, I can tell you. He warned them off in no uncertain terms."

"That's as maybe, but I'll make doubly sure there won't be any repeats. I've a good mind to go round there now."

Belle stamped a foot on the floor. "Mick Boyle, you'll do no such thing!" Then she grabbed her stomach, let out a long groan, and leaned back in her seat. "Oh, that wasn't good. I've disturbed baby."

Boyle quickly knelt beside her. "Are you alright?"

"I feel faint. Can you get me a glass of water?"

As Boyle raced out of the room towards the kitchen, Belle sat up and winked at Jacko. When her husband returned, she sipped at the water and looked pleadingly into his eyes. "Promise me that you won't do anything. If I have to constantly worry about you getting into trouble, it will affect our child. Please don't let that happen."

Her words hit Boyle like a full-on punch to the

gut. Here he was, running off at the mouth, making this about him and not his wife, thinking first about his own feelings instead of worrying about how traumatised she must have been. Part of him understood the Flynns' need for payback if they really thought Boyle had wrecked their compound. But it was one thing to cause damage to property, quite another to assault and threaten Belle. That could not go unpunished.

There would have to be a reckoning, even if it meant keeping Big Paud and his two useless progenies on the backburner. They would get what was coming to them, and then some. For now, he had to be there for Belle. He had to make her believe she was more important than a vendetta. He clasped her hand tightly in his, and spoke tenderly, not caring that Jacko was present. "I'm sorry, darling. I know I've been selfish, and I know you deserve better. I give you my word to put the Flynns out of my mind and concentrate on you, and only you, from here on."

Belle smiled demurely. "You don't need to apologise, Mick, and you certainly don't need to be fussing over me for the next few weeks. It's enough to know I can count on you..." She paused and looked across the room. "Isn't there something you should be saying to Jacko?"

McStravick shuffled his feet in embarrassment. "Not necessary. I think it's time I left you good folks alone." He swivelled and headed for the door.

"Just a moment," Boyle said, rising from his crouch and intercepting the big man as he lurched through the entrance. Boyle held his hand out. "I guess you're entitled to swipe this away. I wouldn't blame you, but you should know how grateful I am for what you did for Belle. Now that I've heard the story, I shudder to think what would have happened if you hadn't turned up. You have my thanks and gratitude and a genuine apology for having to listen to me running off at the mouth."

Jacko took the hand and shook it vigorously. "We were never exactly friends, Boyle, but I've never looked on you as an enemy. I'm glad I could do something for you and Belle, but let's not get all mushy here. I have a reputation to uphold."

Boyle smiled. "Fair enough, Jacko, but I'm beginning to like having you around. I want your word that you'll keep an eye on Belle when I'm at work."

"Don't need to ask," Jacko said.

Big Paud was going through his usual Sunday ritual of a late lie-in, reading the papers, and watching the telly for the build-up to the lunchtime football match on Sky. He'd often thought about buying more shares in the Liverpool club, maybe even become a director with access to his own box. He could afford it. He had more money lying around than he knew what to do with. Yeah, he decided, worth checking into.

The papers were full of the rescue of two girls, a story that quickly changed his feel-good mood. It wasn't so much the fate of the teenagers that caused his dark clouds. It was the over-the-top eulogising of that bastard Boyle. Hero of Castlebar, my arse. There was little detail in the stories, obvious because of the late-breaking nature of the story on Saturday evening. The only photographs were night scenes of a Garda roadblock on the N5, close to where the girls had been discovered. That piqued his interest.

He lifted the television remote and changed channels, just in time for the main one o'clock news bulletin on RTE. This time there were pictures, close-up daytime shots of the burnt-out garage.

Big Paud was hit by a sudden electric shock. He knew this place. It was his! It was one of his stash-drop properties, and here were hundreds of Guards and fire officers stamping around the place. It was surely only a matter of time before they stumbled on his secret chamber under the pigsty.

And then he relaxed. So what? The property couldn't be traced back to him. It was too well hidden among shell companies and phony directorships. He could take the loss. Plenty more where that came from.

The scene suddenly shifted away from the live outside broadcast to a studio where a laid-back announcer was ready with a mouth full of white teeth and a pompous demeanour to let the world know the station had just received breaking news that the police had launched a countrywide manhunt for a suspect in the abduction of the teenagers.

The screen changed again, this time to a grainy black and white driving licence photo of the suspect. The image sent another shock through Big Paud's system. It was more than shock. It was a toe-curling, slap-in-the-face trauma that sent his body into spasms. He could feel the pain welling up in his chest, growing more acute the longer he looked at the screen.

"It can't be. I thought you were dead. How...how the hell is this possible?"

Big Paud's pain grew in intensity. His chest was on fire. He knew what was happening. There was a scare about a year ago when doctors lectured him about his lack of exercise, poor diet, and alcohol intake. He'd brushed them aside. Now, he wished he had listened to them.

Big Paud took one final look at the television. The image was of someone a lot older than Flynn remembered. The subject had changed a lot from the teenage boy he had once been, the freckles and acne airbrushed behind stronger new lines of maturity. There was not much left of the picture's former self, so much so that Flynn had to admit he might've passed the boy on the street without a second glance. But this close, there was no mistake. Three were still enough points of reference to make a positive connection.

Big Paud clutched his chest as another sharp pain burrowed into his cavity. He emitted a long sigh and fell off the chair, his eyes glazed over as darkness descended.

Above Big Paud's prostrate body, his eldest son stared down from the television screen.

Chapter 40

THE GARDA PRESS OFFICE is based in the corporate communications centre at the force's headquarters in Dublin's Phoenix Park.

Unusually for a Sunday morning, there was a full complement of staff on site, including the director who had spent the first hour splitting his personnel into three teams, all tasked with the planning and supervision of the news cycle following the discovery of Megan McGrath and Siobhan Cunningham.

One group dealt directly with incoming emails from journalists and editors across the broad media spectrum, television, radio, and the print press, not just in Ireland but further afield in England and Scotland, where the story was beginning to gain a lot of traction.

A second group manned the telephones. Most journalists liked to avoid emails, preferring instead to buttonhole the right person for the right quotes. Many tried to arrange off-the-record briefings, a backdoor mechanism that suited both parties. Things that couldn't be said openly were often couched in a code that steered reporters into the right areas without any messy legal tie-backs to the press office. Which was why terms such as *it is understood,* or *sources close to the investigation,* found their way into the lexicon of news dispersal.

The third, and most important, team in the building that morning were the strategy planners, the men and women who got to decide how much, or how little, information ought to be drip-fed into the public domain. Police often held back vital clues or key facts as a means of controlling false leads and diversions. Not in this case. A decision was taken early to "pour it out there" – a time-worn phrase used when police needed the public's help.

As the lead investigator, Mick Boyle was consulted on the strategy and agreed wholeheartedly with what was planned.

By mid-afternoon on Sunday, the press office put the finishing touches to a poster campaign centred on Owen Paterson's photograph, now colourised and touched up to HD standard. Alongside the original, a Garda identikit specialist produced two variations, showing Patterson in potential disguises, one of which simply included the addition of spectacles, the other adding a beard and long hair. A first print run of fifty-thousand copies was ordered for distribution to every station and public noticeboard that could be found the length and breadth of the country. Original artwork would be forwarded to the media in time for late evening television bulletins and for Monday morning's front pages.

Put in its most basic form, the strategy was to make Owen Paterson the most recognisable face in Ireland. There had to be nowhere for him to go and nowhere for him to hide. They wanted to make him a pariah.

The press office's soul-searching about how much to release on the identities of Patterson's potential victims, was resolved after a round of haggling, the director finally giving his consent to let the press have file photos of Jennifer Ross and Sally

Gardiner, the Kilkenny and Cork teenagers who were now assumed to have died at Patterson's hands. These pics would sit on newsstands alongside those of Megan McGrath and Siobhan Cunningham, the two who got away.

Confirmation was still awaited from Northern Ireland about the search of the river in Downpatrick. It came through late that evening, which triggered a rewrite of press releases and posters.

Two bodies had now been found at the Quoile River and positively identified, through dental records, as that of Jacinta Wilson and Patti-Ann Weston. Moreover, the PSNI were able to confirm that the bodies had been wrapped in the same hessian-type bag and bound in the same electrical tape as that used on Martina Quigley, whose disposal had been interrupted by the elderly couple back in 2015.

The names of the three Northern Ireland girls were added to the Garda's grim headcount of Patterson's evil.

John Bonnaville had contacted Boyle on his personal mobile number ahead of the official announcement of the river discoveries. The distress in the PSNI Inspector's voice was evident. "This was not what I wanted to hear," he told Boyle, "but I guess deep down it's what I had always feared happened to those poor girls.

Boyle sympathised with his counterpart. "Have you spoken to the girls' parents?"

"Yes, they doted on their daughters and always clung to the hope that someday they would walk back in the door. Part of them is glad to get closure, but after eight years it doesn't get any easier. Breaking news like that is the shittiest part of our jobs."

"Bad business, John," Boyle agreed. "Our only consolation is that we now know who we're dealing with. We're moving heaven and earth to run Patterson to ground."

Boyle promised to send Bonnaville all the updated information, including the poster campaigns. "Maybe you could see about circulating them in the North. Probably not much chance he'll head in your direction, but better to cover all bases."

"Consider it done. I've been put in charge of re-opening all three cases and will move back to Downpatrick for my base, but if you think I can help in Castlebar, I'm willing to travel there."

"Sit tight for the moment," Boyle said. "Maybe you could look again at the witnesses in Downpatrick and show them Patterson's photo. You never know, it might kick something loose, such as old acquaintances or places where he might go. It's a long shot and I promise to keep you posted if anything shakes loose at our end."

The Monday morning scene at Castlebar Garda Station was one of euphoria. The mood of celebration trumped everything, especially so when two large bouquets of flowers arrived at Sergeant Moriarty's desk with messages of thanks from the McGrath and Cunningham families. The teak-hard copper, remembering the sheer delight on the faces of the parents when he'd delivered the good news in person with Superintendent Delaney on Saturday evening, had to sniff back a tear as he read the inscriptions to a packed foyer of uniforms and detectives. *Our eternal love and gratitude to Ireland's best men and women.*

Moriarty tried to hide his emotions behind a quickly issued gruff message of his own. "Alright, you lot, stop loitering about. There's work to be done, so get out there and earn your wages."

He fooled no-one. They all smiled back as they headed for the door.

Moriarty patted his chest pocket and walked to the rear of the building. It was time for a cigarette and to pass on some more good news to Boyle. It had just gone seven-thirty and Moriarty knew the Rav4 would already be slotted into its usual parking spot.

Boyle had just mounted the first of the five steps leading to the rear entrance when Moriarty stepped out and held out a cigarette. Boyle shook his head and laughed. "If Belle could see how you lead me astray, she'd have your guts for garters."

"Yeah, well even Belle would understand that you need a celebration drag."

"Please, Sarge, not you too. I've had enough pats on the back and attaboys to last me a lifetime."

"Not that you don't deserve it," Moriarty said, leaning forward to offer Boyle a light, "but this is something else entirely different. Think you might like it."

"Well, c'mon, get if off your chest."

"It's to do with your old friend, Big Paud Flynn. Seems the bugger upped and got himself a heart attack yesterday. They don't think he's going to pull through."

Boyle frowned at the news, not quite understanding why he didn't feel the need to celebrate. Yes, Big Paud was one of the worst types of gangster, someone who deserved to be locked up with the key thrown away for good measure, but it somehow didn't seem right that he should go out with a whimper. Did this mean Boyle felt cheated out of the pleasure of slamming the cell door? Did he believe that dying was too good for Big Paud? Or was it because he simply wanted to go toe-to-toe with the big man one last time?

"I'm not sure how to respond to that," he finally told Moriarty. "It all seems a bit of an anti-climax to the work we've put in to nail the bastard on something substantial. I guess the Lord really does work in mysterious ways."

"That's as maybe," Moriarty said, "but the real good news is that his complaint against you goes out the window. I hear your appointment in Dublin has already been cancelled indefinitely. They can't investigate when the complainant is no longer able to provide evidence."

"Still doesn't mean they won't be wanting answers from me about why I was in the locality when Big Paud's compound was vandalised. We both know that doesn't look right, and it could yet come back to bite me in the ass."

Chapter 41

PUBLIC SIGHTINGS OF Owen Patterson were expected to clutter and bewilder the hunt for him over the next few days. Boyle knew their best chance of catching the fugitive was a phone call that pinpointed his location, even if that meant chasing down a hundred false leads before they got the one real nugget they were after. He saw a statistic once that proclaimed the success rate in capturing on-the-run criminals was down to tip-offs in eighty-five percent of all cases. That was true, not just in Ireland, but also across Europe and the United States of America. Which was why such great store was placed on the Garda's poster and media campaign, likely to be refreshed every few hours to keep everyone interested.

That didn't mean detectives would sit back and wait for the vital breakthrough. Not when Boyle was around. "We go back to basics, we work the angles, and we find the most likely place where Patterson will surface. There are always clues or pointers or inconsistencies. Our job is to find them."

Pep talk over. Down to the detail, he decided, staring across a room of animated faces and seeing renewed enthusiasm, mixed with a determination to close the investigation as soon as possible. Rescuing two teenagers from certain death was a powerful morale uplifter for policemen anywhere in the world.

Boyle decided to split his team into three groups, each responsible for distinctive lines of enquiries.

He glanced down at George Armstrong, reclined on a seat with his feet on the desk in front of him. "Custer, you get the shit-end of the straw. I'm putting four others with you to monitor incoming tip-offs and potential sightings. You don't need me to tell you that you'll be chasing your tail all over the country, running down blind alleys, and generally running into brick walls, but it has to be done."

"Aw, boss, how come I get all the fun jobs?"

"The truth is that you're a details man, Custer. I trust you to treat every sighting as if it's the real thing. Work with uniforms and plainclothes wherever in the country an alert springs from, making sure we deliver a fast and measured response. Chances are that if we run Patterson to ground, it will be because your team does its job."

Armstrong's chest puffed out. "Gotcha, boss."

Boyle turned his attention to Roisin Munn. "You're next up. I've rota'ed three others to join with you in finding out all there is to know about the cottage and grounds at Glencool Forest where the girls were located. Patterson set fire to the place to wipe out fingerprints or DNA, which was a pretty wasted exercise since we'd already learned who he was. What we haven't yet learned is who owns the property and whether this tells us anything about why Patterson chose it for a location to stash the girls. The safe bet is that his name isn't on anything to do with the site, but maybe if we track the real owner we can determine what dealings he or she had with Patterson, or whether they have other similar properties. You never know, maybe our fugitive is using one of these other places to lie low."

"What about the burnt-out Audi?" Munn

asked. "Want us to check back on its purchase to see if there's anything it might tell us?"

"Good idea," Boyle beamed. "We have the full motor vehicle history of all Patterson's cars from the time he first surfaced in 2008. Check with all the dealers, find out what addresses he used on the paperwork, whether anyone accompanied him to the garages, and what payment method was used. He might have used different banks or company accounts. Maybe he got careless and left us a thread to pick at."

The longer the briefing went on, the more animated the room became. Boyle quieted the murmur of voices. "Okay, we move on to the biggest missing piece of the jigsaw. Who the fuck is Owen Patterson and where was he before 2008? What's his history? What did he do with himself for the first twenty-odd years of his life? Our psychiatric consultant tells us it's likely that some traumatic or life-changing event occurred in his formative years to lead him on a path to murder. I'm inclined to agree with her, more so now that we know about the gap in Patterson's history, one he has been careful to hide. We have to connect the dots. Everything hinges on understanding who we're dealing with and where he came from."

"Not going to be easy," Brogan said from behind Boyle's shoulder.

"That's where you come in, Sergeant. You're the third leg of this investigation and the job of your team will be to peel back the layers to show us just who Patterson really is, or should I say, was. How did he become an architect? Where did he study? What name was he using? If need be, show his picture around every university in the country. Some lecturer or registrar has to remember him."

Brogan nodded, impressed by Boyle's train of thought. "It's not every Uni that offers courses in architecture, so maybe it's not as big of a needle-in-the-haystack idea as it first appears."

Boyle smiled. "Plus, there's the added bonus of you being able to go back to stalking the halls of academia. It'll make you feel right at home."

That brought a chorus of laughter, which Boyle quickly tamped down with a wave of his hand. "Okay, that's all for now. Let's get cracking." He turned to Brogan and nodded for him to follow as he made his way out of the room and down the corridor to his office. When they were seated, he asked Brogan. "Think that went okay?"

"You were in top gear, Mick," Brogan responded. "Don't think you missed a trick in there."

"That's as may be, but I still can't shake a notion that we've overlooked something. There's a nagging sensation at the back of my head, but I can't bring it forward."

"A psychiatrist friend once told me that the best way to deal with a situation like that was to empty your mind and try not to think about it. If it wants to reveal itself, it will do so in its own good time."

"That friend wouldn't happen to be a certain Dr Connie Dunne, would it?"

"As a matter of fact, it was."

Boyle smirked. "What's the history with you two? I can tell there was something."

Brogan reddened slightly. "We dated a few times at Uni. Nothing serious. Kind of drifted apart because of our different careers. Just good friends these days."

There was a huge grin on Boyle's face when he leaned forward. "I think it's time to bring you two back together again. I need Dr Dunne's advice on dealing with Megan McGrath and Siobhan Cunningham. We have to get full witness statements, but I'm conscious of the girls' vulnerability. Think you can get Connie back in this afternoon for a chat?"

"Listen, Mick, don't you go trying to play matchmaker."

"Perish the thought. The more I think about it, the more convinced I am that Dr Dunne should sit in on the interviews with Megan and Siobhan."

Connie Dunne was having none of it. "Are you mad in the head? You seriously want to bring these girls into a police station separately for the purposes of recorded and written interviews? That's not the way to go about this."

She was sitting in Boyle's office two hours after receiving a call from Brogan, who sat beside her on the opposite side of Boyle's cluttered desk. "No," she insisted, "you have to take the formality out of it or run the risk of putting these children into a state of catatonia. They are still trying to recover from a horrendous experience, one from which they probably had no hopes of survival, and one they will certainly not wish to revisit anytime soon. Can't this wait for at least a week?"

Boyle shook his head. "I'm afraid not. Much as I sympathise and agree with what you've said, the fact remains that they are material witnesses against a man responsible for five murders. There might be something, no matter how small or tenuous, that we can learn from their interactions with their kidnapper."

"They won't be ready for this," Dunne said with emphasis. "To tell you the truth, I'm not sure when they will be ready. I would need to do a thorough psychological analysis before I could hope to answer that question."

"We don't have the luxury of time. Owen Patterson is still on the loose and could be targeting his next victims as we sit here. As head of this investigation, I need to know if there's any way those two girls can help find him. I asked for you to come here because of the sensitivities involved and I need your help in finding a practical way forward."

"That's just it, Inspector, there are no practical ways forward. You can't take shortcuts with the mental wellbeing of these girls. Believe me, I know the pressures you're all under, but I have to advise that you stay well away at present."

Brogan swivelled to face Dr Dunne. "What about you carry out an assessment of Megan and Siobhan? They were released from hospital this morning, apparently doing rather well, all things considered. Doctors say they were malnourished, and one had a slight infection, otherwise they are physically in good shape. How about you visit them at home, purely on your own professional basis, and let us know if interviews are out of the question."

Dunne paused before answering. "I can agree to that on the condition there are no Guards involved. I won't go into any detail with them about their ordeal, nor will I attempt to get them talking about it. This will be a purely clinical assessment. I will let the girls set the agenda and see how far they are prepared to go. Also, because this will be a professional visit, I can't and won't let you know what we talk about."

"Don't expect you to," Brogan responded. "We simply want you to clear the way for an interview, or at the very least, let us know if and when one is possible."

"Just so long as it's understood, I'm no Trojan horse."

"Never considered it for a moment," Brogan said.

Boyle interrupted the conversation. "It seems we are in agreement. Always thought you two make a great team."

Chapter 42

BY THE TIME BOYLE knocked off work at shortly after nine in the evening, his head was spinning. Updates and reports seemed to fly in and out of his office every two minutes, some warranting follow up action, the majority signalling one dead end after another.

Custer Armstrong was the most frenetic visitor, recounting forty-eight reported sightings of Patterson, mostly in various parts of Mayo or Galway, and none of which proved to be the man they were looking for. They were genuine enough tip-offs, though Custer did wonder how an eighty-seven-year-old man, or a seventeen-year-old teenager, could have been mistaken for the face and details that were splattered across the appeal posters. But all forty-eight were chased down and discounted. The bad news was that they would get to do it all again tomorrow when the count was likely to rise even further as more and more people tuned into the appeal for help.

The detectives chasing down Patterson's car history had something more positive. In three of his five purchases over the past twelve years, Patterson had used cash, a total of fifty-five thousand spent on top-of-the-range vehicles. In two other deals, he'd used an account linked to his business in Wexford. Paperwork on the outstanding deal was still being chased down.

Boyle wondered how an architect, even a

successful one, could constantly come up with that amount of cash. Walking into a showroom with a pocket or briefcase crammed with twenty-thousand Euros, as was the case in one of the purchases, was not exactly common practice. Moreover, it was a risky business, especially for someone who wanted to cover their tracks. Cheques or credit cards were bland, almost impersonal, transactions. But people tended to remember a large brown envelope crammed with cash. So, why shine a spotlight on himself?

Ownership of the cottage was proving more problematic to tie down. The building, plus fifty acres of forest, had been bought in 1998 by a company that was initially registered in the Isle of Man. Since then, the business, which was originally listed as an investment brokerage, had bounced addresses to locations in London, France, and the Seychelles. Tracking down owners and directors was outside the pay grade of rural detectives, leaving Boyle with no choice but to ask the NBCI in Dublin to assign special fraud officers to examine the trail.

The one spark of good news came from Dr Connie Dunne, who had returned to the station after meeting separately with Megan McGrath and Siobhan Cunningham. To her surprise, the girls had been in excellent form and were willing to discuss with police what had happened to them. Dr Dunne had tentatively set up a meeting for the following afternoon at the Cunninghams' house and insisted on being present. Boyle had readily agreed and assigned Detective Dunn to lead the interview.

For his part, Brogan had a fruitless day. He had visited five universities that offered degrees in architecture, but none had Patterson's name among their alumni, nor did anyone recognise his photograph. Brogan had decided to abandon the search in local counties in favour of starting over again in Dublin, the most likely backdrop, he decided, for a man who didn't want to be found. On hearing that Dunne had set up a meeting with the teenagers, Brogan instructed two of his men to head immediately to the capital for an overnight stay and an early round of visits tomorrow.

Boyle straightened in his seat in an attempt to ease the stiffness in his bones. Not much point hanging around here. Another long day awaits. He grabbed his coat and headed out of the station, stopping at the Incident Room to tell his troops to do the same.

As usual, he entered the bar and restaurant through the rear door, noting with a frown that Belle was the sole barmaid for the evening. He pulled up a seat and gladly met her lips when she leaned across the counter. "Nice to have you home."

"Nice to be here, although I didn't expect my pregnant wife to be on her feet at this time of the evening."

"You really are a fusspot," Belle said through a smile. "It's slack this evening and I wanted to give Andrea and Johnny a bit of time off. They do all the heavy lifting during the day, which is when I need them the most."

Boyle nodded in acknowledgment and glanced around the bar. There were only five people spread thinly across the room. One of them was the unmistakeable shape of Jacko McStravick, his back to Boyle and his thick paw wrapped around an almost finished glass of Guinness.

Boyle turned to Belle. "Pour me two pints," he

said, "his eyes casting sideways towards Jacko.

"With pleasure." She returned a few minutes later and set the glasses on the counter. "Seeing as how they are for a good cause, they're on the house."

Boyle was still smiling when he drew up a seat opposite Jacko and pushed a glass across the table. "Mind if I join you?"

"Looks like you already have," Jacko responded with a raised eyebrow. "To what do I owe the pleasure? If you start being nice, the shock will probably kill me. Besides, I've got a reputation to consider."

"You and me both," Boyle said as he clinked glasses. "Imagine the talk when it gets out that one of An Garda Síochána's finest officers is socialising with a known lawbreaker?"

Jacko drained a third of his new pint. "I think the expression you were looking for is *suspected* lawbreaker. Never anything proven, never had anything go against me in court. Pure as the driven snow, that's me. Thanks for the pint, by the way."

"My pleasure," Boyle said. "I needed one myself and somehow it always tastes better in company."

"Even my company?"

"Especially yours. Thanks again for what you did for Belle. Now, stop being a drama queen and change the subject."

"I take it you heard about Big Paud?"

"Hard not to around a small parish."

"Talk is they put him through a triple-bypass today. Can't believe they actually found a heart to operate on. Wouldn't be surprised if the bastard actually pulled through."

"Such is life, Jacko. You ever had many dealings with Big Paud down the years?"

"Here, are you fishing for info?"

"Just conversation, Jacko. Remember, it was you who brought up the subject."

"So it was. Nah, there was never much need for our paths to cross. When he first came to Castlebar, he was already a big shot. Plenty of money and his hand in every pie. Tried to muscle me once for a percentage from my little antiques shop, but I was having none of that. He called it protection money, leastways that's what the geezer he sent called it. Me needing protection!"

"So, what happened?"

"I sent his man packing with a couple of black eyes."

"And Big Paud never came back at you? I find that hard to believe."

"It surprised me too. Kept looking over my shoulder for months until I realised nothing was coming. Guess he had a lot bigger fish to fry than old Jacko, although I always did wonder if he really left me alone so that I could keep the Guards occupied with my little shenanigans."

Boyle shook his head. "Yeah, you really were a pain in the ass. I still think you were lucky there were no repercussions. Big Paud isn't known for his forgiving nature."

"You can say that again. When he first arrived in this neck of the woods from Dublin, he was a mean bastard, always looking for ways to inflict hurt. There was talk in the early days of bodies going missing and people ending up in the casualty room, and all because his wife walked out on him."

"You can't be serious?"

"That was the talk," Jacko said. "Apparently she upped and done a runner one day, leaving Big

Paud to raise three kids. She was never heard from again. Some say she went to America and started a new life."

"Wait a moment," Boyle cut in, "did you say three kids? Thought Big Paud only had two sons?"

"No, there was a third. He was the eldest boy. Apparently, he died in America, some sort of a car accident. Rumour was that he'd gone there to find his mother. You ask me, that's what finally tipped Big Paud over the edge. I don't think he minded the wife's loss, but the son was another matter."

"Jesus," Boyle said, "and you think you know everything there is to know about people."

Jacko shook his head from side to side. "You Guards only know what the folks on my side of the tracks think you should know. If you ever need the right way of things, just give old Jacko a call and he'll put you to rights."

Boyle burst out laughing. "You're spewing shit, Jacko. Hell, you're even starting to talk in the third person."

"Maybe that's because there's two of me. How do you know I haven't got a twin? How do you know which twin you're talking to?"

"Oh, believe me, I'd know if there were two of you, but then, I guess, stranger things have happened. I'm getting another drink, so it's time to decide which of you twins is getting one."

"Eh?"

Chapter 43

BOYLE'S HEAD WAS thumping on Tuesday morning. That was quite a session with Jacko last night. He began to suspect there *must* have been a twin who took over from the big man at some point during the proceedings. Nobody could shift that amount of Guinness and whiskey and still look as fresh as a daisy at midnight. Boyle admitted quietly to himself that he had enjoyed McStravick's company as the perfect release for the tension of the last few days.

It didn't help the headache, however. It was pounding away, urging him to pull the sheets back over. Another few hours of shuteye couldn't hurt. He looked at his watch and frowned. It had gone past 7.30am, already the longest lie-in he'd had for quite some time. He fought the temptation and climbed from the bed, careful not to wake Belle, who was lying in her new side-on position, which, she said, gave the baby the most comfortable angle to while away the last few weeks.

He was showered and dressed and out the door within thirty minutes, conscious that he really shouldn't be driving this soon after a bout of heavy drinking. That's all he'd need. Being pulled over by a uniform for drink-driving would put the tin hat on his disciplinary record. Besides, there was the safety of other road users to consider. He decided to play safe.

Custer Armstrong answered his mobile almost

immediately. "Morning, boss, where are you?"

"I need a lift, Custer. Can you swing by this way and pick me up?"

"On my way."

Armstrong lived less than a mile from Boyle's location, but Boyle knew the chances were the detective was already at the station, earphones plugged in, and beginning another long stint listening to messages on the hotline.

Oddly, it took Armstrong twenty-five minutes to draw up alongside Boyle.

"Sorry, I'm late, boss, but I've got some sensational news."

Boyle looked across and immediately translated the euphoric look on Armstrong's face as news of only one thing. "Tell me we've got him."

"I think we might have. Got a message through late last night and it was one of the first few I listened to this morning. This one jumped out. The caller owns a small backstreet hotel on the South Circular Road, near the Kilmainham Gaol Museum in Dublin. Says he had a guy booked in for a few nights sometime yesterday. Paid cash and looked suspicious."

"Suspicious how?"

"He says the guy showed traces of recently dying his hair. Apparently there were black streaks on the back of his neck and behind his ears. He only had a computer carry bag for luggage and insisted that his room not be disturbed until he left. Claimed to be a writer who needed solitude to complete his manuscript and didn't want breakfast, which was part of the price. He even gave the owner an extra fifty Euros to agree to his wishes."

Boyle started to get fidgety in his seat. "All of

that doesn't make him our man. What prompted the hotel guy to get in touch with the hotline?"

"Sorry, boss, should have said right off the bat. I rang him back as soon as I heard the message and I'm pretty sure he's on the level. Says he saw the posters and television bulletins after the guest signed in and is in no doubt the man is none other than Owen Patterson. Of course, the ledger was signed in a different name, but the owner studied Patterson's picture in detail and is positive, despite the change in hair colour, that he's harbouring our fugitive."

"Is this guest still at the hotel?"

"Yes. Apparently he left just before eight this morning and said he would be away for most of the day doing research for his book."

Boyle let the information sink in for a moment. He would have to contact the NBCI office, and probably let them run the show on their own doorstep. Much as he wanted this for himself, there were just too many breaches of protocol facing him if he went rogue. However, he needed to be there. Which meant he needed to buy a bit of time.

"Custer, tell me you haven't alerted anyone else yet."

"No, boss."

"Good man. We'll rustle up Brogan and Munn as soon as we get to the station. The four of us are taking a trip to Dublin."

"What about getting support from our colleagues in Dublin?"

"Plenty of time to worry about that when we're on the road. Get back in touch with that hotel owner and tell him to keep his head down. It's imperative he does not act suspiciously around Patterson. The slightest thing will spook him."

"Got you, boss, although if this guy is really away for the day there's no reason for the two to be in contact until we throw a net around the place."

"I wish it were that straightforward, Custer. How many times have you seen things go tits up because of the unexpected? Make sure your hotelier keeps a lid on his excitement, otherwise we could end up with egg on our faces."

Two hours into the journey from Castlebar, Boyle prepared for his call to the NBCI. Despite the monotony of the M4 motorway, the time flew. The closer they got to Dublin, the greater the tension was ramped up. Boyle sat in the passenger seat, cradling his mobile as Brogan's Renault Kadjar cruised past Maynooth heading for the city's outskirts. The on-board satnav display showed they were less than forty minutes from their destination.

Boyle needed a plausible reason for being in Dublin ahead of contacting the National Bureau of Criminal Investigation. The answer was staring him in the face. He remembered Brogan telling him last evening that he was sending two men to the capital to check university records for Owen Patterson. It could be argued that the search had taken on greater significance, hence the need for additional support. They just happened to be here when the tip-off from the hotelier was finally checked thoroughly and isolated as extremely promising.

Quite what someone might make at a later date of a tramp around universities by an Inspector, a sergeant, and four detectives was anyone's guess. Most would see it as overkill. A cynic would view it as little more than a convenient bending of the truth. To hell with that, Boyle reasoned. If they got Patterson, no one would be asking questions.

And anyway, he was the lead investigator in the hunt for one of the country's most violent and dangerous criminals. Where else would he be other than at the scene? Stuff procedures and protocols and make the damned call!

He got the main switchboard and asked to be transferred to Inspector Damien Robinson, one of the few officers who had stuck with Boyle through the turbulent last few days of Boyle's sojourn at NBCI. It was Robinson who had insisted Boyle fight for his rights and had offered to stand in Boyle's corner, despite the pressure from above to keep the whole sorry mess of an unfaithful wife under wraps.

Boyle hoped Robinson was still around the place. He got his answer a moment later when the familiar West Cork accent grated down the line. "So, the great Mick Boyle is alive and kicking and remembers who his friends are."

It was typical Robinson humour and Boyle smiled at the memories of some great banter with one of the best colleagues he had ever had. "Well, Robbo, as you know, even Moses had to come down from the mountain now and then to spread a bit of learning and knowledge to the great unwashed. Let's just say I'm in your neck of the woods and in need of a bit of support."

"Don't tell me you've got yourself in trouble again? There's only so much I can do to keep bailing you out."

"Nothing like that, Robbo. I've got a real humdinger. Could put another stripe on that scrawny arm of yours."

Robinson's voice changed from a lighthearted tone to one that conveyed more urgency and seriousness. "Has this something to do with your fugitive? By the way, great job on rescuing those two young girls."

"Thanks Robbo, and you've got it in one. We have reason to believe Owen Patterson is holed up in a Dublin hotel." Boyle continued to fill the NCBI man in on the hotline message and the follow-up conversation with the hotelier.

"So that's why you're here. How come you didn't contact us earlier?"

Trust Robinson to get straight to the point. Boyle trotted out his universities story, realising how lame it sounded when he actually articulated it. "Don't bust my balls, Robbo. This is where I need to be. Now, are you going to help?"

"No need to get defensive with me, kiddo. As far as I'm concerned, this is your case and it's only right that you should be front and centre. But, as you well know, I'm going to have to initiate a full press to lock down the area with our people and make sure there's no danger to the public. How do you see this playing out?"

"How well do you know the South Circular Road, and have you heard of this Brownfill Hotel?"

"Know the area, but never been in the hotel. Don't worry, I'll find out everything we need by the time you get here."

"Our information is that the fugitive is out for the day and won't be back for some time. We need to throw a soft cordon around the place for at least a half-mile in all directions. No cars or checkpoints. Don't want to spook him when he's heading back there."

"We've done this kind of thing before, or have you forgotten?"

"Sorry for stating the obvious, Robbo. Where can we meet?"

"There's a visitor car park close to Kilmainham Gaol on Inchicore Road. I'll meet you there in an hour and we'll decide how to proceed. In the meantime, I'll send a man to the Brownfill Hotel just to make sure things are still quiet there."

Chapter 44

THE FOYER OF THE Brownfill Hotel was a hive of activity. Dustsheets covered the carpet and lounge seats, and the walls were stripped off paintings and lighting fixtures. Only a narrow path leading from the revolving door to the check-in desk survived the preparation work as a team of decorators set about giving the entire ground floor a makeover. Strange that the whole place was repainted less than a year ago. Stranger still, that none of the workmen had ever held a brush or roller in a professional capacity before.

None of that mattered. There were no hotel staff to oversee what was going on. Nor were there any guests around to be inconvenienced by the clutter. A young lady, resplendent in the hotel's familiar brown and white uniform. stood to the left of the main check-in counter, her eyes focussed on the doorway, her hand close to a Sig Sauer pistol, which rested out of sight on a shelf of a large semi-circular pedestal, of the type universally used by concierges the world over. But this young lady was no concierge. She worked for the NBCI and was more accustomed to booking criminals than tickets to the theatre.

The men in overalls around her were a mixture of NBCI officers and members of the detective team from Castlebar. Boyle was there, so too Brogan and Armstrong, trying to look busy with repetitive movements of their rollers, languidly moving up and down the same patches of wall, adding layer upon layer of a hideous green emulsion that did nothing to blend in with the foyer's existing ambience.

Damien Robinson and two of his most senior operatives worked alongside the Castlebar team, hoping that three pairs of workers would not look out of place in the cramped surroundings. Out on the street, Boyle had positioned Roisin Munn with a large team of NBCI officers tasked with keeping an eye out for Owen Patterson and closing the net as soon as he walked through to the hotel.

They were a mixture of phony professionals, which included road sweepers, paper-sellers, telephone engineers perched on poles, traffic wardens, and even a busker, who it turned out was a fair hand at an electric guitar and had a more than passable voice when it came to belting out *Hallelujah* or *Country Roads*. His repertoire was an eclectic mix.

Most of them were roles that Robinson had used before on countless surveillance projects. They had the props and uniforms in storage at headquarters, although when Boyle had suggested crowding the foyer with fake decorators, they had to ask a local company for help with providing overalls, dustsheets, rollers, and tins of paint. The company owner was a willing individual, although his largesse didn't stretch to giving them much choice among his large selection of colours. Hence the awful green, a shade not exactly popular with his normal clientele.

Boyle and Robinson had met up as planned in the car park about a mile from the hotel. They had used a concealed incident-room truck to plan their moves, bent over a table looking at a detailed street map of the area around the Brownfill. It was a simple strategy, based on allowing their fugitive through a tight cordon before taking him down inside the hotel. Too dangerous to try anything on the street. If he was armed, the risk of civilian collateral damage had to be the overriding factor. Unless the target somehow twigged what was happening, they would funnel him towards the hotel and wait until he stepped inside.

The members of the exterior cordon team all carried Patterson's photo. They burned the image into their brains until they were each confident they could identify him. They carried small radio transmitters in their pockets, the kind that could be activated with a simple push-button click. There were no earphones or spidery wires, which were known to have betrayed many a surveillance to those with an eye trained for such things.

Everyone was in place before noon. According to the hotelier, Patterson had indicated he would be away until late afternoon, which, of course, didn't mean he wouldn't arrive much sooner. They had to be on their toes from minute one.

Inside the hotel, the clock ticked slowly, the pace of the rollers slackened, and the watchers grew weary. They had been at it for two hours, finally deciding that as long as one pair of painters was actually doing something, the others could take turns at resting on the dustsheet-covered chairs. Another hour went by. And then another.

Shortly after four o'clock, Boyle decided it was time for a short morale-boosting talk. "Listen up. We are now entering the optimum time for Patterson's return. Anytime over the next hour constitutes late afternoon in anyone's book, so we get back to it as if our target were just outside and we keep this up until he is. Our watchers might only be able to give us little more than a few seconds warning, but we've got to be prepared for them missing him completely, which means he could suddenly appear unannounced. Let's get to it."

Boyle led the way, and the rest of the squad began climbing the paint-spattered A-shaped wooden ladders supplied by the decorating company. The concierge went back to reading a magazine, flipping the pages with her left hand while her right arm continued to dangle below the top of her pedestal, her hand less than six inches from the concealed Sig.

Out on the street, an NBCI officer pruning a hedge at Emmett Lodge, watched six people alight from a Bus Eireann community minibus on the corner of Emmett Road. The group was made up of four women and two men, one of whom carried a computer shoulder bag as he turned into South Circular Road. Right size, right build, black hair, and a face that could be a match for the poster photo.

The detective let the man walk a hundred yards before clicking the transmitter in his chest pocket. *Possible sighting on the South Circular Road, heading for Suir Road. Handing it on.*

Another voice clicked in. *Be advised, I'm at the corner of the Suir Road and Bulfin Road. Visual on target heading towards me. He's crossed the road towards the direction of the Brownfill. Your location in two minutes.*

A few seconds later, the same voice broke through again. *Wait. Wait. Target has stopped and is looking around. Something's wrong. He's turned back...I repeat, he's turned back.*

The airwaves remained silent. Then another message. *Target has gone into shop. I have a visual of both front and rear exits. Target at the counter.*

Another delay. *Target out of shop and resuming his direction towards the Brownfill.*

Inside the Brownfill, Boyle exchanged glances with Robinson and then at the rest of his team. Nothing was said, but Boyle noticed Brogan take his pistol from the pocket of his overalls and rest it out of view on the top step of his ladder. Custer Armstrong was moving his weapon under cover of a wipedown cloth when the revolving door at the entrance squeaked an announcement of someone's entrance.

Boyle fought the urge to turn around. He rolled a fresh run of paint on the wall and tried to squint sideways as a man stepped through into the foyer. The angle was all wrong for Boyle to get more than a partial look at the profile, but he was aware the stranger was standing still and swivelling his head around the room. Then the man turned back to the door and pushed his way outside.

"Fuck it," Boyle shouted, "we've been made." He leapt from the ladder and made a dash for the door, aware that the others were already on his shoulder. He shouted back for someone to call up the watchers to apprehend the suspect.

Custer Armstrong was already ahead of the thought and was shouting into his handset. *Target on the run from the Brownfill. Surround and apprehend immediately.*

Boyle burst through the door expecting to find Patterson in full flight. Instead, he crashed into the back of his target, sending a cigarette pack and a cheap plastic lighter skittering out into the road.

The man stumbled forward, tripped over the drop of the kerb, and fell heavily on his knees. Boyle's momentum took him on top of the figure, pushing him into the ground, and trapping his arms and shoulder bag against the tarmacked surface. The rest of the team appeared at Boyle's side as he flipped the man onto his back and stared at the face below him.

A few specks of blood appeared on one of the man's cheeks where it had grazed the surface of the road. Behind the scrape was the stare of an angry and confused individual who wrestled violently against Boyle, trying to dislodge his assailant like a bucking bronco. "What the fuck are you doing? What's going on?"

Boyle badly wanted to punch his prisoner in the mouth. He wanted to exact revenge for all those dead girls and for Megan McGrath and Siobhan Cunningham, who had escaped his clutches. He wanted to do what all those poor children must have wanted to do but were unable to.

The thought of a serial killer sitting smug in a cosy cell with three squares a day and getting unfettered access to a library and university courses was just plain wrong. At the very least, Boyle reasoned, this guy needed a good smacking to send him on his way.

But he couldn't do it.

Because the face that stared back at Boyle was definitely not Owen Patterson!

Chapter 45

DANIEL FLYNN, aka Owen Patterson, aka a whole raft of other names, was lying back in the first-class seat on the Dublin to Belfast Express contemplating how his life had taken another dramatic turn. It hadn't been easy to secure a seat on the train, not when his face was being plastered just about everywhere he looked.

But Flynn was resourceful. He'd learned from an early age how to dodge under the radar, firstly as a youngster trying to get lost in the mean streets of Dublin, and later as someone in need of a new identity in the heady spinning top that was life in Chicago. That's where he had picked up an underworld knowledge about disguises and false papers and how to take care of himself. He'd been doing it for a long time.

Changing his appearance was the easy part. He had a wooden box of tricks – wigs, spectacles, false eyebrows, colour-tint contact lenses, latex noses, and enough powders and creams to cause even a makeup artist to blush. Then there were the props, the best of which were crutches or neck braces or fake warts or fake scars, all of which could dramatically alter one's appearance. Put enough of these changes in physical appearance together at once, and even someone's best friend wouldn't recognise them.

Flynn had gone for the dramatic. A wig of straight black hair, which sat over his ears, but failed deliberately to hide a ragged scar running down from his left lobe across the top of his chin. The other side of his face sported two ugly black and brown warts, which were calculated to draw attention away from any of his other features. It was part of human nature for people to avert their eyes from noticeable physical disfigurements, a fact which worked in Flynn's favour. Not much chance of them connecting an image from a poster with the face of a man they couldn't bring themselves to glance twice at. The neck brace he wore pushed his chin upwards and added further distortion to a visage that no longer looked anything like the Owen Patterson photographs.

The only black spot on Flynn's horizon was a feeling of being cheated out of killing his two Castlebar captives. But there were plenty more fish in the sea. He would find them in Downpatrick. In many ways, it was like going back home.

His mind wandered back further in time, to a distant memory of a mother who was his whole world as a youngster. It was she who had encouraged him in his studies, helping with homework, and filling him with a passion for improving his mind. She'd taught him to appreciate the finer things in life and opened his eyes to poetry and reading and the opera. He was destined for great things, she had often said, ignoring the background into which he was born, and from which there seemed no hope of escape.

She was a small, gentle woman with bright azure-blue eyes and a head of golden curls that flowed below her shoulders. Despite her slim build, she stood up to her husband's constant bullying, which usually ended in violence, and which put her in hospital on many occasions with broken bones or damage to her kidneys from vicious blows. She had tried hard to keep things going, but nothing she ever did was good enough for the loud-mouthed drunkard she had married.

She had drawn a line at caring for Daniel's younger brothers, two tearaways cut from the same cloth as their father. They had constantly missed school, preferring to spend their time roughing up the other kids, or hanging around their father's shady business deals. She had tried to pull them away from that kind of life, but in the end she simply gave up.

Then one day she wasn't there.

Daniel came down for breakfast, expecting as usual to find her in the kitchen among the smells of frying bacon and sausages. The place was deserted, save for her trademark apron, which hung over the back of a chair like a farewell message. There was no note. No goodbyes. Just a partially cleared wardrobe and that damned apron.

In the days and weeks that followed, it became clear that she was not coming back. Daniel took it bad. To his mind, she had not left the family, she had abandoned him. How could she have pretended to have loved him all these years? How could she have left him behind?

His resentment grew with each passing day. At first, he wanted to find her to ask why she had gone, but later his feelings morphed into hatred, the bitter deep-rooted kind that twisted his mind towards more sinister thoughts. If he ever ran into her again, he would kill her for the selfish bitch she had become.

But first he had to deal with a father whose moods turned blacker with each passing day.

Without his mother's protection, Daniel was forced to run errands, which usually involved delivering packets of drugs and picking up money from some of Kilkenny's worst criminals. He was forced to watch as Big Paud meted out punishment to those who failed to pay up or, as was often the case, simply a beating to send out a message about who was the king on the hill.

Daniel scorned at Big Paud's name. It was a self-anointed soubriquet, designed to add another layer of menace when his dealings were whispered in bars and clubs around the county. And, it had to be admitted, Big Paud knew how to get things done, judging by the bundles of cash that flooded into the family's nondescript terrace house.

At first, Daniel fought against his involvement. It went against everything his mother had instilled in him. But the bitch was no longer here, the love and attention little more than a sham. And so, when he turned sixteen he developed his own plan for life. He threw himself into Big Paud's business and began to make himself indispensable with his ideas for using the mountain of cash that was accumulating on a daily basis. It was Daniel's idea to invest in bookmaker's premises and out-of-the-way properties where secure hordes of cash and goods could be hidden. It was even his idea to prepare special watertight concrete chambers beneath mounds of manure or makeshift pigsties. Over the course of the next year, Daniel was present when three such stores were built at separate rural properties. They would be the nest eggs for his plan.

Several days after his seventeenth birthday, for which Big Paud presented him with a gleaming new Ford Escort, Daniel took Jerome and Seamus to school, not caring whether they did their usual disappearing trick as soon as he'd left them. He had his own disappearing trick in mind.

He drove to one of the cash-dumps and emptied the contents. These were still the days of the Irish Pound, or Punt, which had a rough equivalent value to British Sterling. There was exactly one-hundred-thousand in neat bundles of all denominations of notes. A fortune in the Ireland of 1998.

Daniel headed for Dublin, straight to a building site where he could craft a background while he laid his plans. He stayed in a cheap boarding house and asked around for someone who could provide him with a new identity. Not difficult finding information among squads of men, many of whom had themselves had to use such services.

He went for a top-notch brokerage, a seedy operation that demanded ten-thousand pounds for its services out of an attic in a rundown building near Grafton Street. He could afford it, especially since he was getting not one but two new identities, which included birth certificates, driving licenses, and bonafide social security papers. He left the building site, moved between boarding houses, and sold the Ford Escort in favour of a battered old commercial van. He wouldn't need it for long. He spent the next six months learning the ways of banking, focusing his attention on debit cards, international wire transfers, and investment bonds. He opened four accounts at different banks and began drip-feeding his cash into their systems, which he topped up by raiding another of Big Paud's hidden stores.

In the spring of 1999, Daniel jetted off to Chicago, using one of his new aliases. There was no particular reason why he chose the city, other than its strong Irish connections. Anywhere in America would have done. It was a new start, somewhere he could put his formative years behind him. At that stage, he had no intention of ever returning to Ireland.

He decided on pursuing a professional career. He craved respect and standing, perhaps as a banker because he had already learned so much but decided against it in favour of architecture. He signed up for a three-year degree course at Columbia University, rented an expensive apartment near the campus, and settled into enjoying the best period of his life.

But the dark thoughts soon surrounded him. He couldn't shake loose the image of the treacherous blonde-haired woman who had been his mother. How many other bitches were like her in the world? How much deceit and poison were they spreading in the world? Why should they be allowed to get away with it?

He blurred his way through college and tried to fight down the urges. Every time he saw a blonde student, he thought of his mother. And every time he wanted to pull the bitch into the campus undergrowth and strangle the life away from her.

Flynn befriended a fellow architectural degree student by the name of Roscoe Williams, a native Tennessean who had been orphaned from an early age and had had to learn to fend for himself in constant moves around foster homes. Flynn took the young man under his wing, gave him a rent-free room at his apartment, and generally helped with most of the expenses of student life.

One morning, in a strange quirk of fate, Williams was late for a lecture, one that Flynn had already covered. Flynn tossed his car keys to his roommate and went back to sleep. Later that morning, two officers from Chicago PD hammered on the apartment door.

The bad news was delivered with chilling calmness. Flynn's car had been involved in an horrific freeway pile-up that had left the driver unrecognisable, an understandable result of an oil tanker exploding and turning the vehicle into a funeral pyre. The policemen had traced the chassis number back to this address.

Flynn was never sure why he pounced so quickly on the opportunity. Until that moment he had no intentions of returning to Ireland. To do so he would need to expunge all trace of his former identity, easily done since he still carried his original driving licence and passport, which he handed over to the cops. He explained to them that he had loaned the car to his flatmate, named Daniel Flynn, who was originally from Ireland. There was no next of kin and no one to be contacted about the sad news.

And so, the following day a small paragraph appeared in the Chicago Tribune announcing the death of Daniel Flynn. In the way of the press world, the filler item was picked up and re-run the next morning by one of the daily newspapers back in Dublin.

Daniel Flynn, eldest son of Big Paud Flynn, no longer existed.

Chapter 46

FLYNN HAD JUST one remaining problem. The fake papers he held in the name of Owen Patterson carried the picture of an instantly recognisable Daniel Flynn. He had to change, a decision that required plastic surgery and a visit back to his forger to swap photos on all his paperwork, including Columbia University's academic verification certificate. He hadn't spent three years earning an architectural degree to see it wasted on technicalities. If anyone cared to check his status, the new-look Owen Patterson was there to be seen in official university records.

He returned to Ireland in January 2008 and settled again in Dublin, this time buying a modest semi-detached house near Tallaght, and setting up his own practice in a rented office at St Stephen's Green. The business grew rapidly, forged by Flynn's strong personality and his ability to buy his way into the right circles. His wealth and influence grew and for a time everything was as normal as it could be.

But the demons wouldn't go away.

He fought against them for months on end until finally he found himself one evening back in Kilkenny, not quite sure why he was there or what he intended to do. He had taken on a development contract in the city but had commuted regularly back to Dublin each evening. But this time he stayed put.

There was no pre-planning, just an aimless search for an answer. He cruised the city for several hours, stopping for several long stops to watch people walk by on their way to and from pubs and restaurants in High Street. Later in the evening, at St James's Street, close to the Market Cross Shopping Centre, he spotted Jennifer Ross, in many ways an unremarkable girl, who appeared to be aimlessly wandering on her own far from the main car park.

But there was something about her. Definitely the long blonde hair, but also the manner in which she held her head high and sauntered around with a confident and independent stride that reminded him of his mother. His blood boiled.

The next thing he knew was that the girl was in his car, lying across the backseat, the life choked from her in a mad frenzy that lasted only a few seconds. He'd taken the body well outside the city limits and dumped it in a wooded area. He covered the ground with stones and twigs and leaves, and hightailed it back to Dublin, expecting to hear news of the discovery sometime the next day.

But it never came. Not the next day, nor the next week, nor the next month. He had got lucky. He knew that. From now on, things would have to be planned better, which was why it had taken him almost two years to strike again in Cork, a simple snatch of another blonde-haired teenager by the name of Sally Gardiner. This time he was better prepared for the disposal of the body.

This time he didn't use his own car. He bought a second-hand van, using one of his many aliases, and filled it with the tools and materials of an electrician, a simple choice to make because of his close-up contact with many trades in his profession as an architect. He added in several sets of workmen's coveralls and filled the pockets with small pliers and bits of end-wiring to add authenticity.

The spools of cable wire were ideal for his purposes, as were packs of multi-purpose hessian bags. Sally Gardiner, who was his second victim, became the first to be wrapped in the bags, secured with wire, and dumped in a river.

Flynn decided to search for more jobs around the country. After all, it had worked twice and given him reasons to be in the locations of the missing teenagers. There was one place he badly wanted to go. It took two more years before he finally arrived in Downpatrick as supervising architect at a small housing development in the centre of the town. That move cost Jacinta Wilson her life, as too a similar move two years later resulted in the death of Patti-Ann Weston.

Flynn went back to Downpatrick for a third time in 2015 when he ended the life of Martina Quigley. After that, he called a halt to his trips up North. He was spending his luck at a reckless rate and decided to take a break. He went back to Dublin, continued his work within a twenty-mile radius of the city, and fought the urges to kill again.

But it couldn't last. He had known that. He knew it when he sought work in Castlebar and moved into the area for an extended stay.

Throughout all his time back in Ireland, Flynn had kept tabs on Big Paud. His hatred for his father grew to almost insane levels. Someday he would kill him. For now, he would use and torment him. He knew where to look to check records for Paud's property dealings, despite the obvious smokescreens of shell companies and phony directors. His father had a penchant for old TV westerns serials, which down the years had supplied the names of many of his ventures. Names like *The Ponderosa* or *The High Chaparral* or *Sugarfoot* appeared regularly on many listings. The big idiot couldn't resist the nostalgia – and that's how Daniel found the deserted cottage at Glencool Forest in Longford. The buyer was listed as a Mauritius-based consortium under the umbrella name of *Rawhide Regeneration Inc.*

Daniel had visited the forest on numerous occasions before deciding to set up base there. It was far enough away from Castlebar to enact the next stage of his mission. He would not kill his victims right away, as on the previous five occasions. This time he would toy with them and torment them and savour their helplessness and loss of hope.

He had enjoyed travelling back and forth and seeing his captives cower at each of his entrances. It had made him feel good in a way that the quick kills hadn't. Perhaps that's why, in a state of euphoria, he had a sudden urge one morning to call in at Big Paud's works compound in Castlebar. He'd smiled at the nameplate across the entrance. *P Flynn & Sons, Door & Window Manufacturers.*

Jerome and Seamus were welcome to the acknowledgement. They were no better than their vicious, selfish father. His act of spite in thrashing the place was as much against them as it was Big Paud. It hadn't really given him as much satisfaction as he thought it would. Part of him wanted to discover his father alone on the premises. He imagined the look on the old man's face when he stared at his long-lost son and took in the familiar family Colt Python pointed at his head.

But it wasn't to be. Perhaps another time.

Now, as he sat staring out through the windows of the train as it hurtled towards Belfast, Daniel wondered what the next adventure would bring for him. He had no delusions. He was reaching the end game. He was resigned to it. They would probably capture or kill him. But not before he blazed a final murderous trail.

The train drew to a stop at Belfast Lanyon Place Station, formerly known as Central Station. Flynn stepped down from the carriage and looked around. He spotted the taxi rank and pushed his way through a throng of people, stopping at the hailing point to await his turn. He placed his suitcase on the ground beside him, adjusted the fake surgical collar, and kept his eyes averted from several CCTV cameras mounted on the overhang of a roof shelter.

When his turn came, he lifted the case into the back of the cab and looked through the hatch to a driver in his late fifties.

"Where to, sir?"

"Take me to the Europa Hotel for the night. Then, tomorrow morning, if you want the fare, you can call back at ten to pick me up for a trip to Downpatrick."

The driver's eyes lit up. Fares out of the city to rural towns could be lucrative business. "That's no problem, sir. It'll be a pleasure to take you to Downpatrick."

Chapter 47

BACK TO SQUARE ONE. Not a concept Boyle believed in. Okay, they thought they'd got their man at the Brownfill Hotel. In many ways what looked to be the end of the road proved to be nothing more than a cruel diversion, one which had all but drained the energy from his team. Boyle was more philosophical. Suck it up, move on, and get back to basics. No other way to look at it.

And it was not as if they were starting with a blank canvas. They still had a number of leads. There were still avenues to pursue. All it needed was to reinvigorate the troops and rekindle the fire in their bellies. "Yesterday was a setback, nothing more. Maybe we were stupid to think we'd get lucky so early, but luck doesn't play a part on what we have to do next. Use your training, play your hunches, double-check the ground we've already covered. I know we're smarter than this bastard Patterson. All we have to do is prove it."

It was early Wednesday morning when he delivered the pep talk. The long trek back from Dublin had given Boyle plenty to ponder. He wasn't embarrassed by the outcome of the operation or been left with an egg-on-the-face feeling. It had been a promising lead, one that justified the response that was mounted. To do otherwise, would have been a grave dereliction from normal procedures – and that really would have been the case if the subject had indeed turned out to be Owen Patterson and had flown the net because the sighting hadn't been taken seriously enough.

The hapless civilian who Boyle had wrestled to the ground turned out to be what he said he was, a reclusive writer who had ambitions to be Ireland's next big crime thriller novelist. Dublin's answer to Galway's Ken Bruen! The poor sod had stopped at a newsagents to buy cigarettes on his way back to the hotel and had only turned in the foyer when he suddenly remembered his intention to have a smoke before retiring to his room for the evening. He had not been best pleased about his rough treatment, threatening on several occasions to write about his cuts and scrapes in a blog, which he used to promote his total author output to date – two Kindle books that had sold less than a hundred copies over the past two years.

Nevertheless, he had to be assuaged. The last thing Boyle needed was someone running off at the mouth or sharing the story with local newspapers. And so, he cut the man a deal after explaining exactly what the operation had been all about. The writer agreed to total silence in return for exclusive access to police files when the fugitive was caught. The prospect of a best-seller suddenly triumphed over ruffled feathers and a scraped cheek.

The hotel owner had been easier to bargain with. He was prepared to overlook the hideous green smudges on the walls of his foyer after the NBCI agreed to foot the bill for professional decorators to apply a full makeover. He ended up being the only person who was glad he'd made a wrongful identification.

Boyle returned to his office and stared at the ceiling. *Pep talks are all fine and dandy, but where in the hell do we go from here?* His gaze dropped to a small wipeboard, which was dominated by Patterson's wanted-poster photo of a smug face that seemed to be taunting Boyle. There was a catch-me-if-you-can arrogance to the set of the jaw and the creased lines just above the eyebrows where the forehead was pimpled by the ridges and valleys of someone who looked as if they had been in a few scrapes in their time.

Reluctantly, Boyle forced himself to turn away, his eyes falling on another wipeboard, this one discarded on a floor at the corner of his office. Another face smirked back at him. It was that of Big Paud Flynn. *Don't worry, I haven't forgotten you. Soon as I'm done with Patterson, you go right back to the top of the queue.*

He stared between the pictures for several more seconds before his concentration was broken by the office door being flung open. Paul Brogan stepped inside, carrying a sheaf of papers and a face like a cat that had just raided a creamery.

"You're gonna want to see this, Mick." Those Americanisms again.

"What have you got?"

Brogan drew up a seat and fanned the papers across the desk. "What an idiot I've been. We've been tramping around universities looking for background on Patterson when all the time the answer was staring me in the face. I should have gone direct to the RIAI."

"Back up a bit," Boyle said. "What the hell is the RIAI?"

"The Royal Institute of Architects. If you want

to practice in Ireland you need to be registered with them, and sure enough that's where I found Patterson's records. I'm just off the phone with their Donegal office, which is one of many dotted across the country, and they were able to pull out these details for me." Brogan tapped the sheets of paper and smiled.

Boyle glanced down. "What are we looking at?"

"Patterson first registered with the RIAI in 2008 after returning from Chicago where he got his degree at Columbia University. Apparently, because our regulations and use of certain materials is vastly different from a lot of the building codes and standards they use in America, anyone wanting to practice here as an architect has to undergo a professional update course. Patterson did the course with an approved RIAI provider and has maintained his requisite continuous professional development updates ever since."

"Are these papers telling us anything else?"

Brogan nodded. "The degree course at Columbia was three years, so we can assume that Patterson went there something around or shortly before 2005. We can also assume, since there is no record of an Owen Patterson at any time in Ireland, that he picked up the alias in Chicago and returned here with his new identity and credentials."

Boyle rose from his seat, crossed the room, and slapped his hand against the wanted poster. "Finally, we're getting somewhere. It's only a piece of this bastard's backstory, but it's a great starting point. We need to find out what he did in Chicago. Was he in any trouble with the cops there? Who were his friends and acquaintances? Can anyone tell us anything before this man became Owen Patterson?

Get onto Chicago PD and see if they can help."

"That was my next move. Thought I'd bring you up to speed before going any further." Brogan shifted uneasily in his seat. "Look, Mick, I'm sorry about the time wasted chasing down the universities. I really should have thought of the RIAI as the first point of contact. I've cost us a lot of valuable time."

"Rubbish, Paul, we can't be expected to think of everything, besides which nothing might come of this Chicago connection except to fill in some blanks. If we do get something from it, it will be because you were on the ball when it mattered most."

Brogan shook his head and walked to the door. "Thanks for trying, Mick, but it doesn't hide the fact that I fucked up,"

Boyle decided to change the subject. "Where are we on the property search for Glencool Forest?"

"It's been passed onto Custer Armstrong. All we know at the moment is that the site was bought by a Mauritius-based company with the curious name of *Rawhide Regeneration Inc*. We'll probably hit a brick wall trying to get much more than that, but if anyone can ferret out something it will be Custer."

At that moment, George Custer Armstrong was scratching his head, wondering what to do with the name of a company that was probably buried in an avalanche of bogus names and addresses, which themselves were layered upon false trails and subterfuges designed to stop anyone from finding out what or who was truly behind it.

A succession of international phone calls had yielded precisely zero. Not one person in Mauritius had ever heard of *Rawhide Regeneration Inc*, which didn't come as any real surprise to Armstrong, after he'd navigated through some difficult conversations with unhelpful individuals in the French-speaking Indian Ocean island. The registered address for the company was most likely a vacant site in one of the slum areas of Port Louis.

Armstrong tapped his pen on his desk and wondered where next to turn. Probably best to double-check Irish land records for any cross-reference mentions of the company in other property dealings. It was reasonable to assume that if they had bought a site at Longford, they might have had other dealings in Ireland, although the chances were that these were also hidden behind other made-up Mickey Mouse names.

He sighed and leaned forward to his computer and clicked a Google search for landregistryireland.com.

And resigned himself to what he reckoned would be another wasted few hours.

Chapter 48

THE CHICAGO Police Department is the second-largest municipal force in the United States. It employs twelve-thousand officers and two-thousand civilian support staff and runs up an annual spend of over two billion dollars. That kind of money buys it a lot of firepower along with state-of-the-art databases capable of processing the daily mountain of paperwork that flows through the city's sixty police stations.

Its pride and joy is CLEAR, the Citizen Law Enforcement and Reporting system, which pulls together a network of databases for easy cross-reference information on investigations and crime patterns. Much like the Garda Síochána's PULSE reporting mechanisms, CLEAR stockpiles and assimilates notes and reports from every officer and makes them available for instant review by any employee with the correct log-on accreditation.

Which was why Paul Brogan's request for possible background details on Owen Patterson was dealt with quickly by the sergeant to whom he was referred at the CPD headquarters office on South Michigan Avenue. The Sergeant was used to dealing with queries from all around the country, but a request from a brother force outside the States was a first for him

He was happy to help when he heard about the source of the query. When you had Irish heritage, as most Chicagoans liked to boast about, it was a matter of old country pride to do whatever he could. The sergeant kept Brogan talking about life in Ireland and the changing face of Limerick, the birthplace of his grandfather, while his fingers danced across the computer keyboard. In less than two minutes, the sergeant announced a hit.

Brogan frantically scribbled the details, thanked the sergeant for his help, and leaned back to stare disbelievingly at what was written on the pad in front of him.

Boyle heard the heavy running steps on the corridor outside his office and knew something was about to shake loose. He waited patiently for Brogan's usual rushed entrance and looked for signals in the animated face of his second-in-command. "I just know this has to be good news."

"It's better than that, Mick, it's a freaking jackpot. Chicago PD has just imparted some unbelievable news about Owen Patterson. They had a record of dealings with him and you're never gonna believe what they said."

"I'll tell you what I'm gonna do," Boyle mimicked. "I'm gonna come round this table and belt you if you don't put me out of my misery."

"Look, I've got to tell you this from the start and let you make up your own mind. Bear with me. It appears our Owen Patterson was the flatmate of a guy who died in a multi-car freeway accident in 2007. The cops took a statement from Patterson in which he explained he'd let the friend borrow his car to get to a lecture at Columbia where he was studying architecture. Turns out this friend was burned to a cinder and, according to Patterson, there were no known living relatives. Chicago PD closed the case as just another traffic fatality and, based on Patterson's statement, they didn't do a follow up search for next-of-kin."

Boyle frowned. "Where's this going?"

"Here's the juicy part. According to Patterson, his flatmate's name was Daniel Flynn, a native of Dublin."

Boyle's eyes lit up. "Flynn? As in Big Paud Flynn?"

"That's quite a leap, Mick. Do you have any idea how many Flynns there are in Ireland? I admit that I thought the same, but there's nothing to make a link between the two."

"Maybe I can fill in a few blanks," Boyle replied. He remembered Jacko McStravick telling him about a son of Big Paud's dying in a road accident in Chicago. He grabbed his mobile and rang Belle.

"Honey, sorry for the interruption. No time to talk. I need to speak to Jacko. Is he there?"

"And sure, where else would my minder be?"

Boyle heard Belle shout across the bar and moments later Jacko's voice came online. "Don't tell me I'm in trouble."

"Nothing like that, Jacko. It's about the story you told me of Big Paud's son dying in America. What was the boy's name?"

"It was Daniel, although I think Big Paud always referred to him as Danny Boy."

"Do you remember what part of America this was?"

"Almost sure it was Chicago."

"Thanks, Jacko," Boyle said and cut the connection. He looked up at Brogan. "No doubt about it, the accident victim in Chicago was Big Paud's son, or at least it was made to look that way."

"I'm all ears."

"It's really rather simple. The man we're looking for, Owen Patterson, leaves Ireland to become an architect in Chicago, where he just happens to meet up with Big Paud's son, Daniel, who also left Ireland at around the same time. The unfortunate Flynn meets with an accident, after which Patterson returns to Ireland and picks up his new life as a professional businessman and serial killer. How neat is that?"

"You're saying that Patterson switched identities with Flynn after the car accident?"

Boyle shook his head. "No, Patterson *was* Flynn all along. Can't be any other way to explain it. Think about it. Two Irishmen abroad just happened to end up in the same city, at the same university, studying for the same degree, and, to cap it all, they become flatmates. That's lining the ducks in a row in a way that blows the idea of coincidences straight out the window."

"I'm not saying these events were coincidental, but I still can't get my head around all these aliases."

"Look, Paul, I'll bet if you check deeper, you'll find that Flynn and Patterson shared the same birthday. Even when people switch identities, they tend to stick with the important memory triggers, such as birthdate or the first school they went to. These are questions that can trip you up unless the right answers roll off the tongue as a matter of fact. The best way to be prepared is to stick with the basics."

Brogan didn't look convinced. "I still don't see why it could not be a simple case of switching identities?"

"If you think about what I've said and then add

one more important additional layer, the answer becomes clear. We know that when the Chicago cops checked the address of the crash victim, they found his flatmate Patterson. That was the name he gave them, which means this alias was already in place."

"For that to be true, there had to be one other person involved. To follow your logic, the dead man was neither Flynn nor Patterson. So, who was he?"

"I haven't a clue, and it doesn't really matter. What is important is that his death gave Flynn, aka Patterson, the ideal opportunity to tie up an annoying loose end. It was his chance to make the world believe he were dead, while at the same time clearing the way for him to come back home without the risk of us finding out his true identity. You've got to hand it to him. It was perfect symmetry, both in the timing and the execution."

"But surely his face would still be recognisable?"

"I'm guessing here," Boyle admitted, "but I'd lay odds that he got some plastic surgery, or enough of a facelift to make it impossible for anyone to spot his former self." Boyle got up and crossed to the wipeboard lying on the floor of his office. He tore off the photo of Big Paud Flynn and brought it across to the other wipeboard which held the image of Owen Patterson.

"See any resemblance? I knew there was something scratching away at me, but I couldn't make the connection until now. Look at the high forehead and the narrow set of the eyes. This is father and son. The man we've been looking for is Daniel Flynn, son of none other than Big Paud Flynn."

Brogan blew out his cheeks. "Jesus, Mick,

where the fuck do we go from here?"

"There's only one place we can go. We pay a visit to the hospital and see what Big Paud has to say about his murderous offspring."

Brogan looked aghast. "I'm not saying you're wrong, but we need to tread carefully. You're already facing harassment charges, and possibly more, and the last thing you need is to give Big Paud's barrister any more ammunition."

Boyle smiled. "Don't worry, we'll do a bit more digging before we confront the patient. First, we find old photos of Daniel Flynn. There has to be some from schools or colleges. Then we get our computer guys to use those ageing processing wizardry tools of theirs to see what he might look like now and how that compares with the images we have of Owen Patterson."

"Could be an interesting exercise," Brogan said.

"The next thing is to feed our latest information to Custer Armstrong. There's now no doubt that it was Daniel Flynn using the cottage at Glencool Forest, so what's the connection? Is it just some place he stumbled upon, or did he have prior knowledge of the location? Maybe it was his old man who bought the property through this shell company. Get Custer checking for any tie-ups to Big Paud. Tell him to use our files from the previous surveillance operation when we were trying to nail Big Paud for all kinds of wrongdoing. Something might jump out."

Brogan looked across the desk at the two photos lying side by side. "It's strange how the two biggest cases we've had over recent weeks are suddenly beginning to converge."

"The irony hasn't been lost on me," Boyle agreed.

Chapter 49

BIG PAUD FLYNN sat up on his hospital bed and wiped a small teardrop from the corner of one eye. He was hurting. But it was not from any pain caused by a successful six-hour heart bypass operation. This was a duller, more deep-rooted ache that couldn't be eased by pills or medicine. He clutched a crumpled leaflet and stared at a face he thought he would never see again. *Oh, Danny Boy, what have you done?*

As much as the shock of discovering that his eldest son was still alive, there was the gut-wrenching realisation that the lad was a serial killer, worse still, one who had obviously developed a sick fascination with young girls. *Where did that come from?*

Flynn remembered the anguish of having to deal with the reports of Daniel's death all those years ago. It had been like a dagger through the heart. His whip-smart boy, the intended heir of the Flynn business empire, had been taken from him just when plans were being made to give him greater control and responsibilities within the multi-layered organisation.

Big Paud hadn't minded that Daniel had run away, no doubt to look for his mother, and had cared even less when he discovered the money missing from the hide at Kilkenny. In many ways, he had admired the boy's spunk in pilfering the cash, an act which had demonstrated the kind of ambitious and ruthless energy that Big Paud needed alongside him. The money hadn't mattered. The only important thing was that Daniel would chase his dreams and return home to take up where he'd left off.

There had never been a chance of the boy finding his mother. It was Big Paud who'd sprinkled the stories of her going to America as a means to stop people looking for her. The bitch had run away alright, but she'd made the mistake of going to one of the places where Big Paud knew he'd find her. And find her he did, cowering in a Dublin bedsit and brazenly telling him she intended to go back and take her sons away to a new life. That had been the final straw.

Big Paud strangled her and dumped her body in a disused well at the Kilkenny site where he'd stashed his loot.

Poor Daniel. The boy had gone there to get funds to search for his mother, little realising that she was barely a hundred yards from where he had excavated the underground cash chamber.

Big Paud had done his fair share of killing, all of it, he reasoned, for just causes. It was one thing to murder to protect himself and his businesses, quite another to take a life for perverse pleasure, as his son had done. Try as he might, Big Paud couldn't wrap his head around the concept, finally acknowledging that it was making him sick to the stomach.

The realisation brought clarity to his thinking. His initial instincts had been to say nothing, pretend he didn't know, maybe even try to reach out to the boy to see if he could help. But that had long since dissipated. It would have been better if Daniel had died in that accident in Chicago. One thing was for sure; he was already dead to Big Paud.

A muffled cough at the end of the bed tore Big Paud from his thoughts. He looked up to see a beaming Myles Winstanley standing in his trademark three-piece suit with the usual bulky briefcase dangling at his side. He looked down at his client. "Must say, Paud, you're looking remarkably well for a man who went through major surgery just a few days ago."

"That's as maybe," Flynn gruffed, "but I didn't ask you here for pleasantries. In fact, what I want to discuss is very unpleasant indeed."

Winstanley arched his eyebrows and pulled a visitor chair close to the bed. "I'm intrigued. What could be so important as to require my services in such an unusual setting?"

Big Paud launched straight into his story. He held nothing back, save for the small detail of his wife's death, and ended by flourishing his son's wanted leaflet at the astonished barrister. "I want nothing to do with this. The police should be told, but I can't figure out how to approach them. It goes against the grain to have any dealings with those bastards, but what if Daniel kills again and I might have been able to prevent it?"

Winstanley was momentarily speechless. He'd heard some horrific tales from clients before, but this was altogether new territory for him. "I don't know what to say, Paud. I mean, the bottom line is that if you had no prior knowledge of any of these events, then you've got nothing to fear. In the event that you didn't know what was going on or who was involved, it would be your civic duty to draw attention to Daniel, but I must caution you to be certain not to incriminate yourself by association, no matter the circumstances."

"For Chrissakes, I thought the boy was dead for the past twelve years. How could I have known?"

"Quite so, yet I would like to spend a bit of time going over what we should be telling the Guards. Better safe than sorry."

"So, you agree we should contact them?"

"As an officer of the court, so to speak, I can't and won't advise otherwise. You do know who's leading the investigation?"

"Yeah, Mick bloody Boyle. He's going to get a real kick out of seeing me squirm."

Winstanley shook his head. "I could ask for another officer to interview you. It would be a reasonable request, given your current harassment complaint against Boyle."

Big Paud made a show of fixing his pillows before turning back to the lawyer. "That's another thing I wanted to speak to you about. I think maybe we should drop that."

Custer Armstrong paused outside Boyle's door, wondering for the umpteenth time whether to head back to his desk. He held a single sheet of paper in his right hand, knowing with growing certainty that Boyle would laugh at the content contained in the two short, typed paragraphs.

"I know you're out there, Custer," Boyle's voice boomed from beyond the closed panelled door. "Are you coming in, or are you just admiring my nameplate?"

Jesus, the boss could be freakish at times. Armstrong pushed on the handle and stepped inside. "I'm not sure I should be disturbing you with this. The more I look at it myself, the more idiotic it seems."

"Why don't you tell me so that I can make up my own mind?"

Armstrong toddled sheepishly across the room. "I've been doing my head in trying to find a connection between Big Paud Flynn and the Rawhide company that bought the Glencool Forest property."

"And?"

"Nothing but blind alleys, boss, until I discovered this."

"What is it?"

Armstrong seemed reluctant to set the paper on Boyle's desk, but he finally released it. "I traced one of Big Paud's so-called legitimate property transactions, for a bookmaker's shop in Galway, back to this company, which calls itself *Wishbone Developers*. Flynn is a director of the company, which also owns a number of other properties in Mayo."

"And how does this tie in with the *Rawhide* company?"

"That's just it, boss, it doesn't, except for the name."

Boyle lifted the paper and stared at it. "Sorry, Custer, what exactly am I not seeing?"

"Okay, you're going to think I'm crazy, but my old man never missed an episode of the Rawhide series on TV, you know the one that starred Clint Eastwood as Rowdy Yeats? Anyhow, he made us watch it with him and I got to know all the characters, including the cattle-trail cook who was named Wishbone."

Boyle couldn't help himself. He burst out laughing. "That's pretty weak, Custer, although I'll give you ten out of ten for creativity."

"I thought so myself, "Armstrong said, "so I did a little more digging on Flynn's other business interests. We already had him listed as a major shareholder in a small theatre company in Galway. And guess what? The name of that little venture is *The Favor Foundation*."

"Favor?"

"Yes, the same name as the *Rawhide* trail boss, Gil Favor. How about that for a three-timer?"

Boyle turned serious. "It's still a bit flimsy, but I think you might just have made a case for digging deeper. Christ, we always knew Flynn was a bit of a cowboy, but who would have thought he was acting out old fantasies. Good work, Custer. Now take this to the next level."

"How do you mean."

"Check bank and land records for all these companies. Find me a transaction that links them together. Just one silly mistake by Flynn will suffice. Maybe we'll get lucky and see some payments or receipts floating between one or more of them, which means we can prove that Flynn's sticky paws are all over the Glencool property. If we find that, we can tie him in with his son's serial killings."

Armstrong spun on his heels and bumped into Paul Brogan. "Did he go for it?"

"Took a bit of persuading, but I got there in the end," Armstrong laughed.

Boyle rapped his knuckles on the top of his desk. "You two know I'm listening, right?"

"Listening and paying attention are two different things," Brogan scoffed. "Here's two other pieces of good news. First, Garda Detective Munn has just come from Dr Connie Dunne's interview with Megan McGrath and Siobhan Cunningham over at the Cunningham house. The girls fairly opened up with Connie and told her a lot of things about their captivity. I'll fill you in on the details later, but one thing stood out. According to the girls, Patterson – or Flynn, as we now know – kept mentioning Downpatrick and saying things like that's where it all started for him."

"But that doesn't fit with what we know," Boyle countered. "Surely his killing spree began in Kilkenny in 2008 and he didn't get to Downpatrick until 2012? What do you make of it?"

"I just don't know, Connie says it could be a warp in Flynn's memory, although she figured him for being more methodical and accurate about the details of his exploits."

Boyle shook his head. "We'll have to park it for now. You mentioned two things. What's the other?"

"You were right about the birthdates for both Daniel Flynn and Owen Patterson. They're a match."

"Now we're getting somewhere," Boyle said. "Time to have that conversation with Big Paud."

"Careful, boss."

"Don't fret, Paul, I intend to ask Winstanley to set it up." Boyle picked up his mobile, searched for the lawyer's number, and hit the contact button.

"Myles Winstanley. How may I help?"

"This is Garda Inspector Mick Boyle. I would like to set up a formal interview with your client, Big Paud Flynn."

"What a coincidence, Mr Boyle. I was about to contact you with the same request. Can you come to Mr Flynn's hospital as soon as possible? I'll expect you within the hour."

Boyle stared at his handset long after the call

had been disconnected. "What in freaking hell was that all about?"

Chapter 50

Boyle's visit to Mayo General Hospital was stopped in its tracks at the front desk of the Castlebar Garda Station. Sergeant Moriarty leaned across the counter and beckoned him forward with an urgency Boyle couldn't ignore. Another distraction was the last thing Boyle needed, considering his head was full of thoughts about preparing for his interview with Big Paud Flynn. Somehow, despite Flynn's willingness to agree to a meeting as soon as possible, Boyle knew it would be near impossible to wrangle meaningful information from the conman.

He approached Moriarty's counter, his head nodding from side to side. "It will have to keep, Sarge. There's somewhere I've got to be."

"Won't take a minute, Mick." Moriarty held up a sheaf of papers. "Thought you should know that we've just received a report from the crime scenes people over at Glencool Forest."

"Can't see it telling us much, what with everything at the scene turned to toast. I'll look at it later."

"No, you might want to look at it now, seeing as how you're heading over to the hospital to visit with our old pal."

It never ceased to amaze Boyle how the Sergeant seemed to know everything that was going on at the station, sometimes before they even happened. "I see your antennae is as sharp as ever,

Sarge." Boyle grabbed the report and stuffed it in his pocket. "I'll read it on the way."

"Might want to look at it before you talk to Big Paud. There's an interesting piece of information in section two. I've marked the copy for your attention."

Boyle couldn't help but laugh. It was known that nothing came and went in the Castlebar station unless the sergeant had first sight. "Okay, I'll bite. What's it say?"

"Nah, that would ruin all your fun. Best you read it for yourself."

"Like I said, I'll go through it in the car." Boyle turned and started to walk away from the reception desk."

Moriarty coughed and looked slightly embarrassed. "There's one other thing, Mick. I put up a collection for those wee lassies you found at Glencool. They both lost their mobile phones and I thought it would be a nice gesture if we had a whip-around to help pay for new ones."

"Good on you, Sarge. Now, I really have to get going."

"Hold it, I need your advice. I had circulated the collection to other stations and, guess what, we've got nearly ten-thousand Euros in the account. What am I supposed to do with all that?"

Boyle sucked in a lungful of air. "Whoa, that's really something, but I don't see the problem. Get the girls the best phones on the market, and transfer whatever's left in the account to one of the local charities. Everyone who contributed will be happy to go along."

"You think so?"

"Of course, just send out a circular. On second thoughts, why not use the extra money to pay for a holiday for the girls and their parents? I'm sure they could all use a break after what they've gone through."

Moriarty slapped the countertop. "I knew you would come up trumps! Brilliant idea. I'll get right on it."

"Now that that's settled, can I please get out of here?"

Moriarty watched Boyle and Brogan disappear through the station's rear door. He'd chickened out of telling Boyle why he had stopped him from leaving. The information about the crime scene report and the gift for the girls were handy distractions. When push came to shove, Moriarty couldn't say what he had really wanted to.

Every chance Moriarty had got over the past week had been spent searching for the mole who had tipped off Big Paud about the search warrants for his home and business premises. The Sergeant had taken it personally that paperwork he had handled had somehow found its way to a rat whose tip-off had ruined weeks of legwork by Boyle and his team.

Moriarty had gone back through every scrap of paper, chased down every person with whom it could have come in contact, and followed a circular trail that led him from the offices of the Director of Public Prosecutions, who had agreed to the warrants, to the court officials involved in signing them off, and finally to the offices of NBCI, which was responsible for general co-ordination. There were plenty of names to check, as well as a mountain of emails and telephone log details which had been uploaded into the PULSE system.

Patience was finally rewarded. Moriarty was

confident he'd found the person responsible. It was not one-hundred percent definitive, probably not even provable, but there was enough there for Moriarty to know the source.

And therein was the cause of Moriarty's dilemma.

Boyle would react badly to the information. There was no doubt about that. The hot-headed sod would likely take matters into his own hand and get himself drummed out of the force by his impetuosity. Better to let sleeping dogs lie. Boyle had forgotten all about the mole. No sense in stirring a hornet's nest.

The trip to Mayo General Hospital descended into an argument between Boyle and Brogan.

"All I'm saying, Mick, is that you can't push the bastard too hard. He's got his legal eagle with him, ready to pounce on the least little thing. Don't forget, you're already under the hammer for harassing Big Paud and if we do anything to put his health in jeopardy we'll be accused of all sorts of nasty things."

"What's his health got to do with it?"

"Christ, Mick, he's had a heart attack and gone through major surgery. If he starts clutching his chest, we'd better make ourselves scarce."

Boyle squirmed in the passenger seat. "We have to know what Big Paud knows about his son. Look, I don't believe for a moment that the bastard was privy to what was going on, but at the very least he might be helpful in locating where Daniel is now."

"Think he'll tell us if he does know?"

"Not a chance, which is why I'll have to push him a bit. Remember, Big Paud's still got a lot to answer for in relation to the Glencool property. No matter how you spin it, that's a possible accessory charge in a kidnapping case. What about other properties like Glencool? Who's to say Daniel Flynn is not holed up in one of them, which would make his father an accessory after the fact."

Brogan shook his head. "That's a stretch, and you know it. Besides, Custer Armstrong has got nowhere in tracking down other properties. Could be a dead end."

"Exactly, but we need to know for sure."

"Will you please just go easy?"

"I'm making no promises. If the bastard clams up, I reserve the right to rattle his cage."

"You know, Mick, sometimes I think I don't know you."

Boyle snorted without replying. He dug into his jacket pocket and retrieved the crime scene report from Glencool, flicking through the pages before deciding to read it from the start. When he got to the part where Moriarty had run a yellow highlighter through a half-dozen lines, Boyle's eyes bulged.

Chapter 51

THE PRIVATE WARDS were on the third floor of the hospital. There were eight of them, four either side of a wide corridor that looked like it belonged in a five-star hotel, with tasteful landscapes filling the walls, and large-sized potted plants positioned at regular intervals on top of a carpeted floor. Money really can buy anything, Boyle thought, as he pushed against the second door to his right.

Paud Flynn was out of bed and seated on a generous leather seat beside a window that offered a wide panorama of the Mayo countryside. The king was on his throne and his faithful courtier, in the form of Myles Winstanley, was standing rigidly to attention alongside him. Both men wore false smiles that made Boyle want to throw up.

Instead, he marched into the centre of the room and addressed Flynn directly. "I have some questions. I would advise that you answer them truthfully and without...."

"Just a moment, Inspector," Winstanley cut in. "My client wishes to make a statement. This is for the official record, which is why I've taken the precaution of emailing it in advance to your superiors." The barrister waved a sheet of paper and started reading from it in a monotone voice.

Mr Padraig Flynn wishes to inform An Garda Síochána that the man who goes by the name of Owen Patterson, and is wanted for some terrible crimes, is in fact none other than Daniel Flynn, who is Mr Padraig

Flynn's son. Until now, it was believed that Daniel died in a motor accident twelve years ago in Chicago, but the recently published wanted posters, which are in mass circulation throughout Ireland, showed this was not the truth.

Mr Padraig Flynn, who suffered a severe heart attack three days ago, was not aware of these posters until early this morning, at which time he contacted his legal representative to ensure the information he now holds was passed immediately to the police. Needless to say, Mr Flynn is appalled by the actions of his son and believes he should be apprehended as a matter of urgency. By offering this information, at the first possible opportunity, Mr Flynn is demonstrating that his civic duty outweighs the natural instincts of a parent to protect their offspring.

He also wishes to make clear that he had no knowledge of his son's actions, nor was he aware that he had returned to Ireland from Chicago. In light of that, he has also no information to offer about Daniel's movements during the period from 2008 to the present day and can offer no assistance as to where he might presently be located.

Boyle waited for the statement to end before shifting his gaze between Winstanley and Flynn. He started a slow handclap and walked forward to stand menacingly in front of Flynn's armchair. "You two jokers make a great double act, though I can tell you no-one is laughing. You really expect me to believe this hogwash?"

Winstanley moved across to stand protectively between Boyle and Flynn. "We don't care much what you believe, Inspector. You've been given the facts from Mr Flynn's standpoint and I suggest you leave us now and go about whatever it is you do."

"Here's something for you to chew on," Boyle

said. "We had already made the connection between your client and our serial killer."

"I suppose, on the law of averages, even you would get there eventually." As he spoke, Winstanley smirked at Big Paud.

"Here's another connection for you. It turns out the cottage at Glencool Forest is owned by your client. Who's to say that Big Paud hadn't offered it as a bolthole for his scumbag son?" Boyle watched both men closely and detected a hint of alarm behind Big Paud's eyes.

Winstanley, however, gave nothing away. "You're treading on dangerous ground, Inspector. It's entirely reasonable that Daniel was aware that his father owned the property and decided to use it – entirely without my client's knowledge – for his prurient purposes. There's nothing here for you to pursue."

Boyle moved back into Big Paud's line of sight. "Must make you mad that Daniel torched the place. Think of all those lost possessions."

"No comment," Winstanley quickly intervened.

"I guess the insurance company will cover your losses as far as the buildings go, but what about all those lost drugs? At least now we know how you've been hiding your riches."

Big Paud moved across to the end of his seat and stared at Boyle. This time the alarm in his eyes was replaced by something else. Naked fear. "I...I don't know what you're talking about."

"Nice to see the operation didn't bypass your vocal cords. That was quite an inventive underground chamber you constructed at Glencool. My bet is that you had a lot of cash hidden there as well, and that Daniel helped himself to it. But he mustn't have had much use for the drugs. I'm afraid he just opened all the bags and sprinkled them on the manure covering your clever pigpen camouflage." Boyle was grateful he had taken the time to read the crime-scene report, especially Sergeant Moriarty's underscored section, which detailed the drugs find.

Winstanley jumped in quickly before Big Paud could respond. "If I haven't already made myself clear, let me do so now. This is not an interview and my client is not obliged to answer any of your questions. There are perfectly reasonable explanations for all these matters, but we are not prepared to indulge you in a fishing expedition. This meeting is over."

Boyle ignored him and continued to stare at Big Paud. "You going to keep hiding behind this peacock's feathers? Even you must realise that by now we know all about your shady property deals and the fictitious companies with the cowboy names. I'm betting that when we take a closer look at these sites we'll find other underground stashes."

Paul Brogan shifted uncomfortably beside Boyle. He knew his boss was winging it and that they were not even close to identifying any other Glencool-type properties that could be tied into Big Paud. He decided to say nothing, although he smiled and nodded his head as if they had had a breakthrough.

Big Paud didn't react in the way Boyle had hoped. "If you find anything, be sure to let me know. You never can tell how people will take advantage of vacant properties."

Winstanley beamed. "And there you have it, Inspector. My client has gone on record as declaring he has no control over what happens at his sites.

He's a legitimate businessman, and as such, is always a target of those who would seek to take advantage of his good nature. Now, this really is the end. I would ask you gentlemen to leave immediately so that Mr Flynn can get much-needed rest."

Despite Big Paud's apparent coolness, Boyle knew he'd struck a nerve. There was just enough of a hint of uneasiness to suggest Flynn might want to check things out for himself, or at least get one of his henchmen to do it for him. Boyle made a mental note to put a watch on several key Flynn employees, particularly the two sons, Jerome and Seamus. It was not something he could do officially, but he knew just the man for the job.

Boyle turned and headed for the door, pausing dramatically in the centre of the room. "Just one more thing. Tell me about your wife."

Big Paud's face turned crimson. "My wife....my....what's she got to do with anything?"

"Just curious to know why she left you and why we haven't heard anything since her disappearance."

"She left. Nothing else to it."

"Did you try to find her or report that she was missing?"

"Why would I? The bitch decided she wanted something better. I'd heard she went to America, which I guessed was why Daniel had gone there. There was always something between them two. Good riddance, I say."

Boyle frowned at the response. "Seems to me that a man would want to know what happened to his wife. Unless, of course, you already knew."

"I just told you, didn't I?"

"No, you've told me nothing. There were reports that you physically abused your wife, even sent her to hospital on a few occasions. Who's to say you didn't do her more permanent harm?"

Winstanley stormed across the room. "This is preposterous, Boyle, and you know it. I recommend you leave now before I add a few more paragraphs to our official complaint."

Boyle looked past the lawyer to watch Big Paud's face. The eyes had turned black, as if someone had switched off a light behind the irises, and the crow's feet lines suddenly looked more pronounced. Talk about touching a nerve! Boyle wondered how a throwaway remark could have had such an effect, unless of course Big Paud truly had something to hide in respect of his wife's disappearance.

Boyle brushed Winstanley aside and glared at Flynn. "Just so you know, I'll be following this up as soon as I nab your son. I think you know more about your wife than you're having everyone believe."

"I know nothing, you bastard."

"It'll keep for now," Boyle said. "Tell me, was your wife a blonde?"

The question threw Big Paud. "Why in the hell are you asking that?"

"A simple yes or no will suffice."

"Yes, she was blonde-haired, all natural, and always brushing and combing it down her back."

"Where was she from originally?"

"Her folks came from up north, but she left there when she was a teenager to study at Trinity College in Dublin. Always had airs and graces about herself."

"Where exactly up north?"

"It was a place called Downpatrick."

Chapter 52

AND THERE THEY WERE. The final pieces of the jigsaw. The psychiatrist had been right all along about the choice of victims and the trigger that had made Daniel Flynn into a serial killer. His blonde-haired mother had deserted him, and he had wanted revenge on all lookalikes. Dr Connie would likely explain it better and in more detail, but Boyle was satisfied that the teenager's whole persona had been twisted from love into hatred by the simple act of abandonment.

But more important than that, Boyle had learned the most crucial information of all from his interview with Big Paud. The killer was heading back to Downpatrick. It was where his mother had hailed from, perhaps even where Daniel Flynn tried to find her, and almost certainly why he had chosen the town for most of his murderous activities.

What was it that was reported from Dr Dunne's interview with the two surviving girls who had recalled some of the things their captor had said to them? *He kept mentioning Downpatrick and saying things like that's where it all started for him.*

At the time, Boyle had been confused by the remark. It hadn't made any sense that Flynn could have been referring to the start of his killing spree, because they knew that had begun in Kilkenny. No, what Flynn had really been talking about was his mother's roots. That's where she had come into being and, in a sense, that's where Flynn's troubles were rooted. If she hadn't been born, then neither would he. Which meant he would not have experienced the pain of her leaving or felt the urge to lash out in retaliation. His warped mind had come to blame not just a person, but a place.

Daniel Flynn was in Downpatrick. Nothing else made any sense. Besides, in the absence of any other clues, it was as good a starting point as any. And that's where Boyle needed to be.

But first he had arrangements to make. There were other things still fresh in his mind, chief of which was Big Paud's wife. Had she simply had enough and done a runner? Or had her abusive husband finally crossed the line of last resort? Boyle wanted it to be the latter, aware that he was prejudiced by his utter disdain for Big Paud, and all too willing to believe the lowlife had killed the mother of his children. But where was the evidence?

Boyle left his office and walked down the stairs to the front reception where Sergeant Moriarty was standing sentry in his usual position behind the computer screen. If anyone could ferret out some details, it would be Moriarty. The Flynns had been living in Dublin at the time of the wife's disappearance and it would be interesting to discover whether, as Big Paud had alluded to, there had been no missing report filed. Something surely should have been mentioned or followed up on. There might not have been a formal request made by the family to the police, but that didn't mean there hadn't been some Garda interest in the case.

Moriarty readily agreed to search the PULSE system and to make a few calls to colleagues in various stations in the Dublin area.

Boyle returned to his office and made the first of a number of phone calls.

He pulled the crime-scene report from his pocket and studied the names of the attendant officers. He knew most of them, and one in particular, a woman who crossed all the T's and dotted all the I's, and never took anything at face value. Boyle searched for her mobile number and got an immediate response. She was still on site at Glencool and listened intently to Boyle's theory about a possible body being buried in the grounds, the woods around the burnt-out cottage being the most likely dumping place. Boyle knew it was a long-shot but was delighted to hear the CS officer telling him she would give it her best shot.

Next up was a call to PSNI Inspector John Bonnaville. Delivering the news about Daniel Flynn's potential relocation to Downpatrick was like telling Bonnaville he'd just won the lottery. He positively gushed down the line and rattled off a string of actions that he would immediately attend to. He talked about putting plainclothed officers on street-walks, getting unmarked vehicles to patrol the area, and setting up checkpoints to monitor incoming traffic from both the Belfast and Dublin approaches to the town. He'd flood the area with Flynn's wanted poster and check all hotels in the country for any new single-male arrivals from the Republic of Ireland.

Boyle had to wait for the litany to die down before he broached the subject of his own involvement. He told Bonnaville of his intention to travel to Downpatrick with Inspector Brogan and made it clear they needed to be included in anything that went on. There was no argument from the PSNI man, who promised to clear official hurdles and to set Boyle and Brogan up in a B&B in the centre of the town. Bonnaville also agreed to meet with the Castlebar detectives as soon as they arrived.

Next on Boyle's to-do list was Jacko McStravick. It was a call they both agreed had never been made. If Jacko was surprised by Boyle's request, he didn't articulate it, and responded by pointing out that following Jerome and Seamus Flynn would be a piece of cake. Yes, he understood the need for caution and to pay particular attention to any trips made by the pair outside Castlebar. And yes, he knew he was just to collect address details and not to get too close. Who did Boyle think he was dealing with? A greenhorn?

Boyle smiled and disconnected. His last call was to Belle. He explained about heading north and asked her to put together a bag for an overnight stay. He also impressed on her the need to get her full-time staff, Andrea and Johnny, to stay the night in one of the guest rooms. It would make him feel better, he said, knowing she had company, and she finally agreed.

Job done. Calls made. Wheels set in motion. Boyle slumped back in his seat and stared at the wanted poster on his office wall. "It's time for you and me to meet."

Daniel Flynn stepped through the front door of the Europa Hotel at precisely ten o'clock and walked briskly over to the waiting taxi driver who was parked in the semi-circular drop-off and pick-up lane beside the hotel entrance.

Flynn had changed his mind about needing a taxi. Earlier that morning, he'd decided he wanted to be independent for his trip to Downpatrick and had arranged a hire car through the hotel's concierge. The cab driver frowned at hearing the news but perked up when Flynn offered to pay the full out-of-town fare in return for being taken to the Europcar centre on Grosvenor Road.

It was a short journey, one that Flynn could easily have walked, but the last thing he needed was to draw attention to himself by having an argument with a cabbie about being done out of a booking. Twenty minutes later, Flynn was behind the wheel of a Peugeot 3008, using the satnav to key in the address for a Downpatrick B&B he had earlier booked from his hotel room.

His sole possession in the back seat was a double-strapped shoulder bag, which contained stacks of Euros, a change of clothes, his make-up kit, and the Colt Python. It was all he would need. The surgical collar had been removed, figuring the discomfort didn't outweigh the benefits it offered to his overall disguise, although the ugly warts were still in place.

The towns of Saintfield and Crossgar rushed past in a blur as Flynn made his way to a large roundabout that marked the entrance to Downpatrick. To his left, was a road he knew well. It led to the Quoile River, a place that held fond memories, and one that he promised he would visit again.

He took the second exit to his right and made his way up Church Street, deciding to take a nostalgic tour before signing in at the B&B. He was on autopilot now, branching off on a link road that meandered into Scotch Street, Fountain Street, and Edward Street, his journey ending abruptly at

Ardmeen Green, a three-part estate consisting of lower, middle, and upper rows of terraced houses. He sat in the parked car and stared across at one of the homes in the Middle Green.

He let his mind wander. He could almost see his mother skipping out the door and across the Green where youngsters still played football. She had probably been the centre of attention, a manipulative bitch who got the other kids to do what she said. Part of Flynn wanted to get out of the car and set fire to the whole damned row.

He shook the thought aside, switched on the engine, and glanced at the satnav for the final directions to the B&B.

Chapter 53

CATHAL AND BRONAGH Kerr owned the *Dunleath House* B&B. It was one of the best establishments of its type in Northern Ireland, an architectural gem that featured fully integrated ensuite rooms, each with its own terrace looking out at the backdrop of the Mourne Mountains thirteen miles away in the seaside resort of Newcastle.

The Kerrs were known to be a generous couple, often inviting guests to partake freely in barbecues or drinks evenings in one of two patio areas, which caught the afternoon and early-evening sunshine, and where music and laughter seemed to be always on tap. It was little wonder that their order ledger was full of advance bookings from worldwide travellers who had used the facilities and wanted repeat experiences.

It therefore struck Cathal as odd that their latest guest made it clear he wasn't there to socialise. Looking past the obvious facial disfigurements, the B&B owner saw a brusque, soulless individual who wanted nothing more than to complete the formal sign-in procedures and retire to his room. The guest paid cash in advance for three nights, handed over his passport for formal identification, and retired to his room after receiving keys and information about breakfast times and declaring he would be away for most of the day on business matters.

Cathal watched through his sitting-room

window as the man exited the house ten minutes later, carrying a shoulder bag, which was cinched tightly to his back. The man climbed into a maroon Peugeot, expertly completed a three-point turn in the tight driveway and roared off. Not exactly the type you'd want at a barbecue, Cathal mused, and returned to thinking about his afternoon chore of running a mower over the generous lawns that wrapped around the house. Perhaps he'd wait for his son Conaill to finish work and give him a hand.

Two hours later, Cathal was still in the sitting-room watching a daytime film when the house phone rang. He waited for his wife to pick up the handset, which sat on a hallway table beside the front door, before deciding she couldn't hear it from her usual position in the kitchen, where the symphony of a tumble dryer and dishwasher drowned out all other sounds. He got up from his seat and walked into the hallway.

"Dunleath House B&B, Cathal Kerr speaking. How may I help you?" It was a practiced telephone introduction that his wife had insisted on down the years.

"This is Inspector John Bonnaville of the PSNI. Do you have two rooms available for the night?"

"Yes, you're in luck, Inspector. The tourist season is winding down and our last two rooms are still unoccupied."

"Excellent. Can you book these in for Michael Boyle and Paul Brogan? I'll pick the two gentlemen up later and bring them there at about six o'clock."

Cathal paused and grabbed a pen. "That's confirmed, Inspector."

"Oh, one other thing," Bonnaville said. "We're contacting all hotels and guesthouses to be on the lookout for a single male, possibly with an Irish accent or an Irish passport. Do you have anybody like that?"

The B&B owner's eyes bulged. "As a matter of fact, a man booked in this afternoon. His papers show he's from Dublin."

"Is this man still there?"

Cathal detected a sudden urgency in his caller's voice. "What's going on? Why are you so interested in one of our guests?"

"I'm sorry, Mr Kerr, but this is really important. Is the guest still there?"

"No, he went out again and said he would be away all day. Is there something I should know?"

"I can't go into details," Mr Kerr. "I'm in Belfast at present but will be at your house in less than an hour. In the meantime, I'll send two officers from the Downpatrick station to stay with you until I arrive."

"Just hold your horses, Inspector. Is this man dangerous? I have my wife and other guests to consider."

"Please don't be concerned, Mr Kerr. It's probably nothing other than a routine query that we need to check on. As I said, our people will be with you shortly and will ensure the safety of everyone. Thank you for your help."

John Bonnaville beat his predicted arrival time by fifteen minutes. Flashing lights and a siren tended to clear a route through teatime traffic, leaving Bonnaville with less time to consider what he might discover in Downpatrick. The pragmatic policeman in him urged caution. Probably nothing more than a blind alley, which was what he faced ninety-nine times out of a hundred. Still, there was always that one single chance.

He swept into the driveway of Dunleath House and shook hands with the two detectives who greeted him at the doorway to the B&B. They explained that all was quiet and that the husband and wife owners were waiting patiently in the front sitting-room. Bonnaville marched in and introduced himself.

"I'm sorry you've been put to all this trouble," he told the couple, and took a seat that was offered.

"It's not a lot of trouble," Bronagh Kerr replied, "but we really need you to be honest and tell us what's going on."

"I will, I promise, Mrs Kerr, but first I need to hear a description of your guest from Dublin. What age is he? Does he have any distinguishing features? Even the smallest thing can help."

Cathal Kerr burst out laughing. "Distinguishing features? How about a large scar down one side of his face and the most hideous warts down the other side? You couldn't miss this guy if you were trying."

Bonnaville frowned. It was not what he wanted to hear. "That certainly doesn't match what we're looking for."

"How about if he hadn't got the scar and the warts?" Cathal Kerr announced triumphantly.

"I don't follow."

The B&B man moved papers on the armrest of his chair and held up a single sheet. "Here's a copy of his passport identification. He had no scar and warts when this was taken, which I guess was a long time ago."

Bonnaville bounded from his seat and grabbed the paper. "How did you get this?"

"We always insist on proper identification and we take photos on our iPhones to keep as part of our records. It's a legal requirement that we properly verify and vet all our guests. This says he's calling himself Brian Turner from Parkgate Street in Dublin."

The PSNI Inspector had tuned out, his eyes burned into the image on the grainy passport page. There was something there, but he couldn't figure it out. Eventually, he rose and crossed to a table where he spread the paper and placed a copy of the wanted poster alongside it. Then he turned and asked Mrs Kerr if she could bring him four sheets of plain paper.

When she returned from the hallway and placed the paper on the table, she glanced at the wanted poster. "Oh, my God, is that who you're looking for?"

Bonnaville ignored her and placed single sheets below and above the eyelines on both images. The narrow slits were almost identical, if you ignored the different scales and a few etched lines at the sides of both eyes on one of the pictures. He thumped the table. "Gotcha, you bastard!"

Bronagh Kerr gasped. "Is that the man who killed all those poor girls? I remember what happened here in this town all those years ago. Is he back to kill more young innocents?"

Bonnaville composed himself, suddenly realising he had let his emotions get the better of him. "I shouldn't have let you see this, Mrs Kerr. Now that you know what's going on, I have to ask for your utmost discretion. You can't tell anyone about this, at least not until we capture this man, and I will have to ask you to move out of your home until this is over."

"Move? Are you mad in the head?" The outburst came from Cathal Kerr. "This is our home and we're going nowhere. Your job is to protect us."

"I understand how you feel, Mr Kerr, but this man is extremely dangerous. I can't risk you being here if he shows up unannounced. Please believe me, it will make our job a lot easier if we don't have to worry about your safety. This is not a request. I insist we clear this house immediately."

The couple exchanged glances. "I suppose we could go to our friend Teresa's home. She lives in the next street at Mourne View Court."

"Good, that's settled," Bonnaville said with obvious relief. "Can you relocate your remaining guests in other places?"

"Yes," Mrs Kerr responded, "I'll ring around the other B&B owners and see what's available. There will be plenty of vacancies at this time of the year.

Bonnaville watched the couple walk out of the room and suddenly remembered something. "Wait a moment, I don't suppose you know what type of car your guest was driving?"

Cathal Kerr turned with a smile on his face. "I wrote down the make and number plate."

Chapter 54

BOYLE WAS GRATEFUL for two hours of sleep, albeit folded awkwardly in the passenger seat, as Brogan steered his Renault Kadjar across the invisible land border that separated the Republic of Ireland from Northern Ireland near Lisnaskea in County Fermanagh. They were over the halfway point in their four-hour trip from Castlebar to Downpatrick.

Boyle blinked awake and looked at the tracking line on the satnav. They were scheduled to arrive at their destination by six o'clock in the evening. Outside, he watched at least two-thirds of Ireland's famed forty shades of green roll past his window and studied a road sign that told him the MI motorway was just five miles away.

"Pull over and I'll spell you with the driving," he told Brogan.

"Naw, you're good. An old boy like you needs to rest."

"Less of the old, please, I could still give you a run for your money over two laps at Castlebar Athletic's running track."

"In your dreams."

Boyle shifted in his seat and turned to face Brogan. "Speaking of dreams, how are you making out with our Dr Connie Dunne?"

"Where in hell did that come from? If you must know, this little trip put the skids on a dinner we'd planned for this evening. If you're really trying to be a matchmaker, you need to work a bit on your timing."

"My bad," Boyle said. "Tell you what, as soon as we get Daniel Flynn in handcuffs you can have a week off. Take the good doctor for a romantic break in Paris."

"As if," Brogan snorted, and then added. "You know, if we manage to run Flynn to ground, there'll be a jurisdictional issue with who gets him. I can't see Bonnaville agreeing to us taking him south of the border when there are three killings on the books against him in the North."

"I've already thought about that and I agree it will be a problem. I can see lots of reasons for Bonnaville keeping him, but then again it was our investigation that busted the case wide open. I guess we'll just have to face the problem when we get there. Let's just nab Flynn first."

As if right on cue, Boyle's mobile was activated on the car's multi-system dashboard display unit. Bonnaville's name flashed across the screen. Boyle reached across and hit the green accept button. "Hi John, what's the latest?"

Boyle and Brogan sat back and listened to a detailed recount of the breakthrough at the Downpatrick B&B. Things had moved a lot quicker than Boyle had expected, news that both delighted and made him concerned in equal measures, and he wasn't sure how he should respond. Finally, he said: "We're less than two hours away. Can you hold on closing the net until we get there?"

"Not going to be possible, Mick. I've got people on the ground all over the place. This is a relatively small town, and I would expect a sighting of Flynn's car at any moment now. If we get a call, I'll have to act on it immediately."

It was the answer Boyle had expected. "I understand, John. Can you keep us posted?"

"I'll let you know the moment anything happens. When you get here, go directly to the PSNI station, which is now located at the Downshire Hospital site on the Ardglass Road. I'll text you the postcode, which you can put into your satnav. Chances are I'll still be here, unless of course something kicks loose in the meantime."

Boyle thanked him and cut the connection. He banged the palm of his hand on the dashboard and turned to Brogan. "Can't you go any faster?"

Daniel Flynn eased the Peugeot into the inside lane and turned left at the traffic lights. The signpost read Newcastle on the A7, which seemed as good a place to go as any, particularly for someone who wanted to remain inconspicuous. He'd toured the streets of Downpatrick for almost two hours before finally deciding that daylight was not his friend, not when he kept passing the same areas time and again.

The last of the September days usually turned dark at around 7.30 in the evening, so he still had another three hours to kill. Better to do it away from where he wanted to strike, although for the life of him he couldn't decide on exactly what he wanted to do. Snatching a few girls off the streets was old hat. Too time-consuming, too much that could go wrong. No, if he wanted to make a statement, he'd have to come up with something a bit more inventive.

As he drove towards Clough and Dundrum, the answer wouldn't come. He pulled into a tourist car park outside Newcastle, intending only to lie back for a while and think, but on a whim he decided to change his disguise. He removed the rubber scar and warts from his face, swapped his black wig for an auburn mop, and quickly changed his clothes, preferring an open-necked tee-shirt to the crew-cut jumper that he'd been wearing since early morning.

He re-packed his shoulder bag and drove out of the park, intent on putting together one more piece of his plan. He needed a secondary escape route and somewhere to lie low if it proved impossible to return to the Downpatrick B&B. He'd find an hotel in Newcastle and book in under his last remaining alias, the only one he'd brought with him that had all the proper paperwork. If the cops tracked him to the B&B, they'd have a name, Brian Turner, which they could check at other B&Bs and hotels. It was a chance he'd just have to take.

Flynn cursed himself for letting things get out of control. This was not who he was. Up to now, everything he had done had been meticulously planned and executed down to the last detail. He had never before had to act on impulse, not until those bitches had escaped his clutches at Glencool, and not until he'd learned later, through watching television news bulletins, that the bodies of the three missing girls had been found at the Quoile River in Downpatrick. His face was plastered all over wanted posters, even here in Northern Ireland, and he felt a shiver when he remembered seeing that smug Garda detective, Mick Boyle, issue a news conference pledge to track down and apprehend the culprit. *Here's a pledge for you, detective. You'd better be prepared to die trying.*

Boyle was out of the car even before it stopped

rolling into a parking bay in front of the PSNI station in Downpatrick. There was an annoying wait at the entrance door while he stated his name and business into a wall-mounted intercom and stood for what seemed an eternity for the locked door to spring open. He was in no mood to sympathise with the security paranoia that was a hangover from the old days of the Northern Ireland Troubles.

He dashed into the station with Brogan hot on his heels. It was a new building with high ceilings and too much open space around a black-and-white tiled floor that did little to smooth the blandness of the place. It had an antiseptic look and feel to it. Not the kind of place you'd want to spend any time in, but maybe that's what they were going for.

John Bonnaville was waiting for his guests at a perspex-screened reception counter in the main foyer. He shook hands warmly with both men and ushered them towards a set of swinging doors to the right of the building. "Glad you could make it. Afraid there's nothing to report just yet, so I guess we'll have to sit tight for a while."

Boyle stopped at the doors. "Nothing? Surely the car must have been picked up by now."

"I admit, it's a bit baffling. We have more than thirty officers on foot patrol and a dozen unmarks touring the town in continuous loops, but not a dickybird. For the moment, Flynn seems to have vanished."

"And he didn't go back to the B&B?" Brogan asked.

"No, we have two men inside the building and another two stationed in a parked car close to the only entrance. There's been no sign of him."

Boyle shook his head. "We know he's here

somewhere. How hard can it be to track him down? Could be he's holed up somewhere waiting for darkness."

"That's my thought," Bonnaville answered. "I've asked a few of our drivers to do a sweep outside the town in the hope we come across Flynn's car at some lay-by or picnic area. Still nothing coming through."

"Okay, I think Brogan and I will take a turn at touring the town. One more search vehicle can't hurt."

Bonnaville shook his head. "Hold on, Mick, don't get ahead of yourself. I'd thought you two would accompany me. This jurisdictional thing is a bit tricky. Are you both armed?"

Boyle pushed through the doors and waited for them to fold back into their closed position. What he wanted to say was not for the ears of the policemen in the foyer. "Let's get one thing clear, John. When you came to Castlebar I didn't ask about you being armed, nor did I throw jurisdiction in your face. I gave you unfettered access to everything we had about Flynn and I respected your need for total involvement. Do I need to remind you that if it weren't for my people, you wouldn't be where you are? It was us who tracked Flynn down and discovered his true identity and it was us who pressed for the dredging of the river on your own doorstep. So, don't stand there spouting rule books and procedures at me because as far as I'm concerned you know what you can do with them"

Bonnaville's face reddened. "Jesus, Mick, you certainly know how to punch low. I've no intention of freezing you out, much less forgetting how we've got here. As far as I'm concerned, this is still your show, but I need to watch my back with the people above me, which means I've got to account for your movements while you're here."

"That's easily done, John. Just plug us into your radio frequency and let us get out there. We're not going to catch Flynn by standing around here having an argument that none of us really wants."

"Okay, you win, but first you need to eat. I've had something made up in the canteen. It could be a long night."

Boyle smiled and clapped Bonnaville on the shoulder. "Now that's something we can both agree on."

Chapter 55

IT WAS EIGHT O'CLOCK in the evening when Flynn passed the entrance to the ASDA shopping complex on the Newcastle Road approach to Downpatrick. Cars were still streaming in and out of the service road and ahead of him the lights of the town twinkled against the darkness of a moonless sky.

He travelled for another three-hundred yards and turned left into the area's main car park, directly opposite a busy garage. He could see people walking with shopping bags, others jogging, and still more standing idly outside the main Ulsterbus depot where a kerbside cafeteria was in full swing.

Rich pickings.

Flynn moved a hundred yards into the car park and manoeuvred into a vacant slot among a row of cars. He switched off the engine and reached across to the passenger seat for his shoulder bag. The big Colt Python felt good in his hand. His mind was made up. He would walk from here, find the right group of people, and empty the chamber indiscriminately into them. He would probably have time to reload and repeat the exercise while the frightened citizens scattered in all directions. No reason why he couldn't make all twelve bullets count. What a statement that would be.

He felt a familiar rush of adrenaline as he climbed from the car and fixed the collar on a nylon windbreaker he'd bought earlier in Newcastle along with a dark-blue peaked cap emblazoned with the familiar Nike white flash across the front. The Colt dangled at his side as he turned to walk into the town centre. Suddenly, he heard the sound of laughter coming from a darkened area of the park below a line of trees that reached up to the skyline. These were young voices, their strident tones biting into the still air.

Now, what have we here?

He turned back and headed for the sounds. The closer he got, the more the detail of the terrain began to take shape. Careful to stay in the shadows at the rear of the park, Flynn could see a wooded area to his left and a small clearing filled with about thirty teenagers. They were a mixture of males and females who seemed to be in a party mood, judging by the clinking sound of bottles and the loud vocal roars that echoed across the rooftop of the bus station and nearby buildings.

Flynn could feel his palms getting sweaty and the hairs on his arm starting to bristle. He had to force himself to keep calm. He decided to walk to the farthest end of the park to check the lay-out before doubling back and entering the glade from the side opposite to where he now stood. This could all be over within a matter of ten or fifteen minutes, by which time he would be back in his car and on his way to the hotel in Newcastle.

Boyle and Brogan sat in their car at the entrance to St Patrick's Drive. Directly in front of them was a row of busy shops. They could see a sign that declared the property of *Morrissey Chartered Accountants*, and alongside it an off-licence, a Country Fried Chicken outlet, a sit-in Indian restaurant and a pub that advertised live matches on Sky. All were doing a roaring trade, apart from the accountant, who had probably knocked off early, judging from the darkened interior, and taken his audit books home with him.

The area had seemed as good a place as any to surveil. It was teeming with people, an obvious target group for a predator, and the cut-in road where Boyle and Brogan were parked, afforded an unobstructed view of what was happening. If Flynn were sizing up this street, they would spot him.

"Bit of a long shot this, isn't it?" Brogan muttered from the passenger seat.

"You need to learn patience, young Grasshopper. By the way, that was a direct saying from the film."

"Truly, I am in awe of your knowledge," Brogan responded. "And by the way, I'm not sure that's an actual saying, but it should be."

They both laughed and turned back to watch the throng on the opposite side of the road. Boyle's iPhone vibrated in his hand and he quickly raised it to his cheek. It had been agreed with Bonnaville that this was the best way for them to stay in communication. Boyle pressed the button and said: "What's the news?"

"We've sighted Flynn's Peugeot in a car park."

Boyle almost dropped the handset as he reared up in his seat. "Where exactly? How do we get there?"

"Where are you now?"

"It's a place called St Patrick's Drive. We're staring across the road at a Country Fried Chicken carryout and a....."

"Turn left and then left again at the traffic

lights. The car park entrance you want is about six hundred yards on your right, just past a bus station. You can't miss it."

Boyle was already on the move, cutting across a large brown commercial van as he tore towards the traffic lights. He ignored the red signal and eased into the main road, shifting gears, and passing a row of vehicles on a one-lane route to the car park. He spotted the entrance and swung across the road where he was greeted by a policeman in a high-viz jacket waving him to stop. Boyle ignored him and continued until he spotted a cluster of people standing beside a row of parked cars. He recognised Bonnaville in the middle of the group.

Boyle braked to a stop and buzzed down his window. Bonnaville stepped away from a maroon Peugeot SUV and headed in his direction.

"What have you got?" Boyle asked urgently.

"Just got here myself. One of our patrols sighted the car five minutes ago. No sign of Flynn, but I've ordered everyone to this area. We'll fan out from here and walk the entire town if we have to."

Just then there were two loud thunder-cracks which seemed to emanate from a wooded area directly in front of Boyle's car.

"What the fuck was that?" Bonnaville shouted.

Boyle gunned the engine and took off in a spray of gravel. He switched the headlights to full beam and screamed back through the window. "Gunshots!"

Flynn had taken longer than he intended to explore the area. He had walked the full length of the car park until he'd reached a large building which announced itself as *The Saint Patrick Centre* on blue lettering etched into a glass frontage. To the right of the building was a set of paved steps that stretched out of view towards higher ground where Flynn could make out a row of streetlights.

But it was the area immediately in front of Flynn that interested him most. It was a large square, dotted with wooden benches and framed by small trees and planters. It was heaving with people, visiting a fish and chip shop or a Subway sandwich unit, and right in the middle were two policemen, instantly recognisable by their yellow and green jackets and the utility belts which hung at their waists.

Flynn eased into the shadows beside the corner of the fish shop and waited to see what the cops were doing, which wasn't much, other than stopping and talking with some people as they meandered around the square. At one point they looked to be headed in his direction, but suddenly turned and walked the other way, back towards what Flynn now knew was a secondary entrance to the main car park. He waited for them to disappear and retraced his steps, deciding to head back towards his car before cutting across to the glade where the youngsters were partying.

At the corner of the other end of the park, Flynn froze. Two men were standing in front of his car. One was holding a phone or radio to his mouth. Policemen! How did they know about his car? How had they tracked him? Gone was his escape route. Gone was his chance to head to Newcastle and lie low.

But he was not done yet.

He gripped the Colt tighter in his right fist and walked across the park towards the trees. He moved behind the first trunk and checked back to see if the policemen had spotted him. They were still standing in the same spot, staring at his vehicle, and taking no interest in what was around them. Suddenly another two cars roared into the park and skidded to a stop beside the two men. A minute later, another car pulled up beside the group.

It was now or never for Flynn. His hands were shaking and his mouth was dry. He had never felt like this before. He had always been in control, but the presence of the police had spooked him, even to the extent that he was not sure if he could go through with it. But what other option did he have? One way or another, they would get him. Better to go out on his own terms.

Suddenly, he leapt forward, punching his way through the trees towards the crowd of teenagers, his weapon already raised to shoulder height and his finger taut on the trigger. He bumped a shoulder heavily against one tree and stumbled as soon as he reached the clearing and opened fire. The force of the recoil on the big gun took him by surprise, but he fired a second time, and then...nothing. The hammer fell on an empty chamber. Either that, or the damned thing had jammed, but revolvers aren't supposed to seize up.

A bright wash of light suddenly illuminated the area and Flynn could hear the sound of car tyres screeching across the tarmacked surface not far from his location. He lifted his head beyond the fleeing teenagers and spotted a narrow trail which snaked its way towards the rear of The Saint Patrick Centre, now less than a hundred yards from where he was. He took off in that direction.

Boyle could see lines of panicked youngsters spilling

from the embankment that framed the wooded area. They were screaming and stumbling, some already on their knees trying to crawl away from the area, their faces screwed tightly in what could only be described as utter terror.

He forced himself to look away and tried to focus on what was happening in the trees. There was little light to pick up other than a handful of shapes, but one stood out. It was a larger figure, his head bowed as he ran in the opposite direction from the teenagers' escape route. Boyle wanted to accelerate along the road on a parallel line to the retreating figure, but there was nowhere for him to go, such was the mayhem of running and crawling youths blocking his path.

Boyle cursed and leapt from the car, trying to keep a fix on his target as it disappeared behind the trees. He took off at a run, weaving between the kids, his eyes firmly fixed on a large building where the gunman appeared to be headed towards. There was no doubt it was Flynn. Couldn't be anyone else. *It ends now*, Boyle muttered and picked up his pace.

As he rounded the building, which he now knew from the nameplate was *The Saint Patrick Centre,* Boyle spotted the steps and slowed to watch for any movement. He heard a rustling noise and looked up to see Flynn burst from the cover of trees at the rear of the centre and jump onto the steps. He had an advantage of at least forty risers.

Boyle sucked in a lungful of air and took off in chase, aware that Brogan was immediately behind him. His two-at-a-time sprint slowed dramatically after covering fifty steps, about halfway to the summit where Flynn had already reached. Boyle was aware of a slight push against his shoulder and watched as Brogan rushed past him, still maintaining the double-step assault on the long climb.

Despite the perilous situation they faced, Boyle couldn't help making a mental note to scrap his earlier invitation to Brogan to meet him at the athletic fields in Castlebar.

Chapter 56

BROGAN WAS CROUCHED beside a wall when Boyle finally made the summit. Directly in front of him was a sinister looking large wall, behind which was the Down Museum, formerly an old gaol where they hanged prisoners for the enjoyment of the town's nineteenth century citizenry. To the right of the Museum was an imposing courthouse, which dated back to 1735 and still stood as a dispensary of justice, albeit with slightly less harsh sentences being meted out these days.

Boyle was doubled over, his hands pressed against the top of his knees as he waited for his lungs to refill. Behind him, four PSNI detectives, including John Bonnaville, reached the top step. "Where is he?" Bonnaville asked.

Brogan pointed to his left. "He's just disappeared around the corner of what looks like a church."

Bonnaville stepped forward to join him. "That's Down Cathedral, one of the most recognisable buildings in Northern Ireland, mainly because it's where Saint Patrick is buried. The good news is that it's a dead end. Nowhere to go except an old cemetery. He's cornered."

They all stared at the Cathedral, which was uplighted by a series of ground lamps that bathed it in a yellow glow and brought out its true majesty. It was ringed by a stone wall and a road that wrapped itself around the exterior.

"Any chance he can break into the building?" Boyle asked.

"No," Bonnaville said emphatically, "it's closed for the night and it would take a battering ram to make even a dent in the old oak and iron door."

"You sure there's nowhere for Flynn to go at the rear of the building?"

"Well, I suppose he could scramble through a lot of brambles and stones, which lead to an old railway yard, but it's a fairly steep embankment and chances are that he'd break his neck before he reached level ground. I've already ordered up a helicopter to help us with the search."

Boyle was already sprinting forward. "So, basically we've no time to lose," he shouted back over his shoulder.

Brogan, Bonnaville, and the rest of the detectives followed suit. "Is he always like this?"

"No, John, sometimes he's more impulsive," Brogan answered in a deadpan tone.

Flynn followed the curve of the Cathedral driveway and realised it just looped around to the front of the building. There were no other roads, nowhere left to go. He spotted a small wooden gate that led to a cemetery where tombstones and crypts stood as eerie sentries against a backcloth of darkness and silence.

So, this is where it all ends? The thought was surprisingly comforting. He'd run his course and now he had to face the final arbiter. He had never been a religious man, but these surroundings somehow soothed his soul and made him want to pray. He was not looking for forgiveness, just a final acknowledgement that he had been on a righteous path, one that had been set out years ago and from which he could not deviate.

He clambered over the fence and fumbled his way towards one of the larger headstones. He sat behind it and checked he had an obstructed view of the fence where the cops would enter from. He smiled at the thought of taking a few with him.

His only regret at that moment was that he had chosen to come north rather than have the face-off with his father. He would give anything to be transported back to Castlebar where he would empty the Colt into Big Paud's face.

The scraping of feet brought him to full alertness. He looked across the graveyard and saw the face of that Irish detective prick kneeling behind the flimsy three-strand fence. Flynn brought the Colt up to rest on top of the headstone and steadied his aim at the detective's head.

Boyle was first to reach the fence. He knelt down and waited as the others fanned around him. Bonnaville duck-walked over to Boyle's shoulder and whispered. "Listen, Mick, we wait for the helicopter before we go stumbling about in there."

"How long's that going to take?"

"Should have been here by now."

"I'm not waiting around to find out Flynn has already legged it out the other side and down that embankment you mentioned."

Bonnaville was about to remonstrate when the ground seemed to shake. The unmistakeable rattle of a copter filled the air overhead and a searchlight beamed down on top of the Cathedral building. Bonnaville immediately opened his mobile phone and issued instructions to the pilot. The big machine moved forward, taking with it the beam of light which washed across the centre of the graveyard.

Boyle squinted through the brightness in time to see a gun move away from atop one of the headstones. "I have him." He pointed towards Flynn's position and urged everyone to stay still. Then he stood up in full view, moistened his lips, and shouted across the ground that separated him from his quarry."

"Daniel Flynn, we know where you are. It's time to give yourself up. Put down your weapon and stand up with your hands on top of your head. There's no need for you to die here tonight."

The voice that came back was strong and confident. "I know who you are. You're that fucking Guard from Castlebar. You said you'd get me, and it looks like you were right. The only question is whether you will be alive to enjoy the moment."

"Look Daniel, there's something you should know about your mother."

"You keep that fucking bitch out of it. You know nothing about her."

"I do know that she didn't desert you. She didn't run away, as you've been led to believe all these years."

Silence for a moment. "What, what the fuck are you talking about?"

Boyle detected the hesitation in the voice and decided to press on. "What if I told you she was murdered?"

Flynn's figure suddenly rose from behind the headstone. Boyle noticed with relief that the gun was held by his side. "You're bluffing. How...how...could that have been possible."

"I'm sorry to have to tell you that we believe

your father killed her and dumped her body where no-one would find it."

Flynn sunk to his knees. "No, no, why would he do that?"

"I don't know the answer to that," Boyle admitted. "All I can tell you is that he did it and let you believe she walked out on the family." It was as far out on a limb as Boyle had ever gone. He couldn't prove any of what he'd just said, but he was not about to tell Flynn it was nothing more than a hunch.

"Think about it, Daniel. Why would a woman who was so devoted to you suddenly decide to leave you behind at the mercy of a lowlife like Big Paud? If she had planned to run, surely she would have taken you with her."

Tears started to stream down Flynn's face. "You mean it was all for nothing? All those years of hating her and looking for revenge for something she didn't do. Let me go, Boyle. Let me go back to Castlebar and finish off that big bastard."

"I can't do that, Daniel. You have to answer for your crimes."

Flynn's body was convulsing with rage. His right hand, which held the Colt, rose slightly, causing Boyle to tense before he noticed the big Colt flop down again at Flynn's side. The shaking stopped and Flynn wiped his left hand across his face to remove the tears. When he looked again at Boyle, there was a hint of resignation in the dark eyes.

"Yeah, I guess you can't let me go. I should have taken my chance a few days again when I broke into his compound and trashed the place. Should have waited around until he arrived."

"That was you at Big Paud's yard? I saw you climb over the side wall."

"Fuck, you were there? Why didn't you stop me?"

Boyle shook his head. "Believe me, if I had known it was you, I would have."

"I'm not going to let you take me in, so that leaves only one option."

"Wait, wait," Boyle shouted, his eyes fixed firmly on the weapon, which was still held at Flynn's side. "Why don't we help each other."

"What are you talking about?"

"Tell us about Big Paud's cash-and-drug dumps."

"You know about those?"

"To be honest, we've so far only discovered the clear-out job you did at Glencool, but I'm guessing there are other places like it."

"Yeah, well I also cleared out another one of his places in Kilkenny. That's how I funded my lifestyle."

"Tell us about the others."

Flynn shook his head. "Can't really say for sure where they are. I could take a guess, but why should I?"

"Look, Daniel, there's no easy way to say this. Our guess is that your mother is buried at one of these sites. Help us to find her and ensure she gets a proper burial. She deserves at least that, especially from a son she loved more than anything in the world."

"You really can pour it on, Boyle. I'll give you a few addresses, but I want you to promise me two things."

"What are they?"

"Make sure Big Paud pays for his sins. Put him in a dark hole for the rest of his miserable life."

"It's what I figured to do," Boyle said. "What's

the second request?"

"I want to be buried alongside my mother."

"Can't see how anyone could argue against that. Now, what about those addresses?"

Flynn rattled off the names of two properties, the one at Kilkenny he had already referred to, and another seven miles outside Dublin at Clondalkin. "That's it, I'm done here."

Boyle nodded and asked Flynn to step forward.

"Didn't you hear me? It's over." As soon as the words left Flynn's mouth he lifted the heavy Colt, pressed it against his temple, and pulled the trigger.

Chapter 57

IT TOOK MORE THAN four hours to clean up the two sites where Flynn had discharged his weapon. A crime-scene technician examined the Colt and declared two rounds were still in the chamber, which meant only five bullets had been loaded. Perhaps the empty chamber explained why Flynn had stopped firing at the kids, although the group listening to his report conceded the theory was nothing more than speculation. They'd never really know why the young revellers had been spared.

What was clear was that the two rounds Flynn had fired had failed to hit any of his intended victims. Searchers and beaters would recover the spent cartridges and casings during a daylight search, but for now everyone was thankful for a small miracle. It didn't seem possible that Flynn could have missed at such short range, even allowing for the fact that he was running and stumbling. It was just one of those quirky, fluky occurrences that defied all odds and logic. The revolving chamber had cycled itself to the next opening, meaning a live round was ready when Flynn took his own life.

But if Flynn had stopped shooting at the youngsters because of the empty click, why did he not continue pressing the trigger if he had thought he had more bullets awaiting their turn? He'd obviously thought the weapon had cleared itself when he later pressed it against his temple and fired in the grounds of the Cathedral, so why not earlier?

Had it all been just a bluff? Had he expected another click when he pressed the trigger?

No, Boyle decided. There was no mistaking Flynn's intention to top himself. The look in his eyes in those last moments was a giveaway, as was the faint smile when he pulled the trigger.

Boyle had no regrets about the outcome. He'd have happily dealt with taking Flynn into custody, despite the fact that the killer would mostly likely have had to stand trial in Northern Ireland. This way, everyone saved themselves from a lot of paperwork and months of preparing a case to the satisfaction of the Director of Public Prosecutions. No doubt, a defence barrister would have pleaded insanity, which in turn would have led to a jurisprudence circus among the men in wigs. The result would have been the same. A life in custody, with the only difference being the surroundings in which Flynn found himself.

Boyle contacted Superintendent John Delaney at Castlebar to pass on the news of Flynn's demise, and to ask him to alert the Garda Press Office about the need to agree a joint statement with the PSNI. He had got an earlier acknowledgement from Bonnaville that official news of what had happened would not be released until agreed with their counterparts in Dublin.

There was one other thing Boyle wanted Delaney to attend to. He rattled off the two addresses provided by Flynn, and asked Delaney to pass these on for closer examination by Custer Armstrong, who was still checking for cross references between Big Paud and a series of property companies. It might also be a good idea, Boyle suggested, to put the two sites under surveillance until Custer could make the connections.

Neither Boyle nor Brogan wanted to face another four-hour drive back to Castlebar, so they took up the offer to spend the night at the B&B where Flynn had registered that afternoon. The owners had been allowed back into their home after forensic officers sealed off the room where Flynn had briefly stopped. They didn't expect to find anything, because of the in-and-out nature of the guest's brief visit, but procedures had to be followed.

Mr and Mrs Kerr greeted the Castlebar detectives with a full pot of tea and a plate of sandwiches at one o'clock in the morning. They were naturally inquisitive, and Boyle felt they deserved to know the danger was over. Without going into detail, he explained that the man who had booked with them was indeed the person responsible for the deaths of five teenagers and that he had taken his own life after being cornered by police.

In an attempt to shift the direction of the conversation, Boyle complimented the couple on their establishment, and on the general attractions in Downpatrick. "My wife, Belle, would love it here. She is a big student of Saint Patrick and I think I'll take her here for a short break to visit the centre and the grave at the Cathedral."

"Oh, you'd be welcome at any time," Mrs Kerr gushed. "Just make sure you're not chasing murderers."

Boyle smiled at the humour. "I promise it will be purely for pleasure."

Big Paud Flynn lay on his hospital bed staring out the window. He saw nothing of the clear blue skies, or the orange glow of the mid-morning sun, or the trees that swayed gently in a mild autumnal breeze. It was as if they didn't exist. His mind was transfixed on images of his son, his wife, and a wishing well that might yet come back to haunt him

News of Daniel's death was on all the morning television and radio bulletins. Big Paud heard it first on RTE's nine-o'clock broadcast.

The nationwide hunt for the man believed responsible for the deaths of five teenagers is over. Police have confirmed the man, known as Owen Patterson, committed suicide after being discovered last night in Downpatrick in the North of Ireland.

In a joint Garda-PSNI statement, it has been disclosed that Patterson turned a gun on himself when surrounded by a special taskforce of detectives, which included Garda Inspector Mick Boyle, who led the hunt along with PSNI Inspector John Bonnaville. Further updates are expected at a news conference to be held in Dublin later today.

"Fuckin' Boyle, he's everywhere," Big Paud muttered before clutching his chest and falling back against the pillows. He had taken too much out of himself by getting up and agreeing to meet with Boyle the previous day. Doctors had warned him to take it easy, especially during the first week after surgery, and certainly for another six weeks beyond that. But Big Paud was damned if he'd let Boyle see him in a vulnerable position.

Big Paud felt helpless. How could he just lie here while that fucker Boyle was sniffing around about his dead wife? Was Boyle bluffing when he mentioned about the properties and a veiled link to his wife's disappearance? What was it he had said? *Who's to say you didn't do her more permanent harm?"*

One thing was for sure, Big Paud finally decided, he couldn't just wait for Boyle to come traipsing in with the evidence that would put him away for the rest of his life. But who could he trust? He couldn't very well ask his sons to go to Kilkenny to dig up their mother's body. He hadn't even told them that their eldest brother had resurfaced as a serial killer, although it was only a matter of time before the police released the full details including Daniel's real identity.

But that hardly mattered now. Getting rid of the body in the well at Kilkenny was all Big Paud could think about. There was no-one in his organisation who could be trusted with the task, not if Paud didn't want to face a lifetime of blackmail from one of them. Sure, his crew had done plenty of unsavoury things for him the past, but this would be too good an opportunity for some of them to pass up. They'd want well paid for getting rid of a body. And they would want to keep getting paid for their silence. The whole lot of them would sell their granny for a sixpence and would use their knowledge as a get-out-of-jail card if they ever needed to plea-bargain their way out of future trouble. Which was more than a distinct possibility.

No, his sons were the only option. They didn't need to know details about the body. He could tell them it was an old enemy he had got rid of during the early days of building his empire. Yes, the idiots would take everything at face value. He'd simply tell them that the Guards might be on the trail after all these years and he needed the boys to relocate the remains to a new site where they would never be found.

Big Paud's spirits suddenly improved as he reached across and picked up a mobile phone on top of the hospital bed locker.

Jacko McStravick was sitting in a BMW Series 3 saloon across from the entrance to *P Flynn & Sons, Door & Window Manufacturers*. The car was a temporary loan from one of Jacko's many underworld friends, the kind who never asked a question when they didn't want to know the answer. Jacko had called in a favour, reasoning that to follow the Flynn boys, as requested by Boyle, could not be done behind the wheel of his conspicuous campervan.

He had been on the tail of Jerome and Seamus Flynn since yesterday. They always travelled together and so far had done little but move around Castlebar and Westport, the two towns where their father had most of his business interests. They had arrived at the firms' main complex shortly after ten this morning and were likely to stay inside for a few hours. Jacko was tempted to break-off his surveillance and get breakfast at a nearby café about a mile away.

He was glad he didn't.

The doors to the main admin building, which could be seen through the open gates of the compound, were suddenly flung wide by the unmistakeable figures of Jerome and Seamus who jumped down the steps and raced across to one of the site's many sheds. Jerome emerged minutes later carrying a coil of heavy rope looped over his shoulder, and what looked like a shovel and a yard-long crowbar. Seamus followed moments later, his arms spread in front and cradling two coveralls and two pairs of heavy-duty work boots. They dumped their loads into the boot of their father's parked Mercedes and sprinted forward to open the front doors. The big vehicle reversed out of the reserved spot and tore through the gates, turning left in a tailspin that threw dust and stone chippings into the air. All very dramatic, and about as fast as Jacko had ever seen the brothers move.

Jacko waited until the Mercedes turned a corner out of sight before slipping the BMW into gear and taking off after them. He saw the big silver car take the second exit from a roundabout and accelerate towards the office complex for Mayo County Council. It continued eastwards, dodging traffic and entering the N60 at over seventy miles an hour.

"Now, what has got you boys all fired up?" Jacko murmured as he settled in four cars behind the Mercedes.

The miles quickly peeled away on the carriageway-classed road. Signposts for Drumconlan, Carrownurlar, Milltown, and Belclare flashed by as the cars gorged up the miles. They were now on the N17 heading towards Athenry and the M6 motorway.

Jacko patiently sat a quarter-mile back. After two hours, he decided this was beginning to look promising. For two layabouts, who rarely left the confines of Mayo, to suddenly sprint across the breadth of the country, there must have been something special to put fires in their bellies.

Another hour passed. They were now on the outskirts of Kilkenny. The Mercedes left the motorway at a shopping centre junction a mile outside the city and continued at a more sedate pace along a road, which was signposted as Bothar Hebron. The big car slowed to a crawl, as if the occupants were checking directions at each turn-off, finally leaving the main road at an access lane to farmland.

Jacko stopped and considered his options. He couldn't follow the Mercedes into what might be a dead-end property. He'd just have to wait outside and hope there was no other exit route.

Chapter 58

BOYLE AND BROGAN spent the first hour of Friday morning at the PSNI Station in Downpatrick. They completed short statements, signed a lot of forms, and shook a lot of hands. All necessary, Boyle knew, but he wanted out of there and back to Castlebar as soon as possible. Most important, he wanted to step away from the melee of policemen and call Belle.

John Bonnaville intercepted him at the front door. "I can't tell you how grateful I am, Mick, for what you've done. These cases have been a millstone around my neck for eight years, and then you come along and suddenly everything vanishes. I can now put the past well and truly behind me, thanks to you."

"Nice words, John, but frankly they're a load of bull. I might have done my bit, but don't go downplaying your own contribution. You kept this case alive while I was chasing other things, and had it not been for your final input, I doubt we would have run Flynn to ground so quickly. It was a real pleasure working with you, although I guess we would have had to lock horns eventually over jurisdiction if Flynn had not taken the easy way out."

Bonnaville smiled. "I can always let you have the body if you want."

"No, you're good. He died here, so you can bury him here."

"What about that promise you made about

putting him next to his mother?"

Boyle shrugged. "Seemed the right thing to say at the time. The problem is that we don't know where his mother is buried and, chances are, we'll never know."

The two men shook hands and Boyle walked outside, eager to make a phone call and have a celebratory smoke. Bonnaville followed him out. "Just one more thing, Mick. I heard what Flynn said about breaking into his father's premises and I know you're facing a bullshit harassment complaint about that. I'll type up an affirmation statement about what I heard and email it to your office today."

Boyle shot a look at Brogan. "I see someone has been talking out of school. Thanks for the offer, John, but I wouldn't bother, if I were you."

"No bother at all, Mick, no bother at all."

Boyle tossed the car keys to Brogan and walked away to the side of the car park. He opened a cigarette packet, took out the last filter-tip, and lit up, promising himself it really would be the last. He took three deep puffs before cradling his iPhone and thumbing Belle's number. She answered within two seconds, her familiar voice suddenly lifting his mood. "Morning, darling, is everything all right? Why didn't you FaceTime me? I've missed you."

Boyle guiltily let the cigarette fall to the ground at the mention of FaceTime. "Sorry, honey, but you know how bad I am with all these technologies."

"Never mind, tell me how things are going. I heard on the news that you caught the killer. I'm so proud of you, Mick."

"I wanted to tell you before the news broke, but it was a late night and I couldn't disturb you. We've wrapped up everything here and are heading back.

I'll see you shortly after lunch. How have you been keeping? Did Andrea and Johnny stay with you last night?"

"Yes, they stayed over and even insisted on doing the breakfast shift. Mind you, I didn't argue. Baby had a restless night. I think he or she just wants to make an introduction."

Boyle shifted uneasily on his feet. "You're not coming early, are you?"

"There's still ten days to go, Mick, but you just never know. Nature will take its own course."

"Promise me you'll stay away from the bar today. I'll be there as soon as possible."

"Get a grip, Mick Boyle," Belle laughed down the line. "Nothing's going to happen for quite a while. Just take your time and get here in one piece. I love you."

"Love you too."

Brogan sat in the car and watched Boyle's face go through a range of emotions. Mick really did wear his heart on his sleeve, a quality that was both endearing and dangerous at the same time. He was the best detective Brogan had ever encountered, but sometimes he pushed too hard and took too many risks, particularly with his own career. It was why Brogan saw himself as a kind of minder, the one person who could step between Mick and trouble. His boss didn't really do office politics whereas Brogan prided himself on knowing how to navigate potentially tricky situations.

Which was what Mick was now facing.

Brogan was also on the phone, a call that had started as a simple catch-up with the Castlebar team but was first routed through Sergeant Moriarty. That was as far as Brogan got.

Moriarty needed to get something off his chest, and Brogan had called at just the right time. It was about the mole who had leaked the information to Big Paud Flynn about the search warrants. Moriarty explained how he had tracked the source and had been sitting on the information for several days. But he could sit on it no longer, simply because an email copy of the statement that Flynn's barrister had read out to Boyle in the hospital, had arrived in the Castlebar inbox. Someone, however, had forgotten to hide the names and email addresses of those who had been copied into the original missive.

"And why is that important?" Brogan asked.

"Because the name of the mole is on the list and there is no reason why this guy should have been included in an official notification. It's outside his bailiwick, yet here is front and centre of something that should have been none of his business. Seeing his name there, confirmed what I had already suspected."

Brogan didn't want to ask, but knew he had to. "So, who was it?"

"Chief Superintendent William McCluskey."

"Jesus," Brogan gasped. "Mick'll go spare when he hears this."

"Precisely. Which is why you have to help me make sure that he doesn't hear it."

"How in the hell do we do that? Look, don't circulate that email internally until I get there. I'll have to have a good think about it."

"Thanks, Paul. You know what they say about a problem shared. When do you expect to get here?"

Brogan was about to respond when the

passenger door opened, and Boyle flopped into the seat. "Who are you talking to?"

"Er, just contacting the station for updates. Ah, Sergeant Moriarty, can you patch me through to the squad room."

Boyle reached out his arm. "Let me take this. I need you to get us on the move. I think Belle is going into early labour."

Brogan handed over his phone and switched on the car ignition. "Consider it done."

Colin McCartney took the patched-through call. "Good to hear from you, Paul. Great job in the North."

Boyle cut him off. "Sorry, Colin, this is Boyle. I'm putting you on loudspeaker because I've snookered Paul into doing the driving. What's happening there? Did Superintendent Delaney pass on my message to check two additional addresses."

"Yes, boss, we got the message. I've already sent two men to the Clondalkin address and I figured Custer and Munn would head for Kilkenny as soon as we wrap up the morning work."

"No, no," Boyle said with more than a hint of irritation in his voice. "This is bloody important. You should have covered the Kilkenny address from early this morning. Ring the local boys immediately and get someone to babysit the location until our own people get there."

"Sorry, boss, I'll get on it right away. Then I'll get Custer and Munn to leave immediately."

"No again," Boyle said with rising anger. "I need you and Custer to stay there and co-ordinate things. Send two other detectives and tell me where we're at in respect of tying Flynn to those addresses."

"I'll put Custer on the line while I make arrangements."

Boyle waited impatiently for ten seconds before Custer Armstrong's cheery voice broke the silence. "Hi, boss, I see you finally nailed that bastard Flynn. Can't tell you how much it cheered everyone up."

Boyle couldn't help but take his tone down a few notches. "Yeah, Custer, tell everyone it was a great team effort. Now, where are we with those bloody addresses?"

"Right, do you want the long version or the short one?"

"Custer!"

"Okay, the short one it is. I've been going through the usual hoops of chasing my tail around various mysterious companies, most of which were set up overseas. As it turns out, the Clondalkin and Kilkenny properties were both bought by the same company, one with the imaginative name of *Earp Enterprises*."

"So, it's the same pattern of using names from TV westerns. Have you been able to connect them with Big Paud?"

"Not yet, boss, but I'm working on it."

"Keep at it, Custer. This could be crucial."

Chapter 59

MIDDAY. AN HOUR out of Castlebar. Boyle's brain scrambled with all manner of thoughts, most of them about Big Paud Flynn. The past three hours had flown by while Boyle tried to put things into perspective, not easy when so much remained to be done, and so much could yet go wrong.

And still no updates from Castlebar.

Then his phone pinged. It was Superintendent Delaney. "Where are you, Mick?"

"I'll be at the station by one o'clock. What's up?"

If Boyle had been hoping for a breakthrough in the property search, he has about to be disillusioned in a hurry. "You're needed for a press conference in Dublin at three o'clock."

"Dublin? Forget it. Even if I had the time, I wouldn't go within a mile of that circus. They'll just have to get along without me."

Delaney's voice was calm and reassuring. "This is a big deal, Mick. The bigwigs are about to take public acclaim for a job well done, and they want the man responsible for that job to be there with them. You don't have any options. Besides which, I want Castlebar to get the recognition it deserves."

"Okay, John, then you go."

"Don't be silly, Mick. You're the one who rescued two girls and run a serial killer to ground. It's your face everyone wants to see."

"I wish I could but, like I said, I'm an hour outside Castlebar and it would take another three hours to get to Dublin. I wish I had known sooner."

"Yeah, right," Delaney said. "Who are you trying to kid? As it so happens, you don't have to worry about the timing because they've laid on a chopper to take you to Phoenix Park."

"You're kidding. Look, I can't really leave because of Belle. I'm worried she might go into labour this afternoon."

"Do you even hear yourself? You're like a youngster trying to get out of going to school. I spoke to Belle a short while ago and she's feeling fine. She's got your Sunday-best suit all laid out and waiting. You'll even have time for a quick shower."

Sometimes it's best to know when you're beaten, and Boyle quickly arrived at that conclusion. "Who needs enemies?"

Jacko McStravick got out of the BMW for the tenth time and paced the footpath to relieve the cramp and pains in his legs and arms. Two hours on site, and still nothing. The Flynn brothers had not emerged from the farmland entrance, nor could he see any evidence of a secondary road they might have used to evade his scrutiny. He had earlier walked part-way up the lane and scanned the horizon ahead of his position. Nothing but fields. No telltale hedges to show the track of a possible road, no distant farmhouses that needed to be serviced, no coming or going of other traffic on the site.

He was tired and hungry and thirsty. He had to fight with himself not to take off, even for a short while. He badly needed sustenance. Surely a break for an hour wouldn't make any difference? Aye, try telling that to Mick Boyle, if the Flynn boys decided to leave the area while he was away filling his face.

He had just walked back to the car when a brown Ford Mondeo pulled against the kerb about fifty yards ahead of him. He watched as two men got out of the car and walked across to the laneway entrance. They had that look about them. It was one Jacko could spot a mile off. They were police officers. The men talked animatedly for several minutes before one of them turned into the lane and started walking. His colleague returned to the Mondeo.

It was time for Jacko to make himself scarce. He drove about a mile up the road, surprised to see a garage around the first corner, and promptly pulled into the forecourt. What was more surprising was that the shop attached to the garage sold hot food. Had he known that earlier, he could have saved himself a lot of anguish. Not one for what-might-have-beens, Jacko loaded up with two large cheeseburgers, a bag of chips, and a two-litre bottle of Coke.

He drove back past the parked police car, pulled into a parking lane about a hundred yards away, and started munching on his feast. It was only after he'd demolished the first burger that he decided to phone Boyle to let him know what was happening.

Boyle felt the mobile vibrate urgently in his trouser pocket. There was nothing he could do. Seated at a long conference table on a raised platform in the main hall of Garda headquarters at Phoenix Park with the world's press staring back at him, was hardly the right place to interrupt the Commissioner's opening address by taking out his phone to see who the caller was. It would just have to wait.

It was a surprisingly relaxed affair for Boyle. To be fair, the Commissioner had been keeping things on point and had taken several opportunities to mention Boyle and the Castlebar task force. This was no glory-seeking event, merely a genuine attempt to provide update information and to let the public know there was no longer a threat from a brutal serial killer. Daniel Flynn's name and background was released for the first time, as were some key components of the investigation that had led to Flynn's doorstep. The Commissioner mentioned the role played by Garda divisions across the country and acknowledged the assistance of the PSNI and the Chicago PD.

It was beginning to sound like an international crime thriller, Boyle thought. Maybe someday, somebody would write a book about it!

Boyle was calm and at ease during the follow-up questions section, usually a bear pit as reporters clamoured for an extra juicy bit. Most of the journalists' attention was focused on Boyle who stayed on script and divulged only what had been agreed at a briefing with the Garda press officers before the event.

As soon as the session was ended, Boyle made his way to the wings and pulled out his phone. There were two missed calls from Jacko McStravick. He immediately activated the callback function.

"What have you got, Jacko?"

Boyle listened intently to what McStravick had to say. It was a concise, to-the-point report that made Boyle's eyes light up. "You mean the Flynn brothers are at the Bothar Road in Kilkenny? This is huge."

"You know about this Bothar Road?" McStravick asked.

"Only found out about it since we last spoke. It's a possible stash site used by Big Paud, which would seem to be confirmed by the presence of Jerome and Seamus there. You've done good, Jacko."

"So, do you want me to stay or leave?"

"Best you make yourself scarce. Those police officers you spotted are from our Kilkenny station and they will stay there until our own team arrive on site."

Boyle cut the call and pondered his next move. If Jerome and Seamus were still at the site after more than two hours, if could only mean that they were up to no good. Had they been sent there by their father to remove cash and drugs? Or maybe a body?

But what the hell could he do about it? He needed a search warrant to enter the area. How was he going to explain that? Was a dying man's declaration enough to convince a judge to let the police take a close look at the properties? Superintendent John Delaney would know the best way forward, but in the meantime he had to make sure the officers already on the ground did not let the Flynn boys out of their sight.

"Ah, there you are, Boyle. Come out here and talk to Assistant Commissioner Quinn who has a proposition for you." Boyle looked up and saw the Commissioner standing with his deputy at the corner of the platform.

The Commissioner shook his hand for the umpteenth time that afternoon. "Great job, Boyle, and I don't just mean with the investigation. You handled yourself like a real pro with that baying mob of journos. I'm beginning to think we're wasting your talents by leaving you out in a limb over in Mayo. Have a word with the Assistant Commissioner to see if we can do something about that."

With that, the Commissioner walked off, leaving Boyle open-mouthed and staring at the man now approaching with his hand out. "I'll get quickly to the point," Quinn said. "You're being put forward for a well-earned promotion and we want you back at NBCI to be a part of a restructuring we've been thinking about for some time. What say you to that?"

"Sir, I'm sorry, this is bad timing. I have a number of urgent calls to make, especially about my wife's condition. I really need to get back to Castlebar."

"Is your wife alright?"

"Yes, sir, we're expecting our first baby and...."

"Enough said, my boy. Get yourself out of here. We can talk about this matter another time."

Chapter 60

THE EUROCOPTER 135T2 touched down in the athletic fields at Castlebar an hour after it left the grounds of Phoenix Park. Boyle had been tempted to ask the pilot to divert to Kilkenny, but quickly concluded there was little he could do to affect things on the ground. It could be hours yet before the surveillance on the Flynns was wound down, let alone for police to find out exactly what the brothers were doing at the location.

Boyle knew his time would be best served by being at Castlebar, chasing down warrants and pushing his team to make the connections they needed to finally nail Big Paud Flynn. There was also a more important reason for being back on home soil. He wanted to see Belle.

Brogan was waiting with transport at the athletic fields and promptly whisked Boyle across town to the bar and restaurant premises. Brogan stayed in the car as his boss pushed open the rear gate and rushed through the cluttered yard.

Belle was nowhere to be seen in the kitchen or bar area. The barmaid, Andrea, smiled at Boyle's entrance and pointed at the ceiling, which meant Belle was in the upstairs living quarters.

"Is she alright?" Boyle asked, trying to mask his trepidation.

"Yes, all good. She went up a few hours ago for a lie-down. Ask me, it won't be long now."

Boyle brushed past her and slowed down at the

foot of the stairs. If Belle was asleep he didn't want to wake her with heavy footfalls. He walked gingerly up the steps and was surprised to see Belle sitting on an armchair in the main lounge. "Thought you were lying down. How are things?"

Belle spread her arms in an invite for an embrace. "I saw you on TV. You looked really great and you spoke so well. I didn't expect you back for hours."

"Stop changing the subject," Boyle scolded as he knelt beside her and wrapped his arms around her in a tender hug. "I asked how you were. Shouldn't you be lying down?"

"I've been resting all day. I contacted the maternity unit this afternoon and a midwife is going to call sometime in the next hour. They think everything sounds normal, but it does seem as if baby is going to come earlier than expected. The nurse will check me over and let me know what she thinks. She did say over the phone that I should prepare myself for admission sometime over the next few days."

Boyle frowned. "That's good news, isn't it?"

Belle laughed. "Yes, Mick, it's all good. An early arrival will suit everyone."

"I'll stay around until the nurse comes."

"You'll do no such thing. I love you, darling, but I need you out of my hair for a few hours. Don't worry, I've got this. I promise to call you as soon as the nurse leaves."

Boyle knew there was little point in arguing. He leaned forward and kissed his wife. "Okay, I've got a few things to do, but nothing that I can't drop immediately."

Boyle entered the station with thoughts of search warrants, Big Paud Flynn, a potentially missing body, and a child wanting to make a first appearance into the world, all fighting for his attention. He wasn't sure he had the energy to cope with anything other than the arrival of his son or daughter.

He was heading for Moriarty's reception desk when Superintendent Delaney burst from his downstairs office and stopped in his tracks. "Mick! Thank goodness you're here. Quick, follow me, there's a bit of a flap on."

Delaney turned on his heels and walked back into the office. Boyle and Brogan followed, each shrugging their shoulders as they stood in front of Delaney's desk. "What's got you so riled, John."

"You're never going to fucking believe this, Mick. I just got a call from Kilkenny. Two of their officers arrested Jerome and Seamus Flynn a short while ago, apparently in possession of a large sum of cash, a bag of drugs, and, get this, a pile of human bones."

"You've got to be kidding me," Boyle whistled. "How the hell did they manage that?"

"One of life's little ironies. The pair were involved in a bad road accident and lo and behold the plastic bags just spilled out from a damaged rear end. The two officers on the scene couldn't believe their luck."

Boyle nodded. "I'd say it was a bit more than luck. Did this happen at the address on the Bothar Road?"

"From what I gather, it was about a hundred yards from the entrance to the site. But here's the real funny part, Mick. The driver of the other car involved in the collision was our very own Jacko

McStravick. What do you suppose he was doing there?"

Jacko had remained parked for ten minutes after his conversation with Boyle. He was still hungry and wanted to finish the remnants of the burgers and chips before hitting the long road back to Castlebar. He'd done his bit, for what it was worth, and now it was down to the Guards to take over.

He glanced in his rearview mirror to note that the unmarked police car was still in position, close to the entrance lane and facing in the opposite direction to Jacko's car. He thought about what Jerome and Seamus Flynn were up to at the farmland site but shook the notion from his head. Not his responsibility anymore.

Jacko gathered together the various cartons that had contained his meal and stuffed them in the brown paper carrier bag that had been supplied by the garage. He'd get rid of it at the first kerbside wastebin he came across. He settled into his seat, buckled up, and switched on the ignition. One last look in the rearview as he started to ease the BMW away into the main road.

His attention was suddenly drawn to the appearance of the silver Mercedes at the laneway entrance where it stopped before moving into the main carriageway at a more sedate pace than it had covered the miles from Castlebar.

There was no sign of the policeman who had walked into the lane earlier, nor was there any sign that his colleague in the Mondeo was doing anything about the disappearing Mercedes. Surely, they're not going to let the Flynns leave the site without checking what they were doing there?

Jacko waited until the Mercedes drove past his position. "Fuck it!" It was a shout of resignation as Jacko gunned his engine and sprinted off in pursuit. He kept the boot to the board as he moved up the gears and rammed the rear of the Mercedes at almost sixty mph. He saw the boot of the big car spring open as it fishtailed across the carriageway before slamming into a garden wall.

Jacko sat behind the wheel of his stationary BMW and watched for a reaction from the Flynn brothers. Finally, the passenger door opened, and Seamus fell out onto the road, his face partially covered by blood seeping from a cut in his forehead. He sat on the tarmac like a rag doll, looking around in a daze, but clearly unable to focus on anything.

The sound of running feet made Jacko swivel to his right where the Mondeo policeman was running. The man skidded to a stop behind the Mercedes, then looked across at Jacko.

"How the fuck am I going to get out of this?" McStravick whispered to himself.

Delaney and Brogan stared wide-eyed as Boyle explained why Jacko McStravick had been at the site of the Flynns' arrest. "I asked him to keep an eye on their movements, but I never expected this. I thought they might lead us to some of their father's hidden properties around Mayo. It was a long shot, and I knew Jacko would be discreet."

"There was nothing discreet about the way he rammed their car and put one of them in the hospital with severe concussion," Delaney said. "If he is seen as one of our agents, and I use the term loosely, then it could jeopardise the case against the Flynns. What if they argue that anything found at the scene is inadmissible because we had engineered the whole thing as a kind of entrapment?"

Boyle banged the table. "How about you stop all the negativity and start batting for our side? The simple fact is that without McStravick we wouldn't have nailed the bastards, so how about we just concentrate on making the case stick instead of looking at loopholes that don't exist?"

Delaney's face reddened with temper. "I don't deserve that, Mick, especially from you. I want the Flynns as much as anyone, but the simple fact remains that McStravick is a fly in the ointment. Who's to say our Kilkenny team wouldn't have followed Jerome and Seamus and watched them dispose of the plastic bags in another location. We could have moved in then and got a clean arrest. As it stands, this is anything but clean."

Boyle slumped into one of the seats and stared at Delaney. "I'm sorry about the outburst, John, I truly am. It was uncalled for. Yes, the Kilkenny officers might have been able to do as you've said, but equally they could have lost the Flynns in a car chase. What McStravick did was to give us the bird in the hand. Without him, the horde lifted from the farmland site might have remained hidden from us forever. Now, we use what we've got, and we build a case, starting with getting those bones identified. We both know they will turn out to be the remains of Big Paud's wife."

Delaney nodded. "I'm with you all the way. Sorry for the Devil's Advocate stuff, but I do worry about how we explain Jacko McStravick's part in all this."

"What if I told you Jacko had another reason for being there? What if I said he had a prior beef with the Flynns and had followed them for some payback after they'd viciously assaulted him?"

"That would certainly do the trick, but how convincing is it?"

Boyle sat back and recounted the story of the Flynns' assault on Belle and how Jacko had intervened, a rescue act that had cost him a few bruised ribs and a slight adjustment to his ugly face.

Delaney leapt from his seat. "The scumbags attacked Belle? Why in the hell didn't you tell us this before now? Was Belle alright? Why didn't you get our boys to arrest the Flynns for assault? How did you keep your cool and not go around there to kick seven bells out of the bastards?"

Boyle marvelled at Delaney's outburst. He knew the station Superintendent was angry at the idea of Belle being attacked and was venting on her behalf. Boyle smiled across the desk. "Let's just say I was persuaded from engaging my base instincts by someone who helps to keep me from flying off the handle, most of the time. Besides, it looks like the Flynns will get a bigger comeuppance than anything I could have dreamed of."

"That they will," Delaney beamed. "That they will."

Chapter 61

HER NAME WAS Angela Doherty. At least it was before she ran into a brutish tearaway, who was making a name for himself plying a lucrative drugs trade between Dublin and his home base in Kilkenny. It was just her bad luck that he chose one particular day to be in the capital and that he happened to be in the bar in Grafton Street when she walked in with some of her friends from Trinity.

For some reason, Angela looked past the considerable deficiencies in manner and appearance and allowed herself to be swept along by the stranger with plenty of money and a lot to say for himself. It was the start of a torrid love affair that ended at an altar within eight weeks. She threw up her studies, moved to Kilkenny, and prepared for the birth of her first son.

By then, she was Angela Flynn, wife of Big Paud Flynn.

It needed dental records, unearthed in Northern Ireland by PSNI Inspector John Bonnaville, to put an identity to the human skeleton spread out on the aluminium tray at Dublin City Mortuary where the State Pathologist had already declared the likely cause of death as strangulation. The absence of the small triangle-shaped hyoid bone was a good indicator, as was the fact that there were no blunt-trauma marks to be found on the skull. Other bones in the body had suffered impact damage, all of which were judged to be old wounds, which would have occurred at various periods, most likely months or years, before Angela's actual death.

The PSNI detective was also able to provide a brief summary of Angela's life, which he had gleaned from parish records, school ledgers, and interviews with some of the senior residents of Ardmeen Green, in Downpatrick where she had grown up. Angela's parents had died in a car accident when she was ten, after which she was raised by an older sister, Violet. It seemed Angela had been a star pupil at the Sisters of Mercy Convent School in Downpatrick and at the Assumption Grammar School in Ballynahinch, a small town situated about eleven miles from where she lived. Angela got accepted to Trinity to study Economics and had left Downpatrick in 1965. Her sister died from a brain clot six months after Angela's departure, although neighbours reported that the younger Doherty, by then Mrs Flynn, had not attended the funeral. There were no surviving grandparents or uncles of aunts.

Bonnaville's email reached Boyle early on Monday morning. He read it twice, shaking his head at the sadness and bad luck that had dogged Angela Flynn's life. It must have been a lonely, depressing existence for a young girl for whom the early days had held so much promise. Her marriage to Big Paud must have been hell, a long journey of abuse and subjugation that ended at the bottom of a well with no one, except for three young sons, to even notice that she'd gone.

Big Paud had got lucky with the manner of her exit. The family had moved to Dublin from Kilkenny only a matter of months before her disappearance. There had been no time for her to forge friendships or relationships in her new surroundings, and the absence of a surviving family of her own meant there was no support mechanism to alert authorities to the fact that she was no longer around. As far as Sergeant Moriarty could find out, no reports had been logged about Angela Flynn being missing and therefore no reason why Gardai should have been alerted to potential foul play.

She was a forgotten, overlooked statistic. But not now. Boyle would see to it that Angela Flynn would get the justice she deserved.

Boyle turned away from the computer screen and looked at a large file, which he had carried home from the office on Saturday evening. By that time, it had been agreed to formally arrest Jerome and Seamus Flynn on a variety of charges. Conspiracy to pervert the course of justice by removing a body from a crime scene; complicity in murder after the fact; possession of drugs with intent to distribute; and possession of goods, namely cash, being the proceeds of illegal activities.

Arrangements were being made to transport the brothers from Kilkenny to Castlebar by Monday afternoon. Jerome's concussion was declared nothing more than a severe headache caused by coming violently in contact with the steering wheel when his car was pitched forward as a result of the shunt by Jacko McStravick. A doctor had declared both brothers were medically fit to be interviewed in relation to the charges against them

Now, that was something Boyle was looking forward to.

By all accounts, during their time in custody at

Kilkenny, the boys were cocky and tight-lipped, refusing to say anything until their legal representative was present. Boyle had no doubt that that representation would be in the shape of Myles Winstanley, whose par for the course would be to stonewall at every turn and to look for loopholes, no matter how small, in the Garda's case preparation.

But Boyle reckoned there was a very big ace up his sleeve. Now that the body taken from Bothar Road had been identified as the boys' mother he wondered how they would react to the news. His guess was that Big Paud had failed to mention that little detail when he'd sent the brothers on their dirty mission. It was bound to have an effect, even for two layabouts who muddled through life not caring about anyone but themselves. He hoped the news would finally prise loose what Boyle was really after.

As yet, there was nothing to tie Big Paud to his wife's death. Everything was circumstantial and speculative. But if one of his two sons admitted their father had sent them on the errand to remove the body, it would be enough to prove prior knowledge by Big Paud of its existence. In that event, a murder charge would be a slam dunk.

Boyle tried to rein in his emotions. Don't get too far ahead of yourself. You've come this close. Keep cool and tease out what you need.

"Mick, Mick, come quick!"

He jumped at the sound of Belle's voice and raced into the bedroom. "What's wrong?"

"Get me to the hospital. It's time."

The next two days were a blur for Boyle. His son was delivered late on Monday afternoon, a week ahead of schedule, and sporting a full head of black hair atop an impressive frame of 8lbs and 4ozs. Mother and baby had sailed through the procedure and were back home by Thursday morning.

Boyle cared little about missing the interviews with the Flynn brothers. In truth, he had pushed the whole sorry business to the back of his mind, knowing Paul Brogan would prove to be a probative inquisitor and probably better able to get into the minds of his subjects than he could. Boyle put that down to Brogan's burgeoning relationship with a certain Dr Connie Dunne.

The homecoming for mother and child was marked by a pub and upstairs living quarters bedecked with blue ribbons, balloons, scores of cards from well-wishers, and several large bouquets, one of which was from the men and women at Castlebar police station. There were callers throughout the morning, mostly friends of Belle, who wanted to hold the baby and who gave the proud father ample opportunities to continually lift the boy from his crib for their inspection.

"What are you going to call him?" A repetitive question that Belle fended off with a stock answer. "We haven't decided yet, but we've narrowed it down."

It was late afternoon before the Boyles finally had some time alone. Belle sat on an armchair cradling her son, by now fast asleep after enduring the constant interruptions. "Right, Mick, we need to agree on a name. My first choice was my father Thomas's name, and your first choice was to name him Patrick after your father. How about we settle for a compromise?"

"What have you in mind?"

As she told him, Boyle's eyes widened. Then he

rolled the name around on his tongue and smiled back at her. "I like that. Can't think of anything more appropriate."

At that moment, a shadow fell across the door and the couple turned to look at a sheepish Jacko McStravick, his arms filled with a bunch of flowers and his gaze lowered to the carpet. "Hope you don't mind the interruption. They told me downstairs it was alright to come on up."

Belle beckoned their guest forward and held up the baby. "Jacko, meet your new family. This is Jack Boyle, who is named after you and who will be your Godson if you agree to take on the responsibility."

The big man's eyes moistened. "Are you serious? You named him after me? I don't deserve this, but I'm chuffed to bits, so I am. Of course, I'll be his Godfather, if you're really sure that is what you want."

Boyle nodded and walked to a cabinet at the side of the lounge. He lifted out two tumblers, poured generous measures of whiskey into each one, and crossed back to the centre of the room. He handed a glass to McStravick. "How about a toast to Jack Thomas Patrick Boyle?"

"Aye, I'll drink to that and no mistake." The contents of the glass disappeared in one gulp.

"There's just one thing," Boyle said with mock sternness. "His name is Jack, not Jacko, and if I ever catch you saying otherwise, I'll bar you from the pub."

The big man grinned. "Deal."

"That's settled then," Boyle said and quickly changed the subject. "Tell me, did my colleagues in Kilkenny charge you with anything for that little mishap you had?"

"Funny thing is that they let me go with a caution for careless driving. One of the Guards, the detective who was the one watching the property, swore that the driver of the Mercedes slammed on the brakes for no apparent reason and there was little I could do to avoid a collision. I think maybe someone put in a good word for me."

"I wonder who that was," Boyle said with a straight face.

Chapter 62

IT WAS ANOTHER three days before Boyle returned to work. The Flynn boys had refused to budge from an audaciously ridiculous story that the only reason they had been at the Kilkenny property on Bothar Road was to clean up the site as a surprise present for their sick father who wanted to put it on the market. When they found the bones down an old well, they had assumed these were hundreds of years old, probably relics the local museum might be interested in, which was why they were taking them back to Castlebar.

The cash and drugs had baffled them, the brothers said. They reckoned some local criminals must have left them there. It was a find that they swore they were taking to the police when they were rear-ended not far from the site.

Myles Winstanley's glib patter was all over the Flynns' bizarre version of events. He had coached them well, knowing that unless the Guards could prove otherwise, there was enough there to muddy the waters for a successful conviction.

Both Jerome and Seamus *had* shown brief flashes of horror when they were told that the bones were those of their mother, but they quickly recovered their composures under Winstanley's steadying influence. Nonetheless, Brogan had noted that Seamus seemed a lot more uncomfortable about the news than his brother. Perhaps there was something there to be worked on.

What was illuminating about the interviews was the admission by the brothers that the property belonged to their father. For the first time, Boyle's team had collaborative proof that tied Big Paud to the dump site, although ten chances to one, the information had been volunteered at the direction of Winstanley, who probably figured the Guards would get there eventually.

And he was right. Custer Armstrong finally backtracked ownership through a myriad of companies straight to Big Paud's doorstep. Armstrong found the name hidden in lists of false directors and bank accounts, which showed deposits made by Flynn shortly before the site was purchased. Lumped in with this deal was a similar deal, which tied Big Paud to ownership of the other property at Clondalkin that had been identified by Daniel Flynn shortly before he shot himself.

The link proved sufficient enough for the issue of an immediate search warrant of the premises at Clondalkin. If nothing else, they might uncover another stash of money and drugs, which would confirm a familiar pattern of Big Paud's operations.

But Boyle was convinced he already had enough. He finished reading Brogan's notes on the separate interviews with the Flynn brothers and ordered another formal session with Seamus Flynn. It was set for two o'clock in the afternoon to allow time for Winstanley to sit in.

"**I**'m going to get right down to it," Boyle announced as soon as the various introductions were made. He stared directly across the table at Seamus. "Your version of why you were at Kilkenny and how you came to retrieve the various items found in your possession is nothing more than a fairytale. Because of your failure to co-operate, we are going to relentlessly pursue the charges against you and ensure you spend a minimum of twenty-five years in prison."

Winstanley put a reassuring hand on his client's arm and smiled across at Boyle. "I'd hoped you would be more inventive than resorting to browbeating my client. We've already given a full and honest explanation for why the goods were in his possession. If you really want to go to trial on the basis of what you have, I'm happy to let a jury decide."

"Good for you, counsellor, but you're not the one facing a grim future. Have you really explained to your client what a jury might think of what is commonly known as causal relationship?"

Paul Brogan, sitting alongside Boyle, tried to mask his surprise at what had just been said, but his raised eyebrows showed he had no idea where his boss was going.

Winstanley looked equally bemused. "What in hell are you talking about?"

"In simple terms," Boyle said, "causal relationship is a process by which one event contributes to the production of another event, where the cause is partly responsible for the effect, and the effect is partly dependent on the cause."

Winstanley blew out his cheeks. "In all my years involved with legal matters I've never heard such twaddle. Would you care to explain what you just said?"

Boyle smiled. "Let me put it in simple terms. Our people found a drugs and cash stash at property in Glencool Forest and a similar stash, using exactly the same camouflaged chamber, on the Kilkenny site where your client removed the evidence in consort with his brother Jerome Flynn. We are currently searching a third site at Clondalkin, where I'm betting we come across the same thing again. All three sites are owned by Paud Flynn, which gives us the causal relationship we need to prove our case. In short, Paud Flynn knew of the sites and their secrets because it was he who created them. This is no longer about conjecture and flimflam, as you would have everyone believe, Mr Winstanley. It is about supportable facts, including the one that says Paud Flynn ordered his sons to that site with the specific instruction to clean it out."

"We are not prepared to say any more on the subject, Inspector. As far as I'm concerned, this interview is over."

"Not your call, counsellor. This interview is over only when I say it is. Now, I'd really like to hear what your client has to say about the points I've just made."

"He is under my instruction not to comment, as is his right."

Boyle ignored Winstanley and leaned across the table towards Seamus. "Here's the thing, Seamus. Your legal representative has a massive conflict of interest. His first duty is to your father, who pays his considerable bills, and that means he will do everything in his power to keep Big Paud out of prison, even if that means that you do time instead."

"Is that right?" Seamus said. It was the first time he had spoken.

Winstanley shook his head vigorously. "No, no,

Seamus, don't listen to him. I have your full interests at heart..."

"I don't see how that could be possible," Boyle interrupted. "Consider this, Seamus, your father sent you on an errand to dispose of your mother's body. How could any parent do that? And then he sends his expensive legal parrot here to sit in on the interviews with you and your brother, not to protect you, but to protect himself. Would someone who murdered the mother of his children and then callously sent those children to help cover the crime, really care about what happens to them? I think you know the answer to that."

Winstanley rose from his chair and glowered at Boyle. "This is preposterous, even for you, Boyle. I insist you give me time to confer alone with my client."

Boyle ignored him and continued to stare at Seamus. "This is your only chance to get out from under this mess. You don't deserve to go down for this. All you were doing was obeying your father's orders. How can that be worth twenty-five years? Tell us the truth and I promise we will reconsider all charges against you."

Seamus started sniffling. "This isn't fair. He told us to get rid of a body that was supposed to belong to an old rival. He said nothing about our mother."

"Who, Seamus, who told you to get rid of the body?"

"He said we'd also find drugs and money at the site and that we could keep these for ourselves as payment for a job well done."

"Who told you that?" Boyle said.

Winstanley slapped his palm on top of the

table. "Do not say anymore, Seamus. I can fix this for you."

"Who told you?" Boyle persisted.

"I can't....I can't."

"Of course, you can. You want to get this off your chest. You need to let it go."

Winstanley's face was a mask of rage. "That's enough, Inspector!"

"Stay out of this, counsellor. Seamus is the one who has to face up to this."

"I...I don't want to say anymore."

"You have to, Seamus. You have to do it for yourself and you have to do it for your poor dead mother. This is your chance to free both your souls."

"I don't want to say."

"Who told you to remove the body from the well at Bothar Road? If you come clean, all the conspiracy charges go away. Your admission will mean you were not acting in concert but were ordered to do what you did. That alone will save you twenty years. This is your last chance."

"I...I don't know what to do."

"Just tell us if it was your father who sent you to Bothar Road with the express intent of removing a body?"

"I...I...yes, it was him."

"Are you saying that your father, Padraig Flynn, sent you to Bothar Road and told you where to find the body?"

Seamus leaned forward and buried his head in his hands. The upper part of his body was shaking. "Yes, it was my father who sent us."

Paul Brogan sat across from Boyle at the conference table in the squad room. "I can't believe you got him to confess. I never saw anything like it."

"I got lucky."

"C'mon, Mick, what in Christ's name was all that nonsense about causal relationships? Did you get that from Wikipedia?"

Boyle smiled. "As a matter of fact, I did. I just needed something to put Seamus Flynn into a tizzy and I figured it sounded serious enough to make him believe he was staring down the barrel. I knew it wouldn't fool Winstanley, but he was not the target."

"Well, it worked. Seamus's statement has been written up and signed. No surprise that Jerome quickly followed suit when he saw his brother's confession. We've got full corroboration on Big Paud's guilt. He'll go down for what's left of his life, which means his whole empire will start crumbling."

Boyle shook his head. "Someone will try to step into the gap left by the Flynns. It'll be our job to keep an eye on who makes the first moves."

Brogan nodded in agreement. "Can you believe Winstanley immediately recused himself from defending the Flynn brothers? Guess that leaves him free to try to save Big Paud's skin."

"No, I think you'll find our legal friend will start disassociating himself from all the Flynns. Even he couldn't save Big Paud now from a murder charge."

"Speaking of which," Brogan said, "I bet you're looking forward to reading out the charge and putting Big Paud under arrest?"

Flynn got up and pulled his jacket from the back of the chair. "No, again. I've got two more important people to see. You can do the honours while I go back to my wife and son. Isn't life wonderful?"

"Are you sure, Mick? You've earned the satisfaction of seeing Big Paud's reaction."

Boyle was already at the door. "Yes, I'm certain. Life is all about priorities, and I've got mine exactly where I want them."

Brogan shifted uneasily in his seat. "There's something I've been meaning to ask you."

"Fire away."

"There's a few whispers doing the rounds about you being offered promotion back to the NBCI in Dublin. Just wondered if there's any truth to them."

Boyle shook his head. "Rest easy, Grasshopper, you're not getting rid of me that easy. This is where I want to be, and this is where I'll be staying."

Brogan looked genuinely pleased. "That's great news, Mick, the boys will all be glad to hear it."

"Maybe they won't be so pleased when I start kicking their backsides on whatever little adventures are around the next corner."

"You're all talk," Brogan countered.

Boyle shrugged and fixed Brogan with a curious stare. "You know, when you said there was something you'd been meaning to ask me, I thought you were referring to something else entirely."

"Such as?"

"Such as, who was the mole who leaked information about our raids on Big Paud's properties?"

The blood drained from Brogan's face.

"It's alright," Boyle said. "You can stop worrying about me finding out that it was Chief Superintendent McCluskey. I already worked it out for myself, although to be fair I had a bit of help from my old NBCI friend, Damien Robinson, who tracked a few incoming phone calls and emails."

"How...how did you know we had discovered the mole from our end?"

"Now, that really wasn't rocket science. I knew that when I asked Sergeant Moriarty to look into it, he would ferret out the source. Felt strange that he hadn't provided any updates until I caught the furtive glances between the two of you these past few days.

"We were just trying to...to..."

Boyle smiled. "I know both of you were looking out for me. I appreciate it, but you can rest easy. I'm not going to rush off and do something stupid. McCluskey will keep. So will everything else. I've decided to be the modern man and take some proper paternity leave. I'll see you all in about two weeks."

Brogan watched the door, his head still shaking long after it closed behind Boyle.

THE END

Printed in Great Britain
by Amazon